WICKED FAME

SASHA CLINTON

For the me who suffers and the me who survives.

FOREWORD

Content warnings

The female main character struggles with depression and some instances of suicidal ideation are described throughout the book as well as instances of:
    -Drug use/drug abuse/alcoholism/substance use/addiction
    -Gun violence, shooting of the main character as well as a secondary character
    -Knife play (consensual; no cuts/bleeding)
    -Gun play (consensual; no wounds or physical harm caused)
    -Hospital scenes

CHAPTER 1

 rancesca

I OPEN my eyes to an unfamiliar blackness for the third time that week.

Something glistens at the edge of my vision—a dark stream of water with the bright glow of street lamps licking its shiny surface.

I sit up on a hard surface. A slow realization dawns on me as I make sense of my surroundings. I passed out on a bench this time.

Unprotected. Alone. Stoned. Anyone could've done anything to me. Yet, when I pat down my coat, my wallet's still there. As is the rest of me.

It doesn't fill me with any relief to know that I'm okay. Instead, my ribs close around frustration and emptiness. Fear and hopelessness and a thousand strange voices telling me I'm a mess are eating up the inside of my brain. My stomach wails in hunger.

The high wore off. Damnit. Now I'm squarely back in hell.

With a groan, I swing to my feet and check my phone. Mom didn't call. I must've lied to her and said I was staying over at Ella's.

Stories are so much easier to create than art. Sometimes, I wish I'd become a writer instead of an artist. Maybe then I'd be less broken.

"Are you okay?" My neck snaps to the left at the newly-materialized voice, burning a trail of pain behind my eyes down to the base of my spine.

Blurry splotches of a woman's face thread into the black void of my vision. She's shorter than me but beautiful—even if the beauty is hidden under shadows and scars and eyes gone cold with despair. Her teeth are chattering, which is no surprise given that it's January. Now that I think about it, the jacket she has wrapped around her petite frame isn't warm enough for this icy weather. As my gaze moves further down, it snags on her socks. They have a hole in them and she's wearing slippers, not shoes.

My shoulders slump in sympathy for this stranger.

A homeless person. That'd explain what she's doing here late at night.

"I'm sorry for hogging your bench," I mutter, swaying on my feet. I can't even stand still or I'll faint. I really need to cut back on the alcohol. "Is this where you usually sleep?"

The brown-haired woman wipes her wet cheeks. A tiny sob infiltrates my ears. I didn't realize she was crying. I was so lost in my inner drama as usual that I forgot to be sensitive to the people around me. Sure, I didn't know the bench belonged to someone else and I needed it at the time. Thanks to that, I've killed half her night's sleep.

"Really, I'm sorry," I say, wondering if she won't die sleeping out in the cold. It's not snowing today, but the temperature is low enough to numb my fingertips.

2

The lady shakes her head. "Don't worry."

"You're shivering," I note from the way she has her arms wrapped around her torso. The tip of her nose is red. "Take this."

Shrugging out of the $7000 woolen armor wrapped around me like a warm blanket, I settle it over her shoulders. Mom bought it for me when I bagged the commission to paint two pieces to be installed in the brand-new luxury residential development Hudson 241. It has been six months since then and I haven't produced a single artwork. Guilt cracks inside my veins.

And just like that, the blackness that I've held at bay all night cuts my head open once more.

Liar.

Worthless.

Impostor.

I bite down on my lip, my jaw trembling in anticipation of the worst.

"I can't take something so valuable." The homeless woman's voice saves me from getting sucked into the vortex in my head. She fingers the luxurious material that I draped on her and swallows, every crease on her skin giving away her desire. A silvery glint flickers in the depths of her dark brown eyes. "It's freezing tonight. What will you do if you give this to me?"

"I'm immune to the cold. You can keep it." I rub the exposed flesh of my palms. The stranger notices the goosebumps peppering my skin, but she must be desperate because she slips into my coat anyway.

She deserves it more than me. I can buy another one with the money I have. Or I could freeze to death, ending my short and miserable life. Either way is fine.

"Thank you. You're so kind," she says as she buttons the coat. It reaches all the way to her ankles. "By the way, I've never seen you around before. What are you doing here?"

"Don't know." I rub my temples in frustration. I'm made of nothing but ache and hangover right now. Not one coherent thought buzzes inside my useless head. "Where exactly is this place?"

"Howard Beach."

I'm in Queens?

Anxiety crowds my chest. Memories come roaring to explain the disorientation that hangs like a veil over my senses.

The club. Booze. Then the shady guys I got drugs from. After that, I was so high, I raced through the streets before deciding to ride on the subway. Can't remember which train I took, though. I walked for miles when I got out at the last stop because I had so much energy and needed to let off steam. The vague recollection of seeing a few nice houses on my path hits me. I also recall collapsing on the bench. Long story short, I ended up at my present location, which is a place I've never visited. And I've lived in NYC for all twenty-one years of my life.

"Howard Beach?" A groan wells up in my throat. "Isn't that, like, a bad area? They say the mafia still operates there."

The woman sniffles. "Yeah, there are rumors like that. But I'm here with you."

Why do her words fill me with concern rather than reassurance? She didn't deny anything. I must be hyperaware because of the adrenaline still lingering in my system.

The danger is licking the back of my neck. It's late at night; I'm in an unsafe place. But there's no need to panic. All I have to do is order myself a Lyft ride and I'll be out in the blink of an eye. I clutch my phone, flicking my finger over the screen hunting for that familiar icon.

Another sniffle breaks my concentration.

"What's wrong?" I ask. "Are you crying?"

She presses a hand over her hair, flattening the strands. "It's the cold."

"You can come with me," I offer. Her fragility calls out to something in me. "My house is pretty big."

Confusion ripples through her features. Shaking her head, she points at a house in the distance, one that's similar to all the other well-maintained, ranch-style homes surrounding it. Lights peek through the upper windows.

"I live there." Her quiet voice is spiked with warmth.

Surprise steals a breath from me. "I thought you were homeless."

"I might be soon. But for now, I still have a place to go to." She coughs out a hollow laugh.

Before I can ask her for an explanation, the shrill whiz of a crash ripples through the frosty air. It came from the house. The woman charges toward her home and I follow her without thinking. My phone dangles in my grip, and the Lyft app opens without a destination. My teeth carve a swollen line on my lips, sawing back and forth.

Intuition tells me that the woman is in danger. Therefore, I can't leave her alone. Never mind that I might be in danger, too, if I stick my nose into her affairs. The last trace of the drug haze from earlier is pumping courage through my veins. I arrive outside the yellow-painted house before my companion.

Three black cars are parked outside. Badly parked, I may add, like the drivers don't care about anybody else on the street. Moonlight illuminates the silver metallic logo on the front.

Mercedes Benz.

I curl my fingers. Those are expensive.

"Why were you walking around alone if you live here?" The question squeezes through my breathless voice. "And what was that noise?"

The most likely scenarios flash through my mind: *domestic violence, robbery.*

"I can't go home right now." Her chest swells under the

layers of clothing. A single tear slides down her cheek. "I'm scared."

Her thin form trembles. I wrap my arms around her, hating how useless I feel just watching her be miserable. Despite being a black hole of angst, I can't stand seeing other people unhappy. All my instincts scream at me to do something.

"What are you afraid of?" I whisper.

"Them," she answers.

"Who are they?"

The thud of her front door slamming open has the two of us breaking apart. Her face goes pale as a ghost as three dark figures spill out of her doorstep, all wearing black suits. Confusion spurts in my mind as the images slot together. One of the men in suits has a man's body thrown over his shoulders.

"Luca...my husband..." A breathless cry leaves the woman's lips as she crumbles to her knees on the dirty road.

It takes me a beat to realize that she's talking about the unconscious man thrown over the shoulder who is now being tossed into the trunk of a car.

Realization clinks against my skull. He's dead. Or he's going to be. This is not domestic violence or robbery. This is a kidnapping.

Luca's body, lying motionless in the trunk of the car, catches a stray beam from the streetlight. Something red is on his face. Blood.

An invisible dark hand squeezes my lungs. Unconscious knowledge licks the inside of my brain like a reptile in the night.

Not a kidnapping. Something worse.

The woman presses a hand to my knee, nudging me in the opposite direction. "You should leave. It has nothing to do with you. Get out of here quickly."

My fingers scratch the screen of my phone. Should I call the police, my brother Ethan, or a Lyft ride? What's the better option in this situation? "I can't leave you. Come with me—"

The dizziness that has my blood in its grip intensifies. The drugs are still tripping through my system, pumping me with artificial highs and lows. My heartbeat trips. Awareness prickles in every nerve. The sound of keys turning in the ignition of a car rents the air.

Two men are still planted in front of her house. One of them has a scar running along his left cheek. His face is lined, wrinkled, and worn. He's carrying a gun that is casually pointed at Luca. The other one's taller, and leaner, and though his face bears no marks, the very cut of his jaw looks threatening. When his dark eyes flicker over mine, I know I'm in trouble.

He saw me.

I punch my brother's phone number. Ethan's well-connected to unsavory characters in the city so he'll probably get here faster and be more useful than the police. I feel guilty about begging him for help after ignoring him for six months, but I can't afford to get stuck in my conscience right now. Ethan owes me one, anyway. I got him together with the love of his life.

Uncertainty fizzes through my blood. I swallow the lump in my throat. I scroll through my contacts for his number. "I'm calling—"

"Go. Quickly. Hurry up." The woman pokes my thigh. A sharp pain shoots in the wake of her touch. She pokes me again, harder this time. "Run. If these men catch you, you'll be dead."

My head lifts, just in time to catch the threatening duo twisting their bodies in my direction. The dangerous guy from before bares his teeth in displeasure at my fingers playing over my phone screen. He strides in my direction, moving a lot faster than I expected from someone of his size.

A helpless scream rises in my throat, smothered by the fear that chokes my windpipe.

The icy wind whooshes in my ears.

Shadows darken.

Footsteps stab the ground like knives.

I feel it in my bones: whoever they are, they're dangerous.

So I do what I'm best at—running away.

My feet claw against gravity, hands trying to grasp for safety. My pathetic lungs heave with exhaustion. I glance backward. The two men are drawing closer, their strides long and supple, their every step equal to three of mine.

"Stop! Put the phone down!" The one with the scarred face calls out. His gun is pointed at me.

In the blink of an eye, the other man in a dark suit gains on me. As his scent floods my nostrils—cigar smoke mixed with musk and danger—the air crackles with the premonition of catastrophe. Before I know it, a strong, biting grip cuts into my wrist. He spins me around with terrifying speed, making me drop my phone.

A squeal punches through my tight throat. Panic inflates against my ribcage as I come face-to-face with the tall stranger.

Glass-cutting cheekbones and bottomless dark eyes give way to unforgiving lips that send a tidal wave of fear cascading down my spine. Impossibly broad shoulders and defined arms with a hint of black ink peeking over his wrists register in my hazy perception. His presence overpowers me like an invisible force stamping its mark on my skin. The intimidation and lust for power that radiate off his skin are inescapable. But under the cold expression, I sense someone who is as deeply broken as me.

"Get away." I shove at his chest. It's as useless as banging against a solid wall.

Rough hands graze over my clothes.

I drag my nails across his face but my attempt at scratching his eyes out ends in failure when he easily twists and pins both arms behind me. Terror oozes through my veins. Blackness lashes across my vision, flaring between pinpricks of lights.

I kick my captor's knee. The dark-haired bastard doesn't even wince. Instead, he smiles as if I tickled him—before effortlessly flattening my body onto the ground.

"You need to stop hurting yourself, baby. There's no way you're overpowering an armed man twice your size." His muscular legs straddle my hips, pinning me down. Thick, cruel fingers play with my hair before pulling them back from my face.

"Let me go!" I wriggle, hoping to throw him off. I'm hungover, every nerve foggy and laced with too much alcohol. It has dulled my reflexes.

I've never been so wholly, completely dominated by someone's power in my life. His presence is so loud, it eclipses the moon and the stars in the sky, reducing my world to a single black point of hopelessness.

"I didn't do anything to you," I say.

"Not yet," he replies.

"This is illegal! It's assault."

"Yes, missy, I know it's assault." I've known this thug for all of half a minute but the smirk on his face is already annoying me. "I have been doing this job a lot longer than you've been alive."

A cold sweat breaks over my brow as I stare at the slits of his pupils ringed by dark brown. His gaze consumes my body. He assesses me with a mixture of interest and suspicion.

The shattered, staccato notes of my pulse explode in my ears. Sludge is all there is inside my head. Fear has already paralyzed my body. I can't wait for this nightmare to end.

Except, I don't think it's going to stop.

"Take your hands off me!" I cry.

The press of his touch against the hollow of my throat launches a new wave of panic into my bloodstream.

I whimper in response. "Don't hurt me."

He grazes his thumb over his gun. A wordless warning.

"I won't if you tell me your name," he rasps.

My lungs jerk. Breath leaks out of me in a hoarse moan. I remain silent, not sure whether I'd be digging my grave deeper by giving him personal details.

"Your name." Impatience roughens his voice.

My lips wobble, resistance leaching from me. "Francesca Astor."

A deep line forms between his eyebrows. Maybe he has heard my last name before. That wouldn't be surprising, given that my father and brother made headlines for criminal charges against them six months ago. It was on every news channel. Ethan managed to get the charges dropped, but my father is rotting in prison right now. I wish I could say I'm sad for him, but he deserves it.

"I'm the heiress of Astor Hotels," I fill in when the thug keeps mulling my name over. "My brother is Ethan Astor Jr. He's currently the CEO."

"I remember now." The luxurious material of his black pants slides over my leg as he shifts his leg. "Your family is upper class."

The knot of anxiety in my stomach loosens. "Correct. We're rich, so my brother will bury you in lawsuits if you lay a hand on me."

"Is that supposed to be a threat?" The irreverent laugh that eases out of him only serves to heighten the alarm that's stuck to my every cell like super glue. Does nothing rattle this man? "You're cute."

I expel a shaky breath at the slide of his thumb across my lips. It ignites something in me, something I thought I'd lost a long time ago along with my muse.

Anticipation.

"Will you let me go now?" I ask. "Or are you going to kidnap me and demand ransom from my family because I'm rich?"

"We're going to kill you." The other man I saw earlier emerges from the shadows and holds his gun toward me. He's the one with the scar running across his face.

I'm barely audible when I squeak out, "Kill, like homicide?"

"Yes, like homicide," he replies. "You watch a lot of crime shows, don't you?"

This is getting a lot worse than I imagined.

I inhale. Try to find my calm. It's useless. All those Zen meditation videos? They lie. There's no such thing as inner peace. Inner emotional meltdown on the other hand is perfectly real.

CHAPTER 2

 rancesca

A SCREAM WELLS up in my raw throat. The man pinning me down is strong, though Scar Face, who is still pointing his weapon at me, looks a lot older and meaner than him. He's in his fifties, I'd guess.

As Scar Face tightens his grip on his gun, taking aim at me, the younger man pinning me seizes my arm and pulls me to my feet so fast, it gives me whiplash.

Mr. Tall, Dark, and Dangerous snaps his fingers. "No, Antonio. Don't."

"But—"

"Her brother has as many policemen in his pocket as us," he says. "There's no need for pointless bloodshed. We'll monitor her for now."

Monitor me? Is that shorthand for stalking?

"But—"

"I'll handle her." He cocks his head to the man with the scar on his face, the guy he just called Antonio. "You follow me."

Then he taps the back of my knees, pushing me into a forward trot. "Unless you want me to toss you into the trunk, get your ass moving, *Francesca*."

"Go to hell," I spit out.

"Too boring there." A vicious glow lights his eyes. "I like darker places."

The rasp, the undercurrent of a warning, starts a tremor under my skin. An ember sparks in my groin. This man. There's something both magnetic and scary about him. The look he gives me is dyed with wickedness and promises nothing but suffering. Yet, his rough and authoritative manner sets off a sweet burn between my legs.

"Move." Irritation coats his voice. "I don't have all day."

When I resist following his orders, the barrel of his gun digs into one of my ass cheeks. The shock of having something so hard and cold in an expected place short circuits my brain. The uncomfortable heat between my legs gets slicker, coating my inner thighs with moisture.

New kink unlocked, I guess. I seem to have a thing for dangerous weapons.

Thanks goodness I'm wearing a long sweater so Mr. Tall, Dark, and Dangerous can't see my inconvenient reaction. I squirm, pushing my shoulders back forcefully. "Can't you at least point it at my head like a proper criminal?" I say in a scathing tone.

He sinks the lip of the gun deeper into my flesh in response. ""I would, but you're quieter when you're nervous. I like you quiet."

"You can't kill someone by shooting their butt, though."

"Giving advice to a mobster on how to murder?" His smile is broader now, almost friendly. "I've killed more people than you have teeth, baby."

"What're you trying to do, then?"

"Scare you."

"It's not working," I whisper.

"You're not scared?"

"No." I lick my lips, feeling reckless as I blurt out, "I'm turned on."

Scar Face Antonio releases a loud breath, joining his hands in prayer. "This is why I can't stand college girls. They're always horny. Can't we just kill her?"

Mr. Tall, Dark and Dangerous considers me through narrowed eyes. I'm not sure what his assessment is, but his features stay blank and impassive—except for that smug smile drilled into his lips.

"Patience, Antonio." He sighs. "We don't need trouble right now. We're already tied up in enough problems with the feds."

"But look at her." Antonio flashes a disgusted look at me. "Do you think we'll be able to stand her long enough to monitor her?"

"It's just a job. Do it right." Mr. Tall, Hot, and Dangerous suddenly shoves my body toward Antonio who catches me fast then presses his bent elbow against my neck.

This one holds the gun to my head like a proper, upstanding mobster ought to. And just like that, my arousal freezes and vanishes. It would seem like I'm not as into danger as I thought. Perhaps I'm into a very *specific* kind of danger, one with a sense of humor and dark eyes.

My heart wrings out every beat with apprehension as my feet thud on the road. The car with Luca is gone and so is the woman I gave my coat to. I twist my head to search for her, but I am shoved aggressively into one of the remaining two cars. My nostrils flare at the smell of leather mixed with metal. Mr. Tall, Hot, and Dangerous gets in the driver's seat.

Antonio straps on my seatbelt. "Have a good trip, Missy,"

I unbuckle my seatbelt. "You should've handcuffed me because I'm going to escape."

"Try it," Antonio challenges me with a thick eyebrow raised.

Before I can make a sound, cruel hands grab my seatbelt and snap it back in place.

"Stop that or I'll have to knock you out," Mr. Tall, Hot, and Dangerous informs me in a bored voice. "The concussion will be bad and you'll have a headache for days. Trust me, it's best to avoid that."

Despite how disinterested he looks, the dagger-like edge of his unhinged jaw compels me to obey. I shiver at the recollection of how swiftly he pressed me into the ground earlier, how powerfully he loomed over me.

"Can I ask your name?" I say when he turns his keys in the ignition.

The bellow of the engine swells in my ears. "Aren't you a curious girl."

"It's not curiosity. I just don't want to mentally call you a *fucker* in my head while I cuss you out."

I expecting a shove or a slap for that line, but one corner of his lip twitches in a mocking smile. "You're already thinking of me that much?"

There's no sexual undertone to his words, creepiness or lust. He sounds tired, if anything. For a gangster whose job is intimidating people, he has got a real way of putting me at ease and making me forget that I could lose my life in the next few hours if I'm not careful.

"Got no choice," I reply. "You're making my life hard right now."

"Gabriele Russo." He grabs the water bottle from the glove box and empties half the water in it. "That's my name. You can call me Gabriele. Coincidentally, it rhymes with all the cuss words. Lucky you."

Russo. That's one of the big five crime families in New York.

They've been around for generations. They're so famous even I have heard of them.

The revving of the engine purrs in my ears and I lose my last chance of escape when the car blazes away from the spot where it was parked, streaking through the night. It's a good thing I'm wearing my seatbelt or I'd have my head banging against the windshield by now.

Even when we're on the road, Gabriele Russo doesn't slow down. Blurry lights, shops, snow, cars, and clouds all flit in and out of my vision. I want to jump out of the window but he's speeding so much, I'll certainly die if I attempt that.

"Did you drive racecars before this?" I snip at him. "You have an odd concept of speed."

"Nobody ever complained before."

"Perhaps because they were all dead when you gave them a ride?" I suggest helpfully.

Gabriele's lips tick up in a smile. "Could be."

Relief trickles through my pores when he finally slows at a red light. Mostly because there are other cars around us and not even a Russo can mow them down without consequences.

I beat my knuckles against the glass frantically, hoping one of the other drivers will notice me and call the police. God knows these guys don't have good intentions. Mr. Tall, Hot, and Dangerous has the kind of aura that suggests he's very familiar with torture. His talkative nature and willingness to exchange quips with me is likely a mask to throw me off.

There's every chance I'll get sold into prostitution or chopped up into pieces and thrown into the Hudson River by the time tonight is over. I wish the prospect of death pumped my blood with adrenaline and fear. Instead, all I can think is: *will the agony finally be over then?*

My suicidal ideation is halted when Gabriele Russo twists my head around and crushes my face between his fingers. The pressure of his fingers is so powerful, I'm afraid he'll break my jawbone. This guy doesn't mess around. "How much did you take?"

"What?" I sputter, confused.

"The drugs," he says, his tone softer than before. "How much?"

I blink, sawing my bottom lip with my teeth. *Oh god, oh god, oh god, how can he tell?* "Don't remember."

I'm sweating, panic slicing me in wave after nauseating wave. This mobster has easily sniffed out my biggest weakness, baring a part of me that I've managed to hide so well from everyone else.

"Was it good?" Gabriele Russo holds my stare with a look of mild amusement mixed with disgust. The smile hugging his lips is in contrast to the darkness growing in his eyes. He's not impressed.

"Yeah," I say.

Perfect white teeth sneer when he pulls his lips back. "How good?"

"Really good."

"And now that the high is gone? Is it still good?"

That question wasn't surface-level. His wary gaze slides over my skin like a caress. I need him to stop looking at me like that —like he's seeing right into my ugly, fucked-up head. Like he actually understands what I'm going through.

I grimace, hating how sounds pinch the inside of my head. "It feels like my skull's going to split open. I can't stand the pain."

"How unsurprising. Do you know why most people get high?" The three quiet seconds where he's expecting an answer from me pummel my gut. "To avoid facing the truth. To run from pain. Ironically, when the high wears off, agony is all they feel."

The truth in his words is a needle pricking my skin. It stirs up the uncomfortable feelings lodged in my belly. The string of memories that have marred my existence for the last six months pelts me at once.

Canvases full of ugly, meaningless lines of paint.

Cherry red. Indigo. Lemon yellow.

Colors that used to mean something, that used to be vibrant before they turned grey.

My forlorn sobs as I sit in my studio, clawing my skin and screaming at the empty void that refuses to go away.

The lies, the pretenses, avoiding everyone for the fear they'll see through me.

The passion that's become a curse rather than a blessing.

My mind scrolls through the negative comments on social media like I'm physically scrolling through my phone.

You're just using your parents' money and influence.

Privileged.

You don't deserve to be here.

People like you make the world rotten.

Stop. I have to stop. I drag my attention to the man beside me, to his smoke and copper scented body.

"You're a gangster." I croak, because continuing this meaningless conversation with a guy who might kill me is the only way to keep my thoughts away from the darkest abyss. "Don't you do drugs?"

"I'd rather hurt than be numb." A shadow caresses one side of Gabriele's face. "Of course, my favorite hobby is hurting others. Knives, garrotes, cement shoes, water torture, cutting off fingers one by one. I have a varied skillset."

It's at that moment that I know with absolute certainty; he has done all of it. For pleasure. But that's not all. The tight set of his features and the faded scar marks poking from under the folded-back sleeves of his black shirt tells me he has had some of that done to him, too.

The soft, irrational part of my heart squeezes in pity.

"That got way too gruesome for small talk," I mutter.

"You wanted small talk? Should've said so earlier." His voice pitches high, thick with fake cheer. He steps on the pedal to accelerate. I have stopped praying to God already because not even God has the power to save me from the inevitable car crash Gabriele Russo's speeding will get me in. "So, what college do you go to? Let me guess—Columbia?"

"NYU," I correct.

"What do you study? My bet is on something related to arts or fashion."

"Fine arts."

"Throwing paint on canvas and shit?"

"I can definitely tell that you're a great connoisseur of the arts." I exhale, unable to contain my sarcasm. "Which is why you use such specific technical terms like *canvas and shit*."

His thick hair sweeps across his forehead when Gabriele shakes his head. "Most days, I can't even tell blue and green apart."

Neither can I. Because I'm too stoned. I scratch the hem of my sweater, once again poised at the edge of spiraling into self-hate.

"Don't feel like you have to continue asking me personal questions unless you're actually interested," I say, because who could stay quiet with a criminal watching them so intensely as if he wants nothing more than to hear your sweet voice? "Or do you need the answers to plot my murder?"

"I don't plan murder; I simply do it." Tremors snake down my spine. I believe him. "I'm going to keep an eye on you starting today, Francesca. So I want to know everything about you."

I scoff. "Like what? My shoe size? Bra size?"

"Six and 34C." At my surprised gasp, he screws an eyebrow upward.

He got it right. Gabriele Russo acts dumb and cocky but I can sense that he didn't get this far in the mafia by being stupid.

His observation skills rival Sherlock Holmes. He could even tell I did drugs. Not even my mom can tell.

"Anyway, let's talk about your college," he continues. "You like drawing? Is that what you do in your classes?"

The atmosphere grows dense and claustrophobic as the loaded question settles on me like a paperweight.

Do I like drawing? I can't even draw anymore.

"I'm supposed to be a painter," I reply after a minute. "But I haven't created anything decent in a long time."

"Despite being in a fine arts program?"

The voices from cyberspace screech in my head: *Privileged. Worthless. Waste of space.*

I don't like where this is going, so I turn the question on its head. "Have *you* been to college?"

"Never."

"Ever wanted to go?"

"What kind of question is that to ask a mobster?"

"A normal one," I reply. "I'm curious. If you had a chance, would you have gotten a degree?"

"I never considered it. Didn't have that kind of luxury. And I don't see the point."

"The point of college is doing what makes you happy," I say. "It's to become better at what you're passionate about."

He grunts. "You don't look very happy to me, Francesca."

I close my fingers into fists so hard, the crunch of my bending bones echoes inside the car. My entire family thinks I'm content with my life. What gives him the right to see through my lies?

The Mercedes is zooming ahead at an illegal speed. But Gabriele's eyes aren't on what's ahead—they're squarely on me. This guy is hands-down the worst driver I've ever seen.

Digging my nails into my thighs, I try and fail to catch my breath. "Can you focus on the road? I don't want to die at twenty-one."

"I said I'm not going to kill you."

"I wasn't sure you meant it."

"I don't make promises I can't keep." Gabriele's breath hits my bare collarbones when he releases a long, steadying exhale.

Uncertainty about my future chafes under my chest. I want to know where he's taking me, and what awaits at the end of his rash driving.

"Are you planning to do something bad to me?"

"Very." He smiles but his eyes don't. "Very bad."

"Will it hurt? I'm afraid of pain," I confess. I live with enough mental torture as it is.

"Don't be." Gabriele pauses, letting the silence silk into my pores. Then he folds back the sleeves of his shirt to expose the raw scar marks on his hand. "Let me tell you a secret, Francesca: the more you're broken, the stronger you become."

"That's BS," I retort.

My pain isn't like the pain he's talking about. It's not inflicted on me by physical weapons.

The mean assessment from critics, the whispered jealousy of my classmates, the way people on social media judge me more than they judge my art.

Every word is the slash of a blade against my heart.

I can't help feeling other people's emotions strongly. Ella says I'm an empath. That's why, before I knew it, I started to believe that I was simply a rich, lucky girl who doesn't deserve to exist because I don't add anything of value to the world.

Art is my way of justifying my existence, of convincing everyone that I'm talented, too. I'm not a generic privileged girl who rides on a father's coattails but a one-in-a-generation artistic genius.

I hate the burden of defending my right to breathe. I hate the self-doubt that sets in when people resent me for having a life they think I don't deserve.

I hate it when I can't push the voices down.

So I do the only thing I can. I run from them using a miraculous white powder. Because if I become who they think I am, then they can't hurt me for trying.

"Francesca?" Gabriele's voice calls out to me in the depths of my personal hell.

"You're wrong," I scream. "About pain making you stronger. You have no idea how unkind people can be on social media since you're not on social media."

"How do you know I'm not?"

"Because you are too self-confident."

The truth is, the moment you realize that you're resented and hated by people, that they would tear you down without caring for how hard you try, that's the moment your confidence shatters.

Gabriele offers me an arched eyebrow in response. "Was that a compliment?"

"If it strokes your ego, take it as one." I lean back, folding my arms and falling silent. This conversation has stirred up everything I wanted to forget.

I'm glad when exhaustion grips my muscles. My eyelids droop. Consciousness fades and flickers like a candle in the wind. I've had a long day. My head is woozy.

I can barely tell where we're headed since I haven't been looking outside the window. My attention has been focused on Gabriele. I wonder what he'll do to me. If he'll hold me captive in a dark dungeon or torture me. Maybe he'll show me mercy and kill me quickly.

I jerk forward violently in my seat when the car starts to decelerate. What? We're already there?

I absorb the scene outside the window in panic. It's a familiar street, lined by familiar trees and familiar buildings.

Gabriele pulls up in front of my family's Brooklyn townhouse and parallel parks so badly, I feel sorry for the neighbor whose headlights he just smashed. I hope my mom doesn't have to pay for that.

"How in the world did you get a driving license? You can't even park properly." I shake my head in disgust.

"The same way you got yours. Money." His smile is full of teeth, even in the dark. "And connections."

I roll my shoulder in a shrug.

The click of the door unlocking startles me, elevating my pulse. His body tilts toward mine. What now? Is he going to hit me? Spit on me? Cut off one of my fingers after making me promise to stay quiet? I read somewhere that the yakuza still do that. I have no idea what the New York Italian mafia does. If possible, I never want to find out.

Blood surges in my head. Every passing moment heightens the tension that's spun between our bodies like a single, frail thread.

Gabriele tears off my seatbelt. "Hurry home now before your Mama starts missing you."

"You're letting me go?" The sudden relief chokes me, making me sputter and cough. "I don't understand. I thought you were planning to cut me in pieces and throw me into the ocean. But you just dropped me at my front door like a good boyfriend after a date."

Gabriele grins, bemused. Then points to the other badly parked car on the opposite side of the road. Antonio is glaring at me through the window.

"I'm putting you under surveillance," he informs me. "You so much as sniff in the direction of the police, Antonio will shoot you."

I swallow. "So he'll be my bodyguard from now on?"

"Not bodyguard. Leash. He'll be your leash. Don't test me, okay?" He ruffles the hair on top of my head like this is a playful threat. But the tone of his voice leaves no room for doubt. I'll be

23

dead if I take advantage of his mercy. "Get lost quickly before I change my mind."

I scramble out of my seat quickly. "Um...thank you. Gabriele. I'd appreciate it if you kept the thing about me doing drugs to yourself."

"Trust me, I'm not in the business of tipping off the police about wayward heiresses." He yawns. "But this is an exchange, you understand? I keep quiet about your pastime and you forget what you saw tonight."

"Okay, I will."

"Behave yourself, Francesca," he reminds me. "And we'll never have to cross paths again."

I nod, dashing to my front door. Our housekeeper, Ivana, furrows her eyebrows at my sudden arrival after staying out all night but she doesn't comment on my disheveled appearance and missing coat. Mom must be asleep. The lights are switched off. I pad up the staircase to my room quietly. When I check the street outside through my window, Gabriele's car is still there. His elbow is planted against the window, chin angled toward my window.

I quickly draw the curtains.

Call it sixth sense or whatever, but I know deep inside that this isn't the last I'll see of Gabriele Russo.

CHAPTER 3

abriele

I GRAB a fistful of Luca's collar and jerk him forward. The snap of violence echoes inside the windowless cell. Ricardo—the soldier who transported him here in his car trunk—jabs his ribs. The hostage's pained cry twists through the air.

"Who did you sell it to?" I demand, fingers tightening around the soft fabric of Luca Morelli's shirt. That's a dead giveaway, by the way—the high-quality material. A mid-level mafia office guy doesn't make enough to afford something so fine. His clothes were the first thing that made me suspicious enough to get my men to start tailing him. When men like him start to fatten their wallets, they tend to lose their common sense and splurge to make themselves feel like they're bigshots.

"I can't tell you."

I shake his head, the violent impulses inside me itching to

break free. "You'll have to spill eventually. The only choice you have is whether it'll be while all your teeth are still attached to your jaw."

Luca blinks, his irises swimming up and down the whites of his eyes. I swing my head in a decisive nod.

The blood from before has dried between Luca's dark beard but a fresh stream spills when Ricardo slams his fist into his jaw, dislodging a few teeth. Ricardo is one of my best soldiers, very good with his fists. He has been loyal to the Don for more than ten years now.

Luca screams in agony, but he's a tough bitch. He doesn't break easily.

"You know what happens to rats, Luca." I whistle, reaching for the pliers. We're getting to my favorite part now. The part where I remind people exactly why it's a terrible idea to waste my time.

As his gaze flicks to the metal in my hand, the muscles on his neck stiffen, protruding through his tanned skin.

"Kill me," he pleads.

I grab a handful of his hair and jerk his sorry head backward. "Did you forget my name?"

"Torture Demon."

"Correct. This is my favorite part of the job. So don't expect me to show any mercy."

He flinches when the cool bite of metal pinches around his nail. The first time is always the hardest. And it's when they break the easiest. Men are surprisingly vain about their nails.

"They're from the Russian Bratva." He exhales, sweat pricking his forehead. "And they pay better money."

"Names, Luca." I twist the handle, letting him feel the agony of having his nails pulled out from his flesh.

Before I can follow through fully, a knock on the door interrupts me. Nico, the underboss's voice filters through.

"The Don wants to speak to you," he says.

"Tell him I'm busy," I snap.

"Won't take long."

With a grunt, I drop the pliers. They clank on the cement floor. Distractions are bad for getting confessions. They allow the victim a chance to mentally regroup and think up a new strategy.

"Ricardo, keep pressing him," I whisper in the ear of my subordinate before striding out.

Nico is already out of sight so I trudge up the stairs all alone. The heartless bastard. He should at least accompany me after disrupting me in the middle of my job.

At the top of the stairs is a living room which is grandly furnished compared to the underground cells and interrogation chambers we use to torture prisoners and traitors. Chestnut leather sofas and glass-top coffee tables are arranged across the expansive space. A whole collection of alcohol bottles is strewn on top of those tables.

The Don is leaning back against the back of an armchair. My chest immediately softens at the old man's face. Angelo Russo is the boss of the Russo Family, but at sixty-five, with excess fat weighing down his short, heavyset frame, a crooked back, and thinning hair, you couldn't differentiate him from one of the oldies in the care home two blocks down. He's not a scary Don anymore. But he's still a powerful man and he knows it.

"Have you been well? Sorry, I missed today's meeting." I say.

He nods.

A large bottle of whiskey rests at his elbow. He has been getting really friendly with some of the men on Billionaire's Row lately. I guess more money for him means more money for everyone.

Most boys think of their father as their hero.

Angelo Russo is my hero.

Even though I've seen him do unspeakable things.

He claps his hand on my shoulder as I settle myself next to him.

"Gabriele, my son." He calls me his son even though I'm just a poor, homeless brat he picked up in an alley eighteen years ago. "How's it going with Luca?"

"About as well as you'd expect. I'll have the names by the end of the night. They're Russian."

He beckons me closer and pours me a glass of whiskey. The unsaid command is to drink. That's exactly what I do. I could use some alcohol. It might even help me forget about Francesca Astor. Her pretty pink lips and haunted blue eyes have been stuck in my brain like bubblegum on a sidewalk. My fingertips still tingle from when I brushed her skin.

"Don't kill Luca unless he spits out what we need first," Angelo says. "We need to figure out who is trying to undercut us."

I dig my hands into my pockets and dish out a noncommittal shrug. "He's kind of annoying, though."

"Gabriele," he emphasizes. "No killing. He has valuable information."

"Yeah, I got it. Boss." I salute.

To my side, the underboss twists his wrinkled lips in disgust. He has been quiet so far but I can tell he wants to go home already.

All the capos report to the Don weekly at the backroom of one of the illegal casinos the Russo family operates in Queens. As one of the last Big Five crime families still operating in New York, the Russos have a vast network of resources. However, even though I'm a capo, I didn't show up at the meeting tonight. Of course, that's because I was doing my job, but the way the Don is so lenient with me often rubs the other members of the organization the wrong way. Especially since Nico, the under-boss, is his biological son.

I look down at my hand, taking in the trace of blood

smudged between my knuckles. For some reason, my mind immediately travels back to Francesca Astor, to the red sweater she was wearing. To the sadness that hugged her shoulders as they slumped down in my car seat. She's definitely depressed. And I have no reason to care about her mental health in the first place.

"Ricardo said you picked up the girl who witnessed it." Nico's voice fragments my concentration, dissolving all images of porcelain skin and big, wide eyes full of fear. "Who is she?"

"Francesca Astor," I reply.

"The Astors." The Don rubs his nose, the number of wrinkles on his face multiplying rapidly. "That's not good."

"She won't talk. I'm having her watched."

He dips his head in a slow nod. "Why do you look like you swallowed glass, though?"

"Can't stand her type."

"Rich heiresses?"

"Addicts."

"Your Mama was one, wasn't she?"

A sharp, edgy sensation tears under my skin. I never told him about my mother or my childhood, but he must have done a background check at some point. I've been a capo for long enough and the Don is a shrewd man. He'd never let someone into his inner circle without arming himself with every single piece of information. It wouldn't surprise me if he knew all my weaknesses.

I don't hate him for it. When I swore my life and loyalty to him, I meant every word. I have never once thought of betraying this man.

Because nobody has ever cared for me the way he has. Angelo saved my life.

I didn't have the best childhood, to be honest. I don't know who my father was and my mother spent all her money on drugs to escape the harsh reality of her existence. Anything that wasn't her next fix was inconsequential to her. Including me.

I had to start fending for myself pretty early on. When there wasn't enough money at home, I joined a local gang. Cuts, bruises, and violence have been my life since sixteen. I made okay money, but the jobs were dangerous.

On the night the Don found me, I was lying half-dead in the snow in some grimy alley, bleeding out of my stomach after being shanked by a blade and abandoned by the other members of my group. We'd gotten into a skirmish with a rival gang.

Blackness, final and cold, threatened my vision. Angelo's steely eyes were the first and last thing I saw before the icy night sunk its fingers into me and erased the world.

When the darkness cleared, I was sleeping in a warm room in Angelo Russo's fancy mansion. He'd spotted me while exiting a restaurant. Unable to leave me alone, he brought me home. I stayed at the mansion for a week to recover after which he offered me a job. It was a no-brainer to serve him for the rest of my life. Normal people might feel differently, but to me, he was the closest thing to a parental figure I'd ever had. So I pledged everything to him.

Violence and intimidation were woven into my blood by that point. I wasn't good at anything except fighting, so there was only one path for someone like me to climb up in the world —crime.

"Drink some more," Angelo encourages me now, pouring me some more whiskey.

I grab the glass and down it in a few gulps. The burn sears the inside of my throat, stroking the fire in my chest. At the agony that spreads through my insides, the old anger comes back flashing.

I recognize now why Francesca Astor gets under my skin. She's like my mother. Or at least she will be, soon. There's no saving her. She's going to be consumed by the desperate need to escape the ugliness of the world.

I swore to stay away from those types once Angelo took me in.

I don't need a future like my past. I left that miserable life behind a long time ago. Forever.

"Isn't it your birthday next month?" Angelo's casual tap on my knee rattles something deep inside. I straighten my spine, alert. He has never cared about my birthdays before. "How old will you be turning?"

"Thirty-four," I reply.

"And still unmarried. What a loss to the world." He shakes his head, the unsaid threat hanging in the air. Nico's eyes narrow beside me. So *this* conversation was the real reason he pulled me out in the middle of the job.

"Papa, can you get to the point? I'm sure our capo has a task to finish," Nico prods.

"Well..." Angelo hesitates. "I have a friend. A rich friend. His daughter used to be married, but her husband was a bad man. An abusive man. She divorced him last fall. Unfortunately, he's powerful and out for revenge, so she cannot marry again unless her new husband can protect her. I told my friend I know a decent man who treats women well. What do you say to that?"

"I'm humbled by your confidence in my character," I say. "If you were, in fact, referring to me."

"Of course I meant you!" The Don cracks his lips wide in a jovial smile. "Nico's too surly—"

"And I'm married," Nico interrupts.

Angelo clicks his tongue. "What do you say, Gabriele?"

I rub my chin. There's nothing to think about. We all play our roles in this world. And being a capo was the role I chose to play. My future is writ in stone, sealed by the stars, a straight and narrow path filled with orders to obey and violence to commit.

The day I gave my life to Angelo, I knew an arranged marriage was going to be inevitable. If it benefits my standing in the family and benefits the Russos, I have nothing to complain about.

"As long as she isn't an addict, I'm fine with it," I reply.

"No drug issues," Angelo assures me with softness in his tone. He's becoming very sentimental in old age. "She's a very gentle woman who doesn't ask for much. I think you two will suit each other. Both kind souls with a tragic past."

Nico winces at that overly poetic description. He's the type who can't hide his emotions. That's why he always loses in card games to me. His poker face is shit.

"I hope so," I reply.

"I'll arrange for you two to meet. Her father is very worried —she has been through a lot."

I nod quietly—there's no other appropriate response here.

"Great!" The Don slaps his hands on his knees, voice pitched high. "What a fine night this has been."

I exhale. "If there's nothing else—"

"Yeah, go back and grill Luca," Nico grinds out. "We'll hang around a bit longer until you have the names."

"Suit yourself." I slide my glass to the center of the table.

Then I rise and stride away.

* * *

MY LUCK MUST HAVE VANISHED into the ether. Not only does Luca's interrogation end with him dying without coughing up anything worthwhile, but Antonio tells me a week later that he's done with the rich heiress.

"She makes me drive her to school every morning and gets drunk or high every night. I had to haul her up to her room last night. Then she vomited on me. Please. I'm begging you. No more of this job." Antonio lets out a tired sigh. His voice crackles on the phone.

"I told you to observe her, not become her father," I chide.

"I'm going mad, Gabriele! College girls make my skin crawl. Can't you get Ricardo to do this? He likes flirting. Maybe he'll get friendly with her."

"Ricardo messed up with Luca so he's out of the picture for the moment until the Don's temper cools down," I intone in a steady voice, rolling a paperweight between my fingers.

I'm sitting at the desk in my home, going through the web of money laundering transactions Luca completed in the last few weeks, hoping to find a clue somewhere. Intellectual work is not one of my strengths so the progress has been...well, nonexistent.

Frankly, I need to come up with something. A nugget of valuable intel to get back into Nico and Angelo's good graces. Ricardo isn't the only one who butchered his chances for promotion. I was supposed to keep the whole thing under control but I took my eyes off him for a second and it all went to hell in a handbasket.

"I'll do anything else," Antonio pleads. "Just get me out of here."

I don't have men to spare. I could get Ricardo to watch the Astor girl but he'll definitely try to get in her pants. The leap of hot acid inside my chest startles me. Why do I hate the notion of him flirting with Francesca Astor? Why do I detest the idea of someone from my world tainting her life with the darkness that working in organized crime fills your bones with?

In my profession, you see the worst. Before you know it, you *become* the worst. The heiress is a sheltered little girl, barely twenty-one. She's already sabotaging her life with substances. She doesn't need something even worse.

"I'll watch the Astor girl." My throat clamps around the words possessively, wanting to keep my rational mind from taking them back. My fingers drum against the back of my cell-phone, producing a hollow sound that echoes in my ear. "In return, you'll dig into some documents for me. Use your brains to trace Luca's money. I need to know where it was coming from."

Antonio groans. He hates desk work. Everyone does. But he's better than me because he's good at focusing on details. "Alright. We switch at twelve. I want to eat proper lunch for once."

"I'll be there."

Our deal made, I get my ass out of the office chair. There are a series of black jackets hanging in my wardrobe. I throw one on. Black shirt, black pants, black jacket, black coat, and a gold chain to contrast against the ink swarming over my skin. It completes my look. Nobody could accuse me of not looking like a textbook gangster in this outfit.

By afternoon, I have found my way to the NYU campus in East Village. Antonio emailed me his reports on Francesca and other useful information. Yeah, we're pretty high-tech these days in the mafia.

Antonio made a detailed timetable of Francesca's daily schedule. She goes to NYU Steinhardt in the morning and spends all day there until it's time for lunch. She eats at a fancy brunch place a few blocks away. Then goes back to school. Since she's in her final year, she's taking a module called Senior Studio, where she's supposed to work in her own art studio to create a piece to be part of her spring thesis. I can't believe Antonio went so far as to research her course curriculum. He must've been really miserable.

And I must be even more bored than him because I stride right into the building where the studios are located. 75 3rd Ave. My plan? I have none. My reason for waltzing into a building infested with privileged, artsy types? None, except that

I'm itching to look at the pair of sea-glass blue eyes that have been taunting me in my dreams.

A burly security guard checks IDs at the entrance. His eyes narrow at me immediately but some run-of-the-mill threatening works wonders on him and he lets me stroll through. Hate to brag, but I'm pretty intimidating when I decide to be.

I locate the studio number Francesca is at because Antonio never misses a detail in his reports. He even described all the paintings and the length and width of the walls in the room. The man should've been in the FBI, not a soldier for the Russo family. He has real talent.

I kick the door open, impatience fusing with sharp inhales and exhales. For some reason, I can't wait to see the Astor girl. Nothing rational can explain this impulse and I'm not drunk enough to go diving within the deep, dark murkiness of my psyche for all the wrong, inappropriate reasons I want my eyes on her again.

A high-pitched yelp serenades into the space as I close the door behind me.

"What're you doing here?" Outrage colors her voice.

I scan her frozen form, every line and curve of her thrown into relief by the blank canvas behind her.

Fuck. She looks better than I remember. Less like a stoned teenager and more like a woman with a body that practically oozes an invitation to the depths of hell. The shadows in my car coupled with the baggy sweater and clothes she wore made her look practically homeless that night but she has scrubbed up nicely now.

Her tiny tweed miniskirt and jacket combo shows off her toned, tanned, endless legs. The pale blue and ivory color of the co-ord set accentuates the color of her eyes.

"A whole-ass personal studio." I skim my gaze across the white walls and the series of rectangular paintings in various sizes hanging off them. "How bougie. I didn't even have my own bathroom when I was your age."

She rolls her eyes. "Was that supposed to make me feel sympathetic for you? Because it didn't work."

"Wonder why that is."

The sharp lift of her eyebrows is my silent answer.

"Don't hold a man's job against him." I grab the paints lying on a table in her studio and examine them one by one.

Not sure what I'm looking for here. Probably the drugs. She must have them here somewhere.

"Can you please get out? I need to paint," she says, turning around toward the canvas and giving me an unnecessary glimpse of her round ass encased by her tight blue miniskirt. "The spring thesis exhibition is coming up soon."

"What're you painting?" I curve an arm around her shoulder, a deliberate effort on my part to make her feel at ease. But instead of warming up to my friendly gesture, she shakes me off as if I scalded her with hot water.

"Don't touch me." The clipped, shaky voice curls in my stomach like a bad dream. Her shoulders bunch inward like she's curling in on herself. Like she's trying to disappear.

She's scared. She's uncomfortable.

I've never been in a casual social relationship with a girl, and this kind of gesture has an entirely different meaning when it's between the sexes.

"I'm sorry." The phrase breaks past years of conditioning and rips out of my mouth like I'm spitting out a broken piece of glass. The first thing they teach you in the mafia is to never apologize to someone you're trying to control and intimidate because it makes them think they have the upper hand. Guilt is a powerful chain to bind people with. "I wasn't thinking."

The heiress's shoulders drop a notch. Her long eyelashes fan over her pretty cheeks as she closes her eyes and releases a breath.

"As long as you know." Francesca goes back to staring at her painting.

I drag my feet backward, positioning myself on the opposite corner. The studio suddenly feels like a shoebox. Our inhales and exhales are the only sound, and the scents of expensive roses and the filth of the streets mingle until they become inseparable.

I quietly observe her for five more minutes where she does nothing but glare at the canvas. I never claimed to understand art. I understand the confusing explosions of paint Francesca has produced even less than I would a normal watercolor scenery. It's a lot of black and blue with some red and yellow splotches.

"Is that a night sky?" I inquire, keeping my voice low.

She drops to her knees, burying her head in her hands. "I don't know what it is. Or what it's supposed to be."

"Doesn't look bad," I lie, even though I didn't have to. I could have told her the painting's nothing special. But then that shadowy, defeated look I caught that night will crawl into her eyes again.

Francesca Astor's already standing on the edge of the metaphorical cliff, looking for an excuse to jump. I don't want to be the one who pushes her off.

Her teeth tap against each other. "Well, I exist for the sole purpose of impressing you, so I'm happy you're moved by my achievements."

Her sarcasm withers at my answering glare.

I lean forward. My palms find the wall behind her, caging her in. God save me, it's too exciting to intimidate her. The way she scares easily when faced with my power makes the self-loathing I feel at myself worth it. "Wouldn't kill you to be nice to me."

She clears her throat.

"How do you know?" She scoffs. "I doubt you've ever tried being nice to anyone who stalked you."

Soft, feather-light brushes of air from her open mouth tickle my collarbone. Even her fucking breaths smell like a rose garden. What in the world do they feed these rich girls for breakfast every day? A whole bottle of expensive perfume?

"*Stalking* you," I correct, waving my hand up and down to highlight my magnificent body. "I'm still at it. It's not in the past tense yet."

A reluctant smile edges her lips. It transforms her whole face. I can't believe she's still the same dark, hollow addict. Her smile stretches broader, imprinting those beautiful pink lips in my memory once more. Fuck. I need to stop making her smile. ASAP.

"Look at my luck." She pouts. "Of all the gangsters in New York, I end up with the one who is a grammar Nazi. Can I get the previous guy back? He was quieter."

"Then you shouldn't have puked on him. He folded because of that." I finger the starchy collar of my shirt that my house-keeper did a bad job of ironing. I can feel the creases under my thumb. It makes me feel even poorer in front of this rich girl who seems to be woven from perfection.

I close my eyes. Stop. I left that self-pitying, bruised boy back in my past where he belongs.

Francesca's gaze drops, her smile dissolving. She tucks a thick strand of golden hair behind her ear. "I feel bad about that. Antonio didn't deserve it. I drank too much. My head was all blurry. He was just being nice to me. To make up for it, I even bought him a new suit. I wanted to give it to him today but he didn't turn up."

A foreign pain lances through my chest like a needle being pushed through flesh.

I like the heiress more when she's being annoying than when

she's being considerate. Because kind Francesca is someone who makes my chest harden without explanation. I almost forget that she's not like this all the time, that she becomes a hollow, craving creature who seeks escape in the blink of an eye.

There's something about this part of her that demands to be protected. To be cherished. To be treated like a precious gem. I have to remind myself that it's my job to destroy her. Any day, I might have to put a bullet in that pretty head and blow it to pieces if she threatens the Russo family in any way.

"Why?" My pitch rises as my chest tightens. An uneasy anger spirals in my stomach.

"Why did I buy the suit?" She taps her softly carved jaw which reminds me of a sculpture that I saw in one of the other studios as I walked past. "It's only fair that I compensate Antonio—"

"No, the alcohol. Why did you drink so much that you had to throw up on him?"

That question zings the air with a current of silence. A shuffle of feet punctuates the awkward moment. Francesca goes back to scratching her paintbrush against the palette. The pigments on there have already dried. Hasn't she been painting since morning? But what do I know? Maybe oil paints dry out easily.

"Why do you get drunk, Francesca?" I repeat, grinding my shoe back and forth on the floor, hating the volatile tension that has taken hold of the space. It's none of my business. She'll probably lie to me and say her friends made her do it or that she's young. But I can't dissuade myself from digging deeper into her psyche, cracking open more of her facade and seeing the ugly emotions she's hiding spill out into the light. It's a compulsion. Every word I speak is a compulsion when I'm with her. "Tell me."

She rotates her body, dropping her palette on the table. The storm in her eyes has warped her irises into a darker, murkier blue.

"Cause I missed something," she spits out on a shaky breath.

"What?"

"Myself. I missed myself."

I brush an impatient hand over my hair. "What the fuck does that even mean?"

"I…" I'm certain she'll change her mind and swallow the rest of that sentence, but her voice softens as she continues, "I've always loved drawing since I was a kid. It's all I've ever wanted to do. Art was my life. I was always happy when I was painting. I could get lost in the colors, in the vision, in the beautiful picture taking shape in front of me. But ever since I started this program, there's been this huge pressure to be acclaimed by critics, to exhibit my work in an art gallery, to get a commission, and to find fame on social media so I can sell my pieces. But the more I chase success and validation, the less confident I feel that people will appreciate my work. I guess I miss my old self who could paint without any pressure to make a career out of it."

"You have enough money. You won't die without a job," I chime in unhelpfully.

"You don't get it, do you? I want to be *more* than a girl with money. I want to be someone who created something important. I want people to see *me* when they see me, not the Astor fortune." Francesca slumps to her knees. She caresses the surface of the incomprehensible painting. "Forget it. I'm wasting my breath."

The drained, hopeless emotion bleeding from her every pore sticks to me like glue. I don't think I'll be able to wash off the memory of this moment for days even if I try.

I remind myself that she's young. Also, I don't really care about her. I'm only keeping an eye on her so she doesn't cause Angelo any trouble with the law.

Yet, this feels like more than killing time.

Before I can pluck out an appropriate response to her, a jarring ringtone robs me of the opportunity to speak.

Francesca swoops for her phone. Her whole face wrinkles in tension at whatever ID she reads on the screen. She drags the red icon, then throws the device back onto the table in her studio.

The gnawing curiosity that has fueled my fascination for the heiress punctures by ribs once again, burrowing deep under my skin.

"Who was that?" I ask, putting far too much authority behind an innocuous question.

She shrugs her tiny shoulders like she didn't just get screamed at by a terrifying mobster. "No one."

"I heard a ringtone. So it wasn't a ghost."

Her eyes narrow. "Has anyone ever told you that you're overbearing?"

"I don't need you getting cozy with your friends and telling them what you saw." The sounds pour out of my mouth propelled by hot fury.

"If you really cared about that, you'd have thrown me in an underground dungeon, not given me a ride to my house. You're aware my phone connection has been working all week?"

She's clever.

Even if she blabbed about Luca, without any proof of the crime, it would be useless. It'd be a pain to deal with the police bureaucracy, though, but not impossible. Under other circumstances, I'd have done this the hard way.

"Who have you been talking to?" I press.

She knifes her bottom lip with her teeth so hard, it draws blood. "Nobody."

"You're a bad liar."

"I'm not telling you."

"Afraid I'll kill your drug dealer?" The more I want to be nice to her, the more my blood heats with the need to do the exact opposite. My fingers skim the ends of her hair. I've never held something so fine in my life. I almost question whether I even deserve to put my dirty paws on it. "Poor little rich girl. Where would that leave you?"

Her teeth crack when she bares them. She slaps away my hand. I let her.

"Fine. It was my ex-boyfriend—who unfortunately thinks we're still together. Happy? And before you ask, I'm not telling you his name."

An ember of anger stirs in my belly. My heart plummets. The weight of those words settles in my lungs, slowing my intake of oxygen.

"I didn't ask," I say emphatically to make myself feel in control.

I don't care who her clingy ex-boyfriend is. *I don't.*

My heart rate diving is not a sign of disappointment. Or interest.

Francesca grabs her Ivory Chanel purse off the table, putting distance between us as she races to the door faster than I can react. "I'm going to eat now. Fighting with you has made me hungry."

"We were bantering, not fighting," I correct.

"Sure didn't feel like lighthearted fun."

"For the record, I only fight with my fists." I clear my throat before adding, "And I don't hurt women."

It's meant to put her at ease, but it only serves to raise her suspicion.

"Not even if your boss tells you to?" she questions.

"My boss is a better man than that," I say.

"Whatever." She turns her back to me, reaching to open her studio door.

"Are you running away because you told me that you can't

paint and now you think I'm judging you inside my head?" My gaze holds hers, wringing out her silent admission.

"Are you?" Her voice trips on the question. Her mouth is open. Waiting for my answer. Scared. "Are you judging me? Do you think I don't deserve to be here? That my place should be given to a more talented artist and I'm simply here because of my family's connections?"

"Did your parents donate to the university?"

Francesca's eyebrows furrow in irritation. "No. I got in fair and square."

"You must have some talent then." I lean back against the wall, pointing to her half-finished artwork. "Plus, this looks colorful."

"Colorful. What a compliment."

"You really hate when a guy is being nice to you, don't you?" I scoff. "Guess your type's self-absorbed boys like your ex who don't understand boundaries. Bet he never complimented you."

"How did...." She cuts herself off, narrowing her eyes. "Never mind. I don't want your compliments."

"Then try not to look so happy about it next time." I rub my thumb over my cheek. "You've been blushing for the last minute."

"I'm not!" But she is, and she knows she can't lie her way out of this, too. Embarrassed, she turns and trots away, shouting, "Don't follow me. Or I'll really call the police."

Her threat is flimsy, but I think my staying here is the better option, too. Spending too much time with her is a bit draining on my...mental state. The constant push and pull that she initiates in my chest between my rational mind which knows she's a messed-up girl that I need to stay away from and my not-so-rational mind which wants to get as close to her as possible.

No wonder Antonio wanted nothing to do with Francesca Astor after a week. She gets under your skin with her softness and kindness until you start wanting to protect her. I get it now;

why he drove her to school every day. I'm already ready to buy her lunch and I've talked to her for all of ten minutes.

"Go. I'll guard your paintings." I pick up the brush, dipping it in red paint. "Maybe I'll add some color to this canvas myself."

"Don't you dare!" She marches over and yanks the paintbrush out of my hand. "This is going to be my masterpiece."

"Who knows?" I say. "I might have more talent than you. You have an artist's block anyway. I could be your saving grace."

She hisses in disgust. "Doubt it."

"Okay. I'll just scroll through my phone then."

She shoots me daggers through her eyes as she pads back over to the studio's open door.

CHAPTER 4

 *rancesca*

GABRIELE DOESN'T FOLLOW ME. Not that afternoon, anyway.

I inch along the crowded street on my block heels, peeking inside various shops as I make my way toward The Cinnamon & Fig, my regular brunch spot. I always get the Buddha bowl there. It's to die for.

I used to go there with Ella all the time but our schedules don't line up anymore. I have to spend a lot of time at my studio and she only has classes in the evening. After class, she hangs out with my brother Ethan, who is also her boyfriend. I don't want to cut into their time.

But more than that, I don't feel like socializing with anyone anymore. People's words get stuck in the black net of static running through my brain at all times. My whole life is wrapped up around art right now. I obsess over space, distance, colors, and not being able to paint even when I'm outside my studio. It's gotten to the point where I tune out conversations altogether because I can't focus on anything else. It's painful when people feel ignored by me.

So I spare them that experience by avoiding them.

I trudge onward, taking notice of people's expressions as their bodies pass me as if ships lost at sea. Old habits are impossible to break, so I can't keep myself from taking pictures of some of the sights I see on my phone. From a certain angle, the bare branches of the trees look like two people kissing.

The coldness numbs my brain and quietens it for a second. I spin my head in time to catch the blur of vivid shades in the scenery behind me.

Bright yellow cabs.

Prussian window frames.

Red lanterns hanging outside a Chinese restaurant.

An emotion, fleeting yet familiar, caresses my soul.

I find bliss in colors, in wielding them with a brush, in letting them illustrate the unseen corners of my soul.

Sometimes, art is magic. It turns me beautiful, invincible, and magnificent with its power.

Other times, it erases the empty holes in my chest.

Every day, it demands all my devotion and energy like a starved boyfriend.

But art is a selfish lover because it never leaves me satisfied. It never gives me *enough*.

Before I know it, I'm crashing back down to reality; powerless, invisible, and scared. Craving a high no drug can buy me. Chasing it again with a paintbrush, knowing fully well it'll never be mine.

Knowing that even if it were mine, nothing would change.

So why does it feel like my entire life would be worth something if I only had that one moment of glory?

A text from Ella pings into my inbox, cutting past the sting of disappointment spreading in my nerves.

My throat constricts at the name on the screen.

Ella: Hey, let's meet up tomorrow. I found this great dinner spot. You're free after six, right?

Me: I have some school stuff to do tomorrow.

Ella: What about Saturday?

Me: I'll check my schedule and let you know.

That's just code for: *I'm going to ghost you until you forget about this text conversation.* It's not as though I have an actual packed schedule or don't know what I have going on every day of the week.

Ella: Are you okay?

Me: Yeah, this thesis project is really taking up all my time.

Ella: Let me know if I can help you.

Me: Sure. Hope you're doing well.

Ella: It has been ages since we talked. Both Ethan and I miss you.

Ethan and I? They're guilting me as a unit now after all the trouble I went through to set them up? Well, I did it because I wanted them to be happy. They were both so lonely before. Ella's a socially awkward bookworm and Ethan is so cold and ruthless, even Mom is afraid of crossing paths with him.

I type out the most insincere cliché of all time.

Me: I miss you too.

But that doesn't change the fact that I'm still going to avoid her until I complete my paintings.

Ella: You can talk to me about anything. You know that, right? I'll listen to you anytime. And if I can help you in any way with your art, I'd love to.

Guilt snags in the soft flesh of my heart. Ella and I used to be like sisters. She was always there for me. I know she loves me. That's why I don't want to burden her with my problems. She'll try to help because she can't see me suffer. She'll try to fix me. But this is a battle I must fight for myself.

I was the one who chose to become an artist. I was the one who chose to pursue fame and success. I can't expect other people to put up with the fallout from my dreams.

Me: Don't worry about it. I've made some new friends in my art program. We discuss art stuff with each other.

Okay, that was low, even for me. Ella is shy and has no other friends. She would probably feel excluded by that statement. She might assume I don't need friends anymore. But what else can I do? I lack the emotional stamina to face someone I love and pretend to be happy when I'm bleeding inside. Ella will see through that act in a minute.

Being an artist wasn't the path that my family expected me to follow but I chose it because I was passionate. So the people around me expect me to be happy all the time. To show how grateful and elated I am to be able to draw when more often than not, pursuing my dream feels like sliding down the slope into the valley of death. Yet, I can't stop.

Ella's next message plucks me out of my festering guilt.

Ella: That's great that you've made friends who love art as much as you do. See you on Saturday (hopefully).

Moisture gathers in droplets at the corners of my eyes. I simply don't deserve a friend like Ella. I don't deserve anything, the way I am now. Not even success.

Drained by the text exchange, I stuff my phone back into the pocket of my coat, deciding it's better to not reply rather than say something else that might inadvertently hurt Ella.

Sometimes, I think I might be worse than Antonio. At least he's sincere, honest, and has his act together.

Funny that he's the one in the mafia.

CHAPTER 5

 abriele

"WHAT'S YOUR POSITION? Capo? Don? Just a soldier?"

"You've been researching the mafia," I say, cutting a silencing glare at Francesca as she whistles beside me in my car, all giddy that I'm driving her to school instead of her personal chauffer who apparently doesn't exist even though her family has enough money to drown themselves in. Apparently, her mother prefers to drive by herself since she doesn't originally come from wealth.

"I know all organized crime families have some legal business interests as well," she continues, her ballet flats sliding up and down the mat on the floor of the car. "What exactly are you into? Casinos? Money laundering?"

"Mostly I break people's necks." The tires squeal as I hit the break suddenly when the light turns red. "Fuck. Are you okay?"

Francesca points a fork speared with a slice of kiwi in front of my mouth. "I'm fine. Eat your breakfast."

The correct response here is to scowl. But my pride takes second place to my hunger. I gobble up the fruit she's offering quietly.

"Is it good?" she asks.

I nod, cringing inwardly when she offers me another piece of melon and I devour that, too.

I gave Antonio shit for acting like her father. Now look at me doing exactly what he did. It only took two fucking days of Francesca Astor silently coaxing me with those doll eyes. When she brought me breakfast that her personal chef had made this morning, I caved.

The thing is, I don't like owing people favors. So I obviously asked her to hop in when she told me she needed to get to school.

"You sure all your screws up there are tight? Why're you being so generous to a mobster?" My fingers are still on the wheel. "Unless you laced the food with poison."

Francesca puckers her wet lips. "I believe in being kind to all people."

"Christian charity?"

"I'm not religious. But I think charity is good for the soul."

My acidic scoff betrays my sentiments too well.

"Not all people have souls, though," Francesca adds, a naughty glint in her eye. "A pity."

"If you're trying to convert me into a religion, you can quit it now," I say.

"I'm not trying to convert you to anything."

I'm thinking it's a relief when she stops talking, but a mile later, the silence in the car begins to feel oppressive. The best course of action here is to turn on the radio which eliminates any further possibility of conversation but I'm full of self-loathing these days. So I say, "Can't you drive?"

"Not in the city. There are too many cars."

"You can do it if you practice."

"I'm busy with art. Once I'm a world-renowned painter and my art sells for millions—"

"You can't be serious. You'll be fifty years old by the time you become famous."

Her tiny laugh is like a pearl rolling over my skin. "I'm hoping it'll be sooner than that."

"So until then, you're going to charm mobsters into offering you free rides?" I shake my head emphatically, attention diverted from the road to her beautiful, vulnerable face for a moment. "That's the worst idea I've ever heard."

"I think it's a solid plan," she retorts, playfulness bubbling up under her tone. Smiling, she glances out of the window.

I relax a fraction at the thought that she isn't sad today. Her eyes sparkle with brightness and hope instead of being darkened by the usual shadows. Clenching and unclenching her fingers, she shifts restlessly in her seat. I know for a fact that she did drugs yesterday at the club she was at. That might explain the sudden lift in her mood.

Her sunshine frame of mind is definitely not due to a wellspring of creative inspiration suddenly popping out of nowhere. The nervousness that whispers around her like a ghost is still there, visceral enough to prick the hairs on my arms. When I slide my thumb up her wrist, her pulse is hammering away like an endless wave crashing against rocks.

She narrows her eyes even though I barely touched her for a second. "Can't keep your hands off me, I see."

She's almost as good as me at covering her feelings with sarcasm. Almost.

"If you're scared just say so."

"I told you before. I'm not scared of you." The worst part is, I think she actually means what she's saying. I'm supposed to make her shake in fear at my presence. Instead, she's feeding me fruit like I'm her sweet little pet dog. I swear, I have no idea how this happened.

I remove my thumb from her wrist.

"Hot and cold." She clicks her tongue in mock disappointment. "Mr. Russo, I'm still young so don't give me false hope with your mixed signals and break my heart. I'll never forgive you."

A strange emotion wrestles against my ribcage. If I didn't know myself incapable of feeling it, I'd say it was guilt.

I don't intend to involve myself with Francesca so why are my intestines twisting themselves into painful knots over a simple statement?

Don't give me false hope with your mixed signals and break my heart. I'll never forgive you.

My breath breaks into a silent sob when Francesca goes one step further and runs her thumb up my arm casually, leaving a trail of fire over my nerves.

"How you like that?" she adds in a low, quiet voice. "That's how I felt, you know. Like a weird slimy thing was crawling over my skin."

The air thumps with an invisible heartbeat as the suggestion in her tone coils around my neck like a collar. A low buzz of heat echoes in my groin. Damn it. It's been too long since I got laid. But that doesn't mean I'm tempted by this slip of a girl.

Not one bit.

Strangely, her touch doesn't feel weird or slimy as she thinks. It feels warm and inviting.

"You need to watch that mouth of yours." I curl my fingers tightly over the wheel and turn it hard, shaking off her touch. "It'll get you in trouble someday."

"Am I not in trouble already? I'm in a car with a Mafioso who stalks me all day." Alluring. Condescending. Her breathy, smooth tone is far too sexy for a twenty-one-year-old.

It's an invitation to my starved body. A softly whispered

promise that will haunt my dreams the same way her perfect face has haunted them since the day I met her.

I put my foot on the pedal, accelerating. Where the fuck is the building with her studio? Why aren't we there yet?

Francesca's breath hitches like she's about to say something else, but the ringing of her phone interrupts her. I silently thank whoever decided to call at this crucial moment.

She heaves an exasperated sigh at the screen. That alone tells me it's someone she doesn't like. So I'm surprised when she answers the phone.

"Stop calling me. What part of 'we broke up' don't you understand?"

A string of frantic noises breaks free from the other end. Though I can't make out the words, annoyance heats up Francesca's features.

"I don't care," she screams. "Bye."

Throwing her phone on her lap, she presses herself to the back of the seat. Her eyelids draw down, exhaustion creeping out of her mouth in a frustrated groan.

I turn on the radio. Piano notes from a somber ballad fill the space. How appropriate for the mood. But when Francesca's chin dips and she releases a small, frustrated groan, I decide to turn the music off.

"What does your ex do?" I ask, wondering how the hell I ended up making small talk with an heiress. "He seems to have a lot of free time."

"Nothing. His parents are rich."

I snort. "Sounds like you two would get along great. Why'd you break up?"

"I hate how he always assumed I'd never become successful. He kept mentioning working at the various charities his family supports after graduation when he knew I'd have to be painting. It irritated me."

"Don't like people underestimating you?"

"Do you like it when people write off your dreams as impossible?"

"I don't have any dreams. Only orders."

"So much for sympathy." She sighs.

"But I get it. You don't have anything if you don't have respect."

She blinks at me. "Never expected to hear that from a criminal. Is there some traumatic childhood backstory you haven't told me yet?"

I'm saved from answering that question by the GPS navigation's end. Meaning we're at our destination.

"Get out." I reach past her and open the door. "The ride's over."

"Thank you very much for not getting into an accident with your driving skills." She hops out, her gaze lingering on me disturbingly long. "I'm sure that took a lot of self-control."

She doesn't rush off to the building, glad to get away from me as I hoped she would. Instead, the heiress waits around. I'd have thought she'd love to get me out of her hair after that heated...whatever that moment in the car was. It certainly has glued its memory into my nerves.

I twist up an eyebrow, rolling down the window glass. "You need something?"

"If you come with me, I can let the security know that you're with me so they don't ask questions," she says.

I scoff. Look at her being all polite and considerate. To her stalker.

She doesn't realize that the security guard will let me up anyway. He's a smart man who understands how the world works. And I'm a pro at threatening.

"No thanks. I'll be in my car."

I'm thinking I must have imagined the way the shoulders sag in disappointment, but she confirms it with her next word. "Don't you always observe me painting like a creep?"

"I've decided to be less creepy starting today." I don't understand why she's still hanging around. "Unless you're missing my creepiness?"

"As if." She snorts.

Then swivels hard and vanishes, leaving me with a heavy ache in my stomach.

CHAPTER 6

 rancesca

"You stink." Mom turns her nose up at me. I'm slumped on my bed, zoning out, my mind obsessing over my lack of progress as usual. "Take a shower."

When she pulls the curtains apart, bright sunshine spears into my cold skin. It crawls over the expanse of my messy room, exposing the proof of my decay: credit cards and dollar bills strewn on my desk beside a faint dusting of white powder traces leftover from yesterday. Rubbing my eyes, I hobble to my feet, hoping to distract my mother.

I shouldn't have bothered. Mom's unsuspecting, too busy adjusting her pearl necklace to pay attention to the evidence staring at her. She's a good mother, but she thinks she knows me. That's why she ignores the signs. In her mind, her daughter is a good girl who loves art, has nice friends, and is happy and fulfilled.

Sometimes, I wish I could be that person.

"It's afternoon already?" I mumble. Why does it feel like I fell asleep only minutes ago?

"Francesca, dear, what are you doing? The charity gala for the Marini Foundation is today. You have two hours to get into your dress on put on makeup."

A groan wells up in my stomach.

I briefly consider feigning sickness. But I don't want to spend the entire day staring at bleak nothingness. Today's Sunday so I didn't even have to go to college. Which means I haven't seen Gabriele, either. When I looked out of the window earlier, his usual black Mercedes wasn't there.

"Sorry." I rub my nose, trying to catch any stray powder before Mom notices. "My thesis has been intense this semester."

Mom runs her fingers lovingly over my hair. "You're so dedicated. But remember to take care of yourself, too. Want to go to the spa tomorrow?"

"Nope." I tumble into my bathroom, groggy.

These days, I only scare myself by looking in the mirror. The person I'm transforming into isn't something I can handle.

By the time I've slipped into a designer dress and covered every crack in my façade with a thick foundation, I almost look like the daughter my mom believes she has.

* * *

MY HEELS TAP against the marble floor as I drift through a parade of gorgeous dresses and tailored suits. Champagne flutes on silver trays are carried past me by crisply dressed servers. Shiny hair glints beneath soft lights, the smell of money and perfume wreathing the air. The charity gala is for nonprofits fighting blindness. It's filled with the who's who of New York high society.

Mom located her friends among the guests and started chatting with them as soon as we entered, leaving me to wander as I please.

My older brother Ethan haunts the periphery of my vision, looking handsome and deadly as usual. Clad in a black suit that seduces with its sophistication, he stands out of the crowd with his height and powerful physique. His girlfriend Ella is not by his side tonight. Ella hates social events and I can't blame her for it. They suck.

"Francesca." His dry, humorless voice curls around the base of my neck like a dark vise. "I thought you'd moved to another continent without telling any of us."

One of Ethan's most unnerving qualities is that nothing escapes him. I thought he didn't notice me, but apparently he did.

"Sorry." I duck under my brother's friendly pat, avoiding him. "I've been busy with assignments."

Ethan exhales, a long line forming between his brows. He's nonverbally calling me out on my bullshit. As I said, he's perceptive. But I'm stubborn, too. I don't budge. "The commission I received has been so taxing. Plus, there's the spring thesis."

"Wasn't the commission six months ago?"

"Great art takes time." My fingers tighten around each other. I can feel how clammy my skin has gotten despite the cool air circulating inside. Lying used to come so naturally to me. Just like art. Now both feel impossible.

"Elliot's not here?" I ask, craning my neck over the crowd looking for my other brother.

"He's at work." Ethan shrugs.

Elliot has become more reclusive than a hermit ever since he started working for Sharma Ventures, a venture capital firm headquartered in the financial district. Boy, his boss must be a slave driver because he doesn't even have time to call his family anymore.

Not that I've tried calling him, either.

Warmth flickers in Ethan's dark eyes. Elliot and I have blue eyes like our mother, but Ethan is from Dad's first marriage so he had darker features.

"Ella misses you." His voice is laced with gentle concern. "She's lonely. You guys used to be inseparable."

"Shouldn't you be keeping her company if she's lonely?" I ask.

"It's different," he says. "You're her friend."

The sliver of affection in his voice is a sign of how much he has changed compared to six months ago. Before he met Ella, Ethan used to be such a cold-hearted prick that he didn't think friendship meant anything. But look at him now. He has broadened his horizons.

I'm happy I played matchmaker. It was my lie about going to London that made them both travel to the UK. And they ended up spending time together, which led to feelings blossoming between them.

Like I said, I used to be a Grade-A liar in the past.

"I'll try," I dish out, noncommittal before a man in a gray suit shows up to demand Ethan's attention and rescues me from being grilled by my brother.

I clamber to the garden outside the venue which is also decorated for the charity event. Breathing in large gulps of air, I try to return to my equilibrium. Except there is no balanced center inside me. There hasn't been in a long time.

Even the freezing air can't rescue me from me. I knead my temples, looking around until I spot a familiar form—that of my ex-boyfriend. I swivel immediately, hoping to escape. Unfortunately, his gaze latches onto me before I can move.

"Francesca!" The last person I wanted to see tonight sashays up to me, his blonde curls bouncing like bed springs. On paper, Mason Turner is attractive. He has the clean-cut good-boy looks that no mother could find fault with.

Including my own, who has been encouraging me to get engaged to him.

But I don't like men with no hard edges, no imperfections, no depth. No darkness.

Nothing calls out to me like danger and ruin.

And the most dangerous thing about Mason Turner is his low IQ.

"You've been MIA, Francesca." His voice is dripping with accusation. My stomach tightens in defensiveness. "What's wrong with you?"

I evade when he tries to touch me. "I was busy painting."

"That again?"

"We broke up. Why are you even calling me?"

"Because I miss you." He slides his foot between my feet. Crowds my space. His head tilts down, hot breath swooshing over my cheeks. "We were so good together, Francesca. The perfect couple. We both come from the same world. We can have a future together. Don't you see it?"

"I don't care about your money or your family name. Besides, I'm more interested in being an acclaimed painter than getting engaged at twenty-one. So excuse me if I don't see the appeal in your offer."

"Do you have to be so stubborn?" His arm snakes around my waist.

"Yes." I elbow him in an attempt to assert my space. "I told you I'm serious about being an artist. What about it is so hard to understand?"

His features crumple in exasperation. A sigh heaves out of him, depressing his chest. "It's not easy to make it in a competitive field like that, Francesca. Being a struggling painter might seem romantic now, but what do you even know about real struggle? You've been pampered by your parents all your life. People like us should simply stay where we belong."

"I belong in..." My throat closes up as the chorus in my head rises.

Liar.

Impostor.

Worthless.

You don't belong in the world of art.

You don't belong anywhere.

Despair pounds against the walls of my chest. Who am I lying to? Mason? Or myself?

I feel like vomiting when I look at the canvas nowadays. Violent churning starts up in my stomach, the sickness traveling all the way up to my head, pricking my skull with a headache.

Is he right? Am I deluding myself by thinking I can do this forever? Will I eventually get exhausted by the struggle of forcing myself to commit my emotions to the canvas?

If I'm being honest, art has me feeling drained most days. No matter how hard I try, I can't come up with anything worthy of being called a masterpiece.

There's nothing beautiful left inside me anymore. No visions or dreams worth turning into art. Nothing but emptiness and the obsessive desire to be recognized. I was so greedy for fame, for success. But am I ready to pay the price for it?

People's expectations are drowning me. No matter what I do, I hear the voices of my professors and critics in my head insisting I need to be better—more shocking, more magnificent, more than a twenty-one-year-old girl trying to figure herself out. I must show people the ultimate fantasy on canvas, one that will take their breaths away. Something so grand, my mind can't even imagine what it would look like.

"Whatever you say." Mason drags an impatient hand through his hair. "Will you at least come to dinner with my parents next Friday? It's been *two weeks*. Haven't you had enough of your tantrum?"

I should kick him in the balls. I have explained to him

enough times in simple English that we broke up but he simply refuses to listen. He's the type of entitled guy who has been spoiled so much, he thinks everybody secretly wants to marry him.

His finger meets the curve of my neck. He caresses my throat, trailing his fingertip all the way up to my lips. "You always had the most beautiful lips. I can't forget how they feel against mine."

A moment of weakness pulls me under. I should back away. Spit on his face.

But I suddenly remember why I started dating Mason even though he's shallow, self-absorbed, and dim-witted.

He's a great kisser. Great at convincing me I'll be just fine if I give up on my dreams. He makes me forget how hollow and ugly the parts of me I can't bear to face are. My tortured mind longs to sink into the dream he paints with his voice, the one where I'm perfect, we're perfect, and everything is perfect.

"Get away from her," a deep, wild voice shatters my dream.

My blood, flesh, and heart all freeze at the same time. the whole world crashes around my ears when a large, male form tracks past me to slam a hand down Mason's shoulder.

I see him in pieces. The navy suit. The big, rough hands. Tan skin. A hint of ink peeks from under the crisp white collar of his shirt.

The lump in my throat expands like a cancerous tumor.

No way. Gabriele Russo is here.

He's looking all polished in his suit with his hair tamed. What the hell is a gangster doing at a charity event?

Mason clamps his teeth, grabbing Gabriele's arm. I spot the vein popping in the mobster's forehead, sensing the violence that catches in the air like the first spark of fire.

Damn. No.

"Leave," Gabriele orders him. "And I don't want to see you bothering her again. Understood?"

A curl falls over Mason's squinting eyes. "Who are you to butt in between my girlfriend and me?"

"Someone you should be afraid of."

"Francesca—"

"Mason, don't," I warn. "He's dangerous. And he's right—we broke up. You shouldn't be pestering me. I'm not your girlfriend."

With a mask of self-righteousness, I bury my moment of weakness, the shameful awareness that I was about to kiss a guy who has never respected my goals and dreams. All because I'm too weak to endure the self-defeating thoughts inside my head. They exhaust me. And when I'm drained, I turn to escapism. And if I can't escape through drugs or alcohol, I'll take it through any means possible.

Sometimes, I'm scared of myself. Of how low I can fall without realizing I'm falling.

"Fine." Mason huffs, staring down at Gabriele. The mobster is unfazed. "But I'm telling Mother that we're not getting engaged. You can forget about being part of my family now."

"I never wanted to be part of your family," I say. "I don't know where you got that idea."

Pride snuffed, Mason flares his nostrils.

Gabriele releases his grip on my ex. "Go now. And don't look back."

Mason has the sense to do as he's told. He takes off. Once his silhouette vanishes from sight, Gabriele glares at me. I begin walking ahead without a word. He opens the door to the main hall for me like he's a gentleman. All the while, his eyes pin me with a glare that is borderline threatening.

I roll my eyes. "Don't be melodramatic. He was my ex. We were only having one of our usual arguments."

My fingers are coated in sweat. I hope Gabriele didn't notice how I almost leaned in for a kiss with Mason. I mean, there's no reason I should care about what he thinks. But I do. I can't explain. I don't want him to think I'm pathetic.

"No need to explain. I was listening," he says.

"Why am I not surprised? Eavesdropping and stalking are your hobbies." I rub my thumb against the strap of my black satin mini-dress. "Why're you at a charity gala anyway?"

"To meet someone."

"Who?"

"None of your business."

Despite having guided me back safely to the crowd, Gabriele stands in front of me like a wall, not budging despite my best eye roll.

"Are you going to stand here all night?" I ask.

"If I want to."

"How about what I want?"

"It's my body, my feet, and they listen to only me." His breath is like a gust of wind as it blows over my face. "Unlike you, I have great control over my body."

"What do you mean?"

Gabriele's dark eyebrows form a V. "Are you so desperate for a kiss that you'd kiss that slimeball?"

Shit. He saw it. And now he's going to hold it over me. I like when we banter. It's fun and it takes my mind off darker thoughts. But tonight, I just want…warmth. Not electricity. Not verbal sparks. Not mental stimulation. Just the heat of another human to assure me I'm still needed, wanted, and desired, despite how terrible I am at art.

"I don't know what you mean." I move away, but Gabriele moves with me. Looks like he has decided to play Stalker tonight.

I sigh the longest sigh ever.

"What are you thinking now, Francesca?" His gruff, seductive voice shoots into my blood as if he injected it.

I spear him with my meanest glance. "That I wish I hadn't come here."

"What would you have done at home? Drugs?" His opaque, dark gaze is making me feel claustrophobic. How does he know so much about me when he has only known me for a week? Has he been paying so much attention to me? Why does that warm my heart? "Alcohol? Would you have slept alone? Cried? Painted?"

All of it. I'd have done all of it.

"Guess you wouldn't have painted, since you can't," he corrects himself.

Liar.

You have no talent.

No future.

Nothing.

Gabriele retreats and the space between us suddenly floods me with even more anxiety. The itch to get closer to him is as intense as the need for oxygen.

"Don't make fun of someone else's pain," I retort.

I grab his jacket sleeve to push him out of my way, but he seizes my hands. Even though his touch only lasts a minute—before he puts distance between us—I feel the imprint of his roughness against mine like a brand.

Lust licks over my skin. I must have lost it after my professor said my thesis painting wasn't up to par on Friday. Maybe my anxiety is flaring again and I need something mindless to turn my attention away from the clawing thoughts inside my head. That's why I almost let Mason kiss me. A distraction is all I need to bury the acidic downpour of self-criticism pelting my brain.

And the biggest distraction of the century is standing right under my nose, wearing a suit and promising me something dangerous with his silence.

Gabriele smells like a moonless night. Heat inflames my senses.

How long has it been since I felt something other than fear, anxiety, and numbness?

Forever.

"Well, can you make yourself useful and get me a glass of wine at least?" I'm not sure why I say that.

"Do I look like a server?" Gabriele rolls one eyebrow up, folding his arms over his chest.

"Why did I even bother asking?"

Not like I'm incapable.

I wander over to the bar where a cute female bartender pours me a vintage pinot grigio. I try to talk to her, but there are too many people demanding her attention. Defeated, I scurry back, careful to avoid attention from my family.

Ethan's busy talking to some guy and with the back of his head to me, it's easy to slip by unnoticed. I scan the swarm of people for Mom. She's still happily nestled in a small group with her old friends. I suppose most of them are talking to her again. The hotels announced profits this quarter again and the types who only care about money and prestige probably realize that the Astor family isn't going to be reduced to poverty by a small scandal.

I debate returning to the spot where Gabriele is standing like a statue made of marble. I shouldn't go near him. But at the same time, I want to. I have no friends here and I can't cling to Ethan without inviting more uncomfortable questions. Eventually, he'll crack me open and I'll spill my secrets. I can't have that.

So I crawl right back to Gabriele. Funny how he's the only one here who knows about my addictions and demons, even though we're simply captor and captive.

He scrutinizes me wordlessly, studying my wineglass. "Sorry, didn't get one for you," I smirk.

"Didn't ask you to."

"What, you don't drink?"

"Not tonight."

"You're here for a job?" That could be the only possible reason he wants to remain sober. "Who are you going to kill? Who's your target? Please say it's not my brother."

The mobster stays silent. He only talks when he wants to. Too bad I need him to talk now. I could use some pointless banter.

My mind is eating away at my self-confidence.

Being a struggling painter might seem romantic now, but what do you even know about real struggle? You've been pampered by your parents all your life. People like us should simply stay where we belong.

Mason's words haunt my heart. I don't know where I belong. I don't feel at home with other old-money kids. I'm different from them. But I'm not like my classmates at NYU, either. Maybe I'm just a freak.

I'm getting a headache from overthinking, so I mindlessly reach for another class of wine, hoping to numb my brain altogether. I want silence, not this endless conflict, this endless fear that I'm not good enough to do the only thing I've ever wanted to do.

When I drain the second wineglass and charge for the third, Gabriele wrenches my arm back.

My ears ring with the sound of his terse command. "Stop."

"Huh?" I slur. "What're you doing?"

"You've had enough. If you continue, you'll faint and I'll have to carry you out over my shoulder."

Curse him. Why did that visual he painted right now seem so hot? Even though it shouldn't. Damn, the alcohol was a bad idea after all. It has made me forget that Gabriele is someone I should fear, not someone I should want.

"Don't tell me what to do," I yell.

His eyes narrow into slits, magnifying the shadows inside his black pupils. "Escaping what you don't like won't make it disappear, Francesca."

With one statement, he turns me inside out, exposing the festering, grotesque feelings I avoid with intoxicants.

My pulse jumps in my wrist. "I'm not scared."

"You are." Gabriele's voice turns into a hard rasp. A ripple of unease rolls down my spine. "Not of me, though. Of yourself."

I bristle at his confidence. "What gives you the authority to say that? Do you have a Ph.D. in psychology?"

"Snap all you want. But you're only digging your grave deeper."

"Excuse me?" I hiss.

"You've bullshitted everyone and yourself so much, you're scared it's all going to unravel someday. Then you'll have to face the truth."

His words crowd my chest, clawing at the barrier I've erected to protect my sanity. Stealing my shield away piece by piece.

I haven't moved an inch from my spot, but I'm breathless when I say, "What's the truth, Gabriele?"

That one split second of silence, before he answers, perforates my skin like a needle. Anxiety blooms under my skin before he even opens his mouth.

"The truth is that there's no light without darkness. No growth without suffering." Gabriele's mouth squeezes into a thin, malevolent line. "And no art without self-doubt."

Though I'm shaken to my core, I manage to retain my bravado. Years of training. He can't take that away from me. "Didn't ask for a philosophy lesson, Professor."

"Wasn't giving you one."

Yet, he has stripped me naked with his words.

Seen through my lies.

Scratched every bruise.

Stabbed at my greatest weakness.

Goosebumps flare on my skin.

As the corrosive, hollowing sensation builds in my bones, my face immediately whips in the direction of the wine. I am powerless against the heavy emotions that well up in the bottom of my heart. I take the only escape route I know. My legs direct me toward the alcohol like a GPS pointing to its destination.

Something heavy wraps around my midsection. Gabriele pulls me back, his physical strength an inescapable force.

"Don't do it," he warns. If I didn't know better, I'd assume that the gangster was actually concerned for me. That seeing me struggling in my studio must have made him care.

I shake my head violently, curls slapping his face. "There's no other way."

I wish there was. Something less dangerous. Less destructive.

He doesn't release his tight grip on me. Not even when I make an effort to pull away from him.

Thick tension envelops us. His sideways glance settles on my skin like the edge of a knife, threatening to cut away the last link I have to sensibility. A complex game of strategy is unfolding inside his head; I can sense it.

He sighs.

Then opens his mouth and fucks up my brain with one simple sentence.

"Ride my fingers, Francesca."

Fire roars inside me, obliterating the years of cold, dead nothing. I've always craved mindless excitement. It's why I abuse drugs. But this is more than a thrill. It's dangerous. Seductive.

And it's calling my name.

The knowledge that Gabriele could wound me, hurt me, only sharpens the edge of my desire.

"You can't be serious." Someone help me. Even my collarbones are hot at the thought of this sexy tattooed mobster touching me so who am I kidding?

Gabriele sees through my flimsy argument instantly.

He plants a hand on my hips, thumb probing the swell of my ass through the thin material of my dress. "If you want to forget, I'll help you."

"Why?"

"Because I can."

Perfume and sweat collide in the air between us. My nipples pebble into hard, aching points, poking through my satin dress, begging for his touch.

He scans my obvious arousal through narrowed eyes.

Taking a step back, he holds his outstretched hand in front of me. "Come on."

It's clear what he's offering.

Not comfort.

Not compassion.

Not even a guaranteed good time.

But a way out of the loneliness and self-doubt that chews me up from the inside.

A momentary break from the incessant worries in my head.

I take it.

CHAPTER 7

 rancesca

My tiny palm meets his open one and he engulfs it in his warmth. I trip on my heels when he jerks me forward, landing against his chest. He cocoons me with his arms, sweeping me away. Past corridors. Past people. Past the shadows flashing over us.

Until we're standing outside the restrooms.

"We're doing it in the toilets?" I screech. It would be my first time.

Irritation crackles in the snap of Gabriele's fingers. "Would you rather do it out in the open in front of everyone?"

"If those are the two choices, I guess it's going to be the toilets." Clamping down my resistance, I follow him into the women's restroom. I check all the stalls to see if there's nobody else. But Gabriele doesn't let me complete my inspection before he hauls me into one of the empty stalls.

I sniff at the air.

"Don't turn up your nose already." The sound of the bathroom stall door bolting shut vibrates against my ears. "It's about to get dirtier. If there's anything you don't want me to do, any limits, speak now."

There are only a few things I haven't experimented with before, sexually, and I doubt he's going to take it that far. "You can do anything you want as long as you don't make me bleed or bruise me. Not even a tiny cut. And of course, use protection. It's non-negotiable," I say. "You can be a little rough, but not too much. Also, don't choke me."

A tiny smile curls against his lips. The smallest hint of remorse flickers in his expression before hunger and lust overwhelm him as much as they're overwhelming me.

He pulls down my zipper and lowers the front of my dress. The clasp of my bra almost breaks when attacked by his impatient hands. He yanks it off. My breasts spill out into his large palms. He squeezes me, kneading my soft flesh, flicking the hard buds that have been begging for his attention since earlier. I relish the tiny cuts and scrapes that dot the surface of his skin, which add roughness to his touch and make my nipples peak.

His mouth comes down on the bud of my nipple and he kisses the hard peaks, sending flutters of pleasure straight to my groin. The burning hot press of his tongue against my erect bud floods my brain with blissful blankness. Shock clashes with ecstasy. Shivers course through me. It's as close to the feeling of being high as I can get without actually being high.

He turns his mouth to my other breast, biting down this time, gathering me up in his arms easily, holding me in the air as he ravages my breasts until even the brush of cool air against them hurts.

I lean against his shoulder.

He's built like a tank, his body carved with unforgiving muscle and hard lines. I've never done it with such a powerful and violent man. I'm sure he won't be loving or patient. But that's exactly the reason I want this so much.

I brace one hand against the wall and another against his solid chest. He impatiently slides a hand under my dress, cupping my sex, squeezing it through the barrier of my lace panties, drawing out every bit of resistance from me without ever directly touching my skin. My body is flooded by cool, beautiful sensations. My hips rock forward, hungry for his brutal touch.

His dark eyes glisten with naked animosity. The sharp edge of his teeth caresses my earlobe. Thrill lances straight to my core, spreading moisture down my center.

"Antonio was right about you being a horny little slut." His sultry whisper licks a trail of fire through my insides. I moan, coming undone. The bad part about wearing fine lace under-wear is that he can definitely feel the wet spot through the thin fabric.

And he grinds his finger into that exact place, letting me know how much he's enjoying my humiliation. His mouth presses into my cheek so his rasp ghosts over my skin like smoke. "Look at your pussy dripping for a man you barely know. You're dreaming of these rough fingers wrecking your insides, aren't you?"

Warmth and arousal curl at the base of my stomach with every filthy word out of his mouth. It's sick how much I need his brand of raw degradation. I want to be taken hard and fast without any gentleness. So I can forget who I am, where I come from, and what the future holds for a girl like me. I want to stop being me.

I dig my nails into the back of his tailored jacket. "Shut up."

"Why?" He fists my hair with his other hand, pulling my head back and exposing my neck. A scream rises up my throat. "You don't like dirty talk?"

No, I love it.

I shake my head. The eagerness with which I'm grinding against his fingers probably makes words a moot point anyway. My breath stretches taut.

"Will you let me turn you inside out, Francesca?" he asks.

My assent croaks out of my throat as my body surrenders to a wave of pleasure.

But he doesn't give me the sweetness I crave.

My inner muscles clench around emptiness, needing another hit of degrading words delivered in that uncultured, stony rasp. My mind's warping back to that dark place, repeating an endless loop of *Not good enough.*

Even a cold-blooded killer with zero standards doesn't want you, Francesca.

In just a simple power move, Gabriele has revealed the deep cracks in my self-confidence. Was that his intention?

I curl my hand over his unyielding shoulders, bridging the gap between our bodies. "Show me your worst, Gabriele. Let me see it. I have to see it." *So I can stop needing you.*

My hazy brain, addled with insecurity and substance dependence, can't think straight in the presence of something as undeniable and uncomplicated as lust. What's another bad choice when my life's brimming with them?

Gabriele pushes me back until my back's flat against the wall. "You said it yourself. Don't whine to me later."

"I'm not a kid—"

Fear punctures my lungs and squeezes the air out when he rips my panties off. I gasp at the torn scraps when they land around my feet. Shit. I'm going to be bare for the rest of the night.

"You psycho!" I hiss. "I still have to go home."

A hint of humor glitters in his eyes. Judging by the upward flick of his lips, Gabriele finds my attempt at modesty highly entertaining.

"What did you imagine it was going to be like? Did you

expect a mafioso to quote Shakespeare and make love to you gently under the moonlight? I like pain, Francesca. And you're going to learn to like it, too."

Even an idiot could decipher the subtext scrolling through his blown-out pupils: *You can't avoid this pain with drugs and alcohol. I'm not going to let you.*

The hairs on my body stand up. Suddenly, this doesn't feel like mindless sex anymore. He's seen through me into the ugliness nestled under layers of false cheer and polish.

Is this what he meant when he said he'd help me? That he'd help me face my worst parts that I refuse to face otherwise?

Anxiety pecks at my chest. Need tightens into a heavy rock in my belly. But every feeling cuts out to silence when Gabriele's hand crawls back up my thighs. I lock my arms around his neck and spread my legs, opening myself up to his assault.

It takes him no time at all to find my clit. The rough texture of his fingertips abrades my tender, over-sensitized flesh, setting every nerve ending ablaze. One finger thrusts into my entrance, making my legs buckle. His teeth sink into the softness of my neck. He doesn't wait for me to get comfortable before he thrusts two digits into me at once and proceeds to aggressively fuck me, just like I have been waiting for him to. A dark pleasure unwraps in my bloodstream. My nerves sing with satisfaction. God, this feels even better than I imagined. How long has it been since someone gave it to me so good?

"I'm going to screw you like a whore, Francesca." The threat curls over Gabriele's tongue. "Because under all that posh preening, that's exactly what you are, isn't it?"

The slippery wetness dripping down my thighs intensifies. I whimper. This man could make me come with words alone. My back hits the wall every time I jerk against his fingers. I love how trapped I feel between the hard wall and Gabriele Russo's harder chest. This is better than drugs.

"Say you want to stop," he demands. "I dare you to say it."

"No." I grind out through my clenched teeth. Ecstasy is radiating through me. All these sensations chewing my insides are dissolving my pride, my self-preservation, and the very fiber of my soul.

My wet channel eats up his fingers greedily. I stretch for him, yearning to fill the nagging, empty void inside me. My hips move on their own, seeking release in the primal strength of this monster. Pleasure crashes over me, plucking away every self-doubting thought in my head.

Electric shocks shoot in my veins when he curls his fingers inside me, hitting me where I need it the most. My back arches, my body leaning into Gabriele's strong arms. I hate to admit how much I love the solidity of him against me.

These past few months, my world has consisted of impossible expectations and shifting illusions. Highs and lows manufactured by powder and paint. But this moment is real. The pressure of his fingers inside me is real. The depraved words he whispers to me are real. So real it fractures my soul to know I'll never have something like this again.

Moving up and down on his thick fingers, I'm unraveling. Then Gabriele's fingers scissor me and the burn of that stretch catapults me closer to the edge of my release.

A soft sigh escapes my lips. "So good."

"Then why aren't you screaming my name?" he challenges.

"Are you crazy? There might be people here."

"I don't give a fuck if some stranger finds you're a nympho. Scream my name or I won't let you come."

I need to stop before this man wrecks my life with his filthy mouth.

This is so twisted.

He's a thug who stalks me all day.

He has killed countless people with the same fingers that are pressing against my G-spot.

He'll probably shoot me without batting an eyelid if it comes down to that.

Why am I not scared of him at all?

Why in the world am I turned on by how thrilling it feels to be vulnerable in front of a guy who doesn't value life?

The answer twists my gut. It's because Gabriele has no pretenses. He shows all of his darkness without flinching. He accepts his disgusting impulses without condemning himself.

Sure of his place in the world and living for his own validation—he's everything I can never hope to be.

A hard slap against my pussy sucks me away from my overthinking. I bring my teeth down on my bottom lip, tamping down the impulse to cry. To scream. But Gabriele is persistent. His flat palm smacks my tender flesh again and again. Each fresh wave of pain only sends me soaring higher. Coupled with how he's brutalizing my insides, I could come in three seconds flat. But he keeps pulling out his fingers. Stopping. Demanding me to call out his name.

Leaving me no other choice.

"Gabriele, dammit! I will strangle you if you don't stop doing that." The echo of my high-pitched wail reverberates throughout the space. I really hope nobody heard that.

The swoosh of someone flushing the toilet razes my prayers to ashes.

I pale. Great.

Gabriele Russo's smile widens to show teeth. "That made my day."

"You're a sadist."

"You're a prude." His thumb runs across my pussy lips, tracing their edges. The sudden tenderness on the heels of the stinging pain still radiating through my flesh sends shivers to my core. He gives my clit the same gentle treatment, rubbing and pressing and lavishing it with reverence.

Before I can yell at him to go hard and fast again, all the heat and ecstasy wash down my nerves in a rippling orgasm. Pinpricks of waxy light dance in my vision like snowflakes falling from a white ceiling. In that instant, even this grubby bathroom turns into a beautiful scene worthy of being immortalized on a canvas. I pray I'll remember this sight when I'm home at night. And maybe, I'll be able to paint a picture that can capture the bliss I feel when I stare at the grime-flecked white paint while pasted against Gabriele Russo's chest, his thick digits still stuck in me.

Moisture, the evidence of my pleasure, drips from me, gliding down the mobster's knuckles. He brings his hand up to my lips and makes me lick it off. I'm still floating so I do it without a complaint.

One foot eases out of my shoes to venture up his clothed thigh, to where the unmistakable swell of an erection is poking through the fabric. This man is hard for me. Wonder why that makes me feel invincible.

My fingers snag on the button of his pants. I begin to lower myself to the floor, opening my mouth, eager for the weight of his cock on my tongue. "Don't worry," I tell him. "I'll return the favor."

When I look up at him, he's no longer smiling. Dark, nameless rage glitters in Gabriele's eyes. He grabs me by the arm and pulls my body upright.

"This is not a trade," he says.

"I didn't mean it—"

"Stop, Francesca." He rips my hands away from his person, pinning them back to my sides.

Doubt cramps my stomach. Something's wrong. His whole demeanor has changed. The flirtation, the lust, everything has evaporated from him. Leaving behind only anger that smokes against my skin.

His jaw ticks. He bites out the next words through gritted

teeth, "We should stop here. Before you start thinking this is something it isn't."

His statement rings with recrimination, scarring the air between us.

Without an explanation, he bolts out of the stall. The tick of his footsteps mirrors the slow bumps in my heart until they vanish altogether.

When doubt slithers back up my throat, I don't immediately scrabble for the wine they're serving outside.

Instead, I crave the feel of Gabriele inside me.

Slipping out of the bathroom, I hunt for his shadow. He's nowhere.

Disappointment crashes into me.

Looks like I've found an addiction more dangerous than drugs.

Him.

CHAPTER 8

 *abriele*

BOOKS AND MOVIES may have romanticized the shit out of addicts and broken women, but I've seen enough druggies, prostitutes, and headcases in my time as a mobster to know that there's no happy ending with someone like that. A craving like that only grows more destructive with time.

Someone who is in love with an illusion will throw away everything real because nothing has the power to surpass that euphoric, make-believe world of theirs. Sooner or later, sentiments like love, lust, and human connection will lose their allure.

My own mother was such a woman. Men were simply a tool for her to obtain the money needed to feed her true passion —meth.

Francesca is unsalvageable. I come to that conclusion every single time she stares at me with those haunted blue eyes.

There's nothing in them except fear and a commitment to avoid the truth by any means possible. She may be relatively new to drugs, but it'll only get worse for her. She's a disaster waiting to happen.

I may be a mobster, but I've always had a vision for my life: marry a nice girl from a well-connected crime family who will not complicate my life. If she's willing, I'll have kids with her. Otherwise, we'll respect each other's space and grow old together. Marriage is not optional for someone who wants to ascend in the organization. So I've always been prepared for the eventuality.

At least that was what I told myself before I threw my common sense out of the window and fingered Francesca.

Staring at my sorry reflection in the bathroom mirror only makes anger bubble in my arteries. It was a moment of weakness. When she was drinking, I felt her misery like it was mine, felt her pain throbbing in my chest. I simply wanted to take that agony away from her by any means possible.

But then she wanted more. When she came off her orgasm, she had the eyes of an addict who has found a new high. And I realized it wouldn't end with her sucking me off. Because I wanted more, too.

Only an idiot tries to play hero for a woman like her.

I cannot forgive myself for letting Francesca drag me back to my past which I fought so hard to escape. I will not support another woman like that ever again.

Never enable a woman like that again.

Never sacrifice myself for a woman like that again.

A normal family, a peaceful family, even if it comes without love or happiness, is all I want now.

So why was I moved by the wounded vulnerability in her voice after she had a meltdown? What is it to me if she wants to self-destruct?

I need to splash cold, cold water on my face to get myself out of this funk but I dare not approach the toilets because that's where I left my siren of death.

The more time I spend around her, the more I soften toward her in unguarded, unexpected moments.

I'm supposed to marry the woman Angelo has chosen for me. Nico called me yesterday to tell me that she'd be at this charity event. That's the reason I'm here.

"Wear your fanciest suit," he said on the phone. "You need to make a great first impression. Papa is very keen on you two working out."

So am I. As much as I love my own company and banging random chicks when it gets too lonely, I would much rather have a wife who, even if she doesn't love me, can be a reliable presence in my life.

Straightening my tie and wiping away Francesca's wetness from my fingers, I march to where Nico messaged me he'll be.

I blink when I crash into the strong body of another man on the way. He's almost as tall as me. The moment I register his face, a spark of irritation corkscrews into my spine. I rub my jaw, hoping to cut away from him, but he blocks my way.

"Why were you talking to my sister?" he demands in an ominous tone.

"Shouldn't you ask my name first?"

The veins in his throat stick out as he tightens his jaw. "I know who you are, Russo."

And I know who he is—Francesca's older brother and the CEO of Astor Hotels. Ethan Astor Jr.

"She was asking me where the restrooms were," I lie.

He rolls his eyes. Not buying it, I see.

"I showed her the way," I add to my previous statement. I don't give a fuck whether or not he believes me. I need to find Maria Bianchi and get my marriage plans started. No better way to cut away whatever sick thread of lust has me wrapped around the heiress's little finger.

"Took you a long time." Ethan is still carrying out his interrogation. "You better not have hurt my sister."

I did worse.

"Why don't you ask her about what happened?" I run a hand through my hair, laying waste to the hours I spent styling my hair to look less wild. "I'm busy."

Without waiting for his response, I sidestep him and charge forward without looking back until I'm in the vicinity of a thin, pale woman wearing a red floor-length dress. Nico and Angelo bracket her like twin bodyguards.

"You're late," Nico snaps.

"This is Maria," Angelo cuts in, right on cue as the woman raises her hand. I shake her hand. Weird. That was so businesslike. Guess neither of us has any illusions about what's going on.

"A pleasure to meet you, Mr. Russo." Her voice is smooth and cultured. Heavy with fear.

"Call me Gabriele," I tell her.

Her lips work, but it doesn't resemble a smile. She's trying too hard.

I saw her photos before. Maria looks a lot more worn down in real life. Like she emerged from a tornado. Emotionally, that might be the case.

"I'll leave you two to talk." Angelo clears his throat, his cue for Nico to make himself scarce. "Some of my old friends are here."

The two men depart, leaving silence to descend between Maria and me. She gently tucks a strand of hair behind her ear. We stand side by side in solidarity, rooting around for a subject of conversation. I'm no socialite, but I don't remember it being this awkward between Francesca and me, not even when she was my hostage. She had no problems voicing her opinions on my shoddy mobster ethics.

Can't you at least point it at my head like a proper criminal?

I reign in the fluttery feeling in my throat.

"Can I get you anything to drink?" I ask Maria, finally breaking the metaphorical wall of ice.

"I don't drink anymore," she replies. Quickly, lines gather around her mouth as she jerks back from me in panic. "I mean, if you wanted me to, I could, but my head is clearer when I don't."

"That's okay." I prefer women who value their health, anyway.

I inhale, suddenly jubilant. This is going great. Maria seems mature and sensible, a woman who treats her body with respect. The exact opposite of a certain young, reckless heiress who has no consideration for her own well-being.

"I can't have more children. I want you to know that," she blurts out. "I already have a son. My relationship with my ex is complicated. You'll have to protect me all my life. There's not much I can offer you in return except my father's money and connections."

"Angelo told me all that already."

She whips her head upward suddenly. "So I'm wondering what you want from me, Gabriele, if we proceed with this marriage."

"Not much," I answer. "As long as you stay away from addictions, attempt to have intelligent conversations with me sometimes, and keep me company at dinner, I won't ask for anything more."

She swallows, then her frail shoulders shake with laughter.

"They were right about you." She presses her fingers to her chin. "You really are a sweetheart."

"I'm a mobster," I remind her.

"Everybody hurts somebody." Again, a long pause. "I won't hold your job against you."

All I can focus on is that when her lips round into an O, they're nowhere near as luscious as Francesca's.

Hatred clasps around my chest and drives the breath from my lungs. How could I be thinking of another woman when I'm talking to the one that could be my future wife?

Maria is good. Clean, in the way that spring water is clean. She'll be right for me.

"I promise you that I'm not abusive. You won't have to be afraid of me," I say. "There's not much I can offer you, either. My life belongs to the Russo family so work comes first and I'm not capable of romance, but I'll guarantee your safety in every way. If you'll trust me with it."

She nods, though the stiffness of her movement tells me that she doesn't fully believe my words. Scars don't heal overnight, I suppose. "I was expecting a whole lot worse when they told me you were in the mafia."

"Get it all the time," I shoot back.

"So what do we tell Angelo?" she asks.

"Whatever you want to," I reply. "It's up to you."

She nods. "Then I hope I'll see you again, Gabriele."

* * *

THE NEXT MORNING, I take the coward's way out and make Ricardo tail Francesca.

"She threw up on you, too, didn't she?" Antonio says when I slide into my seat at our small office which is essentially a front for one of Angelo's paper companies that he uses to launder money.

I nod harder than I need to, hoping it'll mask my embarrassment at how hot my skin feels at the mention of her name. "The girl's a handful."

"She gets under your skin."

Gets under your skin and makes you feel like you're in heaven. I still haven't been able to put what happened at the gala out of my mind. I woke up hard last night. It has been a lifetime since I masturbated to just the thought of a woman.

The girl's a fungus growing inside my brain. Simply the memory of her is enough to drive me mad. Every time images of her with my fingers inside her assault me, the texture of her skin becomes clearer, the taste of her sharper, and the desire to feel her wet walls clenching around my cock stronger.

"So, any progress on Luca's contacts?" I inquire, rolling a pen between my fingers.

"I'm trying. There's a guy I know. Used to work with him. Good with technology. Want me to contact him?"

"Can we trust him?"

"As long as nobody holds a gun to his head and demands he spills what we made him do."

I bark out a laugh. "So no."

With a frown, Antonio gets back to typing. He's old enough to be my father, if I had to guess, so I'm surprised he manages to use a computer so well. Though to be completely honest, I have no idea who my father is. I'm simply guessing his age at this point. He might have been way older than my mother, an already-married middle-aged man with poor taste in women. She was never sober enough to talk about him.

And I never asked. There was no point in growing attached to a person I'd never have in my life.

"How was your date?" Antonio's gruff voice knifes between the prickly edges of my memories. "The one you got all dressed up for."

"Fine," I reply. "I think it'll work out."

"So whaddya want me to get for your wedding? I need to start saving up now."

A black cloud gathers inside my ribcage at the question. The finality of marriage was something I always understood but it never scared me before.

Now...now I can't forget the feel of pink lips whispering *I'll return the favor* against my ear. The tightening of my stomach muscles is a physical pain that refuses to fade no matter how much whiskey I drink.

"Nothing." I grip the side of my chair tightly, the feel of delicate glass against my skin. The amber liquid swirls inside. I've never drunk so early in the morning on the job before. Damn it. "It's her second marriage. I doubt there'll even be a ceremony."

If this doesn't let up, I'll end up an alcoholic myself. Is this how people get addicted? When they desire something too much and it slips out of their grasp?

Antonio's gaze hardens. "Is that why you're drinking?"

"What? No." Despite the reluctance that bites my insides, I empty the remaining alcohol into the bin and put the glass away. "Maria isn't bad at all."

"A ringing endorsement." Antonio scoffs. Did he always have so many wrinkles on his face or has it grown in proportion to his disapproval?

"Prettier than I deserve," I remark drily, my gaze hitting the empty ceiling before bouncing back to the blank Google page on my computer screen. "She's everything I dreamed of."

Everything I dreamed of and everything I'm realizing I don't actually want.

"If you say so." Antonio's expression could freeze a desert. He rolls his shoulders and gets back to work.

I, too, start clacking keys on my computer. Pretending to be productive is better than pretending to be alright. I'm officially still incurring the boss's wrath for screwing up with Luca, which means I don't have to go to the weekly meetings the capos attend or do any actual jobs. I decide to use the time to look up Maria's ex-husband, the abusive asshole I'll have to deal with eventually.

Christian Ricci

He's a bigshot businessman. Designer suits, gray hair, a smug smile, and eyes that advertise his asshole status more effectively than a neon sign. His billions were made in Hollywood. He's a producer and more than a few actresses have filed sexual harassment lawsuits against him. It confirms that he's human garbage but that's nothing I didn't know already. I'll need useful details if I'm going to keep him in check—such as who he uses to do his dirty work, how much law enforcement he has in his pocket, and how to make sure he doesn't touch Maria again.

I've almost forgotten about Francesca and am deeply invested in tracking down Ricci's closest associates when my phone goes off all of a sudden. I refuse to examine the jump in my heart rate too deeply as I see Ricardo's name flashing on the screen.

He wouldn't call unless something happened with Francesca. I hope she didn't decide to finally spill the beans to the police. Though that would at least get her out of my hair. Fucking an addict is one thing but I have no sympathy for traitors.

"You don't need to give me a report until the end of the day," I say to Ricardo. In fact, I'd prefer it if I didn't have to hear about Francesca Astor ever again.

"We have an issue here, though." Ricardo's breath swishes against my ears through the phone. "She's being pressed by some of our men."

"Our men?"

"Nico's boys," he corrects himself. "She was getting the goods from them. But she forgot to pay them the correct amount so they're going to do the regular drill."

The regular drill involves threatening nonpaying clients, roughing them up a little if it comes to that. If it looks like they can't cough up the money at all, we hook them into prostitution so they can repay us with their earnings. But since Francesca is rich, it won't come to that.

The roiling in my gut gets worse when I hear the rough voices seeping in through the phone line from Ricardo's background. Intimidating, loud voices. And one scared whimper. My fist finds the hard desk to slam into. Anger is a monster inside me, thrashing violently.

I wipe my mouth with the back of my palm, the desire to do physical harm spiraling inside me. I can't believe I want to hurt my own family over a girl. She's a damned nuisance.

"Seems like they're starting." Ricardo whistles.

"And you're just watching?" I scream into the phone. "I put you on the job to..." *To observe her,* I remind myself. To tail her, not protect her.

"There's three of them. They look like they are higher ranked than me. I'm not sure I should get involved."

"Tell them to wait. I'm on my way."

"What're you planning to do?"

"Pay whatever she owes."

My mind whirls like a wound-up clock. The drug business is under Nico's supervision. Nico cannot find out about my interest in Francesca. But I have no other choice. I'm not having her hurt on my watch. Not when the very thought of someone else's hands on her is acid in my throat. I tell myself I would feel this way toward any woman. I'm a decent guy. I don't hurt women. Not unless it makes them come.

"Isn't it better to let things run their course? Her supplier is also from the family," Ricardo breezes on. "If she dies, well, that'll shut her up forever. Problem over."

He should count his lucky stars that he wasn't close to me when he said that. Otherwise, his teeth would be scattered around his feet.

"Did you forget about her background? She's important. The police will be on Nico's trail if anything happens to her. I'm only helping him avoid trouble."

On paper, that sounds like a sensible argument. A hesitant pause from Ricardo stirs up my doubts.

Guilt burns my nerve endings. I should've gone myself instead of sending a soldier.

"Well, when you say it like that it makes sense. No wonder you're my boss." Ricardo chuckles.

"Don't let things spiral out of control before I get there," I say as I dash for my coat and throw it on. Antonio is giving me a pitying smirk from across the room.

Yeah, there's something really wrong with me.

I resent the part of me that cares for her. I resent the weakness that has taken root inside me since the night I touched her, the weakness I thought I'd shed after I left her alone after we finished. I swore to never let someone distress me the way my mother did.

The memory of the longest night of my life, when I lay dead and bleeding in the snow before Angelo found me, loops back. I should've learned my lesson.

I will not lose everything for a woman again.

I will not lose my mind over a woman who doesn't possess the capacity to care for me in any meaningful way.

Once I get my hands on Francesca fucking Astor, I'll make her pay with her life.

* * *

I'm surprised I avoid getting a traffic ticket for my driving. However, the result of my speeding is that I get to the location in twenty minutes. Ricardo is standing outside the building, grey smoke curling from the tip of his cigarette.

"Third floor," he says. "Want me to come with you? In case things turn violent."

"I can handle it," I growl. "Go back to the office."

The metal elevator is old and rickety and makes a bellowing sound as it ascends. My temper has swollen into a mass of violence in the span of my trip here so I punch through the door with no regret.

"Don't fuckin' break our door," says one of the men as I step into their office. Francesca is sitting on the couch, shivering, though I can't tell if those tremors are because of fear or withdrawal symptoms. The low light details a red cut on her face. The bleeding has stopped but she was hurt.

"I said not to touch her until I got here," I grab the collar of the thug who has the misfortune to be standing right in front of me. "What part of that did you not understand?"

The other two men, who had been guarding Francesca, leap at me instantly. As I let go and swing my arm back, my knuckles scrape against the edge of a naked blade in one of their hands. I don't even bother checking if it cut me. I know it did.

"Not our fault. She was resisting too much," the other one explains, as he senses the anger that's a flame in my eyes and pulls the knife out of his comrade's hand.

The rest of the exchange is a blur of words, the incessant hammering of impatience against my bones. Francesca's wide, scared eyes stick to my face and never leave for the six minutes until I manage to get her untied.

I pay her outstanding balance of twenty thousand dollars, which isn't as high as I'd expected. Nico's definitely going to hear of this. He isn't going to like my behavior. My mishandling of Luca is already a sensitive issue. Yet now I'm bailing the only witness to that episode out of her drug debt.

The boys untie her and she hobbles over to me faster than a kangaroo.

"Thank you. Thank you so much. I'll never forget this." Her frail, tear-soaked words press into my chest along with her cheekbone. "I'm sorry I made you do this, Gabriele. But I'm so glad you're here."

Warmth soaks through my skin coupled with a buoyant feeling. Strength. Pride at having protected this frail, innocent, broken thing.

Is that what this is all about, some fucked-up psychological bullshit? I couldn't save my mother from her self-destruction so

SASHA CLINTON

I want to save Francesca Astor? When she's way more hopeless than my mother?

Disgusted, I shake her off with more force than necessary. She wobbles before steadying herself.

"This favor's not free," I bite out in a brutal tone of voice.

"I'll pay you back," she says immediately as she falls into step behind me. This is the meekest I've seen her since the day we met.

"If you had that much money, you'd have paid him," I reply, pointing to the soldier who is happily counting the dollar bills I threw on the scraggy table.

Francesca's inhale is shaky. "I just forgot, okay? With all the things on my mind. I can arrange the money. It'll take a month at most."

"Or you could stop doing drugs?" I stick my hands in my pockets. Irritation clings to my skin when I detect the immediate resistance that stiffens her shoulders. "Just a suggestion."

"I'll try." The low, apologetic note in her voice could easily pass for sincerity. But I know it's just her feeling sorry at the moment. Nothing more. "By the way, why does it make you mad? That first night, too, you were angry at me for being high. Do you realize how much of a hypocrite that makes you? Your own family sells these drugs and profits off people like me. I'm one of your big-time clients."

My lips grow cold. She doesn't need to remind me of what kind of business I'm in. I'm not blind to what I do.

There's no harm in selling a little escapism to people who want and need it, as long as they're paying the right price for it. It's a product, no different from shoes or designer bags.

It's a choice. A lifestyle. In the past, it never bothered me to witness our customers decaying slowly over months and years. Some of them are pretty high-functioning. They never have any problems in their work or life because of the habit. They never get caught, never lose anything. We call them happy endings. They get all the pleasure with none of the side effects.

But Francesca won't be one of them. Because she's like my mother.

This may have started out as an escape for her, but it will take over her entire personality. It will become a replacement for all the things she's losing—her art, her social relationships, her confidence, her mind.

I suck in a breath when we're outside. The sunshine, too hot and sharp for a winter afternoon, burns into my skin with vengeance, reminding me of the dumb mistake that's trailing me, her golden curls catching the daylight. Idiotic thoughts emerge from the cesspit that's my brain: I want to stroke that hair. I want to fist my fingers around it.

"I have a whole repayment plan worked out for you," I tell her instead, charging to my car in long, unceasing strides. No more getting distracted by her pretty face and vulnerable expression. "My help doesn't come cheap."

She gulps. Lowers her gaze. Clasps her manicured fingers in front of her chest. "Whatever it is, I won't stop you from doing it to me."

"It's something you need to do for *me*," I correct, fully aware she'll take this the wrong way. She probably thinks this is going to end with something as cheap as a blowjob.

I make no attempts to clear her misunderstanding. I ought to leave her to find her way back home herself, but I don't need her getting into trouble after I just rescued her so I let her ride with me. I should look into a change in my profession. With this new streak of protectiveness that I've developed, I'm better suited to being a cop rather than a Mafioso.

"Wait here," she says when we pull up at her family's town-house. I was so wrapped up in my thoughts I didn't realize when I drove her all the way back home.

"Don't go. You hurt your hand badly. I'll get the first aid kit."

I check my knuckles in the rearview mirror. She's right. There's a nasty cut there, slashing across my skin. It'd be troublesome if this got infected.

She hurries inside and I wait around, purely out of curiosity. I've never seen what a rich girl's first aid kit looks like.

My disappointment must be evident when she returns with a normal-looking plastic box.

"Were you expecting painkillers or something?" she inquires.

"For a tiny cut? You're offending my pride as a gangster."

Her soft fingertip glides over my skin. "Looks like a shallow wound. Hope this doesn't hurt."

She takes out a piece of cotton and douses it with rubbing alcohol. At the damp feel of it against my skin, at the errant brush of her soft hair against my face, my stomach cramps with a hot, unknown sensation. Her luscious, rose-scented exhales are flooding over my face, filling my nose with the scent of flower petals. When she's being gentle, caring, and kind, she's extraordinarily mesmerizing. And so human. Not just a problematic druggie but a compassionate girl who touches my heart with her small gestures.

"Did you eat lunch?" she asks. "The cook made lasagna today. It's delicious."

"Take your nurse cosplay somewhere else," I snarl, irritated at myself for growing sappy every time she does something nice. "I'm not into it."

"I think you are." A tiny smile curves on her sensual lips.

For a second, I can't take my eyes off their fullness.

My eyebrow molds into a sharp V. "Are you flirting with me, Francesca?"

"Can't I?"

"Wouldn't advise it. Flirting with a man like me leads to bad things."

"I don't mind." Her gaze darkens a fraction when she lifts her head. "By the way, who was that woman you were talking to at the charity gala? You know, after you abandoned me in the toilet."

I retract my hand as the sting of alcohol settles under my skin. She's getting clingy. Or is it jealousy?

"Why're you so interested in my life?" I yawn. "It's none of your business, by the way."

"I don't want to sleep with you if you already have a wife," she asserts, closing her fingers into fists.

"I don't," I assure her, the burn of acid sloshing against my throat. "Also, you're not sleeping with me. You let me finger you. Once. It's in the past."

I'm toeing a dangerous line. I'm *technically* single since the matter with Maria isn't decided yet, nor are we officially engaged or dating. Francesca is technically of legal age. What we did was technically just sex. And technically, having her open up to me lowers her chances of ratting me out to the police.

Why is this scenario built entirely upon flimsy technicalities?

"Once or twice doesn't matter." Her tongue curls in her mouth.

"It was once," I assert.

"What's the big deal?" Francesca says. "It was just physical."

"No, wasn't. It's escapism. Addiction." *Possibly something worse.*

"I felt something for you last night, Gabriele," she whispers. I wish she was a habitual liar, but she hasn't lied to me a single time so far so I assume this is also the truth. "Something deep. I'm not saying it's love. But I needed you."

"You needed to come again," I say, turning my head away. The street is empty. No people. "And I was the only man who could make you."

She shakes her head. "That's not true. What I want...it's not something my body craves. It's something my soul craves. Sounds crazy when I say it, but it's less lonely with you around. I mean, even when you watch me paint at my studio I don't hate it. Because you're witnessing how miserable I really am. You're staring at the real me without flinching. Since I don't want to impress you or be loved by you, I'm free to be myself when I'm with you."

What Francesca said to me before is tightening around me like a noose.

Don't give me false hope with your mixed signals and break my heart. I'll never forgive you.

It's already too late for that.

"You're talking nonsense," I say, though her confession has settled in my bones like a radioactive substance. My inner voice says she's not the only one who is less lonely when we're together. I, too, have grown addicted to her empathy and compassion which has made me show her parts of myself I wouldn't reveal to anyone else. "You still high?"

"I haven't taken anything today."

"Then what's with that confession?"

"It's…I had to say it." I hear the one gasp that tears the steady rhythm of her breaths. Blood rushes in my ears. "Haven't you ever wanted a friend? Someone you could be yourself around?"

"Make friends your age," I advise as she slowly wraps a bandage around my hand and secures it with surgical tape.

"I do have friends my age," she answers. "But I'll disappoint them if I show them my dark side."

"So what? Let them deal with it."

"I guess…I like you more. Can't say why. You're always mean to me, but I suppose you did save me today. So you must be a softie on the inside."

Heat creeps up under my skin.

"I don't like you," I say flatly.

Her jaw drops. "Why not? I'm pretty and kind."

She was pretty, too.

Old memories converge in the present.

"You remind me of my mother." An undertone of bitterness weighs down the air between us.

"Was she a bad woman?" Francesca's hand is a warm touch on my skin. Almost comforting.

I nod. "A druggie like you. An alcoholic, too. Never once did she seek any help. She abandoned me when I was in my teens. Left me to fend for myself."

Her swallow forms a heavy curve, disrupting the smooth line of her throat.

"I'm sorry, Gabriele."

"For what? It's not your fault I was dealt a bad hand by fate."

"For being like your mother." A long, meaningful pause. "Is that why you joined the mafia?"

I sigh. "That's enough of my tragic backstory. Go back home."

She doesn't argue. Gathering her stuff, she gives me a sideways look filled with concern.

"What will you make me pay with?"

"Expect the worst."

"A kidney?"

The cough of laughter pummels its way out before I can do anything about it. Trust her to make a joke out of nowhere.

"I don't want any part of your body. I've had enough of it."

CHAPTER 9

rancesca

COLD SHIVERS LAP under my skin like waves as I cross one heeled foot under the other.

I'm seated in my studio beside my thesis painting, my unexpected guest hovering over me at nine in the morning wearing a navy pantsuit. I forgot her name already. She works for the architectural firm that designed Hudson 241—the same company that commissioned me. She called me this morning saying she had to speak to me.

My lips are red due to my constant nibbling. Irritation surges up and down my spine as she surveys the half-finished picture, prolonging the horrible moment we both know is coming.

"Hope you had a good morning," I start, sounding dumb and confused, scratching my skin because I'm craving something I told myself I couldn't have.

I haven't really been myself since I stopped drinking and

doing drugs ever since Gabriele told me about his mother. I'm grateful that he shared his tragic past with me. Vulnerability isn't in his character for him but he still gave it to me at that moment.

Hearing his story has made me reflect deeply on my choices for the first time. Before, I lived in the moment, equating every hit with artistic progress. I never considered what it'd lead to, long-term. Who I'd become if I kept going like this.

Gabriele's warning woke me up from my dream.

I don't want to become someone like his mom. More than that, I don't want to grow so dependent on drugs that I forget about art. It has happened a lot recently, times when I snort because it's fun and helps me escape the pressure I put on myself all day. Even though I promised myself when I started that I'd only use substances when I absolutely needed them to paint, I've broken that vow many times already.

My control over myself is slipping slowly. It's unmistakable. I can't deny it anymore.

That's why I've chosen to end it. The first day was hell. My aches and pains kept me in bed all day, and at some point, I started to seriously contemplate dying. But I soldiered through with sheer grit. The thing is, I can't afford to go to rehab right now. This is a crucial period for my career. So I'm going to try to quit on my own.

"We begin showing the staged apartment in two weeks, so we need your artwork in the lobby by then," says the lady, turning her slim, pretty jaw to me. "Hopefully that won't be a problem."

My heart nearly tears itself apart with the effort required to pump blood at that moment. No way. This is even worse than I imagined.

"I need more time," I stutter. "We agreed on eight months. It has only been six."

"You should've at least completed one painting by now." The

disapproving smile on her lips unnerves me and splits me open. "Honestly, we only gave you the commission because your brother bought the penthouse and said you were talented. We usually pick more established artists but it tied in well with our youth-oriented charity efforts this year, so the director approved it."

My whole world comes crashing down at that statement. I thought the architectural firm had approached me because they'd seen my paintings on my website and Instagram. I have a hundred thousand followers on the app, which is nothing to scoff at.

"Um...well..." I stammer, the familiar scathing voices coursing through my blood.

Liar.

Nepo baby.

Worthless.

Despite my impending doom, my brain's somehow stuck on the fact that Ethan bought the penthouse. He has lived in a hotel room since he turned twenty-one. The guy used to tell me owning a home was a waste of money because of all the maintenance costs. Ella must've changed his mind. Could it be that he's planning to move in with his girlfriend? Maybe he has finally decided to buy a home and settle down. I wish he'd told me that he was the one who recommended me. But how could he when all I've done is avoid him for months?

"We'd like to have something in the lobby as we show potential buyers around this month. Adds a pop of color. Don't you agree?"

"Yes, of course." My skin is dissolving with anxiety.

I'm cornered from all sides.

My spring thesis submission is in a month. I need to show my professors my progress this week. With the help of a few substance-induced highs, I've managed to keep up with it so far, but every single time I'm alone in the studio, I'm terrified I'll be butchered by art critics and my peers at the final exhibition. They already think I'm a pampered princess who doesn't take art seriously even though I've aced every course since my first semester. But here's the thing with resentment: it doesn't go away no matter how many times you prove yourself.

My background is a brand on my skin, a tattoo I can't erase for as long as I live. That's why everything rides on my success and continuously wowing people with my talent. I don't have any room for mediocrity. Or excuses.

My mind dances over the possibilities of how I can quickly complete the painting. I have a half-finished one from my first year. Maybe I could finish it instead of starting a new one.

"I'll have the painting delivered to you as soon as I can," I say. A tremor moves up my entire body, rattling my resolve to stay off drugs. The desperation is gaining hold of me, the compelling notes of *just one more time* playing on a loop in my head.

"Very good. I look forward to hanging your painting in the lobby," she says, rising to her feet. "I'll call you once it's done so you can take a picture and upload it to your social media."

The moment the lady leaves my studio, my mind leaps to a million paranoid scenarios: they're going to hate my painting. They're going to refuse to display it. My career is going to be over before it has started. I'll be a pariah in the art world for failing to keep promises.

The drug withdrawal, coupled with paranoia makes for a nauseating combo. My nerves are shaky, and my throat is filled with irritation that I can't wait to release at someone. God, I need something strong. Preferably alcoholic. But I swore to quit after Gabriele bailed me out.

I must persevere when it's hard.

I can't let my cravings control me.

I scrunch my eyes shut, gathering my knees to my chest and curling myself up into a ball on the floor. It's one of the techniques I've started using to ride out the lows.

The rasp of shoes against the floor breaks my concentration. Gabriele's broad form slithers in, eyes narrowed in suspicion. "Who was that woman?"

"An employee of Hudson 241. She was here for business."

He cocks an eyebrow in concern. "You look pale."

"I'm trying to get sober," I confess in a thin voice. "It's been hell so far."

He dares to laugh. "Are you stupid? That's what rehab is for. You can't quit by yourself."

"Watch me."

"I *am* watching you. You're shaking."

"I need something to take my mind off the mental agony," I curl my fingers so hard my nails leave nasty marks inside my palm. "You. I need you."

The uncontrollable urge to press my skin against his, to lose myself in his touch has me rising to my feet. I extend my hand to him, the same way he did that night at the gala.

I took it without hesitation then.

He simply scoffs.

"Kiss me," I demand, irate. I'm annoyed often nowadays. I read it's one of the side effects of withdrawal. "Just this once. It doesn't mean anything."

"I know a good rehab facility," Gabriele says drily, ignoring my plea. "I'll text you their address if you want."

"I have to finish my painting in two weeks!" I scream. "I'm not wasting months at a recovery center."

He clicks his tongue in disappointment. "You can't give up the commission?"

"No way. It'll ruin my reputation forever. I've worked hard for decades. I'm not throwing away my golden opportunity for success."

"Even if it costs you everything?"

I press against my aching temples. "I'll deal with it."

Why in the world does my whole body hurt? While I simmer

in hurt over his rejection, he brushes his hand over the top of my head. His slow, quiet statement stings me. "I can't decide whether I pity you or hate you."

"Maybe you're just attracted to me." Locking my arms behind his neck, I tilt up my lips, offering myself to him on a platter. I haven't desired anything as much as I desire the pain he can give me, the exquisite touches that can dissolve all my thoughts. "Wouldn't hurt to give in to your impulses. It can't be healthy to live in constants self-denial."

He arches an eyebrow in suspicion. "What has gotten into you, Francesca? You could have anyone. I'm the last guy you should be begging."

"Because it's different with you," I reply, squeezing my voice to keep myself from sounding too desperate. "It may sound like I'm making this up, but the day after we did it, I could see everything clearly. Something changed. In the toilet where you fucked me, I started to see colors in a different light. What I'm saying is...I was angry when you left me, yes, but I felt inspired when I got home. I started painting something new and finished a lot of the basic details. It was terrible, but I haven't been so productive in ages."

"You think being fingered by me triggered that?" He curls his lips like this is the biggest load of bull he has ever heard. "I think it was your own talent. You own drive."

No way. I have no talent, and these days, I have no self-discipline, either. I'm sure it was the magical feeling that wrapped around me after that orgasm, the way my whole body unraveled after going through such a mind-blowing experience, leaving me vulnerable and open for more wondrous experiences.

Gabriele made me feel pain and that pain broke the parts of me that hold me back.

"Every artist has their muse. You might be mine, Gabriele," I whisper.

He coughs, disbelief threading through the sound. "I'm a gangster, baby, not some mythical creature."

"But you've awakened something in me." I take his hand and press it to my chest, over my beating heart. When he was fucking me, I was ten times more aware of being alive. Of breathing and creating. Of my own beauty as well as my own ugliness. He made me see everything. "I think it might be something good. Why don't we explore it? Also, I have to get the commission painting done and since I have no better ideas, I'm willing to try having sex with you."

"That's enough." He pulls his palm away. "I'm not hearing any more of this nonsense."

My brain works out the details of the proposal right as I'm spitting the words from my mouth. "How about we have an affair? It'll just be sex. No feelings involved. Promise I won't cling. Think about it. You're in the mafia and I'm the heiress of Astor Hotels. We can't date anyway."

"No." His flat refusal exasperates me.

"Hate to brag about myself, but I give a mean blowjob. Shall I show you?" My fingers carve a path down the front of his shirt, my long nails catching on the buttons.

Strong fingers seize my hand before I can get lower. "Don't get carried away. I can still put a bullet in your head any time."

Gabriele separates my clingy arms from his body, fully aware that I'm trying to get him to go further than just a kiss.

I'm too exhausted to fight but too angry to simply seethe quietly. "Why do you hate fun so much? Life's more exciting when you give in to things you're not supposed to."

"If I wanted a thrill, I'd find a whore."

"When I'm offering to do it for free?"

He squares his shoulders. "Learn some self-control."

"There's no point pretending to be mean when I know you care about me." I trail a finger under his chin. "It would have been easy for you to let me get drunk at the gala but you helped me. How is this any different? I'm simply asking you to help me paint. Being a muse is an honor, you know."

Black loathing swirls in his eyes. "You can't keep using me as a crutch, Francesca."

"Why not?"

"Because you can't be saved and I can't save you."

"You saved me before," I say, getting to my knees. "I didn't drink that night. I just told you. I couldn't think of anything but art once I stopped fuming at your coldness."

His eyes are narrow as he registers my statement.

"Get up." The acidic tone accompanied by the hard squeeze of his fingers around my wrist hits me like a ton of bricks. He's probably recalling his mother. How she treated him. Does he think I'm manipulating him? Using him to further my own interest?

The incessant need for another hit transforms into a heavy mass of guilt. He's not wrong. I can't offer him anything but reciprocal sex in exchange for the favor he'll be doing me.

"While we're on the subject of you repaying me, I figured out what I want you to pay me back with." His rasp slides into my blood and makes me shiver from the inside. "For the fifteen thousand you now owe me, remember?"

Please tell me it's sex because I'm so ready.

As if he knows what I'm thinking, he shakes his head. "I want you to paint me a picture."

All the passionate, tingly sensations in my stomach turn to ash.

"What? Are you crazy? Do you think I have the time?"

"I'm not demanding it tomorrow," he clarifies. "I'll give you six months."

"That's still not enough!"

He shrugs, the evil bastard. "It might break you or drive you to insanity. Either way, I'll enjoy the show."

"So you're making me pay with agony?"

I'm scared. I'm already drowning under the weight of three paintings I haven't finished. I don't need one more to add to my burdens. Under any other circumstance, I'd have loved to create something for Gabriele, to have him always hold onto a piece of me through my art.

"I have something very specific in mind," he continues, fishing into his pocket. I blink at the photograph he produces. "Paint me this picture, but make it brighter."

The boy in the photo looks young. He's definitely not Gabriele. His features are completely different. He has a crooked nose and a friendly smile.

"Who is he?" I ask.

"Someone I used to know."

"Brother?"

"Not by blood."

"Name?"

"Not telling you."

A sigh rolls off my lips. "What kind of person was he? I'm only asking because it'll help me decide how I want to paint him."

"He was kind. Helpful. Had big dreams." Gabriele swallows, his gaze sliding down my skin like a hot poker. I want to climb him like a pole and scrape away the sharp edges of my craving. Now that I have the theory that fucking him will make me more productive, I need to validate it. To know there's a way out of the black hole I'm in right now. "A lot like you."

I clear my throat to cover my frustration at my own powerlessness. I've never struggled so much to get a guy interested in screwing me. Usually, they're more eager.

"You still talk to him?" I ask.

Gabriele drags out a heavy sigh. "He's dead."

"How?"

"I killed him."

The air between us grows heavy, burdened by the weight of

106

this revelation. Gabriele doesn't elaborate. A faint dusting of pink crawls across his cheeks.

"You *killed* him?" My jaw comes unhinged in shock. I don't know why this surprises me; he's a professional criminal. But he said the guy was like a brother to him. "I don't get it. Why?"

"Because he betrayed Angelo."

"But he was your friend," I whisper, my heart thundering.

"More than a friend. We were members of the same gang since when I was a teenager. He was the first guy who really cared for me. But there's no mercy for traitors in the family." He grits his teeth and talks in a monotone like he's reciting some arcane law in a cult's rulebook. At the end of the day, I suppose the mafia isn't any different from a cult.

I curl my hand around his. "Did you want to do it?"

"No." One hand cradles the side of his face. "It still gives me nightmares to this day. His face in those last moments."

Light strings through his dark pupils, illuminating his anguish. I can tell he still hasn't forgiven himself for the episode.

My heart shudders. I can feel his regret seeping into me, drowning out the desire for intoxicants, replacing it with sympathy, pity, and the intense need to comfort him.

I know I have no moral high ground, but I'm supposed to be repulsed by the fact that he killed someone. He killed a man. An actual human being. I should be running for the hills, not wanting to rub my body against him and make the miserable expression on his face go away.

He just gave me another piece of himself, a fragment of his past that I'm certain he hasn't shared with very many people. I'm honored he trusts me. It feels good to be useful to someone, to know that he can be as honest with me as I am with him.

For that one brief moment, every thought of need and craving evaporates from my brain. The intimacy we share feels precious like it's the center of the world.

"Then why did you do it?" My voice trips over my shuddering breaths.

"Because I had to survive in the underworld. Because that's the kind of man I am." He steps away from me. "I'm a mobster. Taking lives is my way of life. You keep forgetting that."

"I haven't forgotten it," I murmur, shrinking on the inside. "But you look sad to me, not dangerous."

"I am sad." Gabriele lets out the longest exhale, closing his eyes. When he opens them again, I swear they're so soft, he could be a different man. "God, it felt so good to admit that."

He laughs a little, but the laugh is brittle and melancholic. My heart totally breaks.

Fire burns inside my chest. Regret. Shame. Inferiority. They wash over me in turn. Here I am, pestering him to have sex with me because I can't paint. When he deals with the guilt of killing his best friend every single day, and still manages to not crumble.

"I knew I was drawn to you for a reason," I end up vocalizing my thought.

"And what reason would that be?" Gabriele asks, his voice a touch more playful than usual.

"Because you live with demons, too." It's so quiet, the end of my sentence reverberates in the air. "But unlike me, you never let them destroy you."

"I'm a fighter, Francesca." His gaze is icy, but his voice is passionate. "I learned to be one. By accepting pain and seeing it as a sign of strength rather than a flaw. Hurting is natural. It is the process of being human."

"I hate being human sometimes. I think I'd be happier if I was a frog."

If I was a frog, I wish I could stop feeling altogether. My emotions are intense and uncontrollable. What's a harsh word to someone else is a death sentence to me that I'll replay in my head for weeks. Tides of despair come and go at their will inside my mind.

Gabriele's lips jerk up in a smile. "I'm sorry if I burdened you with my past, but it's not yours to care about. I'll deal with it myself. You have more than enough to occupy your mind. Starting with how you're going to finish my painting."

"You didn't have to say that." I sniff. "We were having a good moment right now."

"No, we weren't. We were having a negotiation about how you're going to pay me back."

"I'll try," I promise. "To do justice to your friend's picture."

Contrary to my statement, my resolve has already crumbled on the inside. I'm playing a losing game. There's no way I can ever be as strong as Gabriele.

"Sorry for telling you such a gruesome story." Gabriele's voice breaks me away from my spiraling thoughts. "You didn't need to hear it. Don't let it affect you when you're painting my friend."

"I'm glad you revealed something so personal to me." I touch his knuckles lightly. Reassuring. "Guess you're growing to trust me despite how you act."

Gabriele doesn't immediately voice his protest, which is a small win.

He rubs his wrist against his side. "Never thought you'd be the person I'd confess to. If any of my men knew, they'd lose all respect for me."

"Because you regret killing your friend?" I ask.

He sighs.

"I'm glad you regret it. Empathy is what separates psychopaths from the rest of us."

A scoff this time.

"So don't hate yourself for being human," I add. "Also, feel free to tell me more of your secrets anytime. You saved my life. The least I can do is listen to you."

"You have a funny way of being helpful," Gabriele says.

When his eyes stay on me a beat too long, thick heat envelopes my senses. The familiar hum of need sings in my bloodstream, the familiar promise of escape. If only he touched me again, breathed heat into my ice-cold veins.

The desire he imprints on my skin with every touch, every glance, and every caress is proof that at least one person in the world *needs* my existence. In a world filled with haters, I only need one lover to give me the will to fight the voices one more day.

"Gabriele, I'm happy you're back." My palm slides against my hips, itching for a touch of him. "I didn't like Ricardo. He was such a jerk."

"That means he did his job well."

I tilt my body closer to his. Before anything can happen, though, his phone rings. The moment his gaze flicks to the caller ID, his easy, nonchalant expression darkens ten notches. Some kind of trouble, I'm guessing, from the lines digging into his forehead.

He massages his temples, not even looking up from his phone as he waves at me and leaves the studio.

Without his magnetic face to gawk at, I'm back to focusing on my unhealthy thoughts.

Darkness writhes in my blood. I force my attention to circle the room, to find another subject to obsess over. And I find it so easily: my unfinished painting. Just like that, I'm back to the exact issue I was trying to escape.

How am I going to complete a whole new painting in two weeks? I haven't even started. I'm going to have to retreat to my studio in the woods. It's more a cabin than a studio, but at least I can drink and get high all I want over there, meaning I'll probably be able to finish the painting faster than at this studio in the university, where I must always appear sober.

Only one problem: I can't go alone. I'm no longer so in

control of myself that I trust being alone in an isolated cabin. I might forget to eat. Or sleep. Or live.

What would Gabriele say if I asked him to go with me?

I exhale. He'll probably refuse.

The noises of him talking fade. I peek and see he's gone. Maybe something came up at work.

My whole being deflates.

Resentment wars with patience. How could he leave me here alone when my negativity is about to devour me? Wait. I must stop. I don't have any right to expect comfort from him. But we were so close. *I* was so close to winning this fight.

Dark noise thrums between my ears.

The answer calls out to me in a single color: *white*.

CHAPTER 10

$\mathcal{G}$abriele

NICO'S EYES are orbs of fire when I slink into my apartment. His legs are crossed as he lounges comfortably on my leather couch.

"What the fuck are you doing here?" I yell. "Did you break in?"

Nico smiles, though his jaw is tighter than a cork in a wine bottle. "Obviously."

The fact that he forced himself into my apartment and is sitting on the sofa like it's something normal tells me how dire the situation is. Nico doesn't usually behave this way. He's the second in command as the underboss so he usually carries himself with dignity.

"Are you going to explain yourself?" I inquire, far too cocky for someone who's about to get chewed out.

"Sit down, Gabriele. We have to talk."

"Regarding?"

"The don...Papa...he was poisoned."

The ground falls from under my feet. It can't be...

"What...is he—"

"He's alive. Recovering. I got him a doctor in time. However," his tone sharpens, "it's clear that the men Luca was involved with had something to do with his poisoning. Which makes this entire thing your fault. Because you've been cooling your heels instead of figuring out who those dirty bastards are and burning down their houses."

"I was told to lay low and reflect on my mistakes." The excuse fills my mouth like shards of glass.

"But you're still part of the family. I thought you'd try to find something and prove yourself. You used to be so eager when you were young. Is it age? Getting older? You have lost your motivation."

"What do you mean?" Anger muffles my tone. "I'm as loyal to the family as ever."

"I wasn't doubting that. But loyalty aside, what else do you bring to the table?"

"The casinos I manage make good money. And I follow every order."

The mafia isn't much different from a corporation when it comes down to it. I'm having to defend my right to stay by reminding him of my achievements. And I'm not even sure why. Angelo is alive and he'd never ask me to leave. Nor would he blame me for this poisoning episode when I wasn't at the scene. But I can't be too hard on Nico. He almost lost his father. He's probably scared and hurt, wanting to blame someone for his own failure.

Nico suddenly comes to his feet and looks me straight in the eye. "You've been acting strange lately. I heard from the boys that you paid for one of the customers who had defaulted."

"It was the Astor girl. Her brother's powerful. If your boys had roughed her up, there'd have been hell to pay. Besides, she's loaded and there's no sense in losing a regular client."

Nico's gaze sharpens. "Even if that's true, you didn't have any business getting involved."

"I was preventing *you* from getting into trouble!" I throw up my hands in exasperation. "We're brothers, aren't we?"

"Instead of looking out for me, do your job," Nico says, cold. "You've been dragging your feet on the matter since you killed Luca. It has been more than a week and there's been no progress. During that time, the enemy seems to have figured out every single thing about us, down to what Papa eats for breakfast. They must have someone close to us on their payroll. The cook swears she didn't poison Papa's dinner and I believe her. She has been with the family too long and gains nothing from his death. Whoever it was is someone very close to the family and high up in the hierarchy. Someone who has access to Papa in his house."

The implication of his words settles on me like stone.

"You suspect me?"

"I suspect everyone. Especially those Papa trusted."

"Those outside his bloodline, you mean," I sputter.

He shrugs. "I won't apologize for being vigilant. The first name that came to my mind when I realized there was a traitor among us was yours, Gabriele. I wondered for a minute if Ricardo killing Luca was more than a coincidence and if you were unable to find anything useful on our enemies all week because that suited you."

Speechless, I gape in horror as Nico wipes sweat off his pale forehead. The realization that he doesn't see me as family dawns on me clear as crystal. He assumes I'm someone he can't trust. After all the years I served him, that hits hard.

"Angelo saved my life," I hiss. "But since you mentioned Ricardo, I admit it was out of character for him to go so far in a fit of rage. He has always had a hot temper, but he never messed up a job. I'll keep an eye on him."

"See that you do." He threads his fingers between each other. The pensive silence in the room balloons into a dark streak of uncertainty. He chooses to omit the obvious: *And I'll be watching you, Gabriele.*

Damn it, is this how Francesca feels when I stalk her? Like she can't breathe?

"If anything happens to Papa, I'll be the next Don," Nico continues.

"I'm aware of your role in the organization." Everyone knows this. Nico is Angelo's only son and he has been in the game for a long time. Nobody is better prepared to take over in the event of Angelo's death.

I cough when Nico closes in on me quickly, his fingers lightly brushing over my suit jacket. He makes it look casual and brotherly but he's fooling no one. The gesture is steeped in intimidation. It's a silent warning, the proof that things between us have changed. That we're no longer brothers but wary allies.

"I don't need you in the family, Gabriele if you can't do your job. Papa might have picked you up, but I have no obligation to keep you."

Animosity hangs heavy in the air between us. A match waiting to be struck.

Those harsh, bitter words soak into the walls. I'm left stunned by Nico's tirade. He's usually so stoic. I'm trying to understand that he's upset and shocked after what happened to Angelo. It could've happened to him just as easily. And he's scared of dying.

But I'm more scared of what would happen to me if Nico kicks me out of the family, or, as he's implying, makes me retire. He did that with one of the other, older capos last year. But that man was essentially useless, too old to take care of his responsibilities anymore. He was a deadweight to the organization. I'm only thirty-four. I'm nowhere close to being done.

"I'm sorry for what happened. Whoever was behind Angelo's poisoning will die a slow and torturous death. I'm going to make the bastard pay."

"Save your apologies. I need real, concrete information soon."

"I'll get it."

He's acting this way because he's shaken by the episode. Yet, my stomach feels like it has collapsed in on itself. The Russo family, this world, is the only stable place I've known. Without it, I'd have been lost in life.

I can't lose my only place in the world. The mere thought makes me nervous, catapulting me back to the cold, uncertain days of my youth when I thought I'd die on the streets like a stray cat. I hoped I'd left that past behind, just like I thought I'd left addicts like my mother behind, but at the moment, the theme of my life is déjà vu.

"Gabriele, here's my advice to you: stop being distracted by pussy. Right now, there are far more important things to take care of."

"What do you mean? I'm not distracted."

"You're spending too much time with the Astor girl."

"It's my job to watch her!"

"I don't care where you stick your dick but be discreet about it at least. Maria is sensitive. And once you're married, it'll have to stop."

"Of course. I would never cheat. Besides, as I said, I'm just watching her. Nothing is going on between us."

Nico's voice curls with a bitter edge as he laughs. "Then why is she at your apartment? It's ten at night."

I snap my head backward, my heartbeat ramping up.

And there she is. Her image is stamped on the video feed from my home security system.

Holy fuck. What is Francesca Astor doing at my front door in a low-cut black dress and the sexiest high heels that must be banned in the state of New York ASAP? I hope she isn't high or drunk or worse—here to beg me for sex. Because there's no chance I'll be able to resist now. Nico's suspicion and raw anger are chomping at my intestines. The fear of losing my only identity, my only home has me wanting to fuck something hard to make the insecurity stop. Am I just like her? The first sign of anxiety, and I bury myself in the unhealthiest addiction I can find.

Also, I'm going to strangle Antonio for giving her my address. It couldn't have been anybody else.

"You might want to open the door," Nico suggests, strolling ahead of me. "For me. I'm leaving."

I chase after him. "She's simply part of the job."

"As long as you marry Maria, I don't care what she is."

Dammit, this makes me look so bad. The furious beast inside me rattles against the confines of my body as Francesca's big doll eyes blink up at me.

I've had enough of her infecting my life like a goddamn virus.

I grab her jaw in a bruising hold before she passes through the threshold of my door. "Are you high?"

Tears fill up her eyes, dribbling down her cheeks. My nails digging in might leave marks on her porcelain skin. I don't give a fuck. My patience has officially reached its end as of three seconds ago.

She exhales an alcohol-laced breath.

Even the numb part of me that usually feels nothing trembles in rage.

"I was scared." The words sound weird because I'm crushing her lips with my fingers. "I blacked out for a bit, then woke up. A guy was tailing me."

"You were afraid of a stalker and you came *here*?" I cough,

117

unable to contain my sarcasm. "I'm your full-time stalker, baby."

"I feel safe with you," she explains. "It makes zero sense. Maybe it's because you're the only guy I know who has a gun. If somebody tries to hurt me, you can shoot them."

"Not your bodyguard," I remind her.

"But you're strong. Plus, you never hesitate."

Is she naïve because she was raised in a sheltered environment or because she never had to suffer the consequences of her actions? It's undoubtedly the second one.

I may feel bad for her artistic struggle from time to time, but that's not enough to make me resent her for humiliating me in front of Nico by turning up at the worst possible time. He's already suspicious of me and she made it worse. Damn, she's just like my mother. All she cares about is her next fix. And now that I'm her muse, apparently, I'm what she needs to get her art career back on track.

I press my fingers into her jawbone, using all my strength, not stopping even when she whimpers.

Irritation fizzes in my blood. I'm annoyed by how easily she trusts me, by how naturally she expects me to help her, and by how codependent she is becoming. I'm even more annoyed by how I let her get away with it. Every. Single. Time.

But that stops now.

I'm not about to be used by her anymore. Muse or not.

I'll use her instead. It's time she got a taste of her own medicine.

"You're so addicted to danger, Francesca." I let my hand drop, satisfied at the red marks left behind on her pale skin. "Because you think you can run before you *really* get hurt."

Those lips. Those juicy, plump lips glazed with pink lip gloss that smells like strawberry taunt my nostrils. Like a decadent dessert waiting to be bitten into.

I claim them with mine in a punishing, brutal kiss. My teeth knife into her flesh, drawing blood. Grabbing her by the ass, I cage her against my body, trapping her in a prison of muscle she can't escape. She doesn't even fight me.

The second her salty taste seeps into my tongue, the gruesome memories, and hollowness I've always carried in my bones fade. The injustice of losing my position fades into an afterthought. The wraiths that inhabit my mind stop clawing at my conscience.

For the first time in forever, I exist without fears, without bitterness. Nothing in the world compares to this feeling.

My fingers melt into her jaw. Skin on skin, it's pure madness, an obsessive craving that erases everything but the desperate clamoring of our heartbeats.

She's addicted to my pleasure but I'm addicted to her pain. The more of her cries I smother with my tongue, the more blood I draw, the more desperately she squirms against me, the better I feel.

I don't need you Gabriele if you can't do your job.

I understand now why Francesca needs substances. It's the only way to escape the weight of powerlessness. When my body is dominating hers, the friction between us erases the reality that haunts me. There's at least one thing in the world I can control. Right now, I need that sense of control. I crave that power, even if I have to use her to get it.

Maybe we're more similar than I imagined.

Another scorching kiss, my tongue diving into her mouth and I forget where I am. Who I am. Wishing it was my cock inside the slippery heat of her mouth, not my tongue.

When we peel our wet, swollen lips apart, I shove her backward into the hallway.

"Go. I'm in a bad mood today. There's no telling how cruel I'll be."

But Francesca has abandoned all common sense, not that she had any, to begin with.

Her body snuggles closer, breasts grazing my torso. Heat swirls through my stomach. I'm hard. Damn it.

"Use me to make yourself feel good. It's the only thing I can give you. I want to make up for all the times you've helped me. Please."

She drags her nails over the back of my shirt, teasing the skin underneath.

"I'm not my mother," I say. "I can't throw away my pride for a fleeting high."

"I know you blame your mother for being an addict and she deserves it, but in a way, you're clinging to her. You don't want to let her go because that'd make you feel abandoned for real." A horde of shivers flutters inside my stomach.

I know that. I've always known that I was trying to convince myself of my mother's affection by holding onto the image of her.

Because those memories are all I have.

And now, I'll overwrite them with ones so dark, there will be no question of my mother ever taking up any more space in my brain.

If I'm Francesca's muse, she can be my grim reaper.

My grip tightens on her waist, sinking into the soft flesh of her hips. God, I want to taste that skin, to drown myself in those beautiful curves.

I can't save her, but I can help her destroy herself.

With one hand, I pin her wrists to the wall above her head. "Guess what? I'm going to make your wish come true."

My free hand clamps around her throat, though I don't squeeze, so she can still breathe easily. Stepping between her legs, I press my bulging arousal between her legs.

"Gabriele?" she yelps, her innocent eyes going wide. But she doesn't resist.

"You're fucked, Francesca."

I drag her into my apartment by her neck before slamming

the door shut. Then I retrieve my firearm from the drawer. I pull out the magazine to show her it's fully loaded before pressing the gun into her forehead. She releases out a soft pant.

I can't believe I'm doing this. I'm a dick. No, I'm actually a lot worse, as she's about to find out.

"Make me come in five minutes or I'll pull the trigger," I tell her. "Don't think for a moment that I'm joking. I've killed people for less."

Francesca stutters. "What?"

"If you can't do it, then run along home to your Mommy now."

Her eyes slant downward. I feel the gears in her head churning for once. She's seriously mulling this over. The ache in my dick intensifies at the thought of her bailing now. Not when I'm finally ready to end this torture she has been putting me through since that night at the gala.

But my Francesca never disappoints. Her streak of self-sabotage runs too deep.

"Okay," she whispers.

"Okay, what?"

"Okay, you can end my life if I don't bring you to orgasm in the next five minutes."

With eager fingers, she undoes my belt, sinking those hands into my boxers and brushing her thumb across the head of my cock. I curse under my breath as her fingers travel across my shaft. Ecstasy boils over inside me and spills through the cracks of my hardened resolve. Her touch is a brutal assault on my senses.

Then she opens that pretty mouth and I nearly lose my mind.

The sight of her puffy, bleeding lips turns me on even more, hardening my cock to steel. Knowing I did that to her, imagining her displaying those bruises to everyone she meets for the next few days gives me a rush. I've always had deviant sexual tastes, but I usually tone them down enough to make it bearable for my partner.

Not tonight. I'm done being considerate of her.

She slowly takes the tip into her mouth, licking up and down. She knows what she's doing. Within moments, pleasure prickles every cell in my body. Her tongue plays up the hard ridge of my erection. Then swallows me inch by inch, deep throating, closing her eyes, and devoting herself fully to my pleasure. Her fingers move against the base of my cock while her mouth tries to take me fully. She settles into a rhythm with her hands and tongue, and every minute of the experience is pure bliss.

Until it's too much for me. I want all of me inside that tight, wet hole of hers. I want to punish her, leave her on the verge of breathlessness, wishing she'd never started this. Wishing she had never laid eyes on me that night we first met.

Cupping the back of her head, I drive my thick, length into her mouth which is too small to fit me. A strangled sound explodes from her. That only fans the fire in my blood, inflaming my sadism until I want to wreck her more.

Her anguished cries, struggling breaths, and the sight of her strawberry-colored lips closed over my erection is my every erotic fantasy brought to life.

"Open wider, baby," I drawl. "I won't come like this. And you don't have much time left."

She winces but obeys. As I thrust into her mouth, hitting the back of her throat with each stroke, her gag reflex makes her choke again and again. Tears leak down the sides of her eyes. Her throat must feel raw and abused. It's probably uncomfortable beyond words. But there's no escaping this hell now. Not unless she's ready for worse. The metal edge of the gun pressing into her skull is a constant reminder of the stakes.

The sensations kick up a notch as I feel an impending climax gripping my insides. The glorious feeling of release crowds my nerves as control unravels from me.

I spill inside her mouth, the fierceness of my orgasm rocking me to my core.

No other woman I've had has made me come faster or harder.

She swallows it all. I assume it's because she's too worn out to spit out my cum. Her fingers are shaking when she wipes the remnants off her lips.

"Congratulations on saving your own life," I say.

I expect her to start the waterworks any moment now, or run out in fear after what she just experienced.

Instead, she grins at me.

"That was exciting." Her face is flushed, her eyes glazed with manic light. "I've never done something like that before."

It takes me a second to fully comprehend what I'm witnessing.

She's happy. Exhilarated.

Is she crazy? Wait, why am I even asking that? She's Francesca fucking Astor. Madness is her personality type.

I'm too speechless to even consider what this means. Who would have thought that Francesca would have the same dark tastes as me? Is that why I've been unconsciously attracted to her since the moment we met? Because I sensed she could make all my fantasies come true since she's just as wicked and twisted as me.

My need to hurt is equal to her need to be hurt.

She has shown me that she can take what I throw at her. Now I need to find out if she can take all of me. "Do you want more?" I ask.

My cock's hardening again.

"What's more?"

"Me inside you."

A twinkle in her blue eyes. "Hell yes."

Her fingertips scratch along the buttons of my shirt.

I move my hands up her thighs, feeling stroking a finger along the wet fabric of her panties. She purrs, arching forward in anticipation. Grinding my finger over her clit through the barrier, I swirl my tongue over the hard tip before biting. She grows wetter and wetter, her greedy channel trying to ride my finger.

But it's not my fingers I'll be stuffing inside that tight pussy tonight.

Lifting her up, I press her back against the wall. Her legs wrap around my waist readily. I slap her ass. She only coils her legs tighter around me. I extract a condom from my pocket and roll it over my length. Holding those round hips in place firmly, I impale her on my hard cock.

She cries out at being penetrated so deeply.

Burying my face at the side of her neck, I drag my lips over the curve of her throat. "Does it hurt?"

"A little."

"It's going to hurt a lot more. Punishment ought to hurt."

Fisting my shirt, she squirms to accommodate me. This is a hard position for her, but I love how deep I hit inside her like this. She's fucking tight and smells like heaven. My lips scrape the side of her neck.

"But Gabriele…?" she gasps.

"Yeah, baby?"

"What are you punishing me for?"

"For showing up at my apartment without warning me. You have no business here. Imagine if I was married, how bad it'd look."

"You're not, though." Her confidence is jarring even though I've never told her that I'm single.

"I might be soon," I confess. I hadn't meant to say it. Nothing is certain between Maria and me so far. But judging by Nico's tone today, it's a done deal.

Francesca doesn't probe me. Her eyelids are draping down in pleasure, her teeth sinking into her bottom lips as she arches her back and fights the heightening pleasure. Even she knows she hasn't earned it.

I slide out and then push back in. Her cry burns my ears. Fire strokes every nerve ending.

"Francesca," I say her name. It's a question and an answer. "Your pussy looks so good taking my cock."

"Yeah? How good?" There's that feisty side of hers, pushing through the pain and tears. This girl is a fighter. I wish she could see that about herself, too.

"Good enough that I could watch it every day." Her nails sink into my shoulders as I refuse to let her catch a breath, pushing into her harder, the rhythm of my thrusts growing more frantic. "Multiple times."

Her shaky breaths meld into a coherent sentence as she continues to take my pounding like a good girl. "I'm going to hold you to that promise, Gabriele."

"I promised you nothing. Don't start hallucinating when I've not even pounded you hard enough to make you see stars."

"You promised me pain," she reminds me.

"And you'll get it," I reply. "I want to feel your pussy spasm around me."

"Mmmmm," she mumbles.

With one more brutal thrust, I push her closer to the edge. Her cries twist into pleading moans. Easing one hand off her lips, I grind it against her swollen clit, hoping it's enough to set her off.

She bursts apart in my arms screaming my name, loud enough to wake up my neighbor's sleeping cat. I love every moment of it. Every second when her head, her throat, and her body are filled with nothing but me.

I wish I could keep her like this forever.

But my body is acting on instinct, hammering into her

faster, seeking its own release. She looks hazy, still in the throes of her orgasm, but she takes me without complaining.

Every clench of her walls around me is a glimpse of paradise. I drown in that tight heat, the pull of her sex squeezing every bit of pleasure until I have no more to give.

Until I'm nothing but an exploding firework inside a human body.

It's an all-consuming experience, made fiercer by me still being inside her. Our bodies are pressed so close together, I can feel her chest rising and falling against me.

I'm not a religious man, but if I was, I'd say it's a spiritual experience.

It takes a while for all the pleasure to ebb from me. Francesca drops her legs and I let her go. Her knees wobble, but she grabs the wall and stabilizes herself.

Those big, innocent eyes arrow straight into my soul.

"Whew. That was intense."

I avert my gaze. I can't stare at her directly, not after what we just did. Not after how deeply we were connected. I'm afraid she'd see that something has changed for me.

Wordlessly, I slink away.

When I get rid of the condom and return from the bathroom, Francesca's not in the living room anymore. I stride into my bedroom to find her curled up on my bed like a cat. She shows no signs of leaving.

"Another round?" I ask just to be polite.

Spreading her arms, she flashes a smile. "Cuddle with me."

Horror widens my eyes. "Why don't you ask me to stab you? That might be easier."

"It's aftercare," she shouts, creases developing between her thick brows. "That's part of sex, too. Gosh, you're so cold. No wonder you're still unmarried. Your wife will leave you if you refuse to cuddle after you just fucked her."

Her statement clubs me in the chest. If things go well, I'm

going to get married to Maria. The thing is, I don't know the first thing about how to treat a wife. I've never dated, only slept with sex workers and willing women who didn't do relationships. I had no idea that I was expected to hang around and coddle them after getting them off, too.

Slithering under the sheets, I grudgingly spoon with Francesca, writing this off as preparation for my married life.

It's only three minutes. Five minutes, tops. It won't kill me.

"Are you happy now?" My gruff voice comes out soft. I just can't damage her. Every time I go there, I end up pulling myself back.

She's too precious to break. Or maybe she's too broken to break further.

Her arm dangles over my body. She drapes one leg over mine. Like she owns me. Like we're actually something.

When she rubs her cheek against my chest, warmth flutters against my skin. I assume it's arousal, but I'm not hard.

She exhales against my collarbone. "If you weren't in the mafia, what would you do?"

She's hitting me in all the vulnerable spots today with her words. With Angelo's health, the issue of succession, and what Nico said...I'm already afraid of how long I have left in the family.

"I don't know. Never thought about it. All my life, I've only been focused on surviving in the streets, doing whatever it took to make myself valuable to Angelo. I may have been born to be in crime," I say. "What about you? If you weren't an artist, what would you do?"

She sucks in a shocked breath. "I've never considered any other career path. It has been my dream since I was a child to be an artist. Guess we're the same."

Neither of us knows or wants to consider anything other than what we've hoped for all our lives, even if it isn't the best course. The safety of the familiar is more soothing than the uncertainty of the unknown. Suddenly, Francesca's obsession with wanting to be an artist to the point of becoming an addict makes sense. I'd do whatever it took to stay in the mob, too. It's the best life I've known; the only life I've known. I fit better here than I fit anywhere else.

But some deep, dark curiosity prompts me to ask: "If I wasn't a capo in the mafia, what do you think I'd be?"

"A soldier in the military. Your physical fitness is extraordinary and I think that you'd be happy doing something that involves physical combat."

I laugh, my fingers groping a strand of her hair. I never considered enlisting in the army, not even when I was young and I wanted a decent life. Doesn't sound as fun as beating up people for a living, but at least I can still work with my body. For a brief second, visions of an alternate life parade through my mind—a life where I live in the light and have medals rather than wounds decorating my chest.

I close my eyes and force the image away.

"That's funny."

"No, I'm serious. It's still not too late."

"The government doesn't pay that much. I'm used to living in luxury," I mumble. "Besides, they'd kick me out the moment they look at my criminal record."

I'm pretty good at this job and it's not like I have a passion or dream I want to pursue. I dare not hope for a life I cannot have again.

"What about me?" Francesca says, looking up from my chest. It's still a little ridiculous to me that we're cuddling after sex, but it's too comfortable with her body nestled against mine. It feels right. Uncomplicated. I'm going to enjoy it for now. "If I wasn't an artist, what do you think I'd be?"

"An heiress."

She punches me in the chest. "That's not a career!"

"Let's see...a fashion designer or a model. You have good taste in clothes."

She perks up. "Was that a compliment?"

I shrug. "If you're so desperate for validation, I guess it could be."

"Oh, shut up. Why did I even ask?"

I rest my face over hers. The sex has satiated me but also drained all my energy. Sleep is curling its dark claws around my consciousness.

Before I realize it, I pass out with her in my arms.

CHAPTER 11

I'D NEVER DESCRIBE Gabriele as a nice guy. Strictly speaking, he's evil. A bad person. He sells drugs, runs illegal gambling dens, kills people, and freely engages in a dozen other morally contemptuous things.

He's also making me breakfast.

I settle my legs under his dining table, watching his back muscles flex as he fries up an omelet, I give up on trying to hate him. He's my addiction. Addictions are supposed to be toxic. If I could be addicted to healthy things, I'd be a gym rat, not a substance abuser.

"You're quiet," he notes, a few minutes later.

"Enjoy the peace while it lasts," I answer, rubbing the headache from my mild hangover. I didn't drink that much. By the time I was on my third glass, my mind had skipped over to Gabriele. In my imagination, I was running my nails down those carved abs, tracing the edges of his scars. So I left the bar early. He doesn't even know how many times thoughts of him have held me back from going over the limit.

Is it good or bad that I lust for him more than I lust for alcohol now? I can't tell which one is worse.

"You were drunk yesterday," his gruff tone cuts out my replay of last night's events at the bar. I think I saw Ella there but I dodged her before she could catch me. God, I hope Ethan wasn't with her. He'd have a *lot* to say if he figured out what I was up to. "Don't hate me now because I took advantage of you."

"I was only mildly intoxicated." I curve my eyebrow. "I remember everything we did clearly. Starting with how you threatened me with a firearm to blow you and how hard my mouth worked to suck that massive cock of yours. And...can't forget that you spilled inside my—"

He blocks his ears, clicking his teeth in disdain. "You have a dirty mouth."

"Yours is dirtier," I remind him. "Should I repeat the things you said to me last night?"

"Shut up and drink this." He slams a glass of what looks like tea on the table in front of me to cut me off. "It'll help with the hangover."

This is why I can't get him straight in my mind. He's supposed to be terrible, and sometimes, he's just that. Rude and closed off. But other times, he's normal, no different from any other guy I've dated in the past. If I'm being honest, he's a lot nicer and more considerate than most guys I've dated. It's bizarre how the man who almost killed me last night for not making him come can be fussing over fixing me breakfast now. The contrast is insane.

Warmth sizzles through my heart. I need to stop analyzing him so deeply, or I'll just start seeing more of him that I like. I love complex people. They fascinate me, like a painting with hidden meaning.

But I can't love Gabriele. There's no future for the two of us. He's about to get married. I don't know if what we're doing is right, even if he's going to have an arranged marriage in the future.

"Never thought you cooked," I say.

"I'm handy with knives." He spins the blade he's using in my direction. "In more ways than one."

"Was that a covert suggestion for knife play?" I plant my elbows on the table and lean forward. "Because I'm down for anything with you. The more dangerous, the better."

Gabriele's eyebrows cross over. He doesn't answer my question, but turns back and continues cooking. I suppose he's still not the type to talk openly about his vulnerabilities. Including his kinks. Or maybe he's still beating himself up over the fact that he fell asleep on me last night, and made me stay at his place.

When he's torturing himself with his own conscience, he's a treat to stare at. The way the corners of his eyes crinkle, how his mouth turns down…it's satisfying to watch him act human.

He slides a plate with an omelet and two slices of toasted bread under my nose, then grabs ketchup from the fridge and deposits it next to my plate of hot breakfast.

I examine the plate before me like a slide under a microscope. The aroma infiltrating my nostrils is appetizing, but there's no telling if it'll taste good.

"Will I get food poisoning if I eat this?" I say to lighten the mood.

"Why don't you give it a go and find out?" he challenges.

I do exactly that. I'm pleasantly surprised by how soft the omelet is. Delicate, perfectly balanced flavors coat my tongue. It's better than the one the chef at our place makes. And she's a professional.

"I take back what I said yesterday." I put down my fork. "Forget the military. You should be a professional chef."

"I'm not going to be anything other than a mobster." Gabriele's teeth grind down a little too hard. He goes surly all of a sudden. "Why is everybody trying to get me to retire?"

"Is your boss tired of you, too?" I inquire. "Not surprised."

"I'm not talking about my job with you. Eat up and leave. I have shit to do today." Without warning, his face morphs into a storm cloud. I saw another man leave when I came in last night. They probably talked about something related to work. Bad news, if I had to guess. It'd explain why Gabriele's expression was dark and menacing when he fixed his eyes on me. Also, he was more volatile than usual, which is why he let me get to him so easily after flatly refusing me that very morning.

"So where do we go from here?"

All I get in response to that is the efficient hiss of chopping and frying. When I repeat my question, he grunts.

Clearly, communication isn't one of his strengths.

"If this is a one-time, thing, that's cool," I say, wondering if he can hear the undercurrent of disappointment threaded through my syllables. "But I hope it isn't. What we did together was so different from anything I've experienced before. You made me access emotions I have a hard time dealing with, like fear. And I enjoyed it."

The slightest wobble in Gabriele's efficient motions gives away the crack in his armor. "You have to learn to deal more healthily."

"Sex is good for health," I argue. "It burns calories."

Gabriele's short bark of laughter lights up the whole room. "Only you could say that."

Suddenly, he blinks like he's trying to stuff down what he's feeling. When he turns away, I rise out of my chair.

"Gabriele, don't fight your feelings," I plead, drawing on every bit of authority I possess. "Or you'll end up like me."

He steps away from me, his eyelids dropping shut. He runs

his tongue across his lower lip, grinding his hand through his hair.

Breath empties from my lungs when he falls to his knees on the floor, right beside me, fingers clenching around the arm of my dining chair for support.

"I'm weak Francesca," he murmurs. "I thought I was strong but you've fucked with my head and my willpower. Now I need you—I need your body, your lips, your touch—just as much as you need me."

The declaration is quiet and straightforward. Which makes it more powerful. For moments, stillness beats between us like a broken clock.

It hits me in a rush.

Gabriele's addicted to me, too. And he hates it. He hates it but he can no longer deny it.

The calluses on his fingers generate delicious friction when he drags them across the planes of my jaw. He's looking into my eyes—something he never does—and I'm looking back. The air is charged with intimacy, with the silent knowledge that the dynamic between us has changed.

All this time, he was the one who looked inside my head and clearly saw my demons.

Now I'm looking inside his.

There's no mistaking the hint of self-disgust. He probably thinks he's turned out just like his mother. Also, he probably pictured being with a different kind of woman: serene, stable, wholesome.

Not broken, reckless, and emotional.

I gather his face into my arms, holding him against my chest. The agitation heating his skin cools. The weight of him against me feels intimate in a way that's not sexual, but just as addictive. This small, intimate bubble of silent acceptance where we provide space for each other's turbulent emotions to settle is precious. I could drown in this closeness as easily as I could drown in soul-shattering orgasms.

"If you need me then take me." My lips move against his silky hair, my mouth ghosting over the top of his head.

Gabriele squirms free from my grasp. A draft of cold air caresses the places where his skin was against me seconds earlier. He rises to his feet. "Not today."

He draws away from me, and the safe cocoon I was ensconced in vanishes like a puff of smoke. Focusing on reality, I pick up my fork and knife and began digging into the remainder of my breakfast.

"Come with me to my cabin if you're not busy," I say around a mouthful of food. Rubbing my sweaty palms on my dress, I barely hear the words I'm speaking over the gunfire of my heartbeat. "It's near Woodstock. I'm going up there to paint during the weekend. We'll be all alone."

"You want me to watch you paint? I'd rather die."

"No, I want you to be there so I don't slip like I did yesterday. I'm really trying to quit. And I think I can. If you help me out a little."

"By fucking you every time you crave escape?" he completes for me.

"I'll make it worth your while." I wink. "I promise. Plus, you're my muse and I work better when you're close to me."

It's an unconventional method, for sure, but I don't know anything else that has worked for me so well before.

"Let me think about it," he says at last. "There's a pretty important job I need to complete this week. I can't afford to be distracted."

"I'll wait for you."

I finish eating quickly after that.

"It's time for your classes," Gabriele reminds me. "I could drive—"

"No. I'll take a cab," I say, even though I have only taken the subway a couple of times and hate being inside a crowded train. "You said you have something."

I'm almost out of the door when his footsteps rock closer. "Wait."

My body obeys his voice instinctively. I turn around. His thumb presses across my lower lip, coming away with a smear of ketchup.

I burst out smiling. The action is so uncharacteristically caring. He's displaying a side of him that I've never seen before.

"Thank you, Daddy." I tease.

He frowns. Not a fan of Daddy Kink, I see.

The heat of his forehead burns my skin when he taps his head against mine. "I don't want other men looking at your lips and getting ideas."

"We never agreed we were going to be exclusive. So tell me why shouldn't they get ideas?" I say, knowing it'll get a rise out of him.

"Because you're mine, Francesca. It's so obvious it doesn't even need to be said." Shivers unfurl in my stomach as his breath strokes my ears.

At that moment, I feel it—the fierce truth clasping around me like a physical shackle.

I am his. I have been from the moment I lost the ability to feel alive without him.

* * *

IT FEELS odd to be in my studio without Gabriele's safe presence lingering in the corridor. Either he decided I wasn't enough of a threat anymore, or he was telling the truth about having an important job. Neither Ricardo nor Antonio is here. They must be on an important job, too.

Still, I don't miss them.

My work is proceeding surprisingly well. Yesterday night's

intense sex refreshed my mind. I was able to feel excited for the first time in forever. It has opened up parts of my brain that I couldn't access for a long time.

Gabriele might really be the muse I've desperately needed.

Looking at my half-finished thesis painting doesn't automatically trigger all the critical comments and hate in my head.

The shadows of our bodies moving, the residue of pleasure coursing through my veins envelops my mind in a soft haze.

Possibility shimmers around me. I'm back in the mental space where my ideas unspool into breathtaking visions, where anything can be created and anything can be destroyed without effort.

My brush glides across the surface of the canvas. For one glorious hour, I drown in my dreams, bathe in the masterpiece taking shape before my eyes. However, at the first moment of tiredness, the barbs of criticism poke through my skull again.

Putting down the brush, I stretch my fingers. I've already accomplished more than last week. All in a single day. It looks pretty great, too, if I say so myself.

This is the high I've desperately sought. A euphoria you only experience when you pour your heart and soul into something.

A flicker of pride drips down my chest. It's almost time for lunch so I grab my purse and head out. I'm mentally planning to stop by my favorite coffee shop when the hum of familiar voices in the corridor makes me freeze.

At the other end, two of my classmates are digging into their Doritos near the vending machine, their conversation too loud to ignore.

"Did you notice? Francesca Astor has been acting so shady, coming and going to her studio as she pleases. Plus, there's that scary guy who's always with her. I'm sure he's the one actually painting her thesis."

The saliva sliding down my throat freezes. Gravity isn't

working anymore. The joy of creative release crashes into the abyss of self-doubt.

Shakily, I press my palms to my ears, but the acoustics in this building don't work in my favor.

"While we work hard, she just pays a professional and takes the credit. I can't stand her. Acting all sweet on the outside while she's scheming in that head of hers," says another one of my classmates. I remember her well because she smiled at me and pretended to be nice to me during the first semester. I had no idea it was an act.

This is what you get when you pretend to be perfect all the time.

"Girls like her shouldn't be here." The conversation continues. I should dash quickly across the hallway before they spot me. But my inner sadist is waiting to be flayed by more cruel judgments. "It's unfair for the rest of us."

Girls like you shouldn't exist.

"God, I hate her."

The world would be better if you were gone.

The voices from my youth come back to me, a constant loop I cannot eliminate. I grew up insulated, with other rich kids who didn't think my wealth made me a threat to them. But I attended an art camp when I was in high school.

It's there that I first realized being rich didn't mean I'd be popular.

Because everybody wanted this as badly as I did—the fame, the success, the lifestyle of a full-time artist. Everybody was as passionate as me. Yet not everybody could be successful. We knew that even then.

But those who couldn't make it blamed it on me.

You're only here because your parents are rich.

It started with that, then grew worse until I began to question whether I even deserved to dream. Because I couldn't refute anything.

Everything they said was true.

But it wasn't the whole truth.

I was there because my parents could pay the course fees, but also because I was talented, serious about getting into art school, and because I'd worked hard to build a great portfolio.

Having never been around other artists before, I was desperate for peer validation. Their hatred seeped into my soul until it colored my own perception of myself. Until I was nothing more than the rich, spoilt, imposter they wanted me to be. Things tipped downward once I got into college.

I hear stuff like this every few weeks. The constant onslaught of envy has dug its claws into my non-existent self-worth. I can't undo it, and it drags me deeper into fear every day. What if everyone in the world thinks the same of me?

What if everyone hates my art because *I* created it?

I scrunch my eyes shut, struggling to breathe louder and fade the judgment corroding my insides like acid.

In the darkness under my lids, I see his face.

If Gabriele was here, what would he tell me?

Fuck them. Yeah, probably that.

But that's because he has never been resented for existing. He might be a criminal who kills without thinking while I'm simply a girl with rich parents who support my dreams, but between the two of us, it's me society loves to cut down.

I suppose being evil is better than being lucky.

My legs are shaking by the time I claw across the corridor. My classmates are already gone by then. There's a hole in my chest. The fear I fought all morning is taking over me again. Defeat leeches the joy of having made progress on my painting. At the end of the day, I can never win.

I sprint to the coffee shop, thinking my day can't get any worse, but in the line, I spot the last person I want to see.

Composure peels from me like layers of an onion.

My brother Elliot. Why is he here? He doesn't work in this area. My heart beat drums in my ears like a 90s rock song someone forgot to turn off as I watch him through the window glass from the street.

I step back, but the motion only alerts him. He squints up from his phone screen. Our identical blue gazes collide.

Elliot's easily the most conventionally attractive of us siblings. Ethan looks scary, I have a pleasant face but nothing to write home about. Elliot is striking, someone you can't help but turn toward. When he uses that pretty face to his advantage, nobody can win.

"Francesca?" His focus slides from my face to my shivering fingers.

Here's the thing about putting on an act: it's like any other skill. Practice makes perfect. When you've done it long enough, your fake persona snaps on like a switch. Sometimes, it seems more comfortable than my real identity.

"Funny meeting you here." I sidle up to him, all sisterly, fixing a bright smile on my lips. "I thought you'd vanished off the face of the planet for good."

Three months ago, he moved out of our Brooklyn town-house to live on his own in a small apartment. He's unrecognizably suave in the gray suit that peeks from under his long, unbuttoned woolen coat. Those sun-kissed curls of his have been tamed into a uniformly platinum blonde mass that's swept back neatly, baring his forehead.

I suppose he's working hard to fit in with the other people at the office. If I remember correctly, Sharma Ventures is a venture capital company which means they finance startups. I never thought Elliot would end up going into that after studying philosophy in college but he owes a huge debt to Zara Sharma, the founder of Sharma Ventures.

"Me? You're the one who never calls me and never answers my text messages?" He screws his mouth into a displeased twist. "I thought you didn't want to see me ever again."

The searing press of guilt melts my bones. "I was going to call you."

"When we were in our graves?"

"No. Soon. After I was done with my spring thesis."

You're a bad liar. Gabriele's statement echoes in my skull. Heat floods my ears.

"It's okay." Elliot scoops up four cups of coffee from the counter. "I know you haven't forgiven me for what I did to Ethan."

I sigh, tongue-tied, as awkwardness expands like a blood-stain. Things are complicated right now between us three siblings. Ethan, my eldest brother, got into a lot of legal trouble last year thanks to Elliot. Elliot's also the reason my father went to prison. Given the kind of man that Dad was, Elliot almost did a good deed.

"Like my new look?" Elliot says when I remain silent too long. I suppose I must have been glaring at him throughout that time.

"You look like you've sold your soul to a corporation," I answer.

"I'll take that as a compliment." His finger bounces in the air, pointing up and down my form. "You, on the other hand...is everything okay?"

"What do you mean? I look exactly like I used to."

"No, you don't. Your eyes are red."

Brothers are the best lie detectors. Is it because he has known me since I was born?

An icy finger caresses my chest, pumping it full of fear. I don't want Elliot or Ethan to find out what I'm doing right now. They're both overprotective. Ethan will get me committed to a rehab facility before I can take my next breath.

But sometimes, I wonder if I'll ever go back to who I used to be when this dark spell is over. Like Elliot, I want to change and become a better version of myself, but right now, I'm only spiraling toward destruction.

It's like there's nothing where my heart used to be except a yawning hole. Whatever I see, whatever I do, I can't feel anything. My mind keeps looping those same thoughts until I'm nauseous. My head is filled with cruel words that aren't mine. I used to be able to block them out with beautiful images and dreams, but when that was taken from me...I just drowned.

"How's your new job?" I quickly divert him from the topic of my imminent mental breakdown. "I'm surprised your boss hasn't fired you."

"Trust me, she wants to. I do nothing except make her life miserable." His chest rises, then falls. His gaze locks onto his phone where a new message has popped up. "But she needs me to pay back what I owe her."

"You have enough money in your trust fund," I inform him. "Remind me why you're slaving away at an office job again?"

"Because my boss is hot and I like being around her." The dry, humorless tone with which he delivers that line tugs at my heartstrings. It reminds me of the old Elliot who used to crack jokes with a straight face.

"Let's hope she doesn't find out that you have a thing for older women," I add with a nudge of my elbow. Elliot's always had a very clear type—older, successful women. It's the case of opposites attract. Since he's not very ambitious or mature, he's drawn to people who are.

His face freezes into an awkward expression. "She might have found that out already."

"And she still hasn't fired you? She must be an angel."

Elliot shrugs. "Enough about me. You look like you haven't slept in days. Why are your eyes so red? Francesca, are you okay?"

Shit. Elliot used to casually experiment with drugs when he

was much younger and during his partying days. He might be able to pick up the signs if he examines me closely.

I smooth my bangs over my forehead, hoping they hide my eyes.

"Worked all night on my painting." Butterflies are dancing an entire waltz in my stomach. I feel like I'm on the edge of a cliff. "But I'm curious about what exactly *is* your job. You look pretty busy." It's a strategic question, meant to deflect the conversation away from my life.

"I'm her personal secretary," Elliot says. "I do anything she needs me to do."

"Including getting coffee," I finish, observing him tap his fingers against the edge of the counter.

"I like this part of the job the most." Elliot yawns. "Since it's the easiest."

The weird part is, I don't even know if he's serious about working at Sharma Ventures because he wants to hook up with his boss or if he's using that as a cover to hide his real reason. Elliot is a complete mystery. Out of the three of us, he's the hardest to comprehend. I can never tell what's going on inside his head. His devil-may-care façade hides his intentions really well. In some ways, he's like me. Except my mask may crack a lot easier than his.

"Francesca, let's meet at my apartment and hang out on Sunday. I'll show you my cooking skills," he pipes up.

"You couldn't even boil water when you were at home."

"I've learned new skills since I started living alone." He sighs a little too long. "Don't make fun of me. But I think this is my life's calling."

"Buying coffee?"

"Being a secretary. Serving someone with all my devotion, making their life a bit easier. Ethan's always been the natural CEO, the one who likes to be in charge. He's a control freak. And you're the artist. Dad always groomed me to think I was born to be a master, someone who would give other people orders because I was an Astor, but I'm more comfortable when I'm being given orders."

"There's nothing wrong with that," I say. "I'm glad you found something you enjoy. I was scared you'd waste away your life partying."

Elliot wipes a hand over his forehead. "I was, too."

Cradling the mug holder stacked with hot coffee cups, he juggles his phone in one hand, typing something.

"Looks like you're busy." I step to his side, brushing past him to avoid prolonging the conversation. "Don't want you getting fired and becoming a useless bum who hangs out at home again."

He grabs the cup of coffee he ordered. On his way out, Elliot plants a hand on my shoulder, squeezing. "You don't have to forgive me because Ethan forgave me."

"I have no reason to hold a grudge against you." I swallow thickly, remembering all the drama Elliot caused six months ago when he made Ethan go through hell. "You never hurt me."

His features slacken in relief. "And I won't ever hurt you. You're my only sister. See you on Sunday."

He slips away from me before I can disappoint him by canceling our plans because I'm going to Woodstock this weekend.

CHAPTER 12

 *abriele*

MARIA SCANS the broken glass carpeting the office floor. It leaves a trail all the way across the dark wood like a galaxy of stars. Torn pages and the keyboard that fell off the desk during my altercation with a member of a rival crime family show further signs of a struggle having taken place here. Ricardo and Antonio just cleaned up the body. The man's in the basement, but spatters of his blood spot the room.

She's a wise woman, so Maria chooses to silence her curiosity. "Did pick a bad time?"

She's not the frivolous type, so there must be a reason for her visit.

"Did you need anything from me?" I visually check her for bruises, but she's fully covered in a coat, black pants, and boots. "Has your husband hurt you—"

"No. I came to talk to you. Casually. It's nothing important."

Despite doing her best, she can't hide her shock at the scene before her. She presses her lips. "I met Angelo yesterday. He said he wants to see us married soon. But I want to get to know you better. I will not rush into this like I did with my last marriage."

"Of course. Unfortunately, there's an issue I'm dealing with at the moment." I wave my hands at the chaotic state of the office. "Should be done by Saturday. Do you want to..." My teeth bite my tongue in reflex as Francesca's invitation swims back into my head.

It's near Woodstock. We'll be all alone.

In my brain, there's a version of me doing all the depraved things I've wanted to do with her.

All alone.

I'm imagining a rustic cabin in the wilderness where nobody can hear her regardless of how loud she is. I want to make her scream until her throat is hoarse.

A heavy need settles in my bones. The cold prick of regret stabs the back of my skull.

My body is in this room with the right woman, but my mind isn't. Strawberry-scented lipstick coats the inside of my nostrils.

Though I stand before my future wife, my cock's burns with the fervent need to be inside a different girl.

My time with Francesca is designed to be short-lived, so I'm determined to make the most of it before I settle down. There's something I have felt for the heiress since the first moment I've met her and it demands to be explored. She makes me care deeply for her wounds, makes me want to soothe them. I eat up every haunted look of her eyes. She has no idea how much self-control it takes me to keep my hands to myself when she begs me. Even when I'm angry at her, I can't stay angry for long. Also, since I found out she can take every dark kink I throw at her, I am dying to ravish that luscious body in all the depraved ways. A person like her, so open-minded yet beautiful and sensitive, is very hard to come by.

I'll give her the few weeks and months I have left. The last days of my freedom. And hope it's enough.

I drag my errant thoughts back to Maria who is breathing slowly. "I'll let you know when I'm back," I say.

She makes a small, affirmative gesture by crinkling her eyes. "Angelo said he was poisoned by the enemy. Does that have something to do with it?"

A resentful sign unravels from me. "They've been coming after our territory for a long time. I thought it was the Russians, but turns out it's our old rival, the Bianchi family. Those rats were lying low for a while since their Don and Underboss got arrested in a drug raid last year, so I thought they weren't a threat anymore."

The sudden swish of cloth catches me off guard. Maria dabs her Burberry handkerchief over my forehead, soaking up all the sweat and god knows what else I got on me while I was beating that man who currently is tied up in the basement into pulp. "Am I making you uncomfortable?" She withdraws jerkily. "Seeing blood makes me...worried."

"Not at all." It's nice of her to clean my cut, but her kindness seems cautious. Unnatural. Unlike Francesca who does it as easy as breathing.

"You're busy. I'll go." Abruptly, she turns and saunters away.

I wind my way down to the basement where a shriek rattles the dark-painted walls. I left the questioning up to Antonio this time. Ricardo's just guarding the man, in case he tries to escape.

Unbuttoning my sleeves and dragging them up over my arms, I cast a glance to Ricardo. "Has he said anything worthwhile?"

Ricardo's uncharacteristically serious demeanor is the first sign of a problem. "The underboss's son was the one who engineered Angelo's poisoning. He fled the city yesterday. Probably knows we're coming for his ass."

"Where's he now?"

"He has vacation homes in Miami, San Francisco, and Chicago. It'll be one of those. The hostage doesn't know which one he's currently residing at."

Fear rolls down my spine. He left yesterday? If he leaves the country, if they actually manage to escape...Nico will kill me for not going after them harder.

"Get out, Ricardo," I grind my teeth as I step into the small room, violence surging up my bloodstream. "I'm taking over."

* * *

THE CHEESECAKE TAUNTS ME. Why did I have to buy the goddamn thing just because it reminded me of Francesca? It's like my subconscious mind already decided to go to Woodstock even before the rest of me caught up.

The bartender blinks at me curiously.

"Rough fight?" he asks, scrutinizing the unhealed cuts and wounds tattooed on my face.

"This week was a fucking nightmare," I reply.

I must sound sufficiently violent because he puts a stop to his friendly small talk immediately. Staying a safe distance away behind the bar, he begins pouring the other guest's drinks. For a Saturday night, this place isn't very crowded.

I sip my beer, eyes roaming the crowd for a specific blonde.

The good news is, I finally captured the idiot who poisoned Angelo after a pointless trip to Miami and then Chicago. After getting him to confess, I put him out of his misery. Then killed his associates and sent Nico footage of their corpses.

Nico replied with a one-line message.

Sorry for doubting you were a Russo.

Now the bad news: I don't care. Not about Nico, nor my glorious return as a hero, nor about the ridiculously expensive party that Angelo is planning, not even for the fact that Nico suggested he'd make me the underboss when he becomes the Don.

When I set foot in the backroom of our casino in Queens, the place where all the capos and senior members hold meetings every week, a venue I'd been in more times than I could count, it felt empty. The cheers rang hollow, the praise didn't calm my unease. The alcohol tasted like an expensive luxury I'd lost the ability to appreciate.

Not even Nico's warm welcome could make the place feel like home anymore.

All I could see was the distrusting man who had been in my apartment that night. Something had broken between us, and nothing could put it back. The sense of security, the sense of rightness I'd always felt being a part of this family was gone.

I didn't belong there, which was ironic, given I'd sacrificed my life to prove to everyone that I did.

You'd be a great chef. Your cooking's phenomenal.

Francesca's suggestion from that morning whispered to me like a mirage promising a path out of the endless desert.

To me, growing up in uncertainty, home meant a permanent roof over my head, a clear source of income, and a group of familiar people who cared for me and whom I could call my own.

But is home a safe place or one that your heart is pulled to, even when it makes no sense?

My vision blurs, eyelids begin to droop, but I fight to stay awake. The past few days have taken everything out of me. The fear of losing the enemy, and the devastating consequences if he fled, made sleep an impossibility. I drove myself hard every second.

And all that to ultimately end up here? Life's ironic sometimes.

The moment she enters the bar, my instincts flare to life. I smell her strawberry scent before I see her.

Without fail, every single head—both male and female—turns in her direction. The heiress is very pretty, but in this case, it's her outfit that's drawing all the attention. Designer, as always. In a blue tweed miniskirt and jacket co-ord set, showing off miles of silky smooth skin. It's always blue with her. It must be her favorite color or something.

If I'm a dog that knows the scent of its master, she's a hawk that knows the sight of her prey.

Her bare legs fold under the counter as she slides into the stool next to mine. All I've seen in the last few days is the ugly mugs of Bianchi men, so her angelic face is a welcome change. I stare at it like it's Mona Lisa.

"Never thought I'd find you drinking alone at a bar." My ears tingle at the brush of her voice. "Any reason you picked this specific one, hundreds of miles away from where you live?"

"So I could run into you."

"Seriously?"

I raise my half-full glass of beer. "This is the nicest place in this town and you're still you. You need to numb the pain. So, how's your art coming along?"

The last question is simply to irritate her. Sometimes, her eyes look so cold and lifeless, anger is the only way to breathe fire into them. That's why I banter with her. Annoy her. Force her to think up witty retorts instead of wallowing in her misery.

"I think I want to die," she declares, her voice scratchy.

I hold her hand and guide her up my thigh, loving how her skin flushes and she leans in closer. Until her fingers register the bulge of metal at my side. "My pistol's at your service, in that case."

"You're joking, right?"

"I'll give you three seconds to guess the answer."

"You sound mad."

"Here's a tip, Francesca: next time you invite someone to

your studio, text them the fucking address instead of hoping they're a psychic."

"Shit. I'm sorry. I thought...." She groans. I notice that the usually flawless strands of her hair look dry. The whites of her eyes are meshed with red veins. "I'm out of it nowadays."

Between the two of us, I can't truly say who looks worse. I look like I ran into a truck and she looks like she ran into an artist's block.

Removing her hand from me, I deposit the box of strawberry cheesecake on her lap. "A souvenir for you, all the way from Chicago."

"Cheesecake?"

"Rose cheesecake. I don't know, it reminded me of you. Since you're into beauty, art, and stuff."

My heart pounds in my ears as her passive expression shatters into something unidentifiable.

I curse at myself inwardly. Why did I say something so cheesy? That's not like me. The words poured out before I could contain the warm, cozy sensation that gripped my chest the moment she sat next to me like it was the most natural thing in the world.

Like it was exactly where she belonged.

She didn't need to think about it for even a second.

Things are changing between us. We're growing closer, despite my desire to push her away. That, combined with my own dissatisfaction at not being happier after my great conquest of the Bianchi family snowballs into a hot surge of displeasure. What's wrong with me all of a sudden? Just a few weeks ago, I was so secure in my place in the world, so sure of my future with my perfect wife, and now all my dreams are ash I don't want to swallow.

Francesca runs her fingertips along the paper bag the box is in. "Were you always this sentimental? No, wait. I remember you telling me I need to learn self-control and turning me down just a few days ago."

I scowl. "Let's say the warm Miami sun made my cold heart melt a little."

"Why were you in Miami?"

"Business." I almost want to confess I killed two men and maimed three, just to see those juicy lips parting open in shock, but I resist.

"I'm assuming it's best not to ask about the kind of business?"

"You assume right."

It's too much to hope that she'll drop the line of questioning. "Your face looks like a mess. Are you sure you shouldn't be lying in a hospital? Is it safe for you to move?"

"Don't judge a man's state by his appearance," I say. "I can still throw you over my shoulder and carry you out of here before you finish taking your next breath."

"I see you're wasting no time with foreplay." Francesca tugs at my arm, pouting in the direction of the door. "Consider me charmed by your dirty talk."

I clear my throat, not budging.

"Order your drink," I say. "I'll even be generous and pay for it."

"I'd rather go home now." Her hot exhale kisses my jaw. "There's so much we can do together when we're all alone."

"I know you wanna quit, but it's better to reduce your intake slowly. One glass won't set you back."

"I already had two in the morning."

Of course, she did.

"And how many in the afternoon?" I ask.

Pink stains brighten her cheeks. "One."

"In that case, let's get out of here," I say, afraid she might be tempted by all the free-flowing alcohol if we hang around longer.

As we stroll out with her arm curled around my middle and mine around her shoulder, I wonder what the people around us think of us together. There's no mistaking what we are—a thug and a polished princess. We look wrong together.

When she squirms into the driver's side of a pickup truck parallel parked in front of the bar, my confusion deepens.

"What're you doing? Get in," she says.

"You can drive? Then why did you make me your personal chauffeur?"

"Because I'm always drunk, high, or hungover. I don't want to get into an accident or kill anyone." She unfastens her seatbelt and hops out of the car, handing me the keys. "Actually, it's better if you drive right now. I have a headache."

"You just saw me drinking," I remind her.

"Half a glass of beer. I've had more. We'll be breaking the law either way."

If there's anything I'm a pro at, it's breaking the law, so I get behind the wheel without further protest. There's no better way to relax than to drive on empty rural roads where I can drive as fast as I like.

Francesca has adapted to my reckless driving over the last few weeks because she doesn't even comment when I nearly crash into somebody's fence.

"You said I remind you of roses." Her sweet voice rises over the low hum of the radio. "You remind me of a knife."

"A rose and a knife. That's a weird picture. Those two don't belong with each other."

Neither do we.

This craving, lust, whatever we're experiencing, exists in the sliver of time between irresponsibility and recklessness. We're playing with fire knowing it'll burn us but hoping the burn will be good enough to make it worth it.

Francesca said it herself. It's just sex. Just physical. She won't cling and neither will I.

At the end of the day, she's a rich heiress desperately seeking an escape from the brutality inside her own head. Someday, her illusions about me will be shattered. When they're all gone, she'll leave me. Just like my mother did.

My grip tightens around the wheel. I have to remember that.

"Those cuts look deep." She caresses the bumpy, broken skin over my cheekbone that the doctor stitched back together roughly. "Who did this?"

"He's dead so don't worry about it."

Her lips pucker in distaste. "You killed someone in Miami."

"He's not the first man I've killed." *And he won't be the last.*

"Of course. You're the big bad criminal who has killed loads of people. Are you proud of it?"

The knot in my stomach expands like a balloon with the growing creases on her face. I know she doesn't like my profession. She accepts it because she's blinded by the breathless attraction we share but someday, she'll open her eyes. When she does, she's going to hate what she sees.

"Why wouldn't I be?" I exhale. "I did it to save my family. To save myself."

"And is your family proud of you?"

"I hope so." Maybe Nico's pacified for now regarding my loyalty. But how long will it be until he begins to suspect me again? I saw the resentment on the faces of the other capos who were afraid of losing to me in the succession war. That I have more say in the organization than they do. Is that what brothers should think?

Maybe Francesca's not the only one desperately holding onto illusions to erase the emptiness of her reality.

Maybe it's the both of us.

"You never talk much about your family. I mean, apart from your Mom and your friend whom you killed. Is Antonio your family, too? And Ricardo?"

"They're like my brothers."

"Who is your father?"

"The Don. Angelo Russo. He's a man I respect more than anyone else."

"Wow, it's rare to hear you talk about someone in such positive tones. I need to look up this guy. He must be impressive." Her fingers hungrily scour Google on her phone. Angelo's picture from years ago comes up. The time when he went to prison for tax evasion. It was a brief stint, but he was in the news for it. His hair is still brown in that photo. "Huh, he looks normal. What exactly do you respect about him?"

"That he's fierce, but also gentle and paternal. He takes care of his people even if he has to ruin lives to do it. To me, he's the perfect father, a pillar of strength and support. But at the same time, he's no tyrant. It's a fine line."

Francesca giggles. "He's a lot like you, then."

Pinpricks of warmth stick to my skin. All my life, I've wanted to be like Angelo. He's my role model. To be told I resemble him is the greatest honor.

"I'm nothing like the don." My voice is low, unsure. The coldness in the air pricks my skin. Francesca is staring at me expectantly, waiting for me to tell her more. "I can't change anyone's life the way he changed mine when he saved me at sixteen."

"Saved you how?"

"He found me bleeding after a gang fight and rescued me. Nursed me back to health. Gave me a roof over my head and a job. If not for that opportunity, I wouldn't be here with you."

The feather-light weight of Francesca's fingers settles on my knee. "How did you almost die?" she whispers in a scared voice.

I have never told her about my brutal teenage days. But this car ride is long, and the mood between us is suitably heavy. We have time, and I don't need to focus on the road since it's deserted.

"You know how many times I've been arrested by the police

as a teenager?" I start, trying to lighten up the depressing talk of my childhood with some statistics. "Sixteen. I got involved with a gang after my mother started selling her body to men to pay for her addiction. There would be strange guys over at our apartment at weird hours. Some of them were brutal. They liked hurting a young boy because it made them feel strong. Some men wanted me to stand out in the cold while they fucked her all night. And others…well they wanted to fuck me."

She gasps.

"Is this story too horrifying for a precious heiress who grew up in a safe, perfect home?" I press my foot on the pedal, accelerating, wondering if she thinks less of me now that she knows what sort of background I come from. I'm a dirty, defiled man in more ways than one.

"I'm so sorry." Her voice trembles. I can feel her heavy breath caressing my neck, her upturned face staring holes into me. "I never imagined it was so bad for you. Did your mother allow… those men to…do touch you?"

"She never lifted a finger to protect me, that's for sure." Anger turns my saliva into acid coating my tongue. "When I grew sick of being hurt, I joined a gang. At first, it was because I needed to learn how to defend myself. Fighting is not an optional skill when you have a life like mine."

"On the night we first met you told me you were a fighter," Francesca says, squeezing my knee in sympathy. "It breaks my heart to know you were forced to fight. That you weren't given a choice."

"Life is not about choices, Francesca. It's about making the best of the limitations imposed upon you."

Her breaths are coming in shorter waves, cascading hotly down the side of my face. "I still wish it was different. Your past. If you had a happy home, a happy childhood—"

"I would be someone different. Those years, unbearable as they were, made me strong. I like knowing I survived the worst and that I can survive whatever life throws at me because of what I had to endure. Though, to an heiress like you, I guess my background sounds unsavory."

"Gabriele." Francesca reprimands me, pulling her body back like I've wounded her. "I would never judge you—or anyone—for circumstances outside your control."

She means it. I can see that in the wetness of her lashes, in the tears that are on the verge of spilling from her eyes. Francesca is a bleeding heart, so compassionate to a complete stranger who is only using her for her body and his kinks. Well, she's using me, too.

"I have never met your don Angelo," she continues. "But he must be a great man because he recognized your value and saved your life."

"He taught me a lot," I admit, resenting the fact that I've ended up giving one more piece of my history to her today, one more detail I've never told anyone but her. Angelo knows about my childhood years, but only because he did the research. "I have never missed not having a father. Angelo was everything I could have asked for in a father figure and more."

"You know, I think you'd make a great father, too. You're so protective." Releasing a huge sigh, she leans back against her seat. "If only Daddy Kink was your thing, I could get to enjoy that side of you."

A cough sputters out of me. I tear my attention away from the road to glare at her in disgust. "You had to go and make that sexual?"

"Of course. Because our relationship is just physical, Gabriele. That's what I promised you. Unless you want this to be more than sex?" Her saucy eyebrow arch is a trick, a trap, the door into a universe I can never be a part of. She's teasing me, but it stings.

"How can it be more?" I say. "You're you and I'm me. We

both have our place in the world. And those worlds will never collide."

"You sounded like my ex-boyfriend Mason just then."

"Don't compare me to that dickhead."

"You're a dickhead, too, sometimes—" Instead of completing her sentence, she waves at the approaching structure outside the window. "Here. This is my cabin. Turn right."

It's half-blurred by trees but gets clearer as I approach it. The GPS navigation gives me my final direction.

I swerve the car, parking in the driveway.

"Finally. Home sweet home." Francesca thrusts out her arms at what looks like an average house. It has a wooden exterior. Through the windows, I spy cozy yet tasteful furnishings reminiscent of a cabin.

"This is where you paint? I don't see any paintbrushes."

Francesca leads me behind the house. There's another rectangular building here, a smaller one. It has no windows but when she opens the door, a skylight floods the room with brightness. "No, *this* is where I paint."

The actual studio is in a separate building behind the house, then. It's extremely spacious with grey walls, high ceilings, and canvases of all sizes. Broken palettes, tubes of paint, dirty, stained cloths, and wooden easels are crammed into the space.

But it's the not-so-obvious details that my mind fixates on.

I see things that I shouldn't. Buckets of tears imprinted on the white canvas where there should only be empty nothing. The dangerous push-pull of her shattered mind as she played with the paper-knife now resting on the edge of the table. The depth of her passion for art in the huge number of artworks stacked in the corner and the collection of rough sketches on paper pinned to a board.

I know too much about her, details that make her *my* Francesca rather than just a warm body with a pleasing face.

I hate that my real addiction is discovering the broken parts of her psyche, unraveling her mysteries, and penetrating deeper into her heart and mind than anyone ever has. Making her give me parts of herself, especially the fragments that nobody else ever had the privilege of seeing.

I lie and tell her it's her body I'm into, it's her tight cunt, her pretty lips. But the question that she asked me earlier, the one that I evaded, still lingers in my head.

Unless you want this to be more than sex?

I cannot answer that yet so I point to the collection of canvases full of color that are leaning one in front of another like a stack of dominoes waiting to collapse. The ones in the front have a thin layer of dust, but underneath it, they're all vivid splashes of color. Beautiful, mundane sights are elevated into magical experiences through a soft and romantic style of art.

A brook with flowers blooming beside it.

A bouquet of roses on a table.

The nightscape of a town as seen from atop a hill.

"How many years did it take you to finish all of this?" I say.

"Six," comes her instant reply. "But most of them are terrible."

"Which one is your favorite? Show me."

"So you can tell me how childish it is?"

"I'm just curious. Besides, I don't know a thing about art so how can I judge if it's good or not?"

She considers this, nodding.

Her ass cheeks bounce up in the air as she bends to retrieve a small painting from the back. It's the image of two koi fish swimming around each other in water painted in bright, vivid colors. Their orange spots are hard to miss even from a distance. The greenish-blue water has been rendered sparkling and transparent through some sorcery that I will never decode. Even the small weeds under the water's surface are visible. It's easily one of the most gorgeous images I have looked at in my life.

"This one's from when I was fourteen. Took me a week to complete. I was so proud of it, I hung it in my room and boasted to all my friends. Until I couldn't stand to look at it anymore."

My gaze locks onto the picture, my eyes refusing to blink.

Breath shudders in my lungs. It's as breathtaking as a clear stream or vast mountain, something so perfect only the divine ought to have the power to create it.

"How could a human have done this?" The question in my mind trips over my tongue.

Francesca's smile spreads slowly across her whole face, bringing the light back to her lifeless, hungry eyes. "That might be the most extra compliment anybody has ever given me."

I clear my throat, pulling my features back into a rougher, more intimidating expression. I can't be going all soft and mushy around her. I'm already opening up to her way more than I open up to anyone. And every single detail she knows about me is a weapon she can use against me.

"It's nothing like what you're into these days," I remark. "I can't figure out your spring thesis but I appreciate this. It's simple and beautiful."

Francesca tilts her head, a frown screwing the corners of her lips. "That's because I've grown as an artist. I'm trying more challenging projects, doing more abstract stuff that will win me awards and acclaim in the future."

There it is, her desire for validation and fame. Burning a hole in the air. Burning a hole in her soul. Burning her real self to ashes in the process.

Why is she so determined to become what other people want her to be when her natural self is so magnificent? I'll never understand. "Whatever you say."

Her heels click in a slow drumbeat as she saunters toward me, extending the painting out to me. "Last time I was at your apartment, the walls looked bare. This matches with your couch Will you take it if I give it to you?"

She's giving me artwork that means so much to her? A warm feeling nuzzles my stomach. What would it feel like to have a piece of her in my living room, to wake up every morning and see something she poured her heart and soul into staring back at me? To feel her invisible presence? A part of her, the fourteen-year-old who loved to draw, is forever imprisoned inside this picture.

I'll never stop thinking of Francesca if this thing is in my line of vision every single day.

It's both a blessing and a curse.

"I don't need it," I say gruffly.

"It's free. So you might as well take it."

"I said I don't need it."

"Come on, you're offending me. Is my painting that ugly?"

"It's not ugly. I..." My complex feelings are forming a web in my brain. This is an equation that will take years to solve, so I quit while I'm ahead. "Okay, give it to me."

"It's yours. I'll hold it in reserve and deliver it to you later."

She puts away the art piece. The dim lights work her angles, chiseling her features into a more perfect version of themselves. I follow her to the main house where the large living room is littered with books and the walls are crammed with her artworks. Once again, they're all completely different from the work I've seen her doing. There's something magical about these. I'm baffled and surprised as I take in each one.

My awestruck expression probably conveys more than flattery could. Francesca edges closer to me, her soft head burrowing into my chest.

Before I know it, her fingers are playing lazily with my hair.

"There's only one bedroom here." Her raspy whisper injects desire into my veins. My self-control begins to dissolve, little by little.

"So?"

I'm never seeing Heaven once I've done everything I plan to do with her.

She crooks her finger in a come hither motion. "I want to show my number one fan a good time."

"I'm not your number one fan."

"I see the way you look at my artworks," is what she says, but her pupils expanding inside those sparkling blue eyes speak a different language. *I see the way you look at me.*

"How do I look at them?"

"Like you can't believe they're real."

I can't believe *she's* real. So talented, so deep, yet so self-destructive. Not many people would treat a criminal the way she does. She was feeding me breakfast before I ever touched her. She was nursing my wounds before I'd ever been inside her.

She was stealing something invisible from me before I realized I was losing it.

"Do you want me to fuck you, Francesca? Is that what you're begging for?"

Her breasts press into my chest so hard, her hammering heartbeat bleeds into my skin. "Exactly. Be rough with me. Do things only a mobster can do. Leave your conscience at the door and rail me like I deserve to be railed."

My nostrils flare. The promise of unraveling her once more, of ripping away yet another part of her mask surges in my bloodstream. I crave the anticipation; the cocktail of fear mixed with hope as I imagine how she'll react when I show her yet another depraved part of me.

Francesca calls out to an unconscious part of me to protect her, and another unconscious part of me to rip her to pieces. Being the asshole that I am, I want to do both. At the same time if possible.

I fit my hand around the back of her neck.

I'm a man who lives by impulses rather than principles.

And she's always my first impulse.

Pulling her close, I crash my lips into hers, the rush of blood crawling in my ears as adrenaline spikes. Her tongue sears my mouth as it brushes over mine.

If I had to describe this feeling…it's like coming home.

CHAPTER 13

 rancesca

THE MOMENT that scorching kiss ends, I slip off my jacket, then my silk blouse. My breasts are tight with need. I hunger for Gabriele's touch to unravel me, to let me slip away from the desperation for another high that's eating at my brain like a worm.

I unclasp my bra under the scrutiny of his narrowed eyes, letting my breasts spill free.

He's looking at me like he's seeing me for the first time.

"Like what you see?" I tease.

"Like?" His teeth are sharp as they flash in a smile. "I want to ruin that pretty body of yours in a million and one ways."

Heat sizzles up my cheeks.

His shoes approach me with light taps. Fevered breaths mingle with fevered moments. His thumb caresses the hard tip of my nipple. Breaching my final insecurity, he reaches down with the other hand, pulling my thong down my legs.

We collide like two burning comets. Mouths mating. Skins merging.

His body overwhelms me. My nerves buzz like live wires. My pulse trips. He's promising me the ultimate escape and my impulsive soul wants to snort it like powder.

His rough touch travels down my throat. He kneads my breasts, traces the curve of my spine all the way to where it meets my ass. Cupping my cheeks, he places a kiss on my forehead. Gently, like he's kissing a delicate flower. The contrast of his hard grip with his soft lips sends tremors up my spine.

How could the man who claimed he'd kill me if I pushed him be the same man worshipping my body like it's the most fragile object in the world? Gabriele's words are cold, but his touch is warm. I can't tell which one is the real him. Yet I'm equally intrigued by both sides of him.

The caring man who saves me from trouble and keeps me company is the one who soothes my shattered heart.

But the heartless criminal who'd put a gun to my head and demand I go down on him burns my demons to ashes.

I need both of them. I'm addicted to both of them.

Gabriele grunts, taking something from his pocket. The red Swiss army knife unfolds with a distinct click. An undeniable knot twists in my belly.

The ingrained paranoia in me yells *no*, but my corrupt soul screams: *yes, yes, yes. Please make me bleed.*

"It's your fault for putting the idea in my head." Gabriele trails the blade underneath my chin. His precise control leaves me hanging on the precipice between fear and arousal. "I won't use this to cut you, Francesca. Only tease you. But if you don't want it, tell me."

Moisture licks down my bare thighs. The headache throbbing at my temples all day is eclipsed by the need throbbing at the apex of my legs. He's doing exactly what I've fantasized about since leaving his apartment. Not in a hundred years did I imagine I would one day be experiencing this in my life.

Please give it to me. Please rip my foolish heart into pieces.

"Why won't you cut me? Isn't that the whole point of a knife?" I moan.

"Have you ever been slit with this?" He holds up the blade so its smooth metal body glints under the bulb light from the lamp. "It doesn't hurt like you think. You can't even feel it slicing your skin. I want to make you suffer, baby. Hurt you until you scream. I won't allow you to escape the pain that comes with what we're doing."

His nails burrow into my wrist. I can't tell if he's begging me or ordering me. We fight a silent war with our gazes.

I stick out my chest, grazing my nipples against the rough cotton of his black shirt. The friction only hardens the already pointed peaks further. "I can take the cuts."

A head shake. "No. I won't go there with you."

I cackle because this is hilarious. "You spill blood for a living, Gabriele."

"You're not my job, Francesca."

"Then what am I? Your whore?" Irritation from my withdrawal coupled with the frustration from having made no progress all day infuses my voice with venom. "Your sidepiece until you decide you want to settle down with a proper wife?"

I shouldn't push him after he has made his reservations clear. After I promised not to cling or make this more than sex. But I'm addicted to the game we're playing. The one where we drive each other to the brink, strip each other naked, and caress the fears and wounds decorating our souls.

Fire kicks in my lungs as Gabriele's wild features grow wilder with fury. His strong hands grab my face roughly, sending jolts of electricity rolling down to my tiptoes. I like being eclipsed by his strength, being at his mercy. Knowing he can snuff out my sorry life with just a snap of my neck, but praying he won't.

"You're the canvas I can paint my twisted desires onto, Francesca." An unholy grin licks his lips. "And God help me, I love you for it."

My heels quake. A man like Gabriele doesn't throw around words casually. That admission is more than I've ever had from him.

Maybe I'm not so unlovable after all.

Hope settles in the grooves left by trauma. "You love me—"

He quiets me by dragging the silvery edge along my bottom lip. With a little more force, he could easily cut my skin open. His control is sexy. Pleasure carves a path to my core.

His low groan hits my groin. "Pick a safe word, Francesca. Say it and I'll stop immediately. When it gets too intense, don't be afraid of pausing to catch your breath. You hear me?"

"Mona Lisa," I mutter, drawing an amused smile from him.

His shakes his head. "That's two words."

"You break the law every day. Don't start being a stickler for the rules now."

"Very well. Mona Lisa it is."

I ache for contact with the cold, unforgiving sharpness of the metal. The promise of death seduces me. The toxic addiction to destruction, danger, death.

The toxic addiction to him that won't go away.

He grabs my hair. A flick of his wrist. The blade slices through my strands, littering the floor with golden locks.

I yelp in surprise. I wasn't expecting that. The ends of my hair poke out unevenly now, proof of his violence. Proof of his hands on me. He has marked me. I'm sure that's what his plan is. To strip away my refinement and dignity bit by bit until I'm nothing more than a mess crying out his name.

"Are you angry at me for cutting your hair?" It's not a question, it's a challenge to oppose him so he can show me who the master is.

"Take anything from me." I flex my neck, surrendering to him. "Anything but your touch."

I don't crave the pleasure Gabriele gives me, I crave him— my muse, a man darker than my imagination, deeper than my obsessions, colder than my shame. I'm sucked in by the desires that haunt the depths of his eyes. I need to know every single one of them so badly that I'll let him play them out on me if that's the only way I can get him to show me.

"We'll see about that." He presses the tip to my flesh, but not hard enough to cut skin. Flutters explode in my belly as he drags the sharp point all the way up my throat. My breaths come faster in anticipation of the sharp point against my lips.

Suddenly, he changes the unwritten rules of the game we're playing.

Withdrawing the blade, he drives the back of the knife into the softest, most sensitive part of my stomach. I grip his thighs tightly, biting back a cry. But that only fuels his cruelty. He seems determined to keep his promise.

Another blunt strike into my upper abdomen, right in my abs. This time, harder. My lungs contract in protest. Tears fountain up in my eyes. Before I can recover from the stinging under my skin, a flower of pain is blooming at the base of my ribs. The back of the knife is rounded and unthreatening; it's the force he uses that makes it so potent.

It's beneath my dignity breaking down in front of him, exposing more of my vulnerability to this manic monster, but the third assault, right under my left rib, frees all the tears I've dammed up. My scream pierces the air.

"Felt that?" Gabriele's knuckles track over the site of the hits. "That's how you bruise with a knife."

In my delirium, I fail to contain my tears. I don't think I've cried in front of him before. It's another shameful secret of mine he's now privy to.

He curls his mouth in disgust at the waterworks.

I could make him stop. *Mona Lisa.*

It doesn't hurt enough for that yet. He hasn't taken enough from me to make me admit defeat.

Besides, it's better when my body is in agony because it quiets my mind. A numb mind is exactly what I need in life to keep myself from snapping.

The mobster grabs my waist roughly. Needle-like stings that erupt over every few seconds when Gabriele's body presses into the bruises left by the back of the knife. The layer under my skin burns with the memory of his recent treatment.

I hear the light, mechanical sound as he folds his knife and places it back in his pocket. He picks me up like I weigh nothing. I slide my bare foot over the stiff outline of his cock poking through his pants, loving the way his Adam's apple bobs when I apply pressure with my toes.

He dumps me on the only bed in the only bedroom in this place.

We fight over undoing his belt, but he wins, sliding out of his pants and boxers.

"Let's make this interesting." The knife slides against my stomach again. I had no idea he managed to grab it before his pants landed beside the bed. He pulls me to the edge of the bed, then gets on his knees, burying his mouth between my legs. With a single lick over my slit, he pushes me right back to the edge.

But his stony voice is what makes my blood erupt with heat. "If you don't come in ten minutes, I'll slice you. With the sharp end this time."

Intoxicating words, those.

Shooting a quick glance at his shadowed features, I let out a shaky breath. "I thought you said you hate blood during sex."

"I'm confident in my skills so it shouldn't come to that. As long as you cooperate."

A powerful current floods my whole system. I feel alive again, like all my cells are breathing air instead of smoke.

What's wrong with me that being threatened turns me on so much? Last time, too, I loved the sense of danger, knowing that he wouldn't show any mercy if I held back.

The velvet glide of his tongue explores my wet heat, asserting his dominance into the most intimate part of me. His teeth graze my wet folds, hinting at pain. Time ceases to exist. The whole world beats to the rhythm of the sensations crowding my groin.

He bites a trail down my inner thighs. His lust envelops me. The intensity of how much and how badly he wants me imprints itself into my nerves with every impatient suck, lick, and scape of his teeth.

His mouth surges against my clit, licking, sucking, teasing. My back arches, my body submitting to him. Bliss makes me curl my toes. The assault on my senses is so overwhelming. My whole body registers every flick of pleasure shooting through the places his mouth touches. Breathing becomes an impossibility.

I'm at the edge. There's only one thing left to do—fall.

Then he gives me the final push, digging the edge of the blade into my skin, reminding me of the stakes.

It sends me spiraling into a supernova. The release slaps hard, harder than ever before, drawing me into a never-ending vortex where pleasure melts into more pleasure until I'm drowning in an ocean of ecstasy.

"Told you I was good." Gabriele wipes the mess I made on his lips, tossing the knife on the floor. Then grabs the back of my thighs, throwing both my legs over his shoulder as he climbs onto the bed.

I'm both ready and utterly unprepared for the savageness of

his cock breaching my wet hole. He fills me completely, bottoming out in a single stroke. As his cock pumps in and out of me with unflinching intensity, I even start to feel the delicious friction of bedsheets shifting against my sore back. Fear of breaking the bed from the force with which he's driving me into the mattress skims my consciousness.

He's wrecking me with his cock, and I want to be ruined.

As his thrusts grow brutal, I squirm, dragging my nails along his back. His mouth covers mine, swallowing my screams. My brain is intensely caught up in his aftertaste of beer on his tongue, in the easy glide of my fingers against the silk of his shirt.

His eyes are open, but he's shutting himself out of this experience emotionally by refusing to look at my face as I bear the brunt of his sadism. He doesn't want to confront the truth: that he likes causing pain.

Maybe he thinks it makes him a monster. Maybe it does. Maybe that's why I'm obsessed with being the object of his desires.

Because the truth I refuse to confront is that I'm in pain. I'm hurting so much on the inside, no damage he does to my body could ever hurt the same way.

I numb the agony with substances because I can't face it. But when I'm in Gabriele's arms, letting him destroy me, I can't deny it, I can't escape it. He won't let me. I can only drown in it, until it's so real it can't be denied.

I'm forced to cope with it.

That's the game we play.

When he makes me aware of the internal agony, when I manage to push past that pain to explode in ecstasy, I realize how strong I am. That while pain is uncomfortable in the moment, I can move past it. I don't have to keep avoiding it.

I can take it and emerge in one piece.

He makes me aware of the strength that's hidden inside me.

Noises part my lips. The raw ache of his strength pounding into me morphs into another release before I see it coming. Beautiful pleasure washes over me, and I let it take everything that I haven't already given him.

Gabriele doesn't stop. He continues to thrust into me, pulling out at the last minute to come on my skin. Wet liquid sprays all over the wounds he left on my stomach and my face as his orgasm hits.

"Your body looks so beautiful painted with my cum." The rough lilt of his voice rolls down my spine, warming parts of me that were starting to cool down. "Now that's what I call art."

I cough.

His depraved actions, dangerous words, and cruel smile should have me bolting for the door. But it has the exact opposite effect. His darkness feeds my soul, sating a hunger I wasn't aware of.

My appetite for this man is endless.

When all is said and done, can I be with someone else after he's done with me? Won't I be disappointed with vanilla sex now? All those upper crust boys with their nice manners, smooth hands, and bland personalities drilled into them at Ivy League universities could never compare to the layered, intense character of Gabriele Russo.

A cold sensation slithers up my back.

This feels like way more than just sex right now. Even though he has filled me and satisfied my body completely, my heart beats around empty space.

I need more from him. More than physical pleasure. More than the emotional distance.

I need everything.

* * *

"What're you dreaming about, Francesca?" He brushes back the hair that's stuck to my sweaty forehead after I've taken a shower to wash off all the traces of him from my skin. "Where's that mind of yours wandering?"

The muscles around my mouth tense but I manage to eke out a sad smile. "I wish finishing my commission came as easy as the chemistry between us."

"Why can't it?"

"I don't know what to draw." I wanted to draw out the mindless, void state of my orgasm for a bit longer, but my brain is already latching onto the unwanted image of the plain white canvas in the studio, waiting for me to fill it with a masterpiece. "I'm completely lost."

"Paint a nice scenery, then. You can do that much, can't you? I've seen how fast your hands move when you're working."

I cough. "That's not art. That's just painting."

"What's wrong with painting?"

"Anybody with a half-decent eyesight can do it. I want people to see that I have *real* talent and vision, greatness beyond technical skill." So they can never accuse me of riding my father's coattails. So nobody will ever ask me when I'm going to pick up another hobby. I want to be Francesca Astor the renowned artist, not Francesca Astor, a hotel heiress with nothing more than a pretty face to my credit.

Gabriele shrugs, playing with my hair, smiling at the jagged ends from the haircut he gave me. His dark eyes dipped in golden light from the wall sconces, hold mine for an interminable length of time. "Two nice landscape paintings are better than nothing at all. In my world, you lose your life if you fail to bring the goods on time."

I appreciate the point he's making. Even if I can't admit it to myself right now. There are only so many lies I can manufacture to cover for my lack of productivity. At the end of the day, I'm a trained artist. Even on my worst days, I can produce an accurate likeness of anything I see on canvas. Indeed, I've always pressurized myself to come up with something abstract, deep, and grand because that would justify that I have *real* talent. Then I'd deserve to be famous, to be noticed over every other struggling artist in the world due to my genius.

"What about subpar goods?" I turn to the huge Mafioso dressed in all black who looks out of place in my colorful studio, like a lion in a dollhouse. "What if you bring mediocre stuff in a rush? Do you get killed for that in the mafia?"

Gabriele's throaty laugh sinks right into my stomach. I've never heard the man laugh before. He drains all the air from the room, replacing it with the endlessly echoing sound of his deep voice. "Nah, you just tell them that if they wanted the good stuff, they should've paid more."

"Sounds just like you." I fail to contain the infectious smile that's unconsciously stretching my lips.

Gabriele Russo is a man with many faces. The more of him I see, the less I understand. He's muddying my feelings with his complexity. It was so much easier to hate him when he was being ruthlessly violent when he was just a villain, not a man who showed interest in my demons and my art.

"Francesca." He snaps his eyebrows together. "Just do what you want and forget about other people."

"I can't."

"You haven't tried hard enough."

I fold my arms in front of my chest. "What if I forget about you?"

"Don't you want to?"

No.

The hard jerk of my heart catches me off guard.

Is it because he's my muse, and sex with him is my only salvation from the prison I'm in? Or is it because he pays attention to me in a way nobody has? When he's around, I'm less lonely. Less frustrated. His perspective helps me see things

174

differently and helps me see myself in a better light. He accepts parts of me that I've hidden for so long, I forgot they weren't guilty secrets.

"You're the only one who makes me take responsibility for my bullshit."

"Responsibility? Even though I almost came inside you unprotected?" He rubs a finger over the arch of my eyebrow. "Don't worry, I know you have an IUD. I'm not that crazy."

"Wait, how did you find out about that?" I blurt out. "I never told you."

"Research." He taps the edge of my table. The click-clacks from his huge silver watch settle between us like tiny gunshots.

"You went through my doctor's records? That's illegal!" I yell.

The silver-tongued thug screws his mouth into an amused curve. "I have my men watching you twenty-four-seven at your house. I've had my fingers inside your pussy. And you want to guilt me over digging up your medical information?"

When you begin to drown, you don't realize it at first. You think you can hold your breath and wait it out. But the water starts to burn inside your windpipe and sear your lungs. It's at that point that you're done for.

Being with Gabriele is the same. All along, I thought this was something I could keep at bay; an event I could draw boundaries around and contain. Only now do I realize how stupid I've been. He has seeped into every part of my life—my body, my mind, even my art. Helpless surrender sedates my nerves the instant that manly scent of smoke and copper floods my nostrils. Parts of me that went numb a long time ago flare back to life in his presence.

I'm drowning in a dense, desperate emotion I don't understand.

A hot flush burns on my cheeks. Breaths fight for space inside my contracting lungs.

My tight knuckles brush against the fabric of my dress. "Why would you go so far?"

He moves lethally. In an instant, he's in front of me, nose mere inches from mine. The delicious pressure of his fingertips at the back of my head threatens to unravel the last thread of common sense I have left.

"I have to know everything about you, Francesca." His smoke-laced breath ghosts over my skin, birthing shivers that slide down my spine to the tips of my toes. His irises are all shadows, no light. Calloused hands slide over my arms, raising all my hair and knocking the air out of my lungs. He locks my wrist in a powerful grip. I may be imagining the fervent note in his voice when he dips his head forward and whispers, "You're all I think about these days."

"Because I might be trouble?" I worry my lip.

"You're already trouble." The rough edge of his finger caresses my wrist in slow, torturous circles. "You have been since the moment I laid eyes on you."

"Funny, that." The spot between my legs is getting hotter, wetter. Dissatisfaction pulses with every rise of my chest because I know there's no way he's going to let me finish the way I need him to. "Let's not forget how you're the one holding a gun."

"There are weapons more dangerous than a gun in the world."

"Like what?"

"Like what you have."

"Sex appeal? Oral skills?"

"Heart. Compassion. Sometimes, a gentle word is all that's needed to bring a man to his knees."

"I have never brought you to your knees, though."

His pupils expand. "Because you're not trying, baby."

"I'm not going to use my emotions to manipulate others. I have better things to do, like create art with my feelings."

I hop off the bed. For some reason, I'm filled with energy as I often am after having intense sex with Gabriele. I feel like I can make some progress on my art. A brilliant idea just struck me, one that originated from what he said earlier.

"Where are you going?"

"To work on my art. Feel free to go to sleep without me. I might stay up all night."

"You'll be alright on your own?"

I nod.

"Gabriele." I fill my lungs with a fortifying breath. "Thank you."

"For what?"

"For being your usual atrocious self."

Satisfaction drips from his expression. "Anytime, baby."

CHAPTER 14

 *abriele*

I SIGH, lying awake on the bed three hours after Francesca has left. My blood hasn't cooled after the sex. Her screams still echo in my ears; her trusting eyes as she let me hurt her are burned into my retinas.

Every thought in my head is *Francesca, Francesca, Francesca*; the way she held me, the way she fit perfectly around me, and most of all, how right everything felt.

Comfortable. Warm. Like home.

I must be going crazy. This is the sleep deprivation from last week talking.

But the bright, hopeful feeling blooming in my chest leaves no room for doubt.

Francesca. With her talent and dreams of being famous, her kind heart and gentle soul that sees the good even in scum like me. If I taint that, I won't be able to handle the guilt. But my hands are bloody and violent, and all I can do is slowly corrode her with every breath she takes in my presence.

I refuse to accept it. I refuse to accept that I feel something more for her than physical compatibility. That I care about her so much that even now, I'm wondering if she's *really* alright in her studio, or if she's simply torturing herself with her demons again.

Burying my face into my hands, I groan.

It's too fast. I haven't known her long enough. She's a user, an addict. It can't be her.

Anyone but her.

If I leave now, if I put an end to this now, it will only be a fling. But if this drags on, then both of us could lose more than we're prepared to lose.

I drill my head into the pillow, praying for sleep to claim me.

Night used to be the time of the day when my mind was the clearest. Now it's when I am assaulted by unwanted thoughts of a future I never imagined before.

A chef with my own restaurant—I haven't been able to get the idea out of my head since she put it there. The pictures grow, bleed, and flow from that starting point. Coming home to Francesca, a home filled with the scent of roses and paint, burying my head in her pretty hair as I whisper, "How was your day?"

Before I can finish my train of thought, my feet betray me. One minute, I'm spread-eagled on the bed thinking about how to steal her car and get back to New York.

The next, I'm turning the door handle to her studio.

"You need to lock the fucking door, Francesca," I boom as soon as I step in. "This place is in the middle of nowhere. Anybody could walk in and kidnap you."

"Is that what you're here for? To kidnap me? Because I might go along with you willingly if you can take me far, far away from art forever."

Her eyes are rimmed with red, the bags under them swollen. Signs of her crying.

A cold fist grips my heart. She's not okay.

My gaze arrows to the canvas. There are pencil marks on it, but nothing else.

Concern incinerates my logic, rationality, and reason.

Reaching around to her back, I wrap her in a hug. "What's wrong, baby?"

"I can't paint."

"Because of the voices in your head?"

"They're endless. I feel scared of disappointing someone the moment I pick up the brush."

"What are the voices saying to you?"

"The same things."

"Who are these people?" I probe because I want to know. "What do they look like?"

"Why does that matter?"

"Because I'll need their names and addresses if I'm going to stuff them in a coffin."

Laughter bubbles out of her. "I doubt that'd help. They're immortal inside my head."

"Then kill them. Take a knife and slit their throats so they can't talk anymore."

Her body shivers under my arms. She wriggles, turning around until her azure gaze clashes with mine. There's heat in those expanding pupils. Heat and fear.

Her greedy fingers coax the muscles in my jaw to soften. Back to her old tricks, isn't she? Trying to escape again.

"Let's focus on art for now. We just had sex."

"I need you now. Gabriele, destroy me again. I have to stop thinking."

"Talk to me. What happened?" Pure animalistic sex doesn't

do it for me anymore. I need to be intimately entwined with the thoughts and the demons in her head while I'm tangled with her body.

I must hear every voice that passes through that mind. I have to rip away every thought that hurts her.

Because only I can hurt her, and I always make it pleasurable.

"It's too hard," she admits. "I got this great idea after I talked to you. I even sketched it, and I felt like I could finally make it happen. But it's so much darker than my usual stuff. I'm afraid it won't be good enough to display in the lobby of an apartment building. I'm afraid they'll hate it and tell me to paint something else. And that will shatter my confidence."

Dropping her paintbrush, she cradles her head against my chest.

"Do you want to be liked by everyone or do you want to be free to draw whatever you desire?"

She double blinks at my question. "Both."

"Here's the thing: you can't control if you'll be famous or if critics will love your work, but you *can* decide if you'll be free."

Her hot breath swishes past my ears. "Gabriele, I'm glad you're here in Woodstock. I love that you're so different from me. You don't look for anybody's validation and do as you, please. Because of that, your perspective is the exact opposite of mine. You make me see things I could never see on my own because my mind doesn't work like yours."

The reverence lacing her voice makes me wrap my arms around her tighter. It feels strange to have someone praise me like this, praise my mind. I've never been told I'm intelligent or my thoughts matter. My body has been my tool of trade, not my brain.

"Why do you want to please people so much? Do you think you're not worth anything if nobody loves you?"

Her lips tremble, telling me I've hit the mark. "I don't know what value I have in the world. If I can't create great art...then how does anyone benefit from me being alive?"

I croak out a laugh. "How do you think anyone benefits from *me* being alive?"

I kill and drag humans into vices like gambling and drug addiction. If they piss me off enough, I even ruin their lives. Yet I've never felt like I don't deserve to be alive. It was my strong instinct to survive that made me choose a life on the streets, then a life of crime. I want to survive by any means possible. I want to live, even if my life doesn't have any meaning.

"I benefit from you being alive, Gabriele." Francesca hugs me back. "This might be hard to believe, but you're an important person to me. These last few weeks...I don't know how I'd have survived them without you. You're my stalker, but sometimes it feels like you're my savior."

"We're going off track," I hiss.

"When I can't sleep at night, I miss your voice. I miss your harsh jokes, and how easy it is to say whatever I want when I'm with you. I don't have to wear a mask or play a role. Sometimes, I wonder why you're the only person who accepts me as I really am."

A cold wave crashes over me. I'm afraid. I'm afraid that she's too emotionally invested in what's simply a sexual relationship. I'm scared she's too emotionally invested in me. But at the same time, I'm elated.

I want her to feel something strong for me. I want her to see me as more than an addiction, more than a muse, more than someone she needs to achieve her dreams of fame and success. I can't pinpoint why I need that when this is just a physical exchange between us but I do.

"This isn't like that," I remind her. "You're imagining things."

"Yeah. Sorry to unload this all on you when you came just for a good time. I'll make it up to you tomorrow."

"We were talking about how pointless my existence is in the world, so how did we end up here?"

"I was just reassuring you that you're needed in the world," she says. Static clings to my skin at the glide of her fingers over my nose. "Your existence is definitely not useless."

I want to reassure her of that, too. But I'm not the kind of man who can lay out my heart in front of a girl who could crush it without even trying.

I swallow, unable to suppress the dream that has haunted me endlessly.

A world where I'm a civilian. A life with morning kisses and afternoon lovemaking and early dinners leading to late-night snuggles. Falling asleep in her arms, day after day.

Coming home to her.

'How was your day?'

And what would be her reply?

In my head, the vision ends there. But the cramp in my stomach demands to go further.

Curiosity pushes the weirdest question out between my teeth. "Francesca, if we were living together and I came home after work, what would you say to me? Like, as soon as you saw my face. What's the first thing that'd come to your mind?"

"Is this some reverse psychology question?"

"Just answer me."

"Well, if you just returned from work, I'd say..." Her palms cup my face. She beams a smile so dazzling, it spins my head. "Welcome home. I missed you and I can't wait to get frisky with you."

Someone must have shot me while I was lost in her eyes because I can't feel my heart beating anymore.

Welcome home.

Why is she so fucking perfect while also being the biggest red flag on the planet?

Is this what they call irony?

Is this what they call destiny?

I should have never come here. There is no way that this won't end badly.

She will wreck me. I will ruin her.

Our version of love won't be romantic; it'll be a twisted aberration.

CHAPTER 15

rancesca

GABRIELE OBSERVES me working from the chair in the corner of the studio. Whenever I stall or stop altogether, he arches his brow. Then his gruff voice drifts to me, asking me if I'm okay, asking me what the critics in my head are saying.

Each time, without fail, he reminds me: "Tell them they can fuck off. Or I'll chase them down and put a bullet through their head."

He never gets vexed at my undying anxieties, the same spiraling thoughts that keep dragging me to rock bottom.

He's my dark knight, protecting me from the chaos inside myself.

Gabriele's undying patience surprises me because of how often he has to hear me repeat the same ugly phrases over and over again.

I'm not good enough. I can't do this.

Everybody will hate this painting

185

I'm never going to have a career.

I'll end up a sad drug addict living in my parents' house forever.

Nobody cares about my art so why am I doing this?

They were right. I should just die.

It's a very exhausting couple of hours for both of us. I'm relieved when I finish half of the painting and the ache in my back and arms forces me to stop for now. Gabriele suggests we head to town and eat at one of the diners. Gabriele is a great cook but he's not a magician—he can't do anything when I have no groceries to cook with.

"What you told me that night at the charity gala has stuck with me. You were right."

There's no light without darkness. No growth without suffering. And no art without self-doubt.

The memory of his penetrating eyes on me, the way he saw right through my nonsense even though he barely spent any time with me gives me chills.

I had so many doubts, I gave up on fighting through them. Because it was too hard. Impossible. I waited for moments of calm and inspiration to come to me, and when that didn't happen, I numbed myself with substances so I could at least feel in control again.

"Thank you for sticking with me through that ordeal. I can be exhausting."

He shrugs. "I've dealt with worse."

"Gabriele, seriously, I mean it. You don't have to tire yourself looking after me. I'll have sex with you regardless."

"I'm not doing it for the sex."

"Then why?"

"I like shooting imaginary people." His eyes sparkle with amusement. "I'm going to make that my new hobby when we go back to New York."

We. Bees drone inside my stomach, clinging to that one honeyed syllable like it's the most precious nectar in the world.

"Thank you for staying with me," I say.

Gabriele shrugs his shoulders, downplaying his patience. "My only other choice is to be alone in that house."

He could desert me and go back. He must be bored already.

"I'll take a shower now, then we can go grab breakfast. I'm sweaty after painting all night." I drop the paintbrush, surveying the half-finished black and red artwork. My inner critic is still judging the choice of colors, unnatural shadows, and technical imperfections but I'm so, so proud of having accomplished so much in a single night.

The shower is perfectly hot to dissolve the aches in my muscles, but I don't spend too long there. I keep waiting for Gabriele to walk in through the door I didn't lock and initiate shower sex, but he does nothing of the sort.

When I step out of the bathroom, his attention settles on my skin like a warm spring breeze. A tremor grazes my spine when his gaze draws all the way down my body, spanning over the black midi dress I'm wearing. It's pretty modest as far as dresses go.

"You're not wearing blue?" Mock surprise stains through his poker face.

"I don't wear blue every day." I pause for effect. "Sometimes, I wear other colors, too."

Gabriele's mouth screws into a frown. "Black doesn't suit you."

"You always wear black, though. Thought I'd match my outfit with yours for today."

"That's because I need to hide the bloodstains that get on me during the job. You have nothing to hide, Francesca. You're pure and innocent."

"Even though I came on your tongue a few hours ago?"

Before I can turn this conversation into a full-blown flirting session, Gabriele sighs. His thick, strong shoulders brush past mine as he arrows into the bathroom.

I hear the lock click.

I suppose he wants to wash up, too.

Despite the buds of craving already unfurling inside me, we manage to drive into town without getting caught up in another mind-blowing carnal fest. I break then, unable to hold back. I'm probably the only one who orders a beer for breakfast alongside my eggs.

The corners of Gabriele's eyes tighten but he doesn't comment.

"I have had some success quitting coke," I say. "I've been clean since I started sleeping with you. But alcohol is harder."

"You have to go to rehab, Francesca. I cannot approve of your method of quitting one addiction by developing another."

"Good for me I don't need your approval then."

His exasperated exhale is loud enough to make the old couple from the next booth squint at us in concern. I wonder what they think we are—lovers, friends, or is it obvious that we're just two strangers who share a dark, ill-fated connection?

A faint wash of pink is smattered over Gabriele's features. Even the tip of his nose is pink. I'm wondering if he came down with something after staying up all night, but his awkward throat clearing, followed by "How're you feeling?" dissolves my doubts.

He must have debated asking me that. It almost makes him sound like a nice guy, after all.

Scratch that. He *is* a nice guy.

The only reason that wasn't more obvious to me is that, like most people, I see the stereotype of the tough, ruthless mafia hitman before I see the man underneath. I remember the rough sex before I recall the gentle moments afterward. I still cannot erase the effect of his profession on my image of him, even though I said I wouldn't judge him.

"Healthy," I reply, grinding my knee against his under the table. "I'm planning to do more work after breakfast."

"When do you sleep?"

"After that." I brush my thumb up and down the length of the ketchup bottle.

"Don't neglect your health just because you're focused on art," he says.

"Gabriele, why do you care so much for my health?"

"Because I've always lived while relying on my body." He clasps his hands on the table. "I would be terrified if something went wrong with my body. I can't imagine how you could be okay with abusing your health. You need your body to continue painting."

"I never thought about it like that."

"You don't think a whole lot," he chides. "You're just reacting to your fears right now, doing whatever it takes to stop feeling them at the moment. That's escapism. Avoidance"

"If sex with you is avoidance, it feels too good for me to stop."

He screws his eyebrows in mild disgust. "It's supposed to hurt, though."

"It doesn't though. It feels great. My ex-boyfriends were all self-absorbed. They played it safe, only caring about their pleasure."

"Not every guy is a dick. I know it doesn't sound convincing coming from me, but there it is."

My heart skips a beat. My fingers curl around his biceps. "I want you to feel good, too. I want to do something for you, Gabriele. Tell me what you want. What do you desire the most in the world?"

"What I desire the most isn't a sexual fantasy."

"I still want to give it to you," I say.

"It's something you can't give me."

"Love?"

"Peace." His breath stutters. "Stability. People I don't have to worry about losing."

The depths of his eyes paint a clearer picture of his desires. He wants to belong somewhere, to have a steady place, a steady person to call his own. I've sensed that about him ever since he told me about his mother. Gabriele was always betrayed by the people he wanted to belong to the most. He never had a safe place to call home because his home was polluted by disgusting men who preyed on him. I don't know how it is in the mafia, but he had to kill his best friend, so I'm assuming it's not a great place, either.

Gabriele is a mystery boxed inside an iron cage. He rarely reveals anything about himself. I've heard about his mother and the friend who had died at his hands, but those were tragic parts of his past. I want to know the good parts, too. His dreams. Hopes. Wishes.

And I want to fulfill all of them for him.

"Did you ever have dreams as a child?" I ask around a mouthful of my beer, which was just delivered to the table by a waitress who gave me a pitying look.

"Don't all children have dreams?"

"What happened to those dreams? Did you already fulfill them?"

"No, I gave up on them. I had to think about other things. Money, survival, the next job, not getting caught by the feds."

I grab one of the napkins from the holder and push it to his side of the table, along with a pen I pick out of my purse.

"Let's do something fun. I want you to write me a bucket list."

"A what?"

"Bucket list of things you want to do the most. Include anything you can think of—food, hobbies, travel, experiences."

"So you can use all that information to blackmail me later?"

"You overestimate my blackmailing skills. I suck at manipulating people." I can't hold back a smile. "You said it yourself: I'm pure and innocent."

"Is that why you can twist my arm into fucking you whenever you want?"

"No, that's because you want it, too. Just admit it."

He doesn't bother denying it. What would be the point when we both know it's the truth? He stares out the window, his fingers drumming against his thigh. Gabriele, despite his very classical-sounding name, isn't classically good-looking. But my whole body sighs at his beauty, every muscle going limp with satisfaction from visually tracing the planes and curves of his features.

The napkin remains spotlessly white and the bucket list nonexistent, so I begin questioning him, hoping I'll wear down the walls around his heart quicker that way.

"Is there anywhere you've dreamed of traveling to?" I tilt my body forward, loose strands of hair sweeping across the surface of the table.

I'm fully expecting my question to be brushed aside, so the low, husky reply catches me by surprise. "Italy. My ancestry is Italian but I was born in The Bronx like my mother, so I have never been to Italy."

"How about next weekend?"

"What do you mean?"

"We can go to Italy for a weekend break. I'll take care of the hotels, tickets, everything. All you need to do is show up."

"It isn't that easy."

"Ahem." I play the fork on the table like a ceremonial drum as I clear my throat. "I would like to remind you that you're in the presence of the heiress of Astor Hotels. I have access to hotels across the world and my network extends far and wide. Nothing is impossible for me."

Gabriele's left eyebrow slopes downward in an unconvinced slant. "Is that why you can't even pay your cocaine dealer?"

"That...that's because my family will suspect me if I make too many big cash withdrawals often without a reason. But if I say that I'm going to Italy with a friend, nobody would blink twice. I do impulsive things like that all the time."

"Except I'm not your friend and you're not going to Italy with me." Gabriele digs his elbows into the table, resting his face on his flat palms.

"You *are* my friend. We hang out together so much."

"I'm your stalker."

"You're my stalker friend."

"I held a knife to your throat just yesterday."

"Fine. You're my knife-wielding stalker friend. Wow, that almost sounded cool."

Scorn laces through his bark of laughter. "There's something seriously wrong with you."

I slide my hand over his on the table, watching the lines on his face soften immediately in response. His skin is cool, but when I touch it, warmth spreads all the way to my heart. This isn't the heat of lust like yesterday. A new dimension has been unlocked in our relationship as a result of the time we shared in my studio. A hidden layer of subtext that makes him seem less like a hot, dangerous guy who fulfills my sexual fantasies and more like a hot, dangerous guy who makes me feel human again. Like I'm more than a failure, privileged princess, or a screw-up.

"You have to let me do this for you, Gabriele." I squeeze his fingers because I want more of the warmth that leaks from his skin into me. "Otherwise I'll feel like a parasite who is always taking advantage of your help."

"I've told you before: I'm not helping you. This is a mutually beneficial sexual relationship."

"You might think so, but you believed in me and stuck by my side last night. That wasn't sex or even related to our physical relationship. When I'm with you, I start to believe in myself."

"Francesca." One terse word that contains a whole universe of emotions inside it. He wants the trip; he wants the dream. He wants it but fear chokes his wishes because his mother was an addict and so am I. Does he think I'll get his hopes up and then flake out at the last minute because I'm too hungover to make it to the airport?

I won't. My ongoing battle with creativity and substances might be intense, but I take my promises seriously.

"Next weekend," I remind him. "Do we have a deal?"

He grumbles, knuckles tracing the edge of the table. I'm certain that's a yes in Gabriele-tongue.

"My bucket list stops right there. I'm not telling you any more of it."

"Not fair. I could turn all your dreams into reality."

"My biggest dream would be for you to stop talking right now."

God must be on his side because the waitress sets down our plates before he can complete that sentence. I'm so hungry that all words die on my tongue instantly. I attack the food, stuffing my face until my stomach is close to bursting.

"You eat like a toddler." Gabriele reaches forward and wipes ketchup from the corners of my lips.

The second our gazes collide, we both freeze, like we were caught doing something illicit, even though it was nothing more than an innocent reflex.

He must be thinking the same thing: our relationship is changing without us being aware of it.

This is the second time he's wiping ketchup off my face and it has a very different connotation than the first time. Once could be a mistake, but twice is deliberate. Becoming acquainted with my chaotic mind last night must have made him feel more protective of me, just like it has made me trust him more.

"Know what's weird?" he continues, pulling back. "Before I met you, I didn't know what I was looking for. I never realized that I needed a place where I'm surrounded by people I can trust. That I need people in my life I can rely on to be there for me."

"Gabriele, you can have all of that. Don't let what your mother did affect your view of the world."

He licks his lips, stalling. "What I'm saying is that you might think you haven't helped me, but you've helped me realize something pretty important."

Happiness crests in my chest, the waves hitting so high, I can't believe it isn't an illusion.

I LABOR over my painting in the morning. Time blurs into a muddy stream of colors and dancing visions. In the afternoon when my energy crashes, I fall asleep on the couch in my studio. Gabriele already went to sleep after we got back from the diner so he's in my bedroom.

Even without him constantly keeping me on track, I manage to push through. When the voices in my head accuse me of being delusional, I fight back with: it's not my idea; it's Gabriele's. And I trust him.

He was onto something with his suggestion that I stop overexerting myself to prove a point to people who aren't even in my life anymore.

The last time art was so freeing and fun was way back before I attended the art camp. When I simply lived for the feeling of getting lost in creating something beautiful.

Did he say a rose and knife make an odd picture?

I'm going to show him they make a masterpiece.

* * *

PAPER RUSTLES IN MY EARS. I don't know what the time is, but the sky is dark. Exhaling, I put the final touch to my painting, fingers trembling as I let my brush rest on the palette.

It's amazing how I finished a whole painting in a day. Then again, with my muse so close to me and all the passionate sex we have been having, I should have expected it. Gabriele truly is magical. He said he didn't want to save me because I couldn't be saved, but he has saved me again and again from falling into despair.

I drag my gaze away from the picture. I might start picking out the flaws in my work if I stare too long. It's my intention to drag out this moment of triumph for as long as possible before I crash back into the valley of self-judgment.

My shoulders and arms are wailing from the labor. My eyelids are drooping from lack of sleep. I haven't stopped or taken a break since breakfast. Gabriele woke up a few hours ago and came around to check on me, but I told him to not disrupt my rare moment of focus so he went back to the cabin.

My fingertips caress the note lying on the table. I thought I heard the door open again after Gabriele visited, but it was barely a whisper and I was absorbed in my art so I didn't pay attention.

You can get through this fear, Francesca.

The writing is sharp and jagged, exactly what I'd expect from a mobster. Still, it's a shocker to find a handwritten note from Gabriele. It feels far too intimate given the nature of our relationship.

"You left this?" I brandish the note in front of Gabriele's face. He's sitting on the sofa scrolling through his phone in his sweatpants.

In his regular black shirt and suit, he looks every inch like a sleek criminal.

But in his gray sweatpants and sweatshirt, he's every inch mine. Only I get to keep this secret side of him.

"Yeah," he replies, lifting his head. "In case you started over-thinking again while I was gone."

"That's sweet."

Gabriele shrugs like it's no big deal. But it means something to me. He made an effort to ensure I wasn't lonely and trapped in his absence. That kind of consideration could only come from deep empathy. Yet, if I tell him that, he'll probably deny it.

I love how much he cares for me and how deeply invested he is in my mental well-being. At the same time, if he continues with these small gestures I'm afraid I'll one-sidedly start liking him, only to feel disappointed later when he doesn't return my feelings.

"What now?" he asks. "You're going to paint more?"

"We're going on a date." I tap his back and he jumps as if I stabbed him. "Stop looking like the sky fell. It was a joke. I need to eat and they sell great hot dogs at the drive-in theatre. And we might as well watch a movie while we're there."

"I'm hungry, too," he confesses. "Your fridge is emptier and colder than Nico's heart."

"Who's Nico?" My Tesla SUV roars as I turn the key in the ignition and reverse it. I didn't drink last night and country roads are much less stressful than city roads.

"My superior and the underboss of the Russo family. He's the one you saw leaving my apartment the day you came over."

"The one who looks like a snake? He's an absolute asshole, isn't he?"

"I wouldn't go that far."

"You're not denying it, either."

Gabriele's knees bump my glovebox as full-body laughter rumbles through him. "I'm glad you didn't major in law or all the criminals in New York would be in trouble. Cross-examina-tion could be your specialty."

"It's the legal profession's loss."

I've only ever been to the drive-in theatre once before with

Mom. She loved the quaint small-town charm it had. It reminded her of her childhood. There aren't many drive-in theatres left. So it's like being in a time machine.

A small number of cars already populate the grassy ground. Mops of hair stick out from convertibles. The big screen in front is white like an untouched canvas. The smell of butter and popcorn permeates the air.

I buy tickets for Gabriele and me. They're cheap, only $10 per person for two films with an intermission in between.

"These movies are PG-13." Gabriele turns up his nose in disgust. "I was down for R-rated with you."

"Get your mind out of the gutter."

"It's not my mind that's in the gutter. When I said R-rated, I meant violence and bloodshed, not sex." His shoulder rises in exasperation. "You're such a nymphomaniac."

I fight the heat filling my cheeks. "What about you? You see enough violence and bloodshed in your day job. Why do you need more?"

"You get enough sex in your daily life, too." His eyebrows cock and it's so sexy. It takes all my resolve not to jump him. He's right. Sex is all I think about these days. "But you still want to see it on screen."

Fair point.

"I guess we can't help liking what we like. Though it might be healthy to change up our routine once in a while." I wave the tickets in the air. "Watching something cute and fluffy might be good for our sanity."

"Doing anything with you is bad for my sanity," he mutters, rotating his head to scan the surroundings. What's he expecting to find, a hidden enemy? Because this is a PG-13 place through and through.

A quick survey of the lot tells me that most of the people here look like they are on dates, except for a few families.

Gabriele and I might be the odd ones here. We look too edgy in black.

Gabriele notices the overabundance of couples too, for his lips draw into a silent line. He marches away, mumbling, "You bought the tickets so I'll buy food. Wait for me in the car."

Earlier, the staff at the ticket counter let me in on how I could use the radio in my car to listen to the sound of the movie playing so I fiddle with that to make sure it's working like it's supposed to.

"Scoot over." Right before the movie starts, Gabriele returns.

He's cradling so much food. Popcorn, cheese hot dogs, cinnamon pretzels, nachos with cheese, two bottles of Iced tea, and chicken breast tenders. My mouth drops open when he hands the bottle of cold iced tea to me.

A smile flickers over his lips, slow and sensual. "You said you needed to eat."

"I'm one woman, not an army." I unscrew the cap on the bottle, relishing the coolness of the iced tea as it washes over my parched tongue. "Also, I'm surprised you bought iced tea when they sell Coke in the shop."

"I know you only drink this," Gabriele says. "It's all you ever get from the vending machine in college."

My eyebrow sharpens in a raise.

He pays that much attention to what I drink?

"Here." He stashes a bunch of candy bars into my glove compartment. "You always nibble on it in the afternoon when your creative inspiration is crashing."

The crinkle of plastic wrappers crunches in my ears as he unwraps one and hands it to me. "Eat."

My throat closes around a lump of emotion. My eyes prickle.

No, I need to have higher standards. I cannot be crying over a guy buying me Snickers. That's just pathetic. Yet this has me in a chokehold.

"Thank you for always looking out for me." I kiss his cheek.

Then the unimaginable happens: he blushes.

Our silences speak louder than words as we look away from each other at the same time. In the last few weeks, I've seen Gabriele act strong, ruthless, determined, sexy, protective, and even brutal.

But it's the first time I'm seeing him being honest, his heart laid bare for me.

The handwritten note from earlier.

My favorite snacks. The fact that he even *knows* what my favorite snack is.

A gift like that has no material value but touches my heart.

That's all I need to regain my footing in the world that spins around me chaotically.

It's all I need to remember that there are people who care that I keep painting, and who want to see me grow and evolve as a person and as an artist.

The loneliness that sits like a rock in my stomach all the time dissolves when he's around.

I need more. I'm not craving drugs right now, nor am I craving escape. I'm craving the warmth and comfort of a beautiful monster who has a heart of gold.

Before I can stop myself, I straddle Gabriele. My lips find him in the dark confines of the car.

His hands roam over the swell of my ass like it's no big deal. Heat ignites between my thighs. "Aren't there rules in this place? Can we do this?" His huskiness casts a spell around me. All I see is him, all I hear is the siren call of his body.

I press one finger to his lips. "We're both rule-breakers anyway."

His throat flexes. His arousal is wedged between my legs, inciting a low flutter in my belly. One hand slips under my bra

SASHA CLINTON

to palm my breasts. The sensation of slowly catching fire travels over me like silk.

I writhe in his arms, whimpering like a kitten lost in pleasure, paying no attention to where I am.

A sharp cry tears out of my throat.

"Shhh," he says as his fingers slide into the wet and ready spot between my legs. Pleasure clouds my vision. He's going to make me come without even trying.

My skin itches with both nerves and delights as his fingers lock around the back of my neck.

The top of his forehead presses against mine. "Francesca, what are you doing to me?"

"Kissing you."

"No, baby, you're breaking your promise. And I'm letting you."

A jarring noise beeps inside my brain, a slow, creeping alarm telling me this is no longer just sex. Not for him.

And I'm letting you.

He's letting me turn this into more. He's a willing participant as much as I am.

As my hand finds purchase in his hair, I'm faced with the one question I still don't know the answer to: What is Gabriele to me when he's not my muse?

CHAPTER 16

abriele

WHEN WE RETURN to New York after that blissful weekend, things aren't the same between us. I've loosened up, lost my resistance to her, and that makes it easier to slip up and reveal soft feelings that aren't lust.

"Get a room." One of the girls in Francesca's program leers at me when I ambush the heiress near the vending machine and kiss her hard enough to make her lips bleed.

There's no stopping my horny hormones, though. I keep wanting to see her. Her face is like sunlight to me, her smile oxygen. I'll die if I have to go without either for too long.

"You don't look as stoned as you usually do," I remark, the day after we return. It's a regular morning: her in her studio, me watching her. "Did you switch dealers?"

"I've been clean for…a few days. I think it's almost five."

"That's better than I expected."

"See? I can do it if I put my mind to it." Setting her paintbrush on the table, she presses herself against me. "Gabriele, we're still going to Italy this weekend. I won't hear any excuses."

"And?" I narrow my eyes. There's something else she wants to say. It's evident in how her torso sways back and forth, restless. "You want to say something else, don't you? What's got you so nervous?"

I'd love to pretend that she's craving me all the time, Francesca gets needier for sex when she's anxious.

"I'm meeting executives from the company who commissioned my painting later today," she informs me. "I'm nervous about what they'll think of what I made while I was in Woodstock. I completed it in a hurry and on the way back to New York, I realized it looks too simple. I should've added more layers—"

I block the rest of her words by pressing the heel of my palm against her lips. "It's beautiful. It's good enough. Repeat after me."

Her fingertips trickle up my cheek, cupping my chin. "It's beautiful. It's good enough."

"Good girl." Despite my desire to play it cool, my hands chase the lush silk of her hair. It's not a sexual touch. It's just... me reassuring myself that she's here and she's mine to touch. For now, at least.

"I could get addicted to your reassurances," Francesca jokes. "That might become my new kink."

"I don't mind."

"Really? You'll reassure me even when I'm being annoying and overly dramatic?"

I nod. "But you'll have to do something for me, too."

"I'll call you Master. Or Sir. Or Boss. Or whatever you want." She ticks her teeth together, a naughty glint in her eye.

I sigh. I shouldn't say it, not with how complicated things are with Maria. But the part of me that used to be sensible has become scarce since the weekend at Woodstock. "I only want you to dine with me every evening after your classes. As great as my cooking is, it gets lonely when I'm eating alone. I'd appreciate some company. Also, it wouldn't hurt if you compliment my food every once in a while."

Francesca's mouth drops open. My heart gallops. Doubt slithers between my newfound happiness.

"Gabriele, that's...." She pauses, giving my anxiety room to mushroom. What if I said it too soon? What if she thinks I'm asking for too much? I'm just her muse. "I'd be delighted. But you're sure it's not too much work for you? To feed me, on top of everything else you're doing for me."

I wave my hand in the space between us. "The rats in my apartment probably eat more than you."

"Hold on." She squeaks, a grossed-out expression pasted on her features. "There are rats in your apartment?" Silence slips between us. Her breasts rise and fall rapidly. Her breathing accelerates. "How big?"

"Oh, did I scare the heiress? Have you never seen a rat, Francesca?" I'm loving how the anxiety on her face is sharpening with my every word, so I take this joke as far as I can. "How pampered did you grow up?"

She cups her palm and shows it to me. "Are they bigger than this?"

"That's the size of a field mouse, baby, not a rat." I fold her palm into a fist before kissing her knuckles. "And this is how big a guinea pig is."

The goosebumps rising over her skin are impossible to ignore when I drag a fingertip over her arm. "So the rats that eat your leftovers are larger than my hand?" She swallows. "I'm not sure how safe it'll be..."

"God, you're so sheltered." I roar in laughter. "I'm kidding, Francesca. There are no rats in my apartment."

I drop the act, gathering her small body into a hot embrace. Her hair smells of me, not expensive shampoo.

Francesca's shoulders sag in relief under the protective shield of my arms. "You had me going for a minute there."

"Yeah, and I loved it. It was fun to see you get worked up over nothing."

Her body that's pressed against mine now seeks more from me, her breasts grinding against my chest, her groin rubbing against my cock, seeking friction.

"You know; I might end up staying the night after those dinners." Biting her bottom lip, she slants her eyes upward in a challenging glance. "Then you'll have to make breakfast for me in the morning, too. You have no idea what you just got yourself into, Gabriele."

She throws in an evil cackle at the end for good measure.

But I'm only fixated on her words: she wants more from me. Just like I want more from her.

But do we want the same more?

"You don't mind spending your evenings with a mobster?" I question, to be certain. I don't need her to agree with me because she's going with the flow. Inviting her into my personal space was a step out of my comfort zone. If this has to be what I want it to be, she'll need to step out of her bubble, too. "Are you sure? It won't be food play or kinky stuff with eggplants if that's what you were imagining. I have a terrible sense of humor but I do talk a lot when I'm eating. And I'll expect you to talk back."

I wish I was the kind of eloquent guy who could talk straight and just tell her I want to have soul-deep conversations with her. But I'm a criminal with stunted emotions and a tough wall, so she'll have to settle for 'I'll expect you to talk back'.

"That's BS." Francesca's lips skim over my collarbone, teasing me through the thin fabric of my shirt. "You're funny and you know it. And I love talking to you, Gabriele. I'm going to pry out all your secrets one by one until you regret having started this."

"You can't make me regret it. Ever."

"That confident, are you?" She makes a groaning sound as the march of footsteps thunders in the hallway outside the studio. Shadows of people flash past us. Francesca unwinds her arms from around me and takes a step back. "Shit. I hope they didn't see us getting all lovey-dovey. I need to get back to work."

Lovey-dovey. It's a strange expression. The flutter in my stomach is even stranger.

"Um..." I stutter. "I have to work, too. I'll see you later."

"At dinner?"

"Not today," I say. "I haven't even bought groceries yet."

"Let me know when we start. I can't wait."

I leave as she gets absorbed in her project. With the whole mess involving Luca wrapped up, I no longer have any reason to keep an eye on Francesca. If I overdo it, Antonio and Ricardo might get suspicious. Since Antonio has a hard time keeping his mouth shut, the news will inevitably find its way into Angelo's ears.

Given how I barely managed to scrape my way back into Nico's good graces, I can't risk another spectacle. So for now, I'll have to settle for meeting Francesca during dinner now. It's better than nothing.

And with that, it's time to face what I've been avoiding all weekend—my future wife.

Maria texted me asking if we could meet up this evening at a restaurant close to her father's townhouse in Manhattan.

I had no reason to turn her down. Which is why I told Francesca we'd skip today.

At seven pm, I greet Maria at the Italian place she picked.

"I hope you didn't struggle to find the restaurant." The beautiful older woman leans in to drop a light kiss on my cheek. A faint floral scent radiates off her. The only thought that comes to me is: it's not roses or strawberries.

"Actually, I got here fifteen minutes ago."

"Sorry to keep you waiting."

The contrast between my previous 'date' with Francesca at the drive-in theatre and this one is like night and day. Where the Heiress wore distressed jeans and a crop top, her eyes red with lack of sleep, Maria beams like a fresh blossom in her elegant pink dress.

"I heard your job in Miami wrapped up successfully." Maria's statement doubles as a veiled question.

"Who did you hear that from?"

"Nico. He visited Papa yesterday. I was surprised you weren't there. Papa wanted to meet you, Gabriele, since you might be marrying me."

"I had other places to be."

Better places, I think but don't have. My mind's been in a tangle since those two blissful days with Francesca Astor. From the cozy sense of home in her arms to how intimate it felt to glimpse her vulnerabilities up close, every moment is a memory that I'll never let go of.

Francesca isn't messed up like I used to think. She's just human. She met the wrong people, trusted the wrong people, and wanted to belong with the wrong people who made her feel worthless. And she's still carrying around their opinions like a collar. It's driving her to ruin.

Despite how heavy Francesca's issues may be, she makes me feel more lighthearted than I have ever felt.

The drive-in movie was fun even if we fucked through most of it. I loved how right it felt to eat popcorn and discuss fictional characters with her afterward.

I mean, she was bred to be a socialite so she can carry a conversation. I was surprised even myself when I opened up to her about wanting to go to Italy.

Then she stole another piece of my sanity when she promised she'd take me.

Maria's gaze adheres to the bruises on my face. "Your injuries are still unhealed."

"It takes a few weeks. I'm sorry I haven't had time for you. It's nice to have this time to ourselves."

When I first saw Maria, she was very withdrawn. That's why it startles me when she beams a smile at me. It brightens her, breathing life back into her symmetrical features.

Maria is absolutely stunning. To the right man, she'd be his Madonna, a face he couldn't tear his dreams away from.

But she does nothing for me.

"I needed a change from staying at home all day," Maria admits. "Somehow, I knew I could find it with you."

We spend the next few minutes chatting about her son. He's sixteen, attends some private academy, is interested in computers, and she's worried because he only eats junk food. Typical.

I pour wine into her glass from the bottle I ordered. "Let's talk about you. What do you like to do?"

"I don't know the answer to that question. Isn't that sad?" Maria ejects a pained laugh. "I've spent most of my life doing what was required of me. I sat on charity committees, looked pretty, threw lavish parties, and socialized with the right kind of people. We vacationed in Europe and Africa every year. My hobbies—I thought I chose them, but they were actually chosen for me—volunteer work and shopping. I thought that was the life I wanted to live, a life where I made the men around me happy. But now I think that was the life he wanted me to live so I would always need him to feel valuable."

That's a loaded answer to my simple question. It's obvious to me that the sadness of losing herself for the sake of an abuser still persists.

"Maria, be honest with me." I set my hands in front of me. Literally putting my cards on the table. "Are you really ready to move on from your past or is that something you're doing because your father wants you to?"

I'm no expert in psychology, but spending time with Francesca has given me the ability to pick out unhealed wounds that sit right under the surface of people's exteriors.

A woeful smile touches Maria's mouth. "I'm still battered from my previous marriage but I have to move on for the sake of my son and myself. I have no idea what's expected of a mafia wife. Can you give me some information about that before I jump into this?"

I refill her wine glass. She doesn't look like a big drinker, but she already finished one glass. "I'm not high up enough in the organization for you to have to attend events with me so you could stay at home and do anything you please," I answer. "As you can guess, getting a job would be out of the question. Apart from being unconventional in the family, it'd put you in danger since your ex-husband owns a corporation. I can't have people tailing you all day, and if you have work trips or travel, that'd make the situation even more complicated."

Another reason I need to quash whatever emotions I've started to feel for Francesca. There's no way she'll ever become a housewife with all her drive and talent.

A meaningful silence reigns for a few minutes. Glasses and plates clink around us. Just as the lack of verbal exchange is turning uncomfortable, Maria twirls her glass, posing a question, "What kind of wife would you like, Gabriele?"

"One who is content."

"Then you're a better man than most."

"We don't have to rush this." *Please don't rush this. I need more time to explore my dark desires with Francesca.* "I can't tell you a whole lot since I've never been married before, but Nico's wife should be able to help if you need more information. Or someone to talk to."

Maria nods. Our food is brought to the table. As we eat, it

seems like a natural point for the conversation to end. Too bad we still have to smile and get through the whole meal.

Can I do this for a whole lifetime? I just told Francesca how lonely I feel when I eat alone but with Maria...it's no different.

A smile creeps past my tight control when Francesca's text message arrives in my inbox.

Francesca: I showed Hudson 361 the painting. They loved it. Thanks. I couldn't have done it without you.

Me: I still haven't seen this painting.

Francesca: Do you want to? It might surprise you.

Me: Show me.

A second later, a picture pops up in my messages feed.

Black background. The glint of a knife. A rose curled around the sharp blade, its petals falling.

Another piece of my sanity shatters. Our conversation in the car. She remembered it. The imagery caught her artistic fancy and she put her career on the line, took a huge risk, all to tell me what? That a rose and a knife make a pretty picture?

That *we* could make a pretty picture, too?

The inner romantic in me is determined to see this as a sign —a wordless message that the heiress wants the same thing as me. In some dark, twisted version of the world, our lives could be intertwined forever.

I want to believe that despite our differences, we're a masterpiece. A singular stroke of divine genius.

Something so rare, we can defy the odds.

Maria blinks curiously, bobbing her head from side to side. "You're smiling. That can't be about work."

"Sorry." I wipe my nose. "I got distracted."

I'm about to put my phone away when three dots flash on the screen, followed by the unmistakable beep of a new message.

Francesca: What do you think of it?

Me: I'll tell you later.

Francesca: *We're meeting up at your apartment, then?*

Me: *In two hours.*

I gulp a whole glass of water before Maria and I resume our conversation.

"Are you seeing some other woman?" So she didn't miss the signs. I'll never be able to cheat on this woman without getting caught. I don't plan to, either.

"It's not serious," I reply immediately. "Just a fling. I'll end it before we get married."

"That's okay, then. I probably don't have a right to expect fidelity in a marriage like this one. It's a bargain I'm striking for my safety."

"No, you deserve it, no matter what kind of marriage it is. And I do, too."

She forces a laugh. "Considering I'm scared of men it won't be hard to stay faithful."

"Glad that we're on the same page."

I always thought of myself as a traditional guy. The monogamous, getting married to one woman and settling down type. But the first thought of Francesca shakes my resolve to the core, igniting my lust, kindling the obsessive desire to meet her right after I'm done with this 'date'.

I know she'll be waiting for me outside my apartment.

I can't wait to go back. I can barely stop glancing at her text messages.

While I'm talking to my possible future wife.

She's temptation personified. A sin I can't avoid committing. A poison I can't stop drinking. Will I really be able to detach from her when I just managed to get her to agree to have dinner with me?

The rest of the evening flows into small talk about our lives, or schedules.

When we part at the entrance of the restaurant, I walk Maria to her chauffeur-driven car. It feels wrong to kiss her, yet, it'd be odd if I didn't. This isn't the first time we're meeting and things are moving forward between us.

So I bite the bullet and do it. It's a chaste peck on her lips. I'm relieved when it's over.

"I was on the fence before this evening, but you've convinced me." Maria cranes her neck. "I'd like to marry you, Gabriele. We should set a date. Papa and Nico are both getting impatient."

"You can pick the date. It'd be my honor to be your husband." The words prick the inside of my mouth like thorns. Maybe because I'm uttering them to the wrong woman.

* * *

My bones feel like lead when I turn the key to my apartment. I should've texted Francesca and called off our meeting for tonight, but spending the end of our days in each other's company has become so familiar, I'd be desolate without it.

Even though she's why I'm conflicted, the reason I'm a ball of pain at the thought of being married to the kind of woman that I've always idealized. A woman who'd be good for me.

Good, but not right. Perfect, but not fulfilling.

I hate that I know what fulfilling means thanks to a girl I should never have met.

I shut down the demonic thoughts shaking the foundations of my character. Angelo expects me to marry Maria. This is no more than what he deserves from me—my complete loyalty and obedience for saving my life. That is what he'll get.

"Bad day at work?" Francesca pounces on me the moment I barrel in through the door, kissing my face like it's oxygen to her.

I've never had a pet dog, but I imagine even dogs aren't this enthusiastic to greet you.

It's ingrained in my instincts to wrap my hands around her

soft hips, to sway to her wild tune as we both slake our thirst with touches and caresses. I don't fight it. It feels too good.

Maria is okay with us seeing each other for now. I can put off telling Francesca about my marriage. There's no date yet. I mean, I'm not even engaged, to be honest.

I roll up her sleeveless blouse and she drags it over the top of her head, giving me ample view of her lacy bra and the hard, rosy nipples peeking through the pattern.

My gaze traces lower, to the ridges of her abs, to the red scars that have turned purple.

It's poetic how she has bruises on her chest from our last time together and I have bruises on my heart from being with her, from losing the last shred of my dignity and control to the merciless, destructive storm known as Francesca.

We're both hurting in the same spot when I push my fingers against the purple mark. Francesca winces, then grabs my fingers and drags them over the hard, aching peaks of her breasts, finding her relief.

I lift her onto the kitchen island, the blunt sound of the gift in my pocket colliding against the marble melting into the desperate, wet sound of our tongues.

"Wait." I slide my hand away from her breast and into my pocket. "There's something I need to give you."

She wiggles her eyebrow in surprise. "You're usually eager to get to the sex part."

"Aren't you confusing me with yourself?"

I press the small red box between Francesca's thighs.

Her delicate fingers wrap around the box. She lifts it up, studying it with a mixture of dread and curiosity. "What's this?"

"Why don't you open the box and find out?"

A ruby ring shaped like a rose. It was the closest resemblance I could find to her painting. I looked for it everywhere after my date with Maria. I found it at an antique jewelry store.

"A ring?" She slams into my chest so hard, her hands locking around me, that I cough for breath. Her laughter, light and full of mischievous humor, is not something I deserve at this moment. Not after I just kissed another woman. "Of course, I'll marry you, Gabriele Russo. This is the day I've always dreamt of."

"Slow down, I'm not proposing to you."

"Why not? Haven't you already fallen in love with me?" I can't even tell if she's serious or joking. "Is there any need to drag this out with pointless pretenses, angst, and a meaningless refusal to admit your feelings?"

The fact that I'm not able to immediately tell her she's wrong about me being in love with her is a bigger problem than this misunderstanding.

I clamp a hand around her waist. "It's not an engagement ring. That would need to have diamonds."

That's the best I can come up with? God, I'm losing my touch.

Francesca crosses her ankles behind my back. "I don't care for tradition."

"Baby, when I marry a woman, I'll do it properly. With the biggest rock possible."

"So what's this ring for?"

"It's a gift for your successful commission project. It reminded me of your painting."

"Oh my goodness, that's true. There's a silver needle stuck through the rose."

"You asked me what I think about it. I was blown away. It got under my skin with its striking colors...just like you do."

I remove the ring from its velvet bed and slip it around her middle finger. It fits like it was made for her, even though I only roughly estimated her size at the shop.

"Were you always this nice?" Francesca raises her hand, captivated by the way light refracts against the crystalline petals of the rose. "Or have I had too much to drink and I'm hallu-cinating?"

"You don't smell of alcohol." I lean in and sniff her, just to be doubly sure.

For the record, I'm extremely nice to women. That's why Angelo wants me to marry Maria.

But Francesca always brings out my dark side.

Still does, when she tempts me with those heavy-lidded eyes and smart mouth.

Surprisingly, she also brings out my romantic side, a side I never knew I possessed.

I don't know if I'm anything more than her muse, fuel for her budding sex addiction. But if the way she kissed me when I bought her fucking Snickers is any indication, I have hope.

And she even faux-agreed to my imaginary marriage proposal. But I could never trap her in my world with a marriage. Not when I know it will destroy her dreams.

"Thank you so much, Gabriele." Breath exits my mouth in a jerky exhale at the sight of her eyes glistening with tears. She isn't usually emotional. But she had the same reaction yesterday at the drive-in theatre. "I'm so happy I have someone to cele-brate my victories with. Most of the time, nobody cares about what I'm doing. I was afraid to hope anyone would. You've made my day with this."

"I haven't got a glass of champagne to toast to your success." I lick the shape of her cupid's bow, offering her my lips instead of a drink. "But here's to hoping you make your dreams come true."

A single tear cuts a trail over the surface of her cheek. I don't wipe it away. She's entitled to her happiness.

"Gabriele." She hiccups. Then pulls her head away, embar-rassed. After a moment, she dried her tears and composed herself. Her sober, clear blue eyes hit mine like laser beams. "I'm so happy right now. When I first met you, I thought it was the worst day of my life but I was wrong. You have surprised me again and again with your kindness."

"So have you. I thought you were an addict with a sassy mouth that was nothing but trouble at first. Well, I still think your mouth is trouble."

Her lips graze the line of my throat. A cold shiver meets the heat in my blood. "Shall I get you off with my troublesome mouth?"

"Only if you want to," I say. "Now that you've successfully completed one painting, do you need inspiration for your next?"

I can't forget that I'm her muse, her new addiction, her escape from her fears and doubts. And that's all I am to her right now.

"You didn't have to remind me that I still have one more painting," she groans.

"Two more. Don't forget my commission. That's your repayment."

She groans louder this time, rocking against my body. Without effort, I've destroyed the beautiful moment we had. Her exuberance vanishes behind the circle of her dark pupils like it was never there.

I'm waiting for her to make an excuse and call it a night when she whispers, "Do you want to know what my painting is called?"

"Why not?"

"It's called Black Swan Theory. If you look carefully at the black background, there's the silhouette of a swan hidden in it."

"You thought to do that in one day?" I'm so impressed by the subtle detail I zoom the picture she sent to my phone to check. It's there. A subtle gray outline. The rose and the knife are in the swan's stomach.

"The Black Swan Theory describes impossible events that come as a surprise and change everything," Francesca continues. "That's what you are to me, Gabriele."

My silence blooms like a strong odor in the living room as Francesca slides off the kitchen island, slips back into her blouse, and carries herself to the door.

"Good night." She opens the door and steps outside. "I'll wait for you at the airport on Saturday."

CHAPTER 17

 *rancesca*

"Can I ask you for a favor?" Gabriele sandwiches my hand between his broad palms as our plane is about to land in Italy. His voice coaxes tender feelings buried under my skin to the surface. "While we're in Italy, don't think about your art. That includes your thesis exhibition, commission, and the paintings you still haven't finished."

"Including the one I need to deliver to you to repay my debt?"

"You can't paint here and you can figure all of that out later. This is supposed to be a break. A retreat to get away from everything."

My lips open with a huge sigh. "You can't tell what I'm thinking about anyway."

"I'll know."

I end up agreeing to it because I want to do everything to make Gabriele feel comfortable on this trip. He was shocked when I sashayed up to him at the VIP lounge in the airport. His knees gave out and he had to grab onto his luggage to stay upright.

"I was expecting you to be nursing a hangover at home." His sarcasm was as sharp as ever.

"I am cutting back on my alcohol intake," I retorted. "Plus, I keep my promises."

We arrived in Italy in the evening and on our first day, we spent all day basking in every luxury amenity the hotel I booked us had to offer. The best Michelin-star dinner. The most relaxing spa experience. A luxurious night of lovemaking with Gabriele eating grapes and honey off my body.

Today morning, we skipped breakfast and started exploring the city of Como, which is on the southern tip of the famous Lake Como in northern Italy. I chose to come here because exploring Lake Como seemed like a relaxing weekend plan. I don't want to wrestle with the crowds in cities like Rome and Milan on our very first trip since my secret agenda is to spend loads of intimate time with Gabriele.

So far, so good. I've been too absorbed by living in the moment to renege on my promise to not think of art.

Time moves at a different pace in a small town like Como which has a very old-world European vibe. Luxurious and expensive villas flicker in and out of my vision, replaced by brilliant blue waters, and cozy streets lined with orange and yellow houses line both sides. I know the pathways like the back of my hand because I've visited Como many times as a kid with Mom and Elliot.

My memories of throwing tantrums for gelato, of Elliot threatening me to behave myself or he'd give me away to child traffickers, Mom's sharp voice scolding him for making me cry. Ethan never vacationed with us because he was always busy with work and him being here would've made things awkward for my mother. She was the reason Dad divorced Ethan's mom.

Still, those are some of my happiest childhood days.

Gabriele mumbles periodically. Mostly, he's looking around like a kid in wonderland, so taken in by the beauty of this place that sometimes, he forgets to keep walking, instead standing in one spot and staring at the picturesque city in front of him.

Given that we avoided the tourist season, the streets are blissfully empty and cozy.

"Isn't this place...unreal?" he mouths after we've strolled the historic center of Como and are wandering along the promenade.

He hasn't let go of my hand at all. He moves over to the other side, protectively shielding me from people and traffic, even though there isn't any traffic here.

The promenade that runs along the lake is home to some fabulous restaurants and sights. Gabriele and I glance at the tranquil waters of Lake Como. It's the third-largest lake in Italy, a perennial hotspot for the world's richest.

"Have you never seen sunshine and water before?" I tease him.

He's so lost in the world around him, he doesn't respond for minutes. My throat contracts.

This is a side of Gabriele I've never had the privilege of viewing. It's so pure, so childlike, that I want to bottle it up and hug it close to my chest.

He is intense, raw, and animalistic when we're having sex. That's why it has been a blessing to witness this softer, more human side of him during our recent getaways together, both in Woodstock and now in Como. When his rough mask chips off and his gentle face peeks through the cracks.

It's also a curse to see this aspect of his character because now I can't go on pretending what we have is only sexual.

His sweet gestures tug at my heartstrings. His awestruck expressions make my stomach somersault. His sincere words and his quiet smiles make every moment of my hellish existence worth it.

I'm so glad I did this for him. I'm so glad I'm trying to quit— even though I packed Valium and Ambien to make sure I have something if anxiety creeps up on me. Coke is too risky to bring to a foreign country. I don't want to get arrested at the border.

"I'm getting hungry," I complain, checking out the restaurants on the promenade. Most of them have outdoor seating and I'd love to have a nice, slow meal right now with the sun warming my skin. Early April in New York can be pretty cold, but here, Mediterranean sunshine pours down on my skin.

We skipped breakfast at the hotel and after trekking all over Como non-stop, my legs are aching. I grab his arm and pull him into a *ristorante* that I visited in the past with Mom and Elliot and it's still in business.

Gabriele leans back in his chair, folding his arms behind his head. He's the stereotypical image of a tourist in his light-colored pants and casual white linen shirt. None of the onlookers whose curious eyes periodically catch on him could guess he works in organized crime.

"I must say, a sexy tan and casual clothes make you look hot." I bat my eyelashes at him appreciatively.

"Are you flirting with me, Francesca?"

"If you've noticed, then it must be working."

My throat is dry even after I've gulped down an Aperol spritz. Nervousness churns in my empty stomach. My hand finds his skin, desperately clinging to its warmth and comfort.

"Don't tempt me or you'll be lying on your back on this table in no time," Gabriele threatens, though his voice is full of humor.

I tighten my fingers around his hand. "I'm down for that."

"That's sweet, but I try not to ruin nice girls like you in public." He produces a lighter from his pocket and flicks it, until the flame's reflection dances inside his pupils. Gabriele doesn't smoke, but I'm afraid to ask what he uses that lighter for. "You come from a good family, yes? Let's spare your parents the shock."

"My dad's in jail and my mom's depressed. One of my brothers was just acquitted and the other one is deep in debt," I say flatly. "Is that your definition of a good family?"

"Damn it." His nail scratches against the lighter. "For a second, I forgot that your family is just as fucked up as you. You look like the poster child for a well-bred, upper-crust debutante."

I snort. "You wish."

The breeze intensifies, lifting the hem of my dress. I don't bother to press down on the fabric. Torturing Gabriele with a peek at my lacy panties is a much more attractive prospect than modesty.

Until he comes over and tucks the loose folds of my dress under my butt. His stubble brushes the shell of my ear as he whispers, "I hate other people seeing what's mine. Do you want me to kill every man who laid his eyes on you?"

Chills roll down my arms. Why is it so arousing to be reminded that I'm his? To be reminded of the violent power he wields over other people as well as my body.

"Then you'll behave," he finishes, pressing a possessive kiss into my cheek.

My blood temperature is soaring after his subtle display of power. I curve my head so his lips line up with mine. Then I sink into their roughness, the unique taste of the criminal that I've grown to love and need more than my friends or family.

This can't last.

He's only in it for the sex.

He's going to get married someday soon and leave you.

Nobody wants you.

You're worthless, both as an artist and as a woman.

Fears gain a chokehold on my throat so fast, the kiss doesn't even register. Before I can push the words away, Gabriele's head is lifting away from mine. It feels like losing a limb.

For the first time, desperately crave to be loved and cherished by Gabriele. His body alone isn't enough. I want him to see me as more than a skilled sex partner, to see me as a part of his soul because he's definitely become a part of mine.

"Would you really murder someone for me?" I ask, rubbing my chest to calm my anxious heartbeat.

Gabriele cups my face with one big hand. "If they laid a hand on you, hurt you, or dishonored you? You can bet I'd do more than murder them."

"Dishonor? That sounds archaic."

He shrugs, with no remorse. "What would you call it then?"

"Sexual assault."

"Too technical. Also, I'm not going to wait around till they actually assault you."

The unkind monologue inside my brain dissolves. I must mean something to him if he wants to protect me. That is going to have to be enough for me. I don't have the right to be greedy. Because why would he choose me?

I'm a distorted mess of a human being with no willpower. Even at this moment, my fingers are sinking into my purse, trying to uncap the bottle with the pills. Hoping to slip one quietly while Gabriele's distracted by the lake.

My scheme is interrupted by the waiter arriving with our order. The familiar aroma of the food I ate as a child with my mother and brother distracts me. Nostalgia clouds my senses as I chew the first bit of duck.

The version of me from the past dances before my eyes.

I wasn't always like this. I used to be happy. Normal. Different.

I can still be like that, can't I?

"Do you like the food?" I inquire, seeing how passionately Gabriele is enjoying his meal. Italy is bringing out the hedonist in him, the man who loves to live and enjoy every moment of life. Also, he must have been hungrier than he let on.

"Thank you for this, Francesca." Gabriele crosses his legs. The breeze has disappeared as if bending to his will. "Just sitting by the lake makes me feel complete."

"I never thought you'd be the type to exaggerate."

Gabriele shakes his head, hooking a finger under the collar of his shirt.

"I'm not. I feel a deep sense of connection to this place even though this is my first visit. It's hard to describe. Do you know the feeling of finding the last piece of a puzzle and then seeing the whole picture for the first time? Realizing it's so much more beautiful than you imagined?" He rubs his shoulder, going quiet for a moment as his gaze trails off to the distant horizon. "It might sound ridiculous, but it makes me so happy to know that my ancestors lived in such a beautiful place. That they walked these streets before me. That their echoes still linger between the branches of these trees and the sparkling waters. That I, too, have roots somewhere in the world."

"New York doesn't feel like home?"

He shakes his head. "Never has. It's too unfriendly. The city will chew me and spit me out if I stop hustling. There's no hustle in Como. Just relaxation."

"That's because you're a tourist."

"Even the locals look like they're enjoying themselves. The pace of life is just different. People are way more focused on the simple joys of life—good food, nature, dolce vita."

Dolce Vita. The Italian term for a sweet life. A life of living in the moment and savoring every moment like it's a sweet bite of a juicy peach.

"Don't tell me you want to move here."

Gabriele's lips squeeze in a half-smile. "If I could. But I can't."

"Why not?"

"I have a job. A family back in New York."

"A family that doesn't feel like family," I surmise.

Gabriele's features thicken with chagrin. This must be the worry that keeps him up, that makes him brooding and surly when he's alone. He doesn't like the world he's living in. Judging from how he described his boss as cold and empty in Woodstock, they must not get along. It sucks to have a mean boss, but it must suck doubly when he also happens to be your sworn brother.

"You can quit," I suggest.

"You can't just quit the mafia, Francesca. They have to kick you out."

"Then get kicked out."

"They'll kill me if I betray them."

"Is there no other way to get sacked? In a regular job, all it takes is to have poor work performance."

"If I break my leg and become useless..." He shakes his head. "No, I've been with them too long. Angelo wouldn't abandon me. I'd probably get assigned to manage money at the casino."

I dig my elbows onto the tablecloth-covered surface of the table. "It's a soul-sucking prison with no escape, isn't it?"

Gabriele releases a noise between his teeth. "Most Americans would describe their job the same way."

"Except my brother Ethan. He thrives on being a CEO. A born control freak who works all day."

"Some people are just lucky."

"Or different."

Gabriele's dark eyes look light brown in the sunlight but his pupils are wide in a silent question. "You never talk about your other brother."

"Elliot? We lived in the same house but rarely saw each other. He's always partying in Ibiza, Florida, or somewhere. He works at a venture capital company now. He says he likes his job—and his boss." I slap my hand to my wet, Aperol spritz-smeared lips. "It's dawning on me that both my brothers love their jobs."

"You love art, too."

"Yeah, but I'm scared I won't have a career as an artist by the time I graduate."

Gabriele's hand comes down roughly over mine on the table. "No thinking about art or your future. You promised me."

His strength shakes away the fears growing like cobwebs around my head. There's no point obsessing over something I can't control. I'll have enough time to lament over my hopeless career once I'm back in Brooklyn.

"Sure. I'm a good girl who always keeps her word." My statement is half-teasing and half-seductive. If he's smart, he'll figure out I'm giving him ideas for later.

We dig into our food again, to finish the last of the scraps. I've noticed Gabriele relishes eating. He probably food is sacred. He looks so happy when he eats like he's deriving pleasure from every morsel of food.

Once again, I'm convinced that someone who respects food as much as he would make a great chef.

Too bad he's only ever going to be a mafioso.

With lunch complete and a small food bump in our bellies, we stroll back down the promenade.

Gabriele's hand shoots to my wrist. He captures it, tugging me back.

"I got this for you." He nudges a long cardboard case in my direction. "It's a souvenir I got at one of the shops during our walk. I want you to remember that we came here."

I'm fascinated by his new moods, and by how much his tenderness toward me has grown since we spent time together in Woodstock. I want to keep this version of him forever.

He's only in it for the sex.

He's going to get married someday soon and leave you.

Nobody wants you.

As I lift the lid of the box, the voices echo louder. Inside the box is a silk scarf with colorful patterns. I know local silk is a specialty of this region. Mom also often bought these for her friends.

"I've never bought anything like this for someone, so I don't know if it's any good," Gabriele says.

My throat is thick with a foreign lump.

I've never bought anything like this for someone, so I don't know if it's any good.

I'm special to him. The thought tickles my dead heart.

Now I realize why all the well-bred rich boyfriends before never satisfied me. I don't need fancy dinners, flowers, and luxury handbags. I can buy those on my own. What I need is someone who makes me feel special, seen, and valued. Someone who takes the time to understand my little pleasures and great challenges.

Gabriele clears his throat. "Are you speechless because you like it or because you're wondering how to get rid of this ugly thing?"

"I love it. Put it on me."

He drapes it around my neck but doesn't tie it.

I twirl around. "How do I look?"

"Perfect."

I feel perfect, too.

"You're not the only one with a gift." I loop my arm around his. "I have one more surprise for you."

* * *

"A FUCKING BOAT?" Gabriele's expression is priceless as he stares at my father's white motorboat.

"Hey, I'm rich. Or at least my brother is."

A uniform line of white boats and yachts lines the harbor of Portofino. Portofino is a fishing village on the Italian Riviera.

It's a favored holiday spot for jet-setting models and other rich and influential people. It doesn't have direct commute links to Como, so we had a bit of a thorny path getting here. It took almost four hours, to change trains and buses.

I've been here many times with Mom, Dad, and Elliot.

I usher Gabriele onto the boat. It's not very big. Neither is it difficult to drive. I have lots of experience from when I was younger.

As I turn the keys and the motor whirs, propelling the boat into the clear blue waters, Gabriele's mouth is frozen in an O.

"Sit back and enjoy the ride," I tell him. "We'll be cruising around Portofino's protected marine area. We can stop anytime you want."

Gabriele's up close and personal with my face by the time I've swerved the boat to avoid collision with another one's path.

"You're supposed to look at the water, not me," I remind him. "There are coral reefs here. And loads of fish and other diverse creatures."

"I wouldn't miss the sight of you captaining a boat for anything." The crinkle of his eyes and the affection in his voice is just like Dad's.

Dad did horrible things to Ethan and other people and for that, I can never forgive him. But he was a great father to me. He cherished me.

"Your mind is wandering, Heiress," Gabriele notes, too sharp to let anything slip past his eagle eyes.

"Don't be creeped out but you reminded me a little of my dad just now. I still miss him sometimes."

Gabriele throws his arm around my shoulder, startling me. The boat jerks to the right. "You must have a thing for criminals."

"Not funny."

"I wasn't making a joke. I was making an observation."

"That I like men with a dark side?"

Gabriele quirks a brow. "Because they feed your dark side."

I want to dismiss it outright, but that could be true.

"Before you, I didn't believe I could have such extreme tastes in sex," I confess. "If my ex-boyfriend had suggested holding a knife to my throat, I'd have called the cops."

"Takes the right man to make it sexy." He beams a smile at me. My heart melts into a puddle right away. He's sexy alright.

Gabriele's teeth look whiter against his newly tan skin. He's enjoying this weekend break way too much.

Eventually, I manage to get him to focus on the purpose of this boat ride—the pristine panorama that surrounds us. The rugged cliffs overlooking Area Marina Protetta di Portofino. The sparkling blue waters.

We live in a concrete jungle. It's a luxury to experience this intimate connection with nature.

Gabriele doesn't need much incentive before he starts acting like a typical tourist and taking pictures. He even takes a selfie with me. I'm going to have to beg him for weeks to send it to me, though.

"I saw a fish that had a jawline like yours," he teases, pointing to an ugly fish with a jaw shaped like a brick.

"You need to get your eyes checked."

"Don't blame me because your plastic surgeon fucked up."

"I have never gotten plastic surgery."

"Those lips can't be real."

"They are very real." To prove my point, I kiss him. A long, sun-soaked kiss that tastes like us.

That shuts him up for good.

In an hour, we have covered almost the entire marine area, so I bring the boat back to the pier.

"That was something special," Gabriele admits as we walk back along the promenade to our hotel. He has often been lost for words during this trip. It's a sign that I'm doing a great job of providing him with memorable experiences that cannot be described using his limited vocabulary. "Thank you."

"You haven't seen anything yet." I soften when his hand covers mine.

With the sun on my face and Gabriele's fingers nestled in mine, the world is an idyllic place where my demons seem destined to wither and die.

Back in our hotel room, he immediately pushes me against the door. His lips break mine with a rough kiss, all sharp teeth and needy tongue. I whimper into him, luxuriating in the mindless, effortless nature of our physical connection.

My brain's beginning to twist into those unwanted alleys of 'you're wasting time here instead of focusing on your thesis', so I welcome the distraction.

For these two days, I've decided to forget about art and focus on making this the best trip of Gabriele's life. I swear, it has been the biggest relief to stop thinking about painting. A burden lifted off my shoulder.

My nipples bead into hard dots as I press my ass against his hard cock. Our bodies move in unison. My panties stick to the wet flesh between my legs, wanting his fingers to rip off the useless fabric.

He can tell the state of my pussy without even touching it.

"Am I going to find you dripping for me?" he questions, lifting my skirt. His thumb rubs my clit through the fabric and he gets his answer.

"Please," I beg. "Take me."

With one touch, I'm soaring. My body chases the rapture of merging with him. My head swims, unable to keep up with all the euphoria spinning around my bloodstream.

He rips away my panties, shifting my body to line up with his hard dick that he just freed from his pants. His hips move fast; he pounds into me hard. It's primal, raw sex, as liberating as it is fulfilling.

My eyes burn with tears as waves of my climax gather in my stomach.

"Don't you wish this could last forever?" I whisper between ragged exhales.

Galaxies spin in front of my eyes. The greatest and most pleasurable mysteries of the universe are all waiting to explode inside my body. I'm at the edge.

Then the boundaries dissolve and the stars break into thousand pieces right before my eyes, releasing their heat into my body.

Gabriele hiccups a laugh in my ear. "There's no forever for you and me. But we have this moment and I'm going to make sure you never forget it."

My entire universe, stars, blah, blah, blah vision of rapture crashes instantly at Gabriele's cold pronouncement. It's always the truth that destroys my illusions.

The uncomfortable, itchy pattern of thoughts inside my head starts up again.

This can't last.

He's going to get married.

Nobody wants you.

Walking all day must have taken it out of Gabriele, so he dozes off as soon as his head hits the pillow. I attempt to read a novel that Ella bought for me last year. I packed it for this trip.

But there's no way a slow literary book is going to keep my thoughts away from the pills in my purse.

I scratch my elbows, attempting to control my urges.

I made a resolution to quit drugs. My limit was that I'd stop when it started to endanger my normal life and routine. I only started two months ago and I only took it once or twice a week when I need to paint. I'm not like one of those druggies who don't even know how bad their case is.

But I hate feeling scared. I detest feeling like I'm losing everything I loved. Gabriele is slipping through my fingers. I feel it. We're getting closer, but at the same time, there's a whole host of new fears in my mind that weren't there before.

I'm growing deeply attached to Gabriele, to his sweet gestures, and to the way he makes me feel desired, needed, and beautiful. But with every little happiness he bestows upon me, I become greedier. Regardless of how much he gives me, I want more. My hunger never dies.

There's no forever for you and me.

Quietly, I seize my purse, slip the pills under my tongue, washing them down with cool bottled water. It's the knight in shining armor I need. My cloudy mind drinks the ecstasy.

I've pushed away the discomfort for now.

But even when I'm swimming in artificial tranquility, I know the darkness will somehow find its way back to me.

CHAPTER 18

 *abriele*

THIS IS PERFECTION.

Is this the place I've been dreaming of? Is this the life that has haunted my dreams? It must be. My heart has been full ever since I landed in Italy. Every day is filled with a sense of rightness, things clicking into place like I was always supposed to find my way back here.

Francesca and I took the train to Milan today. We walked around and she shopped for clothes. As usual, we stopped at a fancy ristorante for lunch. After that exceptional boat ride, this was a more normal day trip, but still great.

On the train journey back to Como, Francesca lays her head on my shoulder casually as she closes her eyes.

"Not protesting?" she moans.

"About what?"

"Me using your shoulder as a pillow."

I move her head to nestle it in the crook of my arm, so her ear rests on the muscled width of my bicep. "Take my arm, too, if you want."

"This vacation has worked wonders for your grumpiness." Francesca snuggles, her velvet-soft hair shifting over my skin. "Or do you like me now because you've seen how rich I am?"

"It's not your money that makes you attractive." It's the hidden depths of her. I may have seen a lot of layers of the heiress's darkness and sexuality and while they were captivating, her lighthearted, fun, playful nature is equally magnetic.

Francesca stretches the corners of my lips with her fingers. "Are you actually smiling?"

"Am I not allowed to?"

"You are, but you can no longer lie that you're not enjoying yourself with me. This trip is amazing, isn't it?"

"I already told you. I love it. Something about these places that we visit just speaks to me. There's a sense of familiarity even though I've never been here in my life."

"I'm glad."

My hand moves on its own will to bracket the side of her shoulders and nudge her body closer to mine. "So what're we doing next?"

"Nothing."

"Don't you have any more boat trips planned?"

"No, but we can play a game." The mischievous glint in her eyes is a challenge I can't resist. "It's a game I've made up. The name's kiss and tell."

"Sounds like we'll be getting up close and personal for this one."

"Wait till you hear the rules. You have to kiss me in the spot where I tell you to. Then I'll tell you one of my secrets. When it's your turn, I'll kiss you wherever you want me to and you have to tell me a secret I ask for."

"You'll kiss anywhere I ask? Does it have to be on my body?"

"I'll even kiss your gun because I'm open-minded like that."

"That's not what I meant." I scratch my nose.

"Then what did you mean?"

"Wait and you'll find out."

* * *

"KISS ME HERE." She points to the junction between her head and the back of her neck. We're back in our hotel room with two glasses of wine and a platter of antipasti laid out on the bedside table.

"Why there?"

"I like being kissed there. Bet you didn't know that."

"I'll remember it." I plant my lips exactly where her finger is digging into her skin.

When I raise my head, spots of light speckle across my vision.

In the momentary play of colors, I see an image as clear as the wineglass Francesca is playing with. She's an artist and I'm just a civilian. In the blink of an eye, she's happy and I'm home. In another dimension, we're a pair of birds flying through the storm and landing on a dry branch.

In this world, though, the water is still drenching our hearts.

She clears her throat. "Your turn now."

"What about the secret?" I ask. "Weren't you supposed to tell me one?"

"Already did." She pulls the covers over her bare legs. "Told you about my erotic spot. Your turn now."

I scoff. "You should start gambling at the casino I manage down in Queens. You'd even beat the card sharps at their game. You're that good at cheating."

Her eyes widen in false innocence. She pops an olive into her mouth, then washes it down with a sip of white wine.

Whatever. She's cute so I forgive her.

I push my hand into her wild, flowing hair, cupping her head and tipping her head forward to my chest. I took off my shirt earlier but before I could undress fully, she roped me into this game. "Kiss me here."

"I thought you'd choose a more interesting spot," Francesca says.

"This is where my heart is. And I've never let you kiss me anywhere close to it."

She's a smart girl so she understands the metaphor.

"Gabriele." Her breath is a wet feather sliding over my cheek. "You can be vulnerable with me. I won't use your secrets or hurt you. I'm more likely to hurt myself, given how much of an addictive personality I have."

The first thing they train out of you in the mafia is trust. Followed by the vulnerability. But from the depths of the prison where I stuffed them at eighteen, both come rushing out at the sound of Francesca's voice.

Like she was always the one meant to open the floodgates and free them.

Her soft, wet mouth lingers on my chest, kissing all over me until I tell her to stop.

"I want to know who your first love was."

"My boss's wife."

"What? That's weird."

"I saw her often when they were courting. Always wished she were mine. She was a true lady."

"So your first love was unrequited?" She massages my back. "How sad."

"It was. But I've moved on from it now," I reply.

I don't dwell on the hard clench of muscle in the spot where Francesca's lips were. Extending my hand, I grab my wineglass. I really need alcohol to get through this game. Vulnerability like this is too addicting. She's cutting me open and I'm enjoying it.

Nobody has been so interested in my secrets, my pains, my past, my heartbreaks.

When she questions me, I can't help but answer.

If she asks me for my debit card PIN now, I won't even hesitate. That's the level of hold she has over me.

"Kiss my feet. I want to feel like a queen." Francesca raises her leg, planting her foot in front of my face, wiggling her toes. They're painted a light pink, as perfectly manicured as every other part of her.

"Sure, Your Majesty." I take her foot and rub my lips between her toes. "Good enough?"

"More."

I trail my mouth over her heel, skimming the hard bulb of her ankle, gliding further and further up. Tracing the curve of her leg, her knee, right up to the flesh of her inner thigh.

She taps the top of my head. "Okay, stop or this won't be a harmless game anymore."

I drop her leg. It lands on the mattress with a soft thud.

Francesca pulls her leg back, folding it against her chest. "Is there any secret of mine you want to know?"

"Your bank account details would be helpful."

"You serious?"

"Consider it charity. Lending a poor criminal a million dollars."

"I'm not telling you my passwords."

"I was joking—"

Her face reddens. "They're too embarrassing."

"*That's* the reason you're not telling me? Not because I work for the mob and could scam you out of your money?"

"Come on. You'd never do that."

I do a slow head shake. "I'm terrified by your lack of common sense."

"Rich heiresses don't have a lot of that anyway."

"Living up to the stereotype, are you?"

"Enough." She rocks her body forward, sending tremors across the bed. "I want to know more of your embarrassing past stories. So tell me where to kiss you next?"

My fingers reach under my pockets for the bulge on my side. I throw my wallet onto the bed.

"On this."

"Why this?"

"So it always smells like you when I use it," I reply.

Francesca picks up the luxurious brown leather and studies it, quickly laying her mouth on it before returning it. She winds her arms around me. "Why do you want it to smell of me?"

I can admit a lot, but not the truth. Not before she does. I long to keep a piece of her because I know I can't keep all of her, no matter how hard I try.

I graze my thumb against her earlobe. "Because you smell good."

"That's a simpler reason than I thought."

"What did you guess?"

"That you wanted to have something that reminded you of me. But I don't know why you would want that."

She's a little too close to the truth for my comfort, so I hide my vulnerability with a sneaky smile.

"I see you so often I don't need to be reminded of you," I bluster.

"But that won't be forever, right?" Her bottom lip is shaking. The quake travels all the way down her neck to her shoulder. She curls her body into a ball. "Let's stop playing this game?"

"What's wrong, baby?"

"Gabriele, I don't want to find out more of your heart-breaking secrets. I don't want you to know more of mine." Francesca's lips clam shut. She studies the mattress quietly, tracing over the edge of the pillow with her nails. "When I'm so scared I can't breathe when I'm so hopeless I can't think of anything else, you're the only one who can make me feel okay.

237

But you're going to disappear from my life someday. I can't afford to depend on you so much."

I click my tongue. "You always overthink this much?"

"Every single day." A smile edges through her answer. "My mind's a terrifying place to be."

"What is that mind thinking of now?"

"About how I've never wanted to give anyone everything, but I want to give you everything, even my bank passwords." Her eyes lift hesitantly. "Is that stupid?"

"That depends on whether you'll regret it." Because I'm desperate for validation that her feelings for me are as strong, as absolute, as mine, I push her further. "Something tells me you're conflicted."

Vulnerability slashes a wound in the air. Fear plays on her pale skin. I've never considered this but she might be as scared of admitting to these weird, nameless emotions as me.

"Gabriele, I love art." She breathes out softly, confirming my hunch. "I gave my everything for art. But it left me with nothing but paranoia and heartache."

The unspoken follow-up question flashes in my mind even though she doesn't voice it.

What if you're the same? What if you take everything from me and leave me with a broken heart, too?

Art is Francesca's greatest devotion, her biggest passion, and yet it is destroying her, breaking her apart piece by piece. Maybe to her, pure passion is a festering wound more than a glorious ecstasy.

"You loved your mother, too," Francesca continues. "You did everything to support her. It ended up killing you. Tell me, do you regret it or was it worth it?"

The cold memories from the back closet of my brain pop up again. She has asked me a complex question to which there is no easy answer. It's not that I regret what I did, I simply regret not recognizing that Mom would never love me back. That she would never see my love for her.

Am I making the same mistake again?

Is she afraid of making me make that mistake again?

"There's nothing in the world worth having that doesn't hurt," I say. "But if you're afraid of losing everything, then there's no point in pushing yourself."

I reach out to caress her cheek.

For the first time ever, she recoils.

That single action brings down the temperature by a few hundred degrees until it feels like I'm in the middle of the Arctic.

The distance between us seems infinite at that moment. An infinite ocean I can't hope to cross. Besides, if I manage to get to the other side, I'll never be able to come back.

This is a one-way trip.

All it'd take to clear this up is one line.

I won't hurt you.

We're both experts at avoiding the truth, though, so I let the chill of our frozen relationship ice me.

"Forget about it. It's not important," I say.

"Yeah." Her nod is all eagerness. "Let's play another game."

We watch television, not speaking a word to each other throughout. When the show's over, we turn off the TV and go to sleep.

Just like that, our time in Italy draws to an end, leaving us both with a heavy, swollen awareness of everything we have got to lose.

* * *

WE'RE FLYING business class on the return journey, too.

"Why did I never get a rich friend before?" I examine the

bubbles in the champagne glass the flight attendant just handed me. "My life could've been so much easier."

"It's not easy to find someone like me," Francesca replies. "I hope you see how lucky you are."

"Again, thanks for this break. It was great to get away from my boss."

I told Nico I was going to Italy on Friday. He was the one who urged me to take a break after I finished the last job, so I did. Though he was surprised by the suddenness of my announcement, he promised he wouldn't call me for work and he has kept his promise.

"I'll never forget the places we saw," I continue, a wistful longing sneaking into my heart as the plane ascends further and further up until Italy disappears under a bed of clouds.

I'll never forget being with Francesca, how magical it felt to experience a vacation with her.

Though I can't afford to leave New York or get a long-term visa to Italy given my prison record, I could have lived with the knowledge that Italy is where my weary soul longs to settle down.

Only now that I'm sitting inside the flight, her fingers threaded in mine, I'm growing aware that the feeling of being in the right place isn't fading.

"Let's come back again when we both have time," Francesca says, popping open one of the three tiny bottles of vodka she got from the flight attendant. "I have to show you Venice and Rome."

No thanks, I want to say. I'd love to erase this entire fucking trip from my memory.

CHAPTER 19

rancesca

TIME RACES once we're back in New York. Gone are the leisurely days soaked in sunlight and strolls down rustic streets. Old anxieties cramp around me, pushing me back into the familiar rut of panic, substances, and a few flashes of inspiration that quickly turn into disillusionment.

My only escape from the cycle is the few hours every evening that I spend with Gabriele at his apartment. Only moments ago, I finished licking my plate clean. The man might be in the mafia but his Pasta primavera rivals the legends.

I spy my phone screen lighting up from the corner of my eye.

I lie to my mother every day that I'm going out with friends. There's no way I can tell anyone in my family about Gabriele yet.

Mom would have a heart attack, Ethan would pop a vein then kill Gabriele for touching me, Ella would be confused, and

Elliot...I have no idea how Elliot will respond to all of this. He's hard to predict.

"Don't you have any friends?" Gabriele asks tonight, his head close to mine. The tantalizing brush of a lock of his hair against my skin sends a rush of blood down my spine. An obsessive craving begins its slow climb up my throat, reaching my lips, begging to be satisfied.

I meld my mouth to Gabriele's. A short kiss. Just enough to keep me from drowning.

"I do have one friend. Her name's Ella."

"She must be a terrible friend," Gabriele says. "You've been suffering alone all this time and she has never bothered to pay attention."

Pain clusters around my mouth, paralyzing my muscles with guilt. "She's not the terrible friend. That would be me. I've ignored her calls and evaded her messages for months now. I think she has just given up on me at this point."

"Call her, then."

My gaze skips up to his. "What, now?"

"No better time than the present."

"We were supposed to have sex now."

"We can have sex later."

"I didn't think you were so interested in my social life."

"I can't bear to watch a poor, friendless girl eating at my apartment." He grabs my phone off the table and holds it in front of me. "Come on."

The phone's weight feels cool in my palm. My trembling fingers resist opening contacts and pressing Ella's name though. She'll definitely want to meet. And I don't know if I can yet. "Why are you doing this?"

"Because I want you to try. You don't have to avoid people forever. I won't be around forever and you need other people who can support you."

The way he drifts off is a sign. A bad omen I can't ignore.

Cold dread churns along with my stomach acid. "Are you going somewhere, Gabriele?"

"I'm going to get married." The silence that follows his announcement punctures the air like a gunshot. All the saliva in my mouth dries up in shock. "Eventually, I mean. We'll have to stop meeting. You should have someone else you can lean on."

He gave me a heart attack there. I'm certain there's something he isn't telling me. Has he already found someone to marry? Is that why he's preparing me to live without him?

I wish I could ask him but I can't. I have no right when I'm an addict who can't offer him anything. Marrying someone else would be the better option for him. I know it's what he wants.

I told myself I wouldn't stand in the way of his happiness. I really love my evenings with Gabriele and I pray they never end, but if that's what he wants, I won't take away his freedom.

"Okay. I'll call my friend." With a deflated downward slope of my shoulders, I give in. When he's around me, I don't feel as paranoid as I do when I'm alone.

I pick Ella from my contacts list.

She answers the phone in two rings.

"Hey, Francesca. I'm so glad you called me. I heard you went to Italy."

"Ethan has been talking, I see."

"How was your trip? You were with a friend, weren't you?" There's no disguising the sliver of disappointment in her voice. She's my best friend, my only friend. But I never even asked her if she wanted to come. The last vacation I promised to take with her to London was a hoax. "Was it someone from your course?"

"Um…sort of," I lie. Ethan definitely doesn't know who my 'friend' is and I'd like to keep him in the dark for as long as possible. Given that Ella is his girlfriend, anything I confide to her will eventually find its way to him.

Damn it. Why didn't I consider this complication when I was setting the two of them up?

"Francesca, are you okay? I didn't want to egg you on because you have your exhibition coming up, but this isn't normal. You're avoiding me and I don't know why. Is it because I'm dating Ethan? Are you uncomfortable—"

"No, it's not because of that..." I trail off. Shit. I spoke without thinking. The truth may be far worse, but I can't have Ella feeling bad about being Ethan's lover. Given her sense of loyalty, it'll kill her.

Gabriele's hand engulfs me, his touch relaxing my tense shoulder.

I snap my head up.

Tell her. He mouths. *Tell her the truth.*

I shake my head, mouthing back, *Are you crazy?*

"You can't lie forever." This time, he whispers into the space between us. "If she's your friend, she'll understand."

Oh my god, I'm not prepared for this. I'm nowhere near ready to open myself up and show my disgusting weaknesses to my best friend who thinks I'm perfect.

I admit it's unfair. Ella confessed her worst demons to me six months ago. She tearfully revealed her scars and pains: about being sexually abused as a teenager, about her mother's depression. She admitted to loving Ethan despite him wanting to keep their relationship a secret at the time.

I felt entitled to that confidence. As her friend, I even asked her why she hadn't told me earlier.

I'm such a hypocrite.

Nerves dance in my belly. I can't go all the way, but I have to take the first step or it'll be unfair for Ella. Also, I think I'd feel better if I knew Ella was supporting me in my journey.

It's just that I'm afraid she won't once she hears the whole truth.

"Ella, I'm sorry for my behavior. I didn't mean to hurt you. I hope I haven't." I put one word in front of another carefully. Gabriele leans back with a wide smile. "I've been struggling with something. I can't tell you what it is, but it's something big. Don't worry, I have someone to help me."

"What is it, Francesca?" Ella's breaths are harried. She's anxious, too. Oh my goodness, this is the reason I avoided telling her. She'll push herself to exhaustion worrying about me now. "Why can't you tell me?"

"Because you'd tell Ethan."

"Ethan loves you. You're his sister. He would never hurt you"

"Yes, but I want to get through this problem in my own way, at my own pace. Ethan will push me to conform to his standards, to do it how he wants me to do it. If he doesn't get his way, he'll tattle to Mom to force me to go with his plan. You know better than anyone that Ethan can be overprotective when it comes to the people he loves."

"Okay, I won't tell him." Ella's swallow is so audible I hear it through the phone. "I promise."

I draw in a large gulp of air, steeling myself. The moment I release my greatest secret as sound, my chest lightens like a load has been lifted off me. "I can't paint."

"But…I don't understand," Ella stutters. "You turned in your commission for Hudson 241 a few days ago. You mean that wasn't your work?"

"I'm not plagiarizing or using a ghost painter, if that's what you're worried about. I wish I had. It'd have saved me so much heartache."

God, if only I'd talked to Ella before. She could have suggested the idea of having someone else paint for me. Though I hate cheating, it'd have been better than the months of endless despair and self-hate I've endured by forcing perfectionism on myself.

"What do you mean?" Ella probes. "What have you been doing Francesca?"

"Drugs." I come out and say it. Gabriele's watching me like a hawk. His slow nod of approval fills me with the courage to go on. "I've been doing coke, Ella. I need to be high to paint. Even then, I can barely cope. I'm scared. I'm scared I'm going to fail and lose my dreams before I ever have a shot at them. I'm scared I'm turning into someone I don't know."

The other end of the line is pure silence. The weight of my fear and my truth charges the atmosphere. Gabriele's steady gaze is firmly fixed on me. That stability puts me at ease as uncertainty swarms me.

"Ella?" I call her name, my voice echoing.

"I'm here, Francesca. Don't be afraid. We'll figure something out. Can I come over to your place? I have to see you. Where are you right now?"

"I'm with my friend." I debate over telling her about Gabriele, but decide I can't say that over the phone. "Don't worry. I'm fine. We can meet later. I have to tell you something else, too."

"Where? When?" I can hear her knocking over something in her room. "I don't have classes on Wednesday."

"Let's meet on Wednesday. At your place." Mine would be risky with Mom hanging around. And a public place where anybody could hear us would be even worse.

"Sure. Will you be fine until then?"

"Ella, are you disappointed that I'm not as happy and perfect as you thought?"

"I never thought you were perfect. Nobody is. But I'm not disappointed in you, Francesca. I feel terrible that you've carried this burden all alone and I didn't notice or help you. I don't understand much about art, but I'll try my best. I think Mom knows people who were addicts. Should I ask her?"

Ella's mother, Hannah Faber, is an actress. Obviously, she knows a lot of people.

"No, don't tell your mom. I want to keep this between us," I say.

"I will."

"Thanks, Ella. I'm tired so I'll call you again later, but I'm grateful to you for listening to me."

"You can call me anytime. I'm always at home reading books. You know that."

"Yeah, have you read any good books recently?"

"Lots."

We slip into the small talk before I hang up. Staring back at Gabriele, it's like I just climbed a mountain.

"Your friend doesn't seem bad," he says. "But I didn't know she was dating your brother."

"I set them up," I reply. "Without meaning to."

He beckons me closer with a motion of his hand. I curl myself up on his lap like a cat, arms easily curving around his shoulders. "So how does it feel now that we're not the only two people who know about your problems?"

"My head is clearer," I admit. "I forgot how smart Ella was. How easy it is to feel comfortable around her."

There are tremors in my heart that have no name. Treacherous sensations invade my stomach. It isn't fear frothing over, threatening to spill. It's like something has been released and my body is gradually adjusting to the new equilibrium.

The ever-present tightness in my chest has loosened.

"Gabriele, thank you for pushing me out of my comfort zone. I couldn't have done it without...you." The word love gets stuck in my throat like a pebble I accidentally swallowed.

You're my sanctuary in the storm, my oasis in this unending darkness.

I lied in Italy when I said the reason I couldn't love was that art had drained every emotion from me. It doesn't matter what my dream takes from me because he gives me back everything I've lost. Even when I'm empty, my emotions overflow at the warmth in his eyes, the smokiness of his voice, and the beauty of the invisible bond between us.

The reason I can't beg him to be more than my muse is because I don't deserve him.

It'd be selfish to make him pour any more of his time and energy into me when I might never get over this toxic cycle of ups and downs, highs and lows, hope and despair.

I may be a disaster, but I'm not heartless enough to drag Gabriele down this hellhole with me.

OUR EVENING RENDEZVOUS continue the following weeks. It's something I look forward to every day: relaxing at his apartment, eating the delicious food he makes, talking to him about my day, and hearing about his. Most of the time, we end up having passionate sex, but there are days when we simply enjoy the warm intimacy of each other's bodies without needing to make it sexual. I enjoy those moments the most because they satisfy me more than the physical intimacy. I underestimated the soothing emotional effect spending time with someone I trust can have on my psyche.

And Gabriele is certainly living up to the hype as my muse, because the more time I spend with him, the more my productivity skyrockets. My spring thesis progresses better than expected in the run-up to the final exhibition. For the first time, I'm actually kind of excited about people seeing my art, even though my familiar friend anxiety is always quietly seething under the surface of my newfound confidence.

The fact that my projects are progressing splendidly adds a spring to my step. I hop along the crowded street.

Ever since we came back from Italy three weeks ago, Gabriele and I have settled into a routine. We meet at his apartment on weekday evenings to dine together unless he has something going on.

On Saturdays, we go out for lunch. I'm afraid to call these

dates, but that's exactly what they feel like. And it was Gabriele's idea, too.

All my exes were rich so they wined and dined me at fancy places where I couldn't let my hair down and had to always act perfect in case I ran into someone from my parents' social circle.

Gabriele and I always come to this quaint Italian place in Little Italy near Chinatown.

The food at this family-run restaurant is fantastic and the table for two is small enough that our knees are smooshed against each other's throughout. I luxuriate in the cozy realness of our relationship nowadays. In this place surrounded by regular people, in these moments plucked from ordinary days, Gabriele and I are simply another couple enjoying each other's company.

Not criminal and civilian, nor an artist and crime boss, but two people.

"Your hair smells gorgeous." He exhales at the top of my head as I arrive at the table he's already waiting at, fingers rolling down the smooth wave of my hair.

These days, I get a pang of guilt when he touches me sweetly. Because my traitorous heart easily misinterprets his kindness as something more. A sharp longing edges between my ribs. Gabriele has my emotions confused with these dinners and dates and whatnot. I don't believe he loves me or wants anything more than easy companionship with me but it's easy to feel like he sees me as special when he lavishes so much of his time and attention on me.

The more of these sweet moments he gives me, the greedier I become. I want a whole lifetime of them.

But how long do I have left to bask in his warmth, to savor his rough touches and heady orgasms? Four weeks? Four months? He'll at least come to see my painting at the spring exhibition, won't he? It feels wrong for him to be missing. He was the sole reason I stayed on track and fought through my artist's block.

"What'll you be having today?" the waiter asks, trading a friendly grin with my partner. He knows Gabriele. I suspect he knows Gabriele's profession, too but he simply doesn't let that affect his view of Gabriele as a man. Or a customer.

"Pick for me," I say.

"The same as me," he informs the waiter.

When the waiter's gone, I free my feet from my shoes. My toes climb up Gabriele's muscled legs, kneading his thigh. "You know what I like about this place? The tablecloths are long enough to cover what's going on under the table."

Gabriele's hand grabs my foot. "Not here."

"You're no fun."

"I have something to tell you."

"Nobody's stopping you." Taking a sip of wine that Gabriele ordered earlier, I rotate my head to the window.

"I'm getting married." The bomb he has dropped makes no sound, but my chest convulses in pain as he goes on, "To a woman my boss picked. There's no date for the wedding yet but it could be as soon as next month."

The unspoken ending to that statement vibrates between us.

We're breaking up in a few weeks.

I tuck a strand of hair behind my ear with sweaty fingers. The thumping of my heart is deafening. "Does...your fiancée know about me? Is meeting you here like this wrong?"

"Maria doesn't mind me seeing you until the wedding but after that, we stop. Okay?"

Her name is Maria. She might be Italian, too. I wonder what she looks like if she's prettier than me. Even if she isn't, she must be a lovely person for Gabriele to have picked her.

He didn't pick you.

Nobody wants you.

Worthless.

The alcohol is too close at hand for me to resist. I drain the glass in minutes.

"Francesca, baby, don't start drinking now." He slams his hand down on my glass, making it impossible for me to lift it off the table. "I didn't want to lie to you or keep you in the dark, but don't make me regret telling you."

"It's too sudden," I say. "When you asked me to eat with you and then asked me out to lunch, I thought we were more than friends. Don't you feel that way?"

The old Gabriele, the one who was gruff and surly, would have denied his feelings with a snarky remark. But he's no longer that man.

His shoulders sag in defeat. "I have no choice. I like you, Francesca. More than you can imagine. I would be more than your lover in a heartbeat if you tell me that's what you want. But tell me honestly, do you think you can survive my world, a world where women stay at home and don't pursue careers that could lead to them being seen, let alone famous? Is that the life you want? Because that's the only future I can give you."

Icy coldness seizes my chest, freezing all my hopes to nothing. Reality is a horrible, inescapable prison. I can't refute a single point Gabriele has made. He's right about everything. As long as he's in the mafia, we cannot be together. This conversation is a dead end.

"But," I start, only to be cut off by him.

"You grew up safe and sheltered. No matter how naïve you are, baby, you must know that I have more enemies than teeth. Those men won't hesitate to hurt you, kill you, or rape you. I protect you now, but there may come a time when I cannot. Can you promise me you won't regret giving up your safe, comfortable life for one filled with violence and uncertainty?" He folds the napkin on the table, waiting for my answer. I have nothing for him, though. My heart desires nothing more than to be with Gabriele, but the life he's describing doesn't sound like

251

me at all. He knows it, too. "You cannot give up on art nor do I want you to. You've fought for it, baby, and you must persevere even if I'm the one standing in your way."

Even though he could easily threaten me to give up everything for him if he wanted to, he doesn't. He values my art, my future, my goals. Most of all, the way his eyes widen suggests that he's hoping—no, he's predicting—that someday I'll get all the success and validation I ever wanted. Does he think I won't need him anymore when that happens?

Because he's more than a muse to me. He's a friend, a lover, a shoulder to cry on, and a man I respect and admire more and more every day. Yet all that will mean nothing if I can't sacrifice my whole way of being for him.

The girl in me is weeping as I admit, "You're right. How silly of me. There's no way I will fit into your lifestyle."

Gabriele executes a slow nod, but stuck in his eyes is a bead of hopelessness. "My place is in the mafia and yours is in high society among the rich and famous. The shadows won't suit you. You're too bright to hide."

It's depressing to think about our relationship ending. The food in my mouth, which was so delicious moments ago, now tastes like cardboard. But what other choice is there? I cannot sacrifice all the things that make me happy for him and he cannot leave the prison of organized crime.

I wipe my lips with the napkin, my other hand quivering on my thighs. "What kind of person is Maria, your fiancée?"

Why not torture me brutally while I'm at it? What have I got to lose at this point? I might as well satisfy my curiosity.

"Mature," Gabriele replies. "Sensible."

"That's all?"

He angles his head toward the windows. We seated right next to them, separated only by a thin wall from the street outside where loads of people walk up and down without any clue.

My blood freezes to ice when I spot the two masculine faces on the other side of the thin glass barrier. The first one exudes intimidation, a tapestry of sharp angles and brutal shadows framed by brown eyes and dark hair. The other is the exact opposite—a golden-haired, blue-eyed Adonis.

I would recognize those features in my dreams.

Ethan and Elliot—my brothers.

Ethan's scowl is beyond angry, every muscle in his jaw tight. Malevolence lurks in his stormy gaze that's pinned on Gabriele.

Elliot isn't the type to love his younger sister in an over-bearing way, so he's grinning in amusement.

Panic stabs me.

"Um...how fast can you run?" I ask Gabriele, shaking my head at Ethan, silently pleading with him to not make a scene. That is a remote possibility given that Ethan gives zero fucks for other people's opinions of him. He's a control freak and massively overprotective. Family is everything to him, even though I'm only his half-sister.

"We're not going anywhere." I catch the bulge under Gabriele's jacket when his palm covers it protectively. He's packing a firearm. Probably a knife, too. "Nobody threatens you in my presence, Francesca."

"Listen, my brothers, have spotted us." I point a finger weakly at the two figures that just barreled into the restaurant. "That's them."

Gabriele scoffs. "Yeah, I see them alright. They won't hold up in a fight."

"No violence," I warn Gabriele through gritted teeth. "I'm going to lie that we're friends and you're modeling for my painting."

The infuriating man simply clicks his tongue. "Mr. CEO won't buy that. He saw us disappear into the ladies' room at the gala. Grilled me about it afterward."

"Ethan saw *what?*"

"He knows what I do."

"Your real job?"

"I have only one job, Francesca."

Sweat pours down my forehead. I'm dead. I'm so dead. Can I pretend to faint? Dramatic as that sounds, it might be the only way out of this mess.

When Ethan aggressively marches into the café like he's a crusader of justice, it's not his ungodly height or strong musculature that grabs my attention, it's the fact that he's dressed in jeans and a sweater. I've never seen him in anything but a suit. He wears formal clothing every time he visits home because he always comes straight from work.

Every clap of his sneakers is like a gong of death as it approaches me. What will I tell him?

To prevent the situation from escalating, I rise out of my chair, jump to my feet, and wave my hands, feigning happiness I don't feel.

Gabriele doesn't miss my acrobatics. "When did this turn into a circus?"

Desperate, I consider texting Ella and asking her to distract her boyfriend with a text or pic or *something*. She's Ethan's only weakness. But we have barely started mending our relationship. It's too early to demand favors. She'll be confused if my first text is *Your bf saw me with a guy and lost it. Calm him down before he turns us into tomorrow's headlines.*

"Francesca." Ethan's bellow is scary even from three meters away.

"Ethan, Elliot, strange seeing the two of you together," I coo. "What brings you to this place?"

Elliot overtakes Ethan to fit me into a snug, brotherly hug. "We're going to therapy to fix our relationship." His teasing tone makes it hard to tell whether he's serious or not.

Behind me, Gabriele snorts out a laugh.

Elliot sighs, peeling himself away. "Wish I was joking, man, but I'm serious."

"You agreed to it?" I gasp at my older brother, who hovers over me like a statue carved from marble. His expression is stony like a gargoyle's. Ethan likes talking about feelings as much as he likes cutting off his fingers one by one. I thought Ella would be the only one he opened up to, but maybe she has changed him for the better. What else have I missed about him in the weeks that I've avoided them?

How much have these two grown while I've decayed?

Ethan folds his arms over his chest, clearing his throat. "Elliot, don't discuss family matters in front of strangers."

"Isn't he your boyfriend? Come on, Francesca, introduce us."

"Hey guys, this is Gabriele..."

I lose my breath and my courage when Ethan gets right up in Gabriele's space, his narrowed gaze blazing down like he wants to roast him alive. Tension explodes when he places a firm hand on Gabriele's shoulder and the two engage in a silent war of hostility. If I was the nail-biting type, I'd have bitten all my nails off by this point.

"Gabriele Russo," my brother drawls in the polished upper-crust Brooklyn drawl that all of us share. "I see you have taken my warning at the gala as a suggestion."

The creases at the edges of Gabriele's eyes indicate that he's pissed. "Your threats couldn't scare a rabbit."

"I didn't want to get the police involved," Ethan says. "But if you want to play it like that, I'll oblige you."

"Go ahead."

Ethan's lips twist in an intimidating smile that acts more like an insult. "It's true what they say about men in the mafia being too dumb to recognize that they can't solve everything with violence."

"Last time I checked Wikipedia, you hadn't been to college, either." Gabriele's eyes glint with triumph as Ethan's frown deepens. "From one high school graduate to another: check your attitude."

As they volley insults back and forth, Elliot taps my shoulder, leaning into my ear to murmur, "Okay, what did I miss? Is your boyfriend Ethan's business rival?"

"Worse."

His jaw drops. "Ella's ex?"

"He's in the mafia."

Elliot pales. "A hitman."

I curve my head down in a slow nod.

"Francesca, you didn't."

"I can date whoever I want, Elliot. You two don't get a say in my life choices. Not that I'm dating Gabriele."

"Tell that to Ethan. Before they kill each other."

Gabriele's eyeing his gun. While I'm too anxious to move, Elliot steps between them.

"Okay, boys, let's sit down and talk like civilized men. And don't forget to listen to Francesca. She's the one who decides what happens in the end."

I clasp my hands. I'm half-afraid they'll both ignore him and continue their pissing match, but he nudges Ethan down onto what was my seat. Gabriele crosses his legs on the seat opposite Ethan's.

"Sister, take it from here." Elliot encourages me with a hand on my shoulder.

I'm grateful he's here to smooth things over. Elliot is a charmer, someone who can get along with anyone. Until he decides to fuck you over like he did with Ethan a few months ago. Then he's the most manipulative snake in the world.

His duality is scary.

"I don't know what you're thinking, but Gabriele and I... we're...we're just..." Oh my god, what was I supposed to say here? What's the correct answer?

We're just sleeping together?

We're just addicted to each other's demons?

He's my fuck buddy?

We're friends?

I love him but he's getting married to someone else?

Why do they all sound wrong? That's not what we are. But what are we?

The ground underneath spins violently. I feel like an orator who stood up on stage for a speech and forgot the lines.

"He's a criminal, Francesca." Ethan forces a heavy sigh into the room. "What're you doing with him? Don't tell me he's selling your drugs. Or taking advantage of you? If he's black-mailing you, you don't have to be scared. I'll protect you."

I hold up a hand. "It's not like that. Our relationship is normal."

"Normal, as in normal friends?" Elliot crooks an eyebrow upward, gaze hopping between Gabriele and me. "Or normal dating?"

"We're not dating," Gabriele interrupts. For one glorious instant, I'm proud of his noncommittal answer. The perfect neutral response that gives nothing away. He should run for president. His opponents would never be able to use his words against him. "She's mine."

I spoke too soon.

"No, she's not." Ethan hisses. Betrayal washes over his expression as his face twists to me. "Right?"

Shame twists in my throat. My relationship with Ethan is already hanging by a thread due to how long I've ignored him.

"I don't know what we are," I admit honestly. "So don't ask me. I'm figuring it out as I go. All I can say is that Gabriele cares about me and my dreams as much as you do, so I want to give him a chance. I hope you can keep an open mind, too."

Ethan's shoulders soften. I might be imagining it, but his chin drops in a subtle nod.

lie so beautifully, it sounds inspiring. Because the truth is that I know exactly what we are.

We're a disaster waiting to unfold. An almost-married man and a girl teetering on the brink of collapse. We're nothing to each other but at the same time, we're everything to each other. It's a relationship that defies labels.

"Is that true?" Elliot surprises me by confronting Gabriele head-on. He must be worried, too. I'm stressing out everyone. I always do. They don't know the true depth of my issues yet.

"I do like her art," Gabriele admits. "She has talent."

"He's my muse," I add because the eccentric artist is the role I've played all my life. I've done worse things for art than sleep with a mobster. My brothers will write it off as one of my bizarre creative rituals. They're not going to scratch under the surface, probe for the truth that's uglier.

"Wow, who would have guessed." Elliot grins. "As long as it's what you want."

"Of course it is. You know how much art means to me. I'm completely devoted to it." I force a tremulous smile, furthering the pretense that everything is rosy.

All the while Gabriele's fingers are digging into the back of my thigh under the table.

Liar.

CHAPTER 20

G abriele

SHE REJECTED ME.

What did I expect? As if she was going to jump with joy at the grim lifestyle I was offering her—no dreams, no art, no joy, no fame, only fear and paranoia chasing her every day as she wonders which one of my enemies will put a bullet into her. It was unfair to dream that she'd ever want to be more than temporary lovers when she has so much promise and potential.

Yet my whole body aches at her rejection, burning up in a fever, alternating between rage and sympathy.

She wasn't mean, cutting, or even direct about her rejection. But the way her shoulders sagged, the quiet but determined, "You're right," that she voiced after I'd listed all the obstacles standing in our way was enough to convey all her emotions.

Part of me prayed for her to say we'd find a way, that we'd

fight the impossible odds because being together mattered more. Because what we had mattered more.

But she gave up, seeing there was no way out of this tunnel.

As I'm torturing myself over my heartbreak, my phone rings.

"Gabriele, it's me, Angelo." Don's statement crackles through my phone's speaker. "We have a date for your wedding."

My heart that was already at rock-bottom plunged deeper into the abyss. I don't want to think of Maria and the whole host of complicated factors in our situation right now.

But duty never rests, not for broken hearts.

"When?" I ask, shifting into a serious tone of voice. I'd segue with small talk but if I speak too much, the fissure in my chest is going to cleave open and spill all my anger.

How can this be happening? I was just starting to...hope for a different future. I admit it; my dreams were unrealistic. But I wanted to dream those dreams for a little bit longer. Because they made me feel like a better man. Whatever Francesca and I have feels right, even when it feels impossible.

"In three weeks," my boss replies, dissolving the last of my hopes for a different outcome. "The fourteenth."

"That's soon. There's no time to prepare–" *To prepare for a goodbye. To prepare for the heartbreak that will follow.*

Angelo cuts me off before I can make a fool of myself. "No need to fret. Maria's handling all the planning. It'll be a simple, intimate ceremony at her father's house. You just turn up, okay?"

"Okay." Agreeing to any demand made by that deep, aged voice is instinct to me.

"And Gabriele?" That one-second pause feels like an age. "Stop seeing that girl now."

"Which girl?"

"Francesca Astor. Maria's ex-husband betrayed her. I won't see her disappointed again."

The verbal punch comes out of nowhere, connecting

straight to my heart, and igniting a visceral, inescapable pain in my body.

"Um..."

I can't stop meeting Francesca. Admitting it, even to myself, is scary. It tilts my perfect, controlled world off its axis, and sends it spinning toward chaos.

But our connection has evolved into something beyond a casual physical attraction, beyond need, beyond addiction, beyond friendship. Hard as I try, I can't make my life before her look appealing. Back then I merely existed. Now I live. Now there are colors in my world that she taught me the names of.

My lip must be bleeding from how much I've pulled at it with my teeth. I still have no answer for Angelo.

"You and Maria must have a successful marriage," Angelo drones on.

I'm not stupid. Angelo isn't suggesting I stop seeing Francesca; he's ordering it. I have never disobeyed a single order before.

My throat thickens with guilt. Facts and memories tick by in front of me like a newsreel.

Our first electric time at the charity gala, her pained eyes coming to life when I touched her, the power coursing through my body when I managed to dissolve the sadness that hung around her like perfume.

The images grow brighter, and sharper, twisting into me like a knife. The idyllic landscapes of Como, Portofino, and Milan. The quiet cozy nights of staying in and talking. All the times she broke for me and allowed me to break her.

The nascent dreams of someday owning my own restaurant.

Everything collapses like a Jenga tower, taking a whole part of my life with it.

A storm brews in my chest, threatening to rip all the muscles and flesh around it. The struggle feels futile. I can't betray Angelo. Not when his voice is so cheerful. He barely survived that attack. Which was my fault. This is the only way I can make it up to him.

A second passes. My protests pass with it.

"Of course." The agreement is a wraith drifting from my lips. I'm not sure what question I'm answering or why. "Sure. Bye."

My fingers feel icy as the phone drops out of my fingers. All of me is numb. Shocked. Empty. Conflicted.

Francesca barges into my apartment exactly at 6 pm. She's very punctual for someone who drifts in and out of reality most of the time.

My nerves are burning at the sight of her looking so happy when her rejection is stinging holes into my heart. She is on something; she's bouncing around like a ball. Far too much at ease even though it's only a few weeks until Francesca's thesis exhibition. The girl I used to know would be having an emotional meltdown.

She has been doing really well recently with her art even though she keeps using drugs as a crutch. Still, at least it's not as frequent as it used to be. She finished her university project early and started on her second commission painting last week —which meant another opportunity for us to seclude ourselves in her studio for a weekend of mindless indulgence.

She's using me as a model for her second piece. Says I'm her muse.

I don't want to be her muse. I want to be her husband. Instead, I'm about to walk down the aisle with another woman.

In three fucking weeks.

A framed painting is nestled under her arm.

I'm not even curious. All my thoughts are wrapped up in what I'm going to tell her.

Tonight has got to be the last time we see each other. If this goes on, I'm the one who will be left broken. I can't let Angelo down, not after he saved me and gave me a new life. I have to break off this sick, addictive, one-sided relationship we have.

My chest twists into a tight knot, but I tell myself I'll be fine. I tell myself this is the right thing to do. We were a long shot anyway. It was meant to fizzle out eventually.

It's time I admitted defeat. From the beginning, this was doomed.

I wished to help her, I wanted to show her the truth of her pain, I tried to take that pain away.

But she didn't ask for the truth, she asked for an escape.

She doesn't need my love, she needs the validation of critics.

She doesn't want me; she wants to lose herself in an addiction that will consume her life.

Every single time, I've given her what she desires.

Tonight, I'll give her the farewell I want.

Pink lips collapse into a frown as my silence stretches for minutes. "You're so quiet today. Something wrong?"

"What's that you have?" I tap the framed painting she's carrying.

"For you. It's my gift. Thank you for helping me get out of my own way. It's the repayment I owe you. I'm surprised you didn't demand it sooner."

Air squeezes my lungs. I forgot about the photo I gave her. The photo of my brother whom I murdered with my own hands. I admit; I was simply curious to see what she would do. At that time, I couldn't stand the horrible truth I had been hiding. I needed to get that burden off my chest. Part of me was hoping she'd turn away from me after hearing about that part of me. But she came closer instead.

I lay her painting over my coffee table where the light from the ceiling light bounces off it.

Now that I'm actually studying the picture, it's mind-blowing. Where the photo was dark, dull, and filled with darkness, this painting is bright, alive, colorful, and filled with hope.

She used brighter colors. Added pink to his skin. Made his face luminescent. Drew sunflowers around him. Light hits his

263

dark brown hair. His face reminds me of my friend, not of the hollow, desperate man I had to kill.

Francesca took my most guilt-ridden memory and turned it into a beautiful artwork. As usual, her talent astounds me.

I must hang the picture on one of the walls. There are too many bare walls in this apartment.

"Don't look at it too much, okay?" she says.

"A painting exists to be looked at."

"I'm afraid you'll see the flaws if you study it too closely."

"It's mine now so I can do whatever I want with it."

"Gabriele, honestly, do you hate it?"

"It's pretty." I make a half-assed attempt at flattery. The truth is that the beauty of her art is so profound my mind is still mining for the correct praises. "I'll consider your debt paid now."

An unknown sensation bursts in my heart.

"I prayed you'd love it." There's an ominous pause as she dips her head downward. "I wanted to give you something that would remind you of me whenever you look at it. Even if I'm not here."

The mere suggestion that she'd be gone from my life one day incites a flurry of anger and hopelessness. I tell myself to simply accept my fate but my emotions have a mind of their own.

The lump in my throat expands to the size of a football. Excruciating pain lances through my windpipe. Breathing is labor at this moment because every breath I take reminds me of how much longer I'll have to live in a world without her.

I lift my hand to caress her, but backtrack immediately, pulling it away. Tender caresses and false hopes have no place in a breakup.

"You want me to remember you?" A heavy exhale pushes the question from my throat.

"Always."

"As the artist who drew this portrait? As a brilliantly talented painter?"

"No." Her soft, tiny fingers knead her chin. A shaky, high-pitched note shoots out of her mouth but she swallows the truth she meant to voice, replacing it with, "As a girl who was special to you."

Unsaid words and unspoiled emotions circle around our still bodies like a vortex.

"Will you remember me, Francesca?" The rasp at the end sharpens my question.

"There's no way I can forget you."

"As your muse?" My voice grows harsher. "As your addiction? As the best fuck buddy you ever had?"

A blush bruises her pale skin. "I…"

One second turns into two and then three. The words I expect to hear from her never reach my ears.

As the man I loved.

As the man who changed my life.

As the one, I want to be with forever.

I wanted to give her a second chance to overturn that rejection, to change the course of our futures. Once again, she picks the same path.

I let out a savage grunt, combing my fingers through my hair. All my organs vibrate with disappointment. If she had said the words, even if they were lies, I'd have given up everything for her—my job, my home, my status, the promise of a stable marriage. That's how much she means to me.

I should be glad she isn't trying to actively ruin my future. I should be glad she's shallow, that she will never give up on art or her material security for me.

It ends better for both of us if that's true.

Francesca suddenly comes barreling toward me, wrapping her arms around my back, the force of her action pushing us both onto the sofa. "I'll remember you as my dear friend, Gabriele."

It's not good enough for me. Not at all good enough.

"I'll remember you as the light that destroyed my darkness," she continues. "And the most talented guy I've ever slept with."

I crack a bitter laugh. Then pull her down to my lap. If she's so determined to see me as a great lay who revved up her inspiration and freed her from her dark days of unproductivity, that's what I'll be

The most talented guy she ever slept with? She can be certain of that after tonight.

Her ass fits snugly between my legs. It feels far too cozy with her like this. Too domestic. It scares me. Domesticity was something I'd reserved solely for my future wife. The wholesome, sensible, well-connected woman I'm supposed to tie the knot with. But this hotel heiress has been living rent-free in my head for too long.

I clear my throat. "Too bad I won't remember you as the most talented girl I've slept with."

"Oh please." She clicks her tongue. "You know how many guys I've given BJs to in college? Every single one came back for more."

Guys? Plural. I could tell she was no nun, but the scale of this is unexpected. Also, I suddenly have the urge to maim every one of those bastards who touched her before me. Obviously, they were useless, which is why she turned to alcohol and drugs.

"Really?" I drum my fingers on her bare thighs, loving the way she curls into my chest. "Give me their names. And addresses."

"You're planning to strangle them in their sleep, aren't you?"

"I make no promises."

"Do you hate that other men have had sex with me?" Her tiny fingers burrow into the hollow above my collarbone. "Because I don't like double standards."

266

She's right. I have no business being possessive. I'll be marrying someone else in three weeks. She's undoubtedly going to end up with someone else too.

But dammit, even the idea gives me rashes.

I shrug. "It's in the past. But if any of them touches you now...they'd better pick out their coffin first."

Francesca cackles. I don't join in. There's nothing funny about it from where I'm standing. "That was a joke, right?"

I choose to not answer. Silence is undoubtedly the best path here.

"You have a wacky sense of humor sometimes." Sunshine-blonde hair spills over my chest as she leans in closer to taunt me with her maddeningly gorgeous aquamarine eyes. The heavy-lidded, sensual way she rakes her gaze up my face settles in my stomach like a slow-acting poison.

It's only a matter of minutes until she has me right where she wants me—on top of her.

She's art, her beauty made up of more than her actual physical form. I may not be a man of culture but even I can appreciate refinement when it's licking its tongue across my lower lip.

When her rosy lips fit over mine as naturally as a lock fitting into a key, I brush away the flint of protest that burns my heart. Resignation washes over me. I'm worse than an addict when it comes to Francesca Astor. One whiff of her and I'm ready to sell my soul for another hit.

My future used to be so clear. The sane, sensible wife. The modest home. A promising career path in the mafia.

Yet with the swipe of her tongue over mine, Francesca pulls me hopelessly into a tornado of chaotic passion, warping me into a world woven from beautiful illusions. I stay, despite knowing that this ends in ashes, blood, and destruction. The higher we fly, the harder we'll crash.

Get a grip, Gabriele.

My inner voice blurs between the waves of heat and pleasure rising and falling in waves. The need to feel pain, to cause pain, magnifies into a compulsion. I bite her lips hard, drawing blood, before licking it away with a caress of my wet tongue. She's too lost in the mindless dance of our tongues to notice or complain. We suck each other's lips until it's the only taste left in our mouths. Even oxygen becomes a luxury when pitted against the unending daydream of this soul-sustaining connection.

"You're energetic today," I remark as we part.

The cut I made on her lip is a purple line, a brutal mark I never meant to leave. But part of me is proud of giving her something to remember me by, too. Even if it'll fade in a few days.

She bounces on my lap. "I feel great."

"Did you snort before coming here?"

"I painted, Gabriele." Her brittle laughter is full of confidence. Her skin radiates happiness.

I almost believe her.

But I know her too well.

She's fidgety. Excited. Her whole body crackles with electricity, shimmering with an invisible euphoria. She's acting too secure, too carefree, and out of character. Certainty hardens in my chest.

Francesca slides her palm up my chest. Her nail catches on my button and then she pops it from its hole. She is grinding her ass against my already-hardening length and it's not helping anything.

I grab her wrist.

Whatever we're doing can't go on. I have to make it stop. Before it messes up my resolve to break up with her tonight.

"What are you planning on doing next once you've finished your degree?" I say, hoping we can focus on something other than the throbbing desire that has acquired a life of its own after that kiss. It smokes the air and floods my bloodstream with arousal.

"Right now, I'm planning on seducing you." Her fingers press against the bulge at the front of my pants. "All I think about these days is having you inside me."

My cock is rock-solid and her stroking is only making the torture more excruciating. Francesca flashes me a naughty smile.

She knows my weakness. She *is* my weakness.

My windpipe closes as desire settles in my throat like a ten-pound rock. My voice sounds like the mewl of a dying cat. "I meant what're you going to do with your art, Francesca."

"Let's not talk about that." She shakes her head. "I'm getting sick of it."

The knot behind my ribs pulls tighter. "What do you want from me, baby?"

"I already told you what I want."

Heat fills my bones. My erection threatens to make a hole in my pants if I don't indulge in it soon. "I love hearing such filthy words from that pretty mouth."

"We both love it."

I begin to reconsider if I should even be fucking her, given that my orders are to end things with her as soon as possible. But my hands have already settled on her breasts. I'm palming them through her floral blouse.

I lay my head in the valley between her boobs. "They should ban you. You're more addictive than a Class-A drug, Francesca Astor."

"So are you, Gabriele Russo." She places a kiss on the top of my head. "I want everything you can give me. Especially the pain."

This sofa is starting to seem too small. I haul her body against my chest, every cell going soft at how intimate this feels.

Kicking down the door, I carry her to my bedroom and throw her on my bed. My teeth find the soft flesh of her neck and sink in, eager to taste that softness.

Her soft moan travels down my spine, making me hard instantly.

I grab her skirt to pull it down, revealing the killer curves underneath. Her body is flesh carved to perfection. A treat for the eyes and a feast for my hands.

Flipping her over, I trace her perfect ass cheeks that are exposed by her thong, molding them to fit my palms. When my finger dips lower into her crease, she arches her back with a ragged gasp.

The exquisite sound does me in.

I pray to every deity in heaven and all the ones in hell, too. *Let this be the last time I touch this girl.*

Angels and devils alike desert me at once when Francesca pulls her blouse over her head. The creamy swells of her breasts are right in front of me, hard nipples barely hidden by the lacy pink bra. Lust blinds my conscience once more. I wait for some divine sign, some godly act of self-control. Nothing happens. Guess being a killer means my prayers were never going to be answered anyway.

I nip her wet sex with my fingers, rubbing her clit slowly. Her moans become heavier. She surrenders to my touch. Just the sight of her pink, moist flesh is enough to torture my dick into spilling precum.

Ache pulses inside me. It won't last long. I need to be inside her now.

Moisture leaks out of her opening. She's a wet dream under my fingertips. So responsive. So beautiful. So easy to please and easier to get lost in.

"Want me to be gentle tonight?" I ask. "I can go slow."

"Don't care." She spits out an audible exhale. "All I want is you."

Frustration beads on my back. She doesn't give a shit whether I'm soft or rough with her, only that it's me. It's what I love about her.

"You never disappoint."

I free my erection, unable to hold out any longer. All my control has been eaten up by her eagerness.

Her breath exits in a shaky exhale as I enter her in an unforgiving thrust that will hurt. But Francesca doesn't make a sound. I push aside the strands of hair stuck to her cheeks, noticing she's flushed.

In a split second, the truth I've been avoiding freezes over my heart. Disturbing images of vacant eyes, fingers clawing for packets of powder, irritable arguments, paranoia, and emotion slowly being washed from her features flits through my head. She's spiraling. She didn't quit. I can't leave her alone.

I can't abandon her now.

Her pliant muscles stretch to accommodate my length until I have every inch buried inside her. She's tight and wet and the million and one things a man hopes for. She rocks her hips up. Pleasure zaps through my body.

"Gabriele." The air from her mouth feels like electricity crackling against my jaw. "You didn't use protection."

"I know you have an IUD, Francesca. You got it at the university health center along with a clean sheet for STDs. Antonio's research on you is pretty extensive." I press my knuckles into her wet sex. "And I'm clean, too."

I'll buy her the morning-after pill tomorrow, just in case. The last thing I need is complications before my marriage to Maria.

"If I wasn't so turned on by you, I'd be scared of you."

"I thought you were addicted to me."

Colors paint her cheeks as she drops her gaze. "That I am."

"Addictions are easy to replace with other addictions," I say.

She'll find a substitute for me. Maybe it'll be meth. Maybe it'll be a more dangerous man.

"Don't be mad." I plant a kiss on her knuckles. "But this is the last time."

"What?"

"I'm getting married in three weeks." It sounds so plausible when I say it. As if I can actually make it happen. Like I can have a life where I won't turn my head every time golden blonde hair swishes past my vision. "We can't do this again."

The faraway look on her features transposes to irritability. She bites her lip. "Gabriele, your dick is inside me."

"I don't want to lie to you or hide things from you just to get off. That's beneath my dignity."

She sighs. But no anger. No sadness.

"Will you invite me to your wedding at least?" she says.

I smirk. "Not a chance."

"I thought we were friends."

We're more than that.

"I still keep an eye on you. Did you forget?"

"Are you going to stalk me even after you're married?" The seductive tone of her voice makes it less a question and more an expectation. "I don't have a problem with it."

"Being a drug addict not enough for you?" I press my knuckles between the valley of her breasts. "You want to be a homewrecker, too?"

Francesca falls silent. Maybe it's the single thread of sense and humanity that hasn't been devoured by her addictions. Her elbows fall flat at her sides. She presses her lips into a hard line, not opening her mouth even when I pound her so hard tears slither down her cheeks.

I thrust in and out of her. She's heaven wrapped around my cock.

But there's no chance I'm coming tonight. It'll be easier to forget her if the sex is mediocre. Bitterness sticks more when it has bad memories attached to it.

So I can't allow myself to climax under any circumstance.

I'll let her have her release, though. I want to give her paradise, a brilliant and dazzling finale to this sordid affair with me. Because there's nothing else I can give her—not the validations she needs, or connections, or inspiration, or whatever's required to sate her demons forever.

My body was what I offered when I first said I'd help her at the gala.

And my body is exactly what I will offer to her now.

Francesca's breaths tear. Her skin tightens over her features. She's close. A flush envelops her cheeks.

Please don't forget me. Please don't forget tonight.

It's a vain hope. Her world is full of glittering things and I am nothing but a spot of darkness.

I grind my thumb on her clit, rubbing to hasten her along.

Fresh tears drip from the corners of her closed eyes. Either the sex is intense, or the news of this being our last time has crushed her. Yet she holds everything inside her.

Until the end, when it all unravels and bleeds from her body.

A pained shriek explodes from her mouth. Her sex spasms around my erect length.

"Gabriele." She pleads my name when she orgasms.

Though I swore, though I promised myself I wouldn't give her this, I can't help myself. She takes away my last triumph from me, and milks every last bit of pleasure from my cock. Until I have nothing left to give.

There's nothing except the deep wound of ending left when all light has faded from my vision. It swirls around our naked bodies like toxic smoke.

Silence ticks by, endless like a funeral.

Francesca wordlessly reached for her clothes. Begins

drawing them over her body. Her face is turned the other way so her expression isn't visible.

Not that I'd want to see it. I don't need the stain of guilt on my conscience.

Rotating on her feet, she sashays over and hugs me. The unexpected warm gesture shakes me to my core. I push her away.

"Don't come here again. If you see me outside, don't attempt to talk to me or get close," I bellow. "Understood?"

"I'm not going to destroy your marriage, Gabriele," she whispers. The enthusiasm from before has vanished completely. She's like another person altogether. The shell of her previous self. She wipes her tears away. "I wish you happiness."

"It's useless for me to say this." *Shut up, Gabriele.* "But I hope you get the success and fame you've always chased and you don't lose yourself in the process."

A small smile puckers at her swollen lips. My teeth marks have bruised the lush, pink skin. Did I go that hard? I wanted our parting to be sweet and innocent, a beautiful memory just for her. But I'm too much of a mobster to not break something fragile and precious without meaning to.

This can't get any worse, I think to myself.

As usual, I'm wrong.

Because the moment Francesca leaves my apartment, a gunshot pierces the air.

CHAPTER 21

I DREAM that I'm falling into a red sea. My body plunges into the depths, seduced by gravity. Down, down, down.

I scream but liquid fills my lungs. I will sink to the bottom. I wonder what's at the bottom. What lies at the end of everything?

A sharp pain incinerates my nerves through the darkness.

My eyelids jerk upward. Light floods my vision. Creamy walls, a hallway...I'm still outside Gabriele's apartment.

A shadowy figure approaches me. My chest feels so uncomfortable like there's a shard of glass stuck inside it. My gaze reaches down to my fingers which are stained red. Blood is pooling under my floral blouse, changing the color of the pink roses to maroon.

Cinnabar. Vermillion. Carmine.

Why am I recalling all the shades of red paint right now? Oh, I suppose it's because red is one of my favorite hues.

A choked sound knifes through my throat but there's no air. None at all. I can't breathe. Did the bullet pierce my lungs? Am I going to die?

More than anything, I feel like I'm slowly choking. The worst part is, I can't tell how much of that is due to the bullet lodged in me and how much of it started when Gabriele told me he'd never see me again.

My bones closed around the softness of my hopes and dreams for us as he tore them apart.

I guess it's what I deserve for being a burden to him.

My gaze pulses between bright spots of light and darkness. I can't even see the face of the man who shot me. Who is he? What did I do to him? Why does everybody hate me?

"Francesca, don't move." The intoxicating pitch of Gabriele's voice ruptures my rambling thought bubble. "Dammit! You've been shot."

Gabriele's huge body appears in front of me. His arm is raised. The shiny body of a gun is wedged between his fingers. Without wasting a single moment, he pulls the trigger. Two gunshots shatter the silence.

The shadowy figure before me crumples. Gabriele goes over to him, steps on his hand, and removes his weapon. He says something but I can't hear what.

Oh my god, It's all happening so fast. I can't make sense of anything.

"Don't…" I strain my throat. My chest is about to split open. "…kill him. Okay?"

Gabriele's at my side in a heartbeat. "I promise. Baby, now stop talking."

His coat lands on top of me, though it barely does anything to stop the blood from flowing. There's too much blood, too much of it.

Gabriele's on the phone now, talking to someone in an

angry, scared tone. I hope it's not the hospital. My limbs are failing. I don't think they can save me now.

I may not live much longer.

"I'm sorry. This is my fault. I thought I could protect you...but I failed..." His forehead is bowed against mine. I never imagined I'd see big, bad Gabriele Russo crying but he's bawling out his eyes right now. "Francesca, don't you dare die or I'll never be able to forgive myself. Are you listening? Don't close your eyes, Francesca. Don't give up. You have to live so I can earn your forgiveness."

My brain's hazy. It hurts too much to keep my eyes open so I close them. It hurts too much to live so I hope the pain disappears soon.

Pain becomes numbness. Numbness becomes sleep. My life is draining out of me.

This isn't how I imagined my demise would look like. But it's so much better. I get to die in the arms of the man I love.

The only tragedy is that he'll never know I loved him.

CHAPTER 22

$\mathcal{G}$*abriele*

I SAW the bastard's face.

Nothing in the world can save him from my wrath. I'll torture him slowly, make sure he understands who he fucked with when he dared to hurt what was mine.

The sight of Francesca bleeding punches me in the gut. I called an ambulance as soon as possible. I briefly considered taking her to the private doctor who digs out bullets when I've been shot but he's a quack who doesn't use painkillers and handles patients roughly. I don't want my girl screaming in pain when she's already wrung out.

So I phoned her irritating CEO brother from her mobile. He lorded over me like he was my master, giving me instructions on which hospital to bring her to.

The corridor reeks of gunpowder and death when I return.

Francesca was taken to surgery. I couldn't hang around the hospital, not with the asshole who killed her still breathing.

"Your jaw's swollen," Nico points out, leaning against the wall outside my apartment door. Nico lives on the ground floor. He rode up the elevator as soon as he heard the shots. "I'm assuming her family wasn't happy to see you."

Ethan swung a punch at me the moment he walked in and threatened to do a whole lot more if I ever showed my face near Francesca again.

I'm gracious so I'm letting him rage. For now. Eventually, I'll have to see how Francesca is doing, even if I have to mow down her domineering brother to get to her.

"This is a mess." Nico shakes his head, the silvery strands in his dark hair glinting in the waxy light. His brows are twisted in a dark V as he surveys the blood-stained carpet.

It's a good thing I own this building and most of the residents here also work for the Russo family. So far, we've kept the police out of it.

"Thanks for your help," I say.

When I left carrying Francesca to the ambulance, I made Nico stand guard over the weasel who had hurt her. I'd shot both his legs to reduce his mobility, but I couldn't risk him disappearing. There was no room for mistakes anymore.

Nico acknowledges my thanks with a minuscule nod. "How's the girl?"

"She's in surgery."

"Will she live?"

"Can't say."

"Can you survive if she kicks the bucket?"

No. I'll be livid. It'll have been my fault. The possibility of Francesca being gone forever is harrowing. I could never forgive myself if that happened.

"I'm hoping she'll pull through." My tongue tastes like iron.

Nico's dry lips pucker a fraction. He's judging my optimism but I don't give a fuck who thinks what of me now. Having the girl I love nearly die before my eyes straightened out my brain, snapped my whole world into alignment. I finally understand my priorities.

My first task is to beat the vermin who shot her to within an inch of his life. I can't kill him since I promised Francesca, but it's not my fault if he decides to kill himself once I'm through.

"Where's the guy?" I ask, clawing the door handle of my apartment. "Is he still alive?"

"Ricardo tied him to your dining chair. I called our doctor to dig out the bullets and stop the bleeding. I assumed you'd want him alive when you returned." Nico sighs. "Gabriele, what are you planning?"

"What would *you* do if someone hurt your wife?"

"Castrate him, cut his tongue out, break all his bones, and make him regret ever being born," Nico answers in his characteristic dry tone without missing a beat.

I rub a hand against my neck. "There. You have your answer."

"Wait." Nico's fingers close around my elbow. "I questioned him while you were gone. He's a Bianchi. Thought you should know."

A member of the Bianchi family, our rivals. I killed their underboss a few weeks ago after discovering he had tried to poison Angelo.

"What? How?" I stagger back in shock. "I took care of every single man in Miami."

"He wasn't in Miami or Chicago with the rest of them; he was hiding in Arizona. Word got around to him about what you'd done. Being a loyal soldier, he had to assassinate you to get his revenge. Unfortunately, your girlfriend got caught in the feud. That bullet wasn't meant for her—"

Panic climbs in my chest, crashing swiftly into waves of self-hate as I complete Nico's insinuation with the depressing truth, "It was meant for me."

"That's why he didn't shoot her a second time," Nico continues. "He realized he'd made a mistake. That you weren't the one exiting the apartment."

Shit. It's my own fault Francesca is lying in surgery.

The vicious cycle of violence is never-ending. Once I kill this weasel, the Bianchis are likely to send someone for Nico's head. That's how these feuds go. Eye for an eye. Tooth for a tooth. Underboss for an underboss.

Exhaustion scales my body. I'm sick of the fighting. It never excited me, but now, as the string of potential deaths stretches years ahead, I want no part of this war. Peace is what I need. Home is what I desire.

I want Francesca breathing on my skin, laughing at my quips, pressing that rose-scented mouth to mine.

There's only one answer: I need to quit the mafia. As much as it pains me, terrifies me, angers me. I have to do it for us to have a chance.

Easier said than done, though.

Leaving the hard part for later, I ease my way into my apartment. The living room stinks of antiseptic and sweat. Ricardo is huddled at one end of my sofa, eyes trained on the Bianchi soldier who is squirming and crying in pain. The floor is slicked with his blood and sweat. There's no sign of the doctor. He must have left.

"Can you speak?" My shadow looms over the bound man. As he bobs his face up, a greasy, triumphant smile etched on his disgusting lips, the firestorm inside me threatens to undo my needle-thin civility.

"You sonofabitch," he exhales. If hatred had a smell, it would be the rotting stench of his breath. "You should be dead."

"Sure you're not confusing me for yourself? I'm not the one who shot an innocent girl," I retort.

"Was she your bitch?" His lips draw over yellow, broken teeth. That misshapen, slimy grin widens. "I hope she suffers. I hope she dies and you understand what it's like to lose everything."

My teeth ache from how hard I grind them. He's right about one thing at least. If Francesca dies, I will lose everything.

But right now, the only thing I'm in danger of losing is my temper. The rage rattling inside my ribcage breaks into a squall of adrenaline. I swing a fist at his jaw, but even the crunch of my knuckle connecting to his jawbone and the click of it dislocating doesn't bring me any peace.

"Ricardo, you can leave now," I say. "I'll handle him on my own."

At the edge of my vision, Ricardo's long-limbed form rises. He shrugs. "Should I get a body bag ready?"

I shake my head, withholding a verbal answer. I want the Bianchi rat to die of anxiety predicting what I'll do to him. I want his heart quaking with fear wondering if I'll spare him or rid the world of his unworthy soul.

Once Ricardo has left, I slide the army knife from my pocket. It's the perfect weapon for slow, miserable torture. Part of me rebels at using the same knife I did to bring Francesca pleasure. I don't want to taint her beautiful memory with his filthy blood.

"At least make it quick with a gun," the man says. I detect a pleading note in his voice. Nico's interrogation probably has him at the limit of his tolerance. "We both don't have time to waste."

Too bad I don't care for his comfort.

"Nothing good ever came fast." I lick my lips but my veins are filled with ice. This is revenge, not pleasure. Regardless of how much he screams, nothing can earn me Francesca's forgiveness.

That's all I care about. That she lives, she recovers, even if it's only to hate me in the end.

Misery floods through me at the thought of his incident leaving a scar on her. What if there's damage to her nerves? What if she can never paint again?

My greatest fear isn't her anger or her indifference. It's destroying her chance at happiness. She has fought her demons for so long that she deserves to have the future she wants. The fame she needs.

There's nothing I can give her—money, connections, comfort, not even safety—but I refuse to take everything from her.

"Know what? Small cuts are too good for you." Changing my mind at the last minute, I put away my army knife. Instead, I grab the meat cleaver from my kitchen.

The Bianchi soldier blanches at the sight of it. Good. He knows what's coming for him then.

* * *

"Get out." It's Mr. CEO, standing at the threshold of Francesca's hospital ward like a gargoyle in his slate gray suit. There are bags under his eyes and the crooked set of his lips conveys his deep resentment. "Go before I call the cops and get your filthy ass hauled to prison where it belongs."

Desperation and anger collide into a writhing mass at the bottom of my stomach. I'd love to wring Ethan's neck and push him out of my way so I can make sure Francesca is fine with my own eyes. But he isn't the villain of this story.

I am.

Besides, Francesca would never forgive me if I maimed him and I'm going to have a hard enough time earning her forgiveness already.

"Can I see her?" Humility tastes foreign on my tongue. The meek voice sounds like it belongs to someone else.

"You don't have the right to see her." Ethan's hostile expression conveys everything. Unyielding, firm, with his arms, crossed across his chest. I don't doubt for a second that he's furious. "It's because of you she is in this state. I swear, I should've done something about it when she said you were a friend. You're a criminal. That's what you are. And your filthy, dangerous world isn't a place someone like my sister should set foot in—"

"I know—"

"Then you should have kept her safe."

Bile rises in my throat. I hate that he's making valid points. She'd be healthy if it wasn't for me. She wouldn't be fighting for her life if it wasn't for me.

"I'm sorry. I didn't mean for her to get caught up in mafia politics. Tell me she survived." The backs of my eyeballs sting. Whether from the smell of antiseptic or the fear of losing Francesca forever, I don't know.

Ethan's chin shoots up, making him look haughtier than he already does. "She will. I've already arranged for the best surgeons and they're operating on her as we speak. She's my sister and there's no way I'm letting her die."

The asshole is the most irritating human being to deal with, but he cares a lot for his sister. That's why I put him down as Francesca's emergency contact when she was brought here. I wanted it to be me, but that wouldn't have been right. I'm not sure Francesca will ever want to see me again after what happened. I broke her heart, then she got shot because of my neglect.

"I'm staying here," I tell Ethan, leaning against the wall.

His stony eyes harden. "No."

"Didn't ask for your permission."

"I'm calling the security."

"Do whatever you must to make yourself feel useful." I sneer.

He scoffs. Reluctantly, his shoulders lower a fraction. Judging from the stillness of his posture, he seems to have quit actively trying to toss me out of the building at least. We're not going to be best buddies anytime soon but I'm happy with this temporary truce.

Ethan digs his thumb into his forehead. A cold, dark gaze slithers over my form, from the base of my toes to the spiky hairs sticking up from my head.

"Who shot Francesca?" There's an accusation buried inside that question. He suspects me but he doesn't say it in so many words.

I wish I could lubricate the dry, crackling animosity between us with a quip, a haughty zinger. Diverting people with humor was a whole lot easier when guilt wasn't searing fiery trails through all my organs.

"It was someone from a rival group in the mob. He was trying to kill me but shot her by mistake."

"Must have a shit aim. You're clearly a whole lot bigger than Francesca." A choking grunt. Did he really make a joke?

"I wasn't with her," I say.

"Why?"

"Because I just broke up with her."

If Mr. CEO hated me before, he's going to tear my sorry ass apart with his bare hands after this answer.

"Just when I think my impression of you can't get any worse, it hits rock bottom." He's doing a better job than I ever could at the whole 'dry humor' thing. Either he's planning to ruin me slowly or he is too scared about Francesca's surgery to waste his emotional energy pointlessly lashing out at me.

"Save your cussing until you hear the rest." My masochistic desires rear their head. I want him to hurt me, to pay the penance for my part in this mess. "I'm getting married."

Within a second, Ethan grabbed me by the collar, hot, furious puffs of breath leaking from his mouth and hitting me squarely on the nose. "You fucker. You were cheating on my sister all this time?"

I want to curl into a ball of nothing and disappear.

Shadows stretch beyond the white walls. Nurses and patients come and go, their footsteps like tolling bells. I have no idea how I'm going to live through the next few hours, how I'm going to keep myself from drowning in the sea of anxiety that's pulling me under with vicious ferocity.

Francesca's face is imprinted in my brain, burned into my retinas. Every moment hammers in the uncomfortable realization that I'm not remotely ready to live in a world without her.

I'd rather die with her.

"I didn't cheat on her." I shove Ethan off me, my excuses sounding both stupid and pointless to my ears. "It's an arranged marriage."

"That doesn't change—"

"Ethan, what happened?" A frail brunette wearing glasses and the ugliest patchwork jacket shoulders past me, grabbing onto Ethan's arm. "Is she alright?"

Mr. CEO pauses his tirade against me. He wastes no time drawing the girl into his arms, kissing the top of her head like she's a newborn baby. "It'll be okay, princess."

This must be Ella, his girlfriend.

Regret. Envy. Longing. Nostalgia. Emotions buffet me from every direction.

It's a tender, intimate moment between Ella and Ethan, definitely not something I expected from the gray-suited gargoyle. It reminds me of the cuddles and kisses Francesca and I shared every day in my apartment.

My chest is bleeding from the memories. I should've held her tighter, kissed her more, treated her gentler.

I should've treasured the tiny gestures and realized how precious they were.

I snatch my attention away, pretending to scan my phone. I'm going to rupture an artery from how hard I'm resisting staring at the two of them.

"Are you Francesca's boyfriend?" Ella comes over. She is completely different from Francesca, not stereotypically fashionable or pretty.

"Not anymore."

"Then why are you here?"

A shudder ghosts down my back. The petite, glasses-wearing girl is peering through my soul, cataloging every single one of my lies and flaws. How do I answer her when she already knows the answer?

Ethan doesn't waste any time slamming into me with his hard gaze. "Yeah, why are you still here? Go to your bride. You no longer have anything to do with my sister."

"I..." Words betray me. "Francesca...I have to make sure—"

"Don't call her name," Ethan says. "She deserves better than someone like you. If you can't value her, the least you can do is give her up."

Resistance spins its threads around my neck, tightening like a noose. I could argue. Could protest. Could lie.

But none of that will make me worthy of Francesca's forgiveness. Ethan's right. I can't face Francesca with my half-assed attitude. What can I offer her if not my complete fidelity and devotion?

Her words from long ago gurgle like bubbles of water in my ears.

Don't give me false hope with your mixed signals and break my heart. I'll never forgive you.

I stalk out of the hospital as quietly as I came.

I didn't even get to see her face.

CHAPTER 23

 *rancesca*

Days blur into darkness, the beep of machines, then medicine, followed by an endless stretch of pain.

Between those, there are other images. Mom crying her eyes out, blubbering as she holds my hand in my hospital room.

Ethan and Ella both act way more emotionally than they usually do as they break down in front of me the moment I regain my consciousness after the surgery.

Ethan's was the first face I saw when the anesthetics wore off. It made me feel calmer to know he was here for me because Ethan is the most responsible person I know. Yet part of me wished for a different set of dark eyes to sparkle at the sight of me. My heart squeezed at the memory of our last time together.

"Francesca, thank you for coming back to us," Ethan said, quaking. He must have been worried sick.

My desperation must have silently urged him, because he

added, "I'll tell Gabriele you woke up. But no power in the world will change my mind about not letting him see you."

"It's not his fault," I croaked, clinging to Ethan's hand. "Don't blame him."

"You're lucky the bullet didn't hit close to your heart and penetrate too deep." He patted my head gently. "Otherwise you'd be dead."

"I survived, didn't I?" I retorted.

Ethan wasn't impressed. I doubt he and Gabriele will ever talk to each other again without him threatening legal action. That's a shame. They're both similar in many ways.

Elliot visited me every day once I was moved out of intensive care into my own private room. He even brought me flowers and chocolates I wasn't allowed to eat since I was still being fed through a tube. He nibbled on them one by one while I watched.

"Mmmm, hazelnut praline is the best. Too bad you can't taste it."

Despite my situation, I coughed out a laugh. Elliot's such an asshole but he's the best at cheering me up.

I need all the cheer I can get right now.

"Your life has been eventful lately," he says today, arranging the bouquet of sunflowers and daisies in a vase. I have no idea where he gets these from but they look luxe. "But honestly, Francesca, stop giving me a heart attack so often. I'm only twenty-seven and I need to marry the woman of my dreams before I shuffle off the mortal coil."

"Who is the woman of your dreams?" I tease.

"Someone who'll never look at me." There's a hopeless edge to his statement. Longing—and defeat—are imprinted inside his blue irises which are the same color as mine. Elliot's so surface-level most of the time, seeing him be angsty is like seeing a snowstorm in the middle of a desert.

Spiteful as it sounds, his despair soothes my broken heart

more than kind words could. I'm not the only one who feels like shit. I'm not the only one who can't get the person I love to choose me. I feel less lonely, less like a failure, and less *wrong* when Elliot's here because he's like me.

Not seeing Gabriele for days has been brutal for my anxiety. Ethan deleted his number from my phone. Said it was a request from Gabriele himself. But I suspect he couldn't stand to see me pining over the man he believes is a crook. He's high-handed as ever.

"Elliot, you used to do drugs before, right?" I broach the subject as casually as I can. Ever since I woke up, I've been thinking about how much I've neglected my health.

When I was on the cusp of death, I realized I was terrified of dying. I imagined how my death could have occurred differently—with booze and pills. I couldn't scrub away Gabriele's mournful expression as he talked about his mother.

Terror saturated my blood. I felt the desire well up deep inside me—the desire to change.

I've been toying with the idea of going to rehab. I mean, I'm going to need to spend weeks in bed recovering from this gunshot wound. My career will have to be put on hold anyway. What's a few more weeks?

I'll never stop being an artist or wanting to be recognized but maybe I can take it slow.

I'm going to come out and tell my family about my issues, though. Their help will be vital to my long-term recovery. However, the prospect of being judged by them is more daunting than losing weeks or even months of my career to rehabilitation.

"Once or twice," my brother confesses, with no trace of emotion. "But I haven't touched anything for years now."

I swallow, debating about spilling all the dark details. Ethan still doesn't know about my substance issues. Ella is truly a loyal friend. Between my brothers, Elliot is less likely to judge me for it, so I blurt it out before courage deserts me. "How did you quit?"

"I lost interest. It wasn't fun anymore."

I blink, a mixture of shock and self-hate cascading down my spine. "Everything in life is just easy for you, isn't it?"

"Not everything, Francesca." There's a meaningful pause at the end of that sentence. His expression warps into suspicion. "Why do you ask? Are you planning to give me another heart attack by doing drugs while you're in the hospital? You could become addicted, Francesca."

"I already am," I yell. The tears I've been holding back all these days so I don't worry my family erupts from my eyes, twin waterfalls. "Elliot, I'm already an addict."

"What are you saying?" Confusion colors his face. "Are you confused? How many fingers?"

He holds up two fingers in front of my face. I tell him where he can stick them. "I'm completely sane."

"Since when?"

My story starts with months of colorlessness, with a single visit to a seedy club in Manhattan, meeting a red-haired man with a slimy smile who offered me a way out of my shackles. It ends with falling in love with a criminal who forced me to confront the pain I was causing myself, and who made me realize I was greater than my demons.

I don't leave out a single detail as I bare it all to Elliot. He's the third person I'm telling after Ella, but the second who knows the true depth of my suffering.

"I had no idea," Elliot whispers. "You always seemed passionate about art. So happy to be an artist. I'm sorry I never looked deeper beyond your mask."

I shake my head. "Don't get me wrong, I did have fun. Or maybe I desperately tried to have fun because the only other option was to sink into the abyss. I was always reaching for thrills, for love, for pleasure, for something good because my mind was full of unhappiness and self-hate. But forcing myself to find happiness only increased my awareness of my misery. The harder I tried, the more obvious it became why I was trying."

A sharp burst of pain tickles my bandaged wound. It exerts pressure on my muscles to talk so much. Moving around hurts. They stitched up my chest but even with painkillers, the agony is ceaseless.

A loud, regretful sigh from my brother silences that pain momentarily.

Elliot's forehead is marred by lines. He dumps his hands into his pockets.

"Francesca, why didn't you tell me before?"

"I was afraid you'd judge me. I thought I'd stop once I got my creative inspiration back. But I'm afraid my elusive muse will never return to me. I'm going to have to push through self-doubt and anxiety for as long as I paint." My long, greedy fingers curl and uncurl in my lap, the familiar wave of anxiety rising in my chest. "I don't think I want to paint anymore. I realized this as I was dying that I want to be happy more than anything. Success or fame doesn't mean anything when you're always scared. I just want to get out of the darkness. But I don't know if I can. I don't know if the darkness is something that surrounds me..." I hiccup, the searing pain of the sudden muscle movement tearing my chest apart. "...of if it *is* me."

Elliot's chest balloons as he inhales. The muted sounds from outside the room's window envelop us. My brother who always has a dry quip for everything is struggling to speak. Never thought I'd live to see this day.

Everything is obvious to me now. My mind is clear. Worst-case scenarios are still curling at the edges of my consciousness, but I can no longer avoid what I've been avoiding all this time. After all, I said it myself.

I'm trapped in an endless loop of unhappiness every day. In

the past, I blamed it on a lack of success. I thought it was due to not being validated. Not being talented. Not being productive. Not being famous. Because if I can't tie it to something I lack, that means my unhappiness has no reason. It just is. I had to make it a problem so I could solve it. But there is no solution, no problem, no cause, and no effect—only an emotion that never fades.

"You deserve happiness, Francesca," Elliot says at last. "I may not understand you because I was consumed by my own demons for so long, but I know that once you put your mind to something, you achieve it. Even if it takes decades, I believe you will figure it out."

There's a sharp stabbing at the back of my eyes. "I wish I believed in myself as much as you do."

"Someday, you will." Elliot's reply is so soft, so gentle, I wonder if it's really my sharp-tongued brother. His hand curls over mine and I sink my fingers into the softness of his palm. "Be patient until then."

The hope lounging inside me rises. "Thanks, Elliot. Though I wonder if I should be taking advice from someone who is five million dollars deep in debt and whose greatest accomplishment is having partied his life away."

Sarcasm is supposed to be his strong point, not mine. But I suppose all of us excel at it.

"You're not wrong," Elliot admits. "I'm more like you than you realize. I felt empty and dissatisfied most of my life, too. I had no passion, no goals, no desires. I chased fun and pleasure because it was easy. But one day, I saw someone and it made me aware of what I needed."

"Which was what?"

"I needed to be useful. Not desirable, rich, successful, or adored. I just needed to be of service to at least one person in the world who appreciated me. So, Francesca, what do you need?"

"I need to be free. Free to express my darker emotions and to have them appreciated." I grasp his fingers tighter. He used to have soft hands before but now they're rougher. "Ever since I was young, I was aware of the dark, turbulent emotions inside me. They would've broken me if I didn't have a way of letting them out. Art was my release, a vent for those complex, intense feelings I couldn't express in words. As long as I drew, the emotions were more manageable. Which is why, when I could no longer paint, I started to suffocate."

"Yeah, you were always really sensitive and emotional. You felt things deeply. It didn't take much to make you cry or smile when you were a child," Elliot agrees.

"I think the obsession with success was simply the desire to have my suffering recognized," I continue. "I buried my feelings for so long. I thought I didn't want anybody to see that part of me. Turns out, subconsciously, I wanted the whole world to acknowledge that side of me—because my art was filled with the truth even when I was filled with lies."

Elliot's other hand moves up my hair, stroking it gently. My whole head feels pinched. I press my head into his stomach.

"It makes sense," Elliot says. "Why you were so obsessive about art. Because it allowed you to be yourself—all parts of yourself. In a small way, it healed your pain."

An electric awareness sneaks through my veins. The stabbing at the back of my eyes sharpens. Tears rush forth, running in cold trails down my cheeks.

"Yeah, I think it did," I sob. "That's why I was terrified of losing it."

I began to replace it with other things like alcohol and drugs. But they didn't let me release my feelings, only numb them. I started to get worse. More stifled. More desperate. More volatile.

Gabriele's dark, probing eyes float into my mind like a sudden dream.

Except then, I met Gabriele. When I was with him, I felt the same sense of liberation. He accepted...no, he demanded to see all the sides of me, especially the sad, miserable parts. And he loved and desired them. He made me face my demons again, he made me find a new way of expressing myself with art.

Spending time with him was profoundly healing.

Perhaps that's why, when we were in Italy, my whole body froze up at the idea of losing him. He's the one who made me real, who ripped away my lies and loved my darkness. He was the place where I could be all parts of myself.

Even if we cannot be together anymore, I will always be grateful for everything he did for me.

For all the ways he changed my life and made me aware of who I was on the inside.

His question from the last time we had sex surfaces in my thoughts.

And what will you remember me as?

As the person who changed my life.

CHAPTER 24

 abriele

ANGELO LIVES IN AN IMPRESSIVE MANSION, one that's a far cry from my modest apartment. Then again, he operates the biggest crime family on the East Coast and has multiple legal businesses in Hollywood. His status demands that he lives it up a little.

His old, gray-haired housekeeper opens the door for me. She has worked in this household for decades. That's why, even though I came unannounced, she recognizes me at first glance.

"Is the Don at home?"

Her tired blue eyes blink warily. "You have business with him?"

"I wouldn't be here otherwise."

"His bedroom," she replies, shuffling her feet uncomfortably.

"Is he busy?"

"No. Let me inform him you're here."

296

I follow the housekeeper's lead. One survey of the house is enough to tell me it's no longer what it used to be. There are no flowers to be seen. When I first came here after being saved by Angelo, this house smelled of roses. The décor was brighter, too.

The Don's wife died three years ago which may be the cause of the change. As far as I know, he has been single since then. I don't remember much about her, only that she was a matronly, unremarkable woman. She wasn't flashy. She had no interest in wearing pretty clothes and living in luxury the way most mafia wives do nowadays, Nico's included. But I remembered how caring she was when she nursed me back to health as a teenage boy Angelo had picked up off the streets.

Don is reading the newspaper in the living room upstairs, the one right next to the master bedroom. I can't think of anyone else who reads the paper in this day and age except Angelo Russo.

One gray eyebrow arches at my presence. "Gabriele. Now this is a surprise."

"I have something important to tell you."

"If it's about the shooting of the Astor girl at your apartment, Nico already gave me the details. Nico said you both cleaned it up quietly. Of course, it'd all be for nothing unless that girl survives. We don't want her family to come after you or blame you for everything. How did her surgery go?"

"No idea." Maybe the Don reads what I'm about to say in my expression because he folds the newspaper and lays it down, drawing himself to his feet. "Regardless of the outcome, though, I cannot marry Maria. I'm sorry, Boss to spring this on you when the wedding is three weeks away. I will tell Maria myself. As gently as possible, of course."

With the mere hardening of Angelo's jaw, the temperature seems to drop fifty degrees. He's not pleased about this.

The coward in me, the young boy who lives to please this

great man wants to take those words back. I could simply marry Maria and cheat on her. But I don't want to fall any lower than I've already fallen.

As Ethan said, Francesca deserves better. She deserves a helluva lot better than being my sidepiece. Or a Mafioso's wife. She deserves a safe and happy life, one that's worthy of her wealthy upbringing and beautiful heart. I never want her to be worried about dying again, looking over her shoulder for a gun at every turn. That's something I won't tolerate.

"What's your reason for not wanting to proceed with the wedding?" The Don's tone is deceptively quiet.

Calling off the marriage is only the first bomb I'm dropping on Angelo tonight. I can't backpedal now.

"I don't believe I can be faithful to Maria," I say. "I'll hurt her, only in a different way than her ex-husband did—"

"The real reason, Gabriele."

"I just can't do it, Boss. I can't pretend everything's fine." The fear coursing through my veins makes my voice wobble. "My whole life changed the moment he shot her in front of my eyes."

The Don grinds his slippers into the carpet, muttering something under his breath. It's definitely nothing good. My body screams in panic.

Have I angered him? He could have me killed in three hundred different ways with only a snap of his finger. But I don't fear death anymore.

I fear unhappiness, lack of fulfillment, the endless pretenses.

The air between us is filled with invisible thorns.

A harsh breath whistles out from between Angelo's parted teeth. "You're in love."

"No. I'm madly in love." Every syllable scrapes through my chest. An intense agony grips my throat. "When I think of a world without her, all I see is darkness. If I can't be with her, it's fine. But I don't want to be with anyone else because touching another woman while she breathes would be a betrayal. I thought it was just physical, an intense addiction I could overcome but now my soul feels like it has been torn apart and I'm scared I'll never be happy again."

Angelo's eyes widen in surprise. There's a momentary lapse in the conversation as he processes what my words could mean and I find the courage to be more direct. His voice is gravel when he says, "Do you want to leave the family, Gabriele?"

"I need to. Otherwise, I'll never be able to be with her without worrying about her safety. She isn't from our world and it was my fault for dragging her into it."

A million silent questions and answers loop between our gazes. Decades worth of loyalty and memories, family bonds and promises. The most significant person in my life, my only constant, my father figure, my master, my Don, my savior—I'm throwing it all away for a chance with a girl who has enchanted my heart. It's the ultimate disloyalty.

I'm sure that's exactly what this seems like to him. But I don't care how fickle and ungrateful I seem. I owe Francesca everything. More than that, though, I owe myself a chance to find real fulfillment instead of settling for a dissatisfying future.

A thick swallow swells the curve of the old man's throat. He's doing his best to soften the deep lines carving his skin, bracketing his eyes, and his jaw. Lines of acute disappointment.

"Have I ever told you about my wife?" He clasps his hands behind his back. "We fell in love when we were young. I defied my father to marry her. She rebelled against her parents, too. They didn't want her associating with someone in the mafia. Sometimes, I felt guilty for taking her away from the life she could have had—one where she didn't have to look over her shoulder twice or worry if her children would return alive every time they left the house. Despite all the trials, though, we were happy." A sniffle as the old man's eyes shine with tears. "Every day since her death seems just a little bit darker."

"I'm sorry for your loss. And for making him lose another member of your family."

The breath we both take in unison as we straighten our bodies is drenched with meaning.

"In life, you regret many things," Angelo says. "But let me tell you this: nobody ever regrets fighting for what they believed in."

I take his hand caressing the thin, age-spot-marked skin and the outline of the veins underneath. A cough spurts from his phlegmy throat when I kiss his knuckles. "Boss, you are the best man I know and that will always be true. You were a real father to me. You made me believe in family, in friendship, in devoting my life to serving someone. I will never regret having been a part of this family and I will never harm you or the family in any way, even when I'm a civilian. Meeting you was undoubtedly the greatest fortune I ever had."

"Don't be giving your farewell speech already. I haven't agreed to let you go. Besides, how are you going to survive once you leave? You have enough money, but you can't waste the remainder of your life doing nothing. You're only thirty-four."

The bud of an idea that was sparked weeks ago has fully bloomed inside my brain. "I'm planning to train to be a chef."

"At this age?"

"I like challenges."

"The restaurant business in New York is more cutthroat than the mafia." A light chuckle accompanies his words.

"I'm willing to try my luck."

His eyelids drop for a moment before his clear eyes swim into view again.

"I'll miss you," he says.

"So will I."

"Are you going to talk to Maria?"

"I'll have to."

Angelo considers a moment. "Why don't you leave her to me? She might not want to see your face again."

"In that case, I'm grateful for your help."

"Gabriele, you'll need to stay with the family for at least a few months," Angelo continues "Show Antonio the ropes so he can take your place. You're going to be a hard man to replace but I need competent men on my side."

A few months. That's nothing. I expected him to demand more. The Don has grown soft in his later years it seems.

Francesca will be focusing on her art career after college anyway. I need to have my restaurant set up and operating before I propose marriage to her, too. I wasn't expecting it to be an overnight thing. I'm in this for the long haul.

"I'll always be on your side, Boss, even when I'm no longer part of the family," I say.

Angelo nods. "That you will be."

CHAPTER 25

 rancesca

"Why aren't you asking about him?" Ella says.

I'm in my room, yawning under the covers. Ever since I left the hospital, all I've done is sleep and eat. Mom dotes on me all the time, force-feeding me more food than I actually need because she's scared I'll wither away and die if she doesn't. Elliot has been busier with work of late, but he does visit occasionally. Ella comes over on most days. Now that her final project has been submitted and her exams done, she has nothing but time on her hands.

"Who?" I ask.

"The guy who shot you." She's absently flipping the pages of the book on her lap. She brought it to read out to me. She has been reading it out to me little by little every day. It's a fantasy adventure novel. I'm not big on fantasy but listening to her voice narrating stories is strangely soothing. Also, I have nothing better to do.

"Ethan told me he was part of the mafia and he shot me by mistake," I say in response, slowly sipping water. "I don't want to know his name. It's better if I'm in the dark."

The pages of the book rustle as her fingers crush the edges. "I'm so glad you pulled through that tough surgery. The wound might scar forever but at least the nerves in your hand weren't damaged so you can paint."

"Yeah. I'm grateful," I mumble. Art has been my salvation these past few days.

I decided to focus on my health and leave my career when I was feeling better, but ironically, that kick-started my inspiration. Vivid images and whimsical ideas take shape at the shadowy edges of my mind all the time, promising me they'll be my next genius project. Sometimes, my hands itch to paint. But it still strains my muscles to paint for an extended time so I settle for sketching in my pad.

I've filled up the thirty pages of my A5 sketch pad already. I'll have to ask Mom to buy me a new one.

Ella's gaze swings back and forth between me and the closed pad lying on my nightstand. "Can I see your drawings?"

"Sure."

I no longer feel the impulse to hide the less-than-desirable parts of myself. Regardless, a flash of heat expands across my face the moment Ella starts flipping through the book.

Ella blinks as black and white pencil likenesses of the same deep-set eyes, the same perfect jaw, the same drastic bone structure, and a sharp profile greet her page after page. Portrait after portrait of Gabriele Russo. Smiling as he did in Portofino. Contemplative. Laughing at my jokes. Crying. Hungry as he watches me come.

I can draw him from memory alone in a million poses. All his expressions are like still images permanently framed in the museum of my mind. Every single one is a sketch filled with love. I'm sure she can sense that, too.

SASHA CLINTON

"They're all pictures of him," she surmises. When my brows knit into a questioning V, Ella explains, "I saw Gabriele at the hospital. Many times. Ethan and he argued a lot."

Should've guessed. I'm sure it took every ounce of magnanimity Ethan possessed not to immediately bring a lawsuit against Gabriele.

I curl my spine into the fluffy pillows propped against the headboard of my bed. "I'm only drawing what comes easy."

What I said to Elliot snakes through my consciousness.

My art was filled with the truth even when I was filled with lies.

Longing sneaks into my veins. A craving I can't satisfy with anything except the rough touches of a particular man. I mentally shake myself.

No. I decided to let Gabriele go. I'm grateful for everything that he did for me and I'll love him forever, but that doesn't mean I'm going to ruin his new life. He deserves stability and true love, not an unstable addict to take care of on top of everything else he's burdened with. I won't be selfish like his mother. I won't expect him to bear the burden of my demons.

"Why am I not surprised that all you've drawn is Gabriele Russo? That he's what comes easy to you." Ella's mention of his name sticks like a needle in my already-bleeding chest. "You don't want to know where he is considering he's the reason you went through the horrific ordeal in ER?"

"No. I don't care."

Ella giggles like I made a joke. "You do care, Francesca, or you wouldn't keep drawing him like a teenager doodling their crush."

"Ella, stop. I don't want to talk about Gabriele."

"Why?"

"Because it's hopeless. I can't have him and I want to wish for his happiness from the bottom of my heart. But every time I'm reminded of him, my heart hurts and the desperation I put away comes back stronger until I want to jump into his arms again." I curl my fingers into fists. "I can't afford to do something so foolish right now."

"Are you scared now that you know how dangerous his world is? Is that why you're avoiding him?"

I shake my head. I wish I had common sense. I wish danger put me off. I wish knowing that I could die any moment if I was with him made my love for him go away.

But no. I'd gladly live inside a landmine as long as I can be with him.

The danger isn't my greatest obstacle. It's the promise I made to him. I won't wreck his dreams of domestic bliss.

"Ella, he's getting married." My breath feels cold as it squeezes out of my nostrils.

She releases a peal of laughter. "Gabriele has been hovering around the hospital the entire time you were there. Trust me, I know a man in love when I see one."

"It doesn't matter who he loves." Powerlessness weakens my voice. A blade of pain slices through my abdomen, throbbing in my cells. "He's in the mafia. He can't choose his partner."

Ella's eyes squeeze shut. She opens them again, looking straight at me. "He can and if he's worthy of your love, he will."

"You don't get it. It's I who doesn't deserve him. You know I'm messed up. His mother was an addict, too. He spent all his youth looking after her. It'd be cruel to ask him to watch me spiral."

"You won't spiral." Ella plants her palms over my hands. "You'll get better."

"I'll try, Ella." Uncertainty is a rock dragging me down. "But I don't know how things will turn out. I'm not pressuring myself to get it right the first time. I'll have to be patient. I might require a few stints in the rehabilitation center to kick the habit."

Her eyes widen with renewed hope. "You'll go to rehab?"

"Yeah. Having a brush with death has made me understand

how much I value my life." I breathe out. "I'm going to take a break from the world of fine art. My thesis is finished, so I should be able to graduate. After that, I'll take things slow. I always felt insecure so I pushed myself to be the best as soon as possible."

Being an artist felt like fighting the whole world by myself, a battle against time and society. Healing will not only involve giving up substances but most of all giving up the attitude where I constantly feel the need to prove myself to people, justify my right to be unhappy, and express my hollowness through art. To convince the world (but mostly myself) that all parts of me have value, especially the sad, shameful parts. It's those things that I fear will take forever.

"Francesca, you're unique." Ella rests the book she was holding on the nightstand. "There's no other artist like you in the world. I've always loved your drawings. And I can't wait to see what amazing things you will come up with next—both in art and life."

She leans in closer to me. I hug my arms around her waist. Her warm, slim body is beautiful, but part of me misses the broader, muscled body of Gabriele.

I mentally hiss at myself. I have to accept the reality. I must be happy with what I have. I'm so lucky to have a great friend who accepts me.

"Thanks, Ella," I say. "Sorry for being a horrible friend to you these last few months."

"I understand you were going through your own battles," Ella says. "It took me years to find the courage to tell you what happened to me. These things aren't easy."

"Will you forgive me?"

"Always. Now that you know my secret and I know yours, we'll be closer than ever."

"Of course, we'll be." I press my body harder against her,

306

even though it hurts. "Given that you will become my sister-in-law in the not-so-near future, do I even have a choice?"

"I'm not—" She gasps. "Ethan and I aren't getting married."

"He bought an apartment, though. A very suspicious move," I note.

"I had nothing to do with that decision. But Ethan did ask me to move in with him," she replies, a touch self-conscious.

"Will you?"

A sniffle against my shoulder. "My mother isn't completely well. I can't leave her alone. But in the future, maybe when she's better, I'll think about it."

"I hope it works out. You two have been alone for too long. I hope you both can finally feel a little less lonely in the world now. And be the happiest people alive."

"I want the same for you," she says. "I want you to be the happiest, too."

"That's a tall order—"

Ella grinds to her feet, jerking away from me when someone pounds on my room's door.

"We have a visitor," the maid says in a frightened voice, her head poking through the door. "A man who looks...well, he isn't like our usual guests. I was going to call the police but he claims he knows you. I've seen him around the neighborhood before."

Hope peaks inside my chest. "Is he over six feet, tall, dark, and menacing?"

She executes a quick series of nods. "He said his name is Gabriele Russo."

Ella and I stare at each other, a flood of surprise welling up in my throat.

"I don't know if I should see him," I confess, scratching a hole in my thigh with my nails.

Ella bends over to place a palm on my head. "Francesca, can you forget about him?"

"Never."

"Then stop acting so wishy-washy." That's all she says. She doesn't urge me to call him, to find him, to speak to him. She doesn't have to.

Whatever I do next is my own decision.

I choose to drag my recovering body down the stairs to the front door.

The tall man planted outside the front door doesn't have a bouquet of red roses, a check for damages, or anything. No get-well present or grand gesture.

There's only him, in his usual black suit.

And it's enough. It's enough in a way drugs and alcohol have never been enough. It fulfills me in a way that people's praise of my art never did. The sight of his visage dissolves the scar of uncertainty left by weeks of waiting, wondering, hoping, and despairing.

The fragrant spring air bites my skin.

The feverish second when our gazes tangle stretches interminably. My pussy throbs so hard, I'm afraid it'll burst open. Need blisters my sore opening.

"Gabriele, why did you come here? What if your wife—"

He catches the direction of my gaze and cuts me off before I can finish. "I didn't get married, Francesca. Couldn't. Not when you're the only one for me."

The world crackles and spins around me. Heat is a hornet's nest stinging my stomach.

The mobster advances upon me, his shiny, polished shoes treading over the carpet in quiet whispers.

"What do you mean?" My voice breaks with elation I've never allowed myself to feel since the day we broke up.

"I don't care if your brother kills me, but I'm marrying you." He shrugs. "Eventually. Once I quit the mafia."

My jaw nearly hits the floor. "You're leaving the mafia? Is that even possible?"

"It is and I've already talked to my boss. He said he'll let me go after a year. I never want you to be in danger again, Francesca, not because of me. As it is, I'll have to beg for your forgiveness my entire life. I put you in danger because I was careless. I regret it every single day. I shouldn't have left you unprotected that day. I thought I was doing the right thing by pushing you away, but it was just a coward's way out. I was too deeply in love with you and I knew you didn't want or deserve the pathetic, anxiety-filled lifestyle I was offering you. Your rejection at the restaurant hurt me so I wanted to hurt you back. Immaturity got the best of me."

His words are like a dream come true. Like an invisible finger dragging over my raw, bruised heart. My stomach trembles.

"Don't hate me, Francesca." If looks could reduce someone's resistance to ashes, Gabriele's soft, begging expression would be a smoking grenade. "Believe me. I never intended to harm you. I kept thinking you'd change your mind."

For the first time, I take a step toward him despite knowing that I will lose every shred of control once I'm close to him. I don't care. I've missed him too much. My heart needs the medicine that's his touch.

"I could never hate you." The words eject themselves through the big lump in my throat.

"When I saw you bleeding, I knew that regardless of if you lived or died, I could never forget you," Gabriele whispers. "If you died, I would have gladly grieved you forever rather than spend a single day with another woman. And if you were alive, I swore I'd become a man worthy of you. It's okay if you don't love me. I still love you. I'll wait for you to return my feelings for the rest of my life."

"I already love you, though," I say. "I always have, Gabriele. I adored you since the moment I saw how tender and sensitive you were beneath all your bluster. You notice things about me people never bother to see and you shower every part of me with your love and understanding, even the parts I am still learning to accept. There is nothing more I could ask for from someone."

His intake of breath is audibly surprised. "Do you...really mean that?"

Tears push against my eyes, demanding to be set free. "Yes. I mean it. One hundred percent. I'm so grateful to have met you. Thank you, thank you, thank you." Every grunt erupts out of me more desperate than the previous. "Thank you for valuing the sad, miserable parts of me as much as the rest of me. Thank you for healing my pain and for loving me despite all the ways I've hurt you and messed things up."

"No, Francesca, I don't deserve your gratitude." He lays a possessive palm over my shoulder. "Not when I'm the reason you almost died. But I'm a greedy man, so it makes me happy to hear it."

One step then our bodies are caught up in each other's like tangled threads. Like clockwork, his hand finds my neck, and my arms find the solid weight of his back. He lowers his lips to mine. We meet in an explosive spark of heat, a burning splint of pleasure.

I take his tongue, loving the velvety taste of him, relishing the solid press of his hand between my thighs. Pleasure throbs in my abdomen, heavy and hopeful, a prayer I need to be answered.

Until my lips ache from the roughness of his stubble stroking across them.

"What did you do to him? The man who shot me." I ask, worry snaking between my happier thoughts the moment our lips part.

Gabriele's eyes narrow. "What he deserved. But know this: those hands that hurt you? He's never using them again."

He cradles my face. With his thumb pressing gently on my chin, he kisses me again. When he pulls himself back, his eyes are red. Filled with pain and everything he has held back for so long.

Tears carve hot trails down my cheeks. I swim to the sanctuary of her arms. This is such a beautiful moment. There's nothing spectacular or grand about it but our emotions make it the most gorgeous day of my life.

"Thank you," I whisper one last time. "This is everything I ever imagined but dared not hope for. Now if only you'd make me come. I've been starved of orgasms for days."

Gabriele plants a kiss on my forehead. "I don't think the foyer of your house is an appropriate place for me to undress you. Unless you're into that, too?"

An embarrassed laugh scales my throat. "No, I'm not. Not with my mother around. But Ella's in my room so—"

"I was just leaving. Take care, Francesca. I'll call you later. You two must have a lot to catch up on." Ella marches up behind me, waving me bye-bye as she stealthily glides out of the door.

I'm internally grateful for Ella's mental sharpness because if I had to send Gabriele away, my body would actually explode.

I grab his hand and quietly lead him up the stairs. Mom watches me, a dent of worry carving a line between her brows but I nod to her, mouthing 'It's okay.'

Gabriele is a secret I'm done hiding. He's the man I love. And I don't care what Ethan or my mother think of him, I'm proud to love him and be loved by him. I want the whole world to know that.

The heat between us intensifies the moment the door to my room clicks shut. He locks it. I catch the flicker of hesitation in his eyes. On any ordinary day, he'd be tearing my clothes off but now he hesitates, settling for brushing back my hair with his fingers.

"Don't worry," I assure him. "I'm okay now. I can have sex. Just nothing too rough."

"I'll never hurt you again," he promises.

Still, his reluctance doesn't disappear. Slowly, I lower one side of my dress, revealing the scar from the gunshot wound I suffered. His whole face immediately pinches into a mask of sadness.

"This …" He kisses it reverently. "It breaks my heart to see it. I'm so sorry."

"Don't be. I've decided to see it as a reminder of my victory over my demons." My core shivers at the trail his lips are painting over my collarbone. "I always thought death was the ultimate escape but when it became a reality, I was scared of losing the life I hadn't yet lived. That's why I will go to rehab. I will slowly get myself back. It's not a race to the top. I can get there slowly. I don't need success immediately. I'm no longer going to live my life to prove to people on social media that I deserve to live, too. I just want to have fun painting again."

His hand stills on my thigh. "You're giving up on fame?"

"I'm going to stop pursuing it so desperately. I'll let it come to me. And if it doesn't…well, then I don't want it. Because I have something better." I grind myself against his hand. "I have you."

Gabriele goes quiet for a few moments, using that time to guide me gently onto the bed. I attack the buttons of his shirt, breaking one as I get the shirt off him. One by one, we pluck every article of clothing from each other. I'm hungry, and impatient while he's slow, and patient. His eyes are fixed on me throughout the undressing process.

"I only wish I was half as great as you believe I am. I'll do my best for you, Francesca. Whatever you want, whatever you need, I'll support you. And if my best is not enough, I'll do even better." Gabriele's breath smells like smoke, like the memory of our first meeting, like everything that I've been holding inside my chest afraid the world will judge it.

I let it all out in front of him, baring the new me, the me who plunges into the flame knowing it'll burn me but I'm not cowering anymore.

"Get on top of me. Ride me," he begs, laying on my bed, surrendering his body to me entirely.

I know it's his consideration speaking. He's afraid his weight might bear down too hard on my recovering body.

I do as he says without protest, mostly because I feel confident enough in my skin to try something new with him. For as long as we're together, I'll never stop being surprised by the new parts of me that I discover when we're intimate.

It's the gentlest sex we've ever had. It feels like the warm glow of candlelight under my skin. A soft, luxurious, easy sensation that I sink into effortlessly. He lets me do as I please, murmuring praises. "Good girl. You're so fucking sexy when you're riding me."

We fly so close to the sun together, it's a surprise we aren't burned to ashes.

The bed creaks under our spent bodies.

I close my eyes, letting the glittering sensations conquer every last doubt I have about us.

When the stars stray from beneath my eyelids, leaving only a dense, throbbing blackness, I realize I'm no longer scared of the darkness.

CHAPTER 26

 *abriele*

DESPITE MY TEARFUL confession to Francesca and her admitting she loves me, too, my daily life remains unchanged. I do the same things I used to do. Cycle through the same places I used to go to. The office. The casino. The club. My apartment. Dinner. Sleep. Then the same routine ad infinitum.

I yearn to call Francesca, to listen to her voice, but she said she wanted to be alone while she was in rehab.

"This is a battle I must fight on my own," she said. "I need some space away from the world."

I respect her decision. Rather, I admire her strength in wanting to face her demons so I've tried to be supportive of her choice.

I'm proud of her courage, the courage my mother never had. I can't believe I ever thought they were the same. My mother had no passion, no dreams, no goals, just a corrosive hunger begging to be filled.

Francesca will succeed because she has her dreams and passions waiting for her at the end of this tough journey.

Antonio yawns in the office, staring at the ledger he's supposed to be compiling.

I strike off one more day from my calendar.

Three more days.

The weird thing is, I never owned a calendar before. I bought one just to mark the days until I could be with her again.

My head snaps in the direction of the lone painting hanging on the shabby wall of my office. It's the one she gave me. My payment for the time I rescued her. She wanted it to remind me of her and it has served exactly that purpose for the last twenty-five days.

In a small, mystical way I feel that her spirit is here with me.

Before I know it, it was the day she was due to leave the rehab facility. We haven't talked about meeting up. I don't know where the facility is, but I assume it was outside the city in some nice, isolated place. Her brother wouldn't have spared a single expense in ensuring she got to go to the best place.

After my daily grind and a round of drinks with Antonio and Ricardo at the bar afterward, I stumble into my apartment.

I'm waiting for communication from her. A text. A call. Something. But there's nothing, no matter how often I check.

Hours bleed into each other. Evening turns into night then midnight. Restlessness claws up my bloodstream. I write and delete multiple messages. A niggling worry scratches at me.

What if she doesn't want to be with me anymore? Now that she's alright, maybe she realized she deserved someone better?

Oh god, what if she met someone at the rehab? Someone as rich and sophisticated as her who wouldn't put her in danger. Someone who can understand her mind better than I can.

Within minutes, worry morphs into acidity at the base of my stomach. I swallow an antacid, suddenly remembering I forgot to have dinner.

There's some bread in the fridge. I slap together a sandwich and scarf it down in the dark, lonely box of my room while watching the news. When I turn the TV off, static silence buzzes in my ears.

I promised her I'd wait for her to reach out.

Maybe she's too tired today. Tomorrow, when she's rested, she'll call me. Right?

I chance a last look at my phone. My heart shoots from despair to hope. There's a message. From Francesca. It was sent twenty minutes ago, while I was wallowing in my self-doubt.

Francesca: Can I come over now?

I text her back instantly.

Me: Yes, yes, yes, please fucking come over now. I'm about to collapse from wondering how you are doing. Are you hungry?

Francesca: Only for you, G.

Thunder strikes my heart. Heat coils around my groin. Our reunion will be explosive; I just know it. I root around for condoms so I'm prepared when she arrives.

She usually lets herself in because she knows the passcode to my apartment. Tonight, though, she buzzes instead.

I swing the door open, chest swelling and bursting with relief at the vision of her standing on the other side.

"I hope you weren't traumatized having to walk through the corridor again," I say. "We can go somewhere else—"

"I'm fine." She barrels right into my arms, her head coming to rest on my chest. All the anxiety from this evening dissolves. It feels right. So right. "Good job taking care of the bloodstains."

I hired an expensive cleaning service to get it done discreetly but it was so worth it.

Francesca kicks the door closed with her foot. Her gaze lifts to me. It's hungry, but this is not the desperate craving from weeks ago, a desire to get lost in something and avoid her demons.

This time, she wants me, not an escape. I can feel it.

"I missed you," I say, heat growing under my skin like vines. "How was rehab?"

"Not as bad as I thought. I'm a little better now and I understand what I have to do. I'm so grateful I'm not alone on this journey." She touches her open palm to mine, her silent gratitude filling my body. "Of course, the struggle isn't over because I'm out. They said it'll take two to five years of commitment to be drug-free for life. But I feel more confident than ever that I can do it."

"I know you can," I say.

The dam holding my emotions at bay breaks when a tear quietly trails down her cheek. I give in to the temptation, gathering up her body in my arms, bringing her lips to mine, devouring the taste of her like a starved animal.

If I had any doubts about her losing interest in me, they all vanish when she kisses me back passionately, rubbing her breasts against my chest.

Passion grips us, prolonging the kiss, and turning it into a wordless interlude. My body reacquaints itself with the planes of her soft form, with the heady taste of Francesca Astor, with the scent of roses that was absent for so long.

Every scrape of her body against mine generates enough friction to make me want to rip off our clothes and take her right here and now. But today's not for quick gratification.

Our mouths stay glued together until it's no longer possible for us to breathe. Then we break away, tears welling in both our eyes, the pain of separation and the ecstasy of reunion having broken down all of our walls.

"How about you?" She breathes hard. "Have you decided what to do once you leave the mafia?"

"I want to be a chef and open my own restaurant. I'm

thinking of applying to culinary school. I'll probably be the oldest dude in class. Don't know how I feel about that." I scratch the back of my neck, self-conscious.

I've always been in a position of power, the most successful and respected man in the room. It'll take an attitude adjustment to start from the bottom again. Still, I feel excited about everything that the future holds.

Francesca nuzzles her head close to my neck. "You'll also be the most handsome guy in class. All the girls will be flirting with you."

"Doubt it. I have a menacing face."

"It's dangerously addictive." She licks a trail over the line of my jaw. "I can't seem to get enough of it."

"Who knows if I'll even make it in the restaurant business?" A shiver coasts down my spine as her tongue pushes across my chin. "Angelo says it's hyper-competitive."

"If you find yourself unemployed, I'll persuade Ethan to hire you as a chef at one of our hotels."

I choke. "I'm not working for your asshole brother. I'd rather go back to the mafia."

"I doubt it'll come to that since your cooking is going to win everyone over and make your restaurant a huge success."

Something inside me softens at her faith in me. It's better because I know she means every word. She has been the most ardent fan of my food so far and if my customers like my food half as much as she does, I'll be the most popular chef in no time.

"Someday, our dreams will come true," I say, kissing her on the mouth again. "Yours and mine."

Her shoulders ease up. "Yeah. I want to be here to witness that."

I kiss the top of her head, letting sacred silence wrap around us.

It's a silent vow, a wordless commitment we're making to

each other. To always support and stay by each other's side. I didn't realize until this moment how much I actually want to see more of Francesca's drawings, and watch her receive the recognition she deserves. I'm more eager to see her achieve her goals than to see my own restaurant get off the ground.

She rises to her tiptoes, grabbing my hand and pulling me. "Let's go."

"Where?" I ask.

"To Italy. I've been dying to go with you again. This time, we're staying for a week."

"When are we leaving?"

A wicked smile. "Now."

Thick resistance rises in my throat. "That's—"

Impossible. I open my mouth. Close it. It doesn't matter.

Because if there's anything I've learned it's that when we're with each other, nothing is impossible.

THE END

Loved **WICKED FAME**? Read Ethan and Ella's story in **WICKED FATE**, book #1 in the **Wicked Men** series, already **out now**.

Elliot's story, **WICKED DEBT**, will be releasing in Winter 2023....

Subscribe to my newsletter to get an early preview of **WICKED DEBT** before the release day.

ACKNOWLEDGMENTS

Can't believe I'm publishing my 8th book already! Thank you to the constants in my self-publishing journey, my encouraging beta readers who make my work better—Briana Newstead and Ellie K Wilde. As always, many thanks to my sister—your love is the fuel that helps me power through both manuscripts and real life. I'm grateful every day that you exist in the world because I would be lost without you.

ALSO BY SASHA CLINTON

You're Still the One (NYC Singles #1)

Ashley

He was my first love. My first kiss. My first husband.

Until he broke my heart and left my life shattered beyond recognition.

In seven years, I've barely moved on from the divorce and managed to get my dream job as an editor.

But he throws my life into chaos again when I'm forced to work with him.

He might be a billionaire and hot as sin, but my heart can't survive a second chance with him.

Andrew

It was an instant kind of love between her and me.

But we were young. When things went wrong, I couldn't do anything to save her.

We weren't supposed to meet again. Or work together.

But fate seems to have other plans for us.

The one thing I know is that this time, I'll make sure she stays.

And I'll do whatever it takes to fight for her.

Henry & Me (Henry and Me #1)

Author Sasha Clinton returns with a hilarious new rom-com about what happens when an inept, out-of-work actress is forced to work for the guy she brutally rejected in college...

My name is Maxima Anderson and there are three things I regret in life: being mean to Henry Stone, moving to Hollywood for my acting career, and choosing to become Henry's housekeeper. The third's the worst, though, because I suck at housework. I'm pretty sure Henry hired me because he knows this, too, and wants to see me make a fool of myself while he savors my misery.

Did I mention he's a millionaire and he's paying me a ridiculous amount of money to do a bad job at housekeeping?

But things aren't going according to his plan. Or mine. Because I'm beginning to realize that under his stony façade, Henry has a golden heart. And he's gotten so much cuter since college. Our chemistry sizzles hotter than my burnt pancakes, and his sweet words corrode my resistances faster than bleach corrodes the lime scale in his bathtub. And if I don't do something about it, I might end up falling for the guy I hurt once...and hurt him again.

Henry & Me is an uplifting, hilarious, standalone romcom perfect for fans of Sophie Kinsella, Jennifer Crusie, and Sally Thorne.

Lucien and I (Henry and Me #2)

Grey's Anatomy meets The Hating Game in Sasha Clinton's new #ownvoices rivals-to-lovers fake-dating romcom.

Mira Krishnan is a cardiothoracic surgery fellow whose three big goals in life are:

1. Achieve superstardom in the field of heart surgery

2. Crush Lucien Stone by showing him that she's the superior heart surgeon.

3. Fall in love with someone who is NOT Lucien Stone so she can erase her years-long crush on him.

Lucien and Mira have been rivals since high school, and she'd like nothing more than to wipe that smug, overconfident smirk off his devastatingly handsome face.

But when their rivalry goes too far and they're caught in the middle of a fight by the program director, Mira's life changes. To avoid being expelled from the fellowship for failing to conduct themselves in an appropriate, collegiate manner, Lucien and Mira are forced to lie about dating each other so they can dismiss their behavior as extreme flirting. But going on fake dates, vacations, and spending time together makes them realize that underneath all the jibes and rivalry, there's potential for something more...and perhaps, instead of looking into other people's hearts, they need to look into their own.

Since I Met You

Sasha Clinton returns with a slow-burn, age gap romance written in an introspective, reflective style that will tug at your heartstrings...

Akash

My straitlaced chemistry professor is the last guy I expected to find making out with another man on campus.

And the last man I expected to start growing feelings for.

My life's already complicated without adding in a hopeless crush on my professor.

But the more time I spend with him, the more I want to hold onto the forbidden love that's growing between us.

Rahul

This has to be the worst mistake of my life—getting involved with a student.

And not just any student—Akash Mehta is the #1 troublemaker of my class.

Never mind that he's also the campus hottie. Or that he has more layers than a puff pastry.

As if that wasn't bad enough, he now knows my biggest secret, so I have no choice but to keep acting as his friend and help him get his wreck of a life together.

But somewhere in between assisting him with coursework, consoling him after his dreams are shattered, and listening to his wild ideas on life, I'm actually starting to like him.

Too bad this can only end one way—with the both of us getting hurt.

This is a MM romance set in India and trigger warnings include homophobia, internalized homophobia, imprisonment, and trauma around sexuality.

Wicked Fate (Wicked Men #1)

A fairytale-like, twisted love story between a morally gray billionaire and a girl who is in love with his darkness...

Ella

I made a bargain with a devil two years ago.

I exchanged my body for a favor that allowed me to live a normal life.

But my devil doesn't look like the one in storybooks.

He's a hot, dark thirty-two-year-old billionaire who is my best friend's brother.

He makes my heart twist with desire and longing.

And he'll be my undoing if I let him take away the last thing I have left —my soul.

Ethan

I didn't expect to find myself in London with Ella.

In the same room. Looking for the same person.

It has been months since I last saw her, months since we made the bargain.

And in all that time, I haven't forgotten how quickly she can get under my skin—and into my heart.

WICKED FATE is a steamy, slow-burn romance with a grumpy yet sweet MMC and a strong, introverted FMC who is a bookworm.

Printed in Great Britain
by Amazon